D1253288

Early Modern Literature in History

General Editors: **Cedric C. Brown**, Emeritus Professor, University of Reading; **Andrew Hadfield**, Professor of English, University of Sussex, Brighton

International Advisory Board: **Sharon Achinstein**, University of Oxford; **Jean Howard**, Columbia University; **John Kerrigan**, University of Cambridge; **Katie Larson**, University of Toronto; **Richard McCoy**, CUNY; **Michelle O'Callaghan**, University of Reading; **Cathy Shrank**, University of Sheffield; **Adam Smyth**, University of London; **Steven Zwicker**, Washington University, St Louis.

Within the period 1520–1740 this series discusses many kinds of writing, both within and outside the established canon. The volumes may employ different theoretical perspectives, but they share a historical awareness and an interest in seeing their texts in lively negotiation with their own and successive cultures.

Titles include:

Robyn Adams and Rosanna Cox
DIPLOMACY AND EARLY MODERN CULTURE

John M. Adrian
LOCAL NEGOTIATIONS OF ENGLISH NATIONHOOD, 1570–1680

Jocelyn Catty
WRITING RAPE, WRITING WOMEN IN EARLY MODERN ENGLAND
Unbridled Speech

Bruce Danner
EDMUND SPENSER'S WAR ON LORD BURGHLEY

James Daybell
THE MATERIAL LETTER IN EARLY MODERN ENGLAND
Manuscript Letters and the Culture and Practices of Letter-Writing, 1512–1635

James Daybell and Peter Hinds (*editors*)
MATERIAL READINGS OF EARLY MODERN CULTURE
Texts and Social Practices, 1580–1730

Tania Demetriou and Rowan Tomlinson (*editors*)
THE CULTURE OF TRANSLATION IN EARLY MODERN ENGLAND AND FRANCE, 1500–1660

Maria Franziska Fahey
METAPHOR AND SHAKESPEAREAN DRAMA
Unchaste Signification

Andrew Gordon
WRITING EARLY MODERN LONDON
Memory, Text and Community

Kenneth J. E. Graham and Philip D. Collington (*editors*)
SHAKESPEARE AND RELIGIOUS CHANGE

Jane Grogan
THE PERSIAN EMPIRE IN ENGLISH RENAISSANCE WRITING, 1549–1622

Johanna Harris and Elizabeth Scott-Baumann (*editors*)
THE INTELLECTUAL CULTURE OF PURITAN WOMEN, 1558–1680

Katherine Heavey
THE EARLY MODERN MEDEA
Medea in English Literature, 1558–1688

Constance Jordan and Karen Cunningham (*editors*)
THE LAW IN SHAKESPEARE

Claire Jowitt (*editor*)
PIRATES? THE POLITICS OF PLUNDER, 1550–1650

Gregory Kneidel
RETHINKING THE TURN TO RELIGION IN EARLY MODERN ENGLISH LITERATURE

James Knowles
POLITICS AND POLITICAL CULTURE IN THE COURT MASQUE

Edel Lamb
PERFORMING CHILDHOOD IN THE EARLY MODERN THEATRE
The Children's Playing Companies (1599–1613)

Katherine R. Larson
EARLY MODERN WOMEN IN CONVERSATION

David McInnis
MIND-TRAVELLING AND VOYAGE DRAMA IN EARLY MODERN ENGLAND

David McInnis and Matthew Steggle (*editors*)
LOST PLAYS IN SHAKESPEARE'S ENGLAND

Monica Matei-Chesnoiu
RE-IMAGINING WESTERN EUROPEAN GEOGRAPHY IN ENGLISH RENAISSANCE DRAMA

Scott L. Newstok
QUOTING DEATH IN EARLY MODERN ENGLAND
The Poetics of Epitaphs Beyond the Tomb

P. Pender
EARLY MODERN WOMAN'S WRITING AND THE RHETORIC OF MODESTY

Jane Pettegree
FOREIGN AND NATIVE ON THE ENGLISH STAGE, 1588–1611
Metaphor and National Identity

Fred Schurink (*editor*)
TUDOR TRANSLATION

Adrian Streete (*editor*)
EARLY MODERN DRAMA AND THE BIBLE
Contexts and Readings, 1570–1625

Mary Trull
PERFORMING PRIVACY AND GENDER IN EARLY MODERN LITERATURE

The series Early Modern Literature in History is published in association with the Early Modern Research Centre at the University of Reading and The Centre for Early Modern Studies at the University of Sussex

Early Modern Literature in History
Series Standing Order ISBN 978–0–333–71472–0 (Hardback)
978–0–333–80321–9 (Paperback)
(*outside North America only*)

You can receive future titles in this series as they are published by placing a standing order. Please contact your bookseller or, in case of difficulty, write to us at the address below with your name and address, the title of the series and the ISBN quoted above.

Customer Services Department, Macmillan Distribution Ltd, Houndmills, Basingstoke, Hampshire RG21 6XS, England

The Early Modern Medea
Medea in English Literature, 1558–1688

Katherine Heavey
Lecturer in Early Modern English Literature,
University of Glasgow, UK

First published 2015 by
PALGRAVE MACMILLAN

Palgrave Macmillan in the UK is an imprint of Macmillan Publishers Limited, registered in England, company number 785998, of Houndmills, Basingstoke, Hampshire RG21 6XS.

Palgrave Macmillan in the US is a division of St Martin's Press LLC, 175 Fifth Avenue, New York, NY 10010.

Palgrave Macmillan is the global academic imprint of the above companies and has companies and representatives throughout the world.

Palgrave® and Macmillan® are registered trademarks in the United States, the United Kingdom, Europe and other countries.

ISBN 978–1–137–46634–1

This book is printed on paper suitable for recycling and made from fully managed and sustained forest sources. Logging, pulping and manufacturing processes are expected to conform to the environmental regulations of the country of origin.

A catalogue record for this book is available from the British Library.

A catalog record for this book is available from the Library of Congress.

Typeset by MPS Limited, Chennai, India.

Contents

Acknowledgements

Some of the research for this project was undertaken in the course of a Leverhulme Early Career Fellowship at Newcastle University: my thanks are due to the Trust and University.

Small parts of this work have appeared in the journal *Appositions: Studies in Renaissance/Early Modern Literature and Culture*, and in the online reference work <www.shakmyth.org>: *A Dictionary of Shakespeare's Mythology*. Thanks to W. Scott Howard and Yves Peyré for permission to reuse this material.

For academic advice, help and encouragement at various stages of this project, thanks to Elizabeth Archibald, Robert Carver, Kate Chedgzoy, Ruth Connolly, Ann-Marie Einhaus, Stuart Gillespie, W. Scott Howard, Stephen Jenkin, Nicola McDonald, Rob Maslen, Liz Oakley-Brown, Mike Pincombe, Barbara Ravelhofer, Jennifer Richards, Corinne Saunders, Fred Schurink, James Simpson and Martin Wiggins. For permission to quote from their copyrighted works, thanks to Martin Wiggins and Nicola McDonald. Thanks also to staff at Durham University Library, the British Library, the Bodleian Library, Leeds University Library and Glasgow University Library (in particular, Bob MacLean and Niki Russell in Special Collections). At Palgrave Macmillan, thanks to Sophie Ainscough and Ben Doyle for their patience and help, and to Peter Andrews for his copy-editing.

Finally, thanks to my parents, Dennis and Lizzie Heavey, to Emily Heavey and to Jon Carter, for their unfailing encouragement and support.

Note on the Text

When quoting from early modern editions, j, u, v and long s have been silently modernized. When quoting from modern editions of early modern texts, the editors' decisions have been followed.

Introduction

To discourse of the furious tirannie of the boocherly
Medea, in dismembring the innocent infante *Absyrtus*
her owne naturall brother, and scattering his martyred
limmes in the hie waye where her father shoulde
passe, were but a loste labour ... [Such stories] are but
Ethnicke examples, farre sette, and a wonderfull waye
distant from our climate both by Sea and Lande: and
committed among such <u>barbarous</u> people, that had   *barbarous*
no knowledge of any <u>God</u> nor yet of any sparke of
<u>Civilitie.</u> (Aii^r–Aii^v)   *Guilty*
            Thomas Achelley, *The Tragicall Historie of Didaco*
                        and Violenta (London, 1576)

Dedicating his *Tragicall Historie of Didaco and Violenta* to Sir Thomas
Gresham, Thomas Achelley claims to find no value in the stories of
transgressive classical women like Medea: they are 'Ethnicke examples',
mercifully removed from Elizabethan, Protestant England by gaps of
time, geography and religion. He argues that to 'discourse' of Medea's
story is a pointless endeavour, a 'loste labour'. Having introduced
Medea in the dedication to his poem, however, Achelley seems to find
her difficult to ignore, and, like his source, William Painter, he likens
the murderous, jilted Violenta to 'a vile Medea fell' (Fi^r) as she prepares
for her revenge on her faithless husband Didaco. More than this, as
I shall go on to show, in the tale itself Achelley builds on his source
and on his use of the specific classical example, turning the power of
this horrifying Medea-figure to his own didactic ends, and cautioning
women to appreciate their difference from her, and avoid her alarming
example.[1]

Described as 'wild Medea' by Shakespeare, and 'fell Medea' by Spenser, Medea is frequently identified as one of classical literature's most abhorrent and uncontrolled heroines, by authors and commentators from the Middle Ages to the present day.[2] She features importantly in the works of many canonical early modern authors, including Shakespeare, Spenser and Jonson, and in works by their lesser-studied peers and successors, including Achelley, James Shirley and Alexander Radcliffe. Moreover, though she is most famous as the Euripidean and Senecan sorceress who killed her children after being rejected by Jason, Medea appears not only in early modern tragedy, or in English translations of classical works, but also in comic and political writing, and in prose and verse as well as drama.

What these authors found fascinating about Medea was, first, her power over men and, second, the way in which they could rewrite her story to differentiate the early modern Medea from her classical and medieval incarnations, simultaneously demonstrating their own affinity with the classics and their ability to make a well-known figure like Medea somehow original, both entertaining and newly relevant to early modern readers and audiences. Just as Achelley cannot stop himself from mentioning her fratricide, despite claiming it is irrelevant to his readers, these authors do not shy away from Medea's murderous and magical power, as their medieval predecessors had often done, but they do not present it unapologetically, like the classical authors (primarily Ovid, and also Seneca) who told Medea's story, and who were so keenly read in the sixteenth and seventeenth centuries. Achelley claims that Medea holds (or should hold) little interest for the Christian author or reader in early modern England, but this is disproved by his own use of her story, and also by the number and variety of early modern works – translations, comedies, tragedies and political treatises – that made use of her myth, in the period 1558–1688. Early modern authors who are divided by time, social class, political persuasion and religious faith are united in their approach to Medea, in that they present and apparently revel in her awful power, while often simultaneously undercutting it, or using it to serve patriarchal and conformist ends. A study of the early modern Medea thus demonstrates how English literature had evolved beyond its classical and medieval models; how social and political concerns impinged increasingly on even well-known stories; and how authors' repeated returns to famous classical stories reflect the demands and concerns of what Jonathan Bate terms a 'mythologically literate' readership.[3]

Early modern English authors might have encountered Medea in Ovid's *Heroides*, *Metamorphoses* and *Tristia*, in Seneca's tragedy *Medea*,

mythology like painting

or in Euripides' earlier ancient Greek tragedy of the same name. All
these works of Ovid and Seneca were translated into English during
Elizabeth's reign, in the period 1566–72, and all had appeared in more
than one English version by 1688, with the *Heroides* the most frequently
translated.[4] The non-Latinate reader might also have encountered
Medea in medieval English poems or prose tales by Chaucer, Gower,
Lydgate and Caxton, and she featured regularly as a brief example,
illustrative of either female wickedness or male faithlessness, in a
wide range of poems, plays, reference works and prose treatises in
sixteenth- and seventeenth-century England. The commonly known
details of her story, those that would have been most familiar to early
modern authors and readers, were as follows. Medea, who is sometimes
identified as the granddaughter of Helios, falls in love with Jason,
a prince sent to Colchis by his uncle Pelias to gain her kingdom's great-
est treasure, the Golden Fleece, from her father Aeëtes. Despite the fact
that he has already impregnated the Lemnian queen Hypsipyle during
a previous adventure, Jason swears love to Medea, and she gives him
the potions, amulets and charms necessary to defeat the dragon, fire-
breathing bulls and earth-born soldiers that guard the Fleece. The Fleece
won, Jason and Medea steal away from Colchis with her young brother
Apsyrtus, and, when her father sets off in pursuit, she dismembers the
child and scatters his limbs over the fields of Colchis (or over the side
of the *Argo*) to distract the king. Later, Medea uses her magical power
to rejuvenate Jason's father Aeson, and promises similar benefits to his
tyrannical uncle Pelias: however, she deliberately neglects to prepare the
potion correctly, and, when his daughters follow Medea's instructions
and stab their father to allow the potion to take effect, Pelias dies. This
first half of the story is outlined by Ovid in *Metamorphoses* 7.1–424,
with the killing of Apsyrtus described in detail in *Tristia* 3.9. Meanwhile,
Medea's magic and violence are described in *Heroides* 6 by Hypsipyle,
who rebukes her absent lover, and hopes for Medea's punishment.[5]

Pursued by Pelias' son Acastus after the king's murder, Jason and
Medea flee to Corinth, and to the protection of King Creon. Eventually,
Jason abandons Medea to marry Creusa, Creon's daughter (also known
as Glauce). It is here that Euripides and Seneca take up the story,
though Ovid's Medea, who has heard of his new marriage, writes to
Jason warning of her impending revenge in *Heroides* 12, and it seems
likely that her most famous acts of revenge were included in Ovid's
lost tragedy *Medea*.[6] The plots of Euripides' tragedy and the Senecan
adaptation are broadly similar, though the Senecan version, which also
makes use of material from Ovid's *Metamorphoses* and *Heroides*, and was

far more familiar to early modern authors than Euripides' tragedy, is generally seen as the cruder, and less sympathetic to Medea herself.[7] In both plays, Medea, furious at Jason's new marriage, successfully petitions Creon for one more day in Corinth, before she is sent into exile. Ignoring the pleas of her nurse, and Jason's demands that she accept his decision rationally, she concocts a potion and kills Creusa by sending her a poisoned robe, and, embracing his daughter, Creon is also killed. Jason sets off in pursuit of Medea, and she kills their two young sons. In both plays, she then escapes by taking advantage of her divine origins, and summoning a dragon-drawn chariot: in Euripides' play she seeks sanctuary with Aegeus, king of Crete, an element of the story that Aristotle found particularly dissatisfying.[8] Though he does not dwell on her time in Corinth, probably in order to avoid repeating material from his own tragedy, Ovid's *Metamorphoses* also has Medea fleeing to Aegeus, after her killing of Pelias, but once again escaping without punishment, after an unsuccessful plot to poison his son Theseus.[9]

As even this brief summary suggests, central to Medea's story is the idea of her magical and murderous power, and its repeated destructive impact on men, children and kingdoms. Literature has returned to her for thousands of years as a compelling and alarming woman, utterly resistant to male strictures and control, and to the obedience and passivity traditionally demanded of women in patriarchal societies, whether these are classical, medieval or early modern. Euripides, Seneca and Ovid in particular were fascinated by Medea's murderous will, her command of magic and her refusal to accept Jason's betrayal meekly. The dramatists end their tragedies with Medea escaping in triumph, assisted by her divine heritage, and Ovid concludes her appearance in the *Metamorphoses* by showing her evading punishment at the hands of Theseus and Aegeus. They are all determined to stress her ability to escape the consequences of her crimes, and all three indulge in what Lorna Hardwick terms 'refiguration', adapting the story as they received it 'by the addition of new features'.[10] In Medea's case, the additions that Euripides, Seneca and Ovid make to her story render her all the more powerful and terrifying. Euripides seems to have been the first to have made Medea an infanticide,[11] and Edith Hall suggests that he probably chose to transform Medea from a Greek woman to a barbarian Colchian, and connects this barbarity specifically with her alarming power: 'Euripides' Colchian Medea is the paradigmatic 'transgressive' woman, and her overbearing nature cannot fully be understood without reference to her barbarian provenance.'[12] Ovid makes much more of Medea's devotion to Jason, but in the *Metamorphoses* he also expands greatly on her alarming command of magic and her control over the very fabric of the natural world in ways that exerted famous influence on Shakespeare, among others. Finally, Seneca builds on the magical power he found in the *Metamorphoses* and *Heroides* in his description of Medea's concocting of poisons.[13] He also makes his Medea even more powerfully angry than Euripides', and more clearly capable of atrocity: E. M. Spearing argues that even before the first scene is concluded, she has already declared that her children must die.[14] The threat to male order represented by this 'paradigmatic transgressive woman', the furious, infanticidal barbarian of Euripides and Seneca, and by Ovid's drug-concocting sorceress, who wields power of life and death over all those Jason holds dear, was at once an abhorrent and a fascinating one for classical authors: the extent of Medea's power was paradoxically only emphasised by euhemeristic attempts to undercut or rationalise her various threatening abilities, by ancient authors such as Diodorus Siculus.[15] Medea thus becomes more threatening as she is reimagined by successive classical authors, and this pattern, of refiguration that is also exaggeration, is particularly noticeable in early modern English writing. This often sought first to embellish the already lurid classical accounts, and to make its Medea-figures doubly alarming, because somehow directly relevant to early modern concerns such as witchcraft, the security of government, or women's conduct.

Modern Medea and some strategies for representation

Medea remains a potent and dangerous icon today. While medieval and early modern England was most familiar with Ovid's Medea, today it is the dramatic representations of the ancient Medea, the infanticides of Seneca and Euripides, which are most frequently returned to. Sarah Iles Johnston notes that the twentieth century 'has been particularly captivated by Medea',[16] and into the twenty-first century Medea's myth has proved no less compelling, resurfacing in cinematic releases including *Médée Miracle* (directed by Tonino de Bernardi, 2007) and *Medea* (directed by Natalia Kuznetsova, 2009), and in dramatic adaptations of Euripides' tragedy by Liz Lochhead (2000) and Ben Power (2014).[17] If it is the son-killing Medea of Euripides and Seneca that is of most interest to modern interpreters, however, they approach this terrible figure in two distinct ways. Often, Medea and her crimes are viewed as admirable: Marianne McDonald argues for the modern Medea, as represented by the Irish playwright Brendan Kennelly in his 1988 play *Medea* (an adaptation of the Euripidean tragedy) as a kind of 'revolutionary

symbol'. She is an Irish woman who is as determinedly resistant as her
Euripidean forebear to the limits that men attempt to impose on her,
and in fact she is able to surpass her original: McDonald argues that
'[i]n Euripides' play, Medea's power was ambiguous; in Kennelly's play
she wins'.[18] Kennelly substantially adds to Euripides in his adaptation,
but the revolutionary power of the modern Medea can hold true even
when she remains Euripides' heroine: McDonald notes that

> [I]n Africa, Haiti and Ireland, as in other colonized countries, perfor-
> mances of *Medea* are staged as an affirmation of liberty. The play of the
> oppressor (since *Medea* is from the colonizer's literary tradition) is co-
> opted as a weapon directed at the oppressor's heart. The performances
> elate the oppressed.[19]

Such works celebrate not only Medea's violence and ruthless will triumphing over either Jason's cruelty or Creon's attempts to control her
but also reflect outwards onto the audience, promising a similar prospect of escape from tyranny.

Medea's power is more complex than this, however, and in her discussion of Mikis Theodorakis's opera *Medea* (1991) McDonald highlights
the second modern strategy for dealing with Medea's power, demonstrating that, in such works, the modern Medea can be a figure 'whose
suffering is emphasized more than her triumph'.[20] While McDonald has
shown how, in the hands of a playwright like Kennelly, the power of
the fifth-century BC sorceress can be appropriated and celebrated, and
turned to the ends of the oppressed society which performs or views it,
John Kerrigan notes other modern and anachronistic attempts to see
Euripides' Medea as punished and held accountable for her crimes. He
shows how this desire to weaken Medea accords with trends in her classical, medieval and Romantic manifestations:

> A succession of pathetical Medeas runs from Ovid's *Heroides* to
> Chaucer's *Legend of Good Women*; but her distresses were hugely
> elaborated by Romantic dramatists such as Grillparzer, and a suicidal
> heroine achieved full scope in Cherubini's *opéra tragique* of 1797.[21]

Speaking of the numerous contemporary retellings of her story, Iles
Johnston notes that 'Often, these modern versions of the myth show
considerable sympathy for Medea', but sympathy, like an emphasis on
Medea's suffering, runs the risk of blunting the power she demonstrates
over the male community, and modern renderings which make Medea

sympathetic run the risk of rendering her unrecognisable.[22] In fact, even the most apparently triumphant modern manifestations of Medea's power can be stymied in surprising ways, and ways that acknowledge the greater power of patriarchal strictures. Kerrigan has shown how feminist authors including Fay Weldon (*The Life and Loves of a She-Devil*, 1983) and Andrea Dworkin (*Mercy*, 1990) have created heroines who are akin to Medea in their ruthless will and desire for revenge on men or on love-rivals: but he points out that, in the cases of Weldon's Ruth and Dworkin's heroine Andrea, female resistance to control or subjugation through acts of violence or revenge is, simultaneously, subtly and devastatingly undercut.[23] The former of these two Medea-figures, Weldon's She-Devil, is forced to undergo extensive plastic surgery, aligning herself with a male-oriented female ideal, in order to carry out her plots against her husband and Mary Fisher successfully, before eventually realising that her dead rival enjoys the real victory. Meanwhile, in Dworkin's work, Andrea's verbal and physical attacks on random men are at the last perversely reliant on the existence of male power: they 'are apt precisely to the extent that they reproduce the offences (and macho idiom) of patriarchy'.[24]

Works like Weldon's and Dworkin's accept, on some level, that the power of the Medea-like woman has its limits, operating as it must do within a patriarchal society, and while they present the ruthless and terrifying potential of the slighted woman, they also undercut or destabilise that potential, even as they represent it. Such works thus constitute a third modern approach that is neither wholly celebratory (in that it limits the power of the Medea-figure) nor apologetic (in that it does not seek to make such a figure sympathetic, because passive and suffering). The current work explores how early modern English authors adopted a similarly bifurcated strategy in their approach to Medea, presenting her as powerful but not praiseworthy, and suffering the consequences of her crimes, without necessarily becoming sympathetic. Medea's various literary and artistic incarnations have received much attention in recent years, and works that consider the English Medea include Nicola McDonald's thesis, Ruth Morse's monograph (both on the medieval Medea) and Diane Purkiss's essay on Medea on the English Renaissance stage.[25] Most critics or collections move from classical manifestations of Medea to continental authors like Pierre Corneille and Franz Grillparzer, however, and thence to twentieth- and twenty-first century representations in film, theatre and art.[26] The early modern English Medea is thus under-represented in comparison with her continental, Romantic and modern counterparts, but this work will show that the issue of how

Her reading a blanket generalization

to negotiate Medea's alarming power was approached in particularly innovative ways by a wide range of English authors in the sixteenth and seventeenth centuries. Neither praising Medea's power nor sympathising with her, authors including Shakespeare, Spenser and Drayton, and lesser-studied contemporaries like Thomas Achelley, Richard Robinson and Edward Ravenscroft, sought not only to outline Medea's threat but also to appropriate, punish or diminish their Medea-figures as Euripides, Ovid and Seneca do not, and in ways that are highly suggestive of the period's anxious masculine attitudes towards women, witches and foreigners.

Similarity and difference: Medea as cautionary example

In her assessment of Medea on the early modern English stage, Diane Purkiss argues that

> the English Renaissance was not particularly interested in, even alienated by, the Medea of Euripides and Seneca. Eventually some exceptional writers, even dramatists, began to take an interest in Medea, the child-killing avenger, but the standard Renaissance Medea was a treacherous and passionate young *girl*, a girl who helps a hero on his way in exchange for marrying him.[27]

As my focus on her power implies, however, early modern authors are more interested in Medea as a sorceress and a ruthless murderer than this argument might suggest. In her discussion of the ancient Corinithian cult of Hera Akraia, Sarah Iles Johnston describes how, after the deaths of Medea's children, the Corinthians, advised by an oracle, founded the cult and erected a statue of an ugly old woman, not to celebrate Medea but to ward off the threat to their own families and society that they perceived from child-killing demons.[28] Likewise, to come to terms with the fears that Medea encapsulates so potently, early modern English authors confronted these fears directly, first emphasising Medea's threat before exploring strategies for dealing with it. At the forefront of these fears are anxieties about the nature and capabilities of women, anxieties which had surrounded Medea from the time of her very earliest incarnations. Edith Hall notes that the classical Medea is unusual among barbarians (not just barbarian women) because of her 'intellectual powers', though she suggests that Euripides steps back from making Medea's intelligence too close to the ideal of the more civilised Greeks, arguing that for Euripides and his audience 'subversive barbarian guile is not the same as the Greek power of reasoned persuasion through speech-making'.[29] In Seneca's tragedy, Creon, king of Corinth, is at once horrified and fascinated by Medea's combining of 'feminea ... nequitia, ad audendum omnia / robur virile est, nulla famae memoria' (a woman's evil willingness to dare anything, along with a man's strength, and no thought of reputation) (267–8).[30] Stephen Orgel has suggested that in early modern thinking 'the line between the sexes was blurred, often frighteningly so', and Medea's masculine qualities were certainly alarming to early modern authors: but, as Creon notes, Medea is horrifying not just because in her murderous violence she takes on masculine characteristics but also because, through her interaction with her children, her love for Jason, her command of magic and of poisons, she remains recognisably and troublingly feminine.[31] In fact, Dolores M. O'Higgins notes that as far back as Euripides and the Greek poet Pindar (fifth century BC), Medea 'appears both exceptional and typical of all females, as they were generally perceived'.[32] She is fascinating because she is a grotesque exaggeration of women's anger at male control over their destinies: but she is profoundly alarming because she is an exaggeration based on very real male fears, about women's plotting, their witchcraft, and their designs on male bodies, either through their passion or violence.

Modern productions such as Kennelly's, or feminist or post-feminist readings of modern female characters viewed as Medea-figures, might seek to build bonds of affinity between Medea and the reader or audience member, particularly if the reader or audience member is disenfranchised in some way, as the Corinthian Medea is rejected by Jason and Creon.[33] In contrast, male authors in the Renaissance were far more eager to stress how their wives, daughters and sisters were essentially unlike Medea, in their silence, their obedience and their commitment to family. Always present, though, is the spectre of this potential similarity, and the early modern authors who present Medea, like Achelley and Richard Robinson, often challenge their male and female readers or audience members to discern how early modern women are comfortingly unlike Medea, but that this is only because they are constantly under pressure and scrutiny from a society that recognises and understands such alarming examples. For early modern authors this issue of similarity and difference can also extend beyond issues of gender, and be applied to the practice of reading and interpretation, and to England's national identity. So in Chapter 4, I discuss how authors attempting comical treatments of Medea rely on their readers discerning where they remain faithful to their models, and where they deviate from them, thereby allowing the 'knowing reader' to enjoy what Linda Hutcheon has called 'the doubled pleasure of the palimpsest'.[34] In Chapter 5, I show how authors sought to bolster support for Elizabeth, for James I and for Charles II, by comparing Medea to terrible but ultimately unsuccessful threats to England's monarchy, such as Guy Fawkes, or the regicides of Charles I. Here again, the reader is encouraged to perceive both similarity and difference, to recognise the amplified terribleness of those rebels or enemies of monarchy who are deliberately and provocatively likened to Medea, and to enjoy the comforting, retrospective knowledge that they did not achieve the same lasting success, in their efforts to overturn monarchic power.

Profit and delight

Including Medea in their literary works, or translating her story into English, gives early modern authors the opportunity to confront and exorcise some of their deepest fears about threats to England, and to early modern patriarchy. However, she held other attractions too: a commendatory poem by A. F., which prefaced Edward Sherburne's translation of Seneca's *Medea* (1648), supposed that the ancient dramatist's scenes were 'presented on the Roman Stage', where they would 'a horrour, mixt with pleasure, raise' (A3ᵛ), and, as this would suggest, the sensational aspects of Medea's story were never far from authors' minds or pens, in the early modern period.[35] Sixteenth-century authors were increasingly preoccupied with the question of how to differentiate their works from the masses, and entertain and educate their readers: in his *Discourse of English Poetrie* (1586) William Webbe gives Horace's advice, 'that the perfect perfection of poetrie is this, to mingle delight with profitt in such wyse, that a Reader might by his reading be pertaker of bothe' (D3ʳ).[36] Authors of comic, tragic and political works, through the sixteenth and seventeenth centuries, shared Horace's concerns, and, determined that their readers should both learn and enjoy, they sought to represent Medea's power over men in ways that were both entertaining and edifying. In his *Mythologiae* (first published 1567), the Italian mythographer Natale Conti gives his readers explicit guidance over how to read mythological stories, explaining how both the entertainment and the lesson should be kept in mind when classical figures are read in the early modern period. So he sums up his detailed account of Medea's magical powers by bluntly telling his readers 'of course none of these things ever happened, then or at any other time'.[37] Rather than a real witch, Medea should be understood allegorically as good counsel or advice, good counsel that forgets itself when it pursues anything pleasurable (represented by Jason) too assiduously. Alternatively, Medea can be read simply as an example of a wicked woman. Either way, Conti explains: 'whether we think of Medea as counsel or prudence, or as a criminal woman, it's clear that the ancients used this myth to teach us something about decency and integrity' (p. 490). For Conti, as for later English authors who made enthusiastic use of his handbook, the value of Medea's story is that her alarming propensity for magic and murder can be made to serve his own authorial agenda, and can entertain, while also teaching his readers lessons about how to conduct themselves. As is often the case with the goriest and most melodramatic manifestations of Medea's power, the entertainment and the lesson are of equal importance, and the former may be used to smuggle in the latter: in his introduction to the work, Conti explains, 'That is why these stories are so enjoyable to read, as they explain the principles of honest living, ideas that we would otherwise reject were it not for the stories' charm' (vol. 1, p. 4).

If Medea's story can entertain through its sensationalism, as Conti suggests, however, its graphic nature simultaneously made it difficult for early modern authors to engage with to the extent that they might wish. Authors who used print as their medium in the sixteenth and seventeenth centuries, like Achelley and Robinson, did often linger with glee on the gruesome crimes committed by their Medea-figures. They even extend this voyeuristic representation of violence into imagining Medea's own punishment: simultaneously representing her power, turning it to their own instructive ends, and entertaining a bloodthirsty readership. It was much more difficult for early modern playwrights to dwell too extensively on the worst of Medea's crimes: translations of Seneca's tragedy were performed scarcely ever (if at all), and onstage, the typical Medea-like revenger will either fail to emulate the model they invoke or will do so in a compromised fashion. So in Shakespeare's *2 Henry VI*, Young Clifford swears to ape Medea's killing and dismemberment of her brother, in his slaughter of 'an infant of the house of York' (5.3.57), but when he realises this ambition, in *3 Henry VI* 1.3.427, he stops short of cutting the young Rutland into 'gobbets' (5.3.59), as Medea does to Apsyrtus. More importantly, though, his similarity to Medea, demonstrated first by his invocation of her as a model and then by his killing of Rutland, is balanced with his own death, a punishment for barbarity that Shakespeare's Elizabethan audience would fully expect, but which Medea never suffers.

Sixteenth- and seventeenth-century playwrights might also get around problems of dramatic propriety by having characters describe, at gruesome length, their determination to outdo Medea, or their delight in

Shakespeare
Medea as murderer

crimes they have committed offstage: a striking example of this approach may be seen in William Alabaster's Latin tragedy *Roxana*, performed at Trinity College Cambridge in the 1590s, and translated into English in the first decades of the seventeenth century.[38] In fact, even if her crimes could not be shown, on the early modern stage there was perverse enjoyment to be gained from the staging of a Medea-like woman in particular (as opposed to the rarer spectacle of the male Medea-figure), because of the spectre of similarity, combined with reassuring difference, that has been discussed above. Lisa Jardine argues that when a Medea-figure is brought onstage, such representations may have been intended to titillate the male members of the audience, and may, paradoxically, be enjoyable as well as alarming, allowing the male audience member to reflect that: 'No woman of *his* will ever get thus out of hand.'[39] Confronted with women who are explicitly or implicitly likened to Medea – Shakespeare's Lady Macbeth, or Alabaster's Roxana, or Edward Ravenscroft's Tamora – the male audience member recognises the threat that the barbarian, the witch and the child-killing woman might pose to his own society. He is horrified by the dramatic representation of such a woman, and yet understands that she is just different enough from the women in his society to allow him to relax: and, because of this comforting realisation, as Jardine argues, 'the representation is equally a source of delight'.[40]

Nevertheless, the lesson is important too, and as Jardine's comments suggest, Medea's story holds lessons not just for women but also for the early modern men who should control and police their potential for transgression. Mark Breitenberg points out that in early modern writing by men, 'deep structural and ideological tensions in society are conveniently located and addressed in the figure of the unruly or disobedient woman'.[41] In fact, as a witch and a barbarian as well as a woman, Medea is a particularly useful tool for male authors engaged in what Stephen Greenblatt terms 'self-fashioning', a process that all but demanded the presence of a Medea-like figure against which to react. He suggests: '[S]elf-fashioning is achieved in relation to something perceived as alien, strange, or hostile. This threatening Other – heretic, savage, witch, adulteress, traitor, Antichrist – must be discovered or invented in order to be attacked and destroyed.'[42] Male authors comforted themselves with the idea that they (and their female dependents) were fundamentally unlike Medea, but key to this comfort is a seemingly paradoxical necessity to stress the danger of such a figure. Medea's power seems to have been most pleasurable for readers and audience members when it was represented, but then undermined or controlled, and when this authorial control over her power might contain a lesson for the reader about their own identity, an assurance that they are (or can be) unlike Medea. For example, on the title-page of the *Rewarde of Wickednesse* (1574) Richard Robinson boasts that the reader of his poem can expect to find

> the sundrye monstrous abuses of wicked and ungodlye worldelinges: in such sort set downe and written as the same have béene dyversely practised in the persones of Popes, Harlots, Proude Princes, Tyrauntes, Romish Byshoppes, and others. With a lively description of their severall falles and finall destruction. (A^r)[43]

Medea is one such 'Harlot', and Robinson takes it upon himself to describe at length her horrible torments in Hell, and her regret at her crimes, in the hope that this radical revisioning of Medea (who is never punished like this in classical or medieval English literature) will prove 'Verye profitable for all sorte of estates to reade and looke upon'. Predictably, Robinson sees in Medea, in her punishment and her regret for her crimes, a lesson for women, about the dangers of unrestrained desire, or the wickedness of magic. As I shall show in Chapter 3, however, Robinson's Medea is also intended as a caution for men: for the brothers, fathers and husbands who must control the women in their lives, as Aeëtes, Jason, Pelias, Creon and Aegeus could not control Medea. Whether an author's focus is instruction, entertainment, or a mixture of the two, her frightening power must be foregrounded, so that authors, readers and spectators alike can consider their own conduct in comparison with hers.

Creating and interpreting Medea

As Robinson's dual focus on her well-known crimes and her invented suffering suggests, Medea is troubling and inspiring in equal measure for early modern authors who come to rewrite her story. Again focusing on ancient and modern (rather than early modern) writing, Kerrigan articulates the relationship between Medea's career and male creativity:

> since Greek antiquity, she has stood for the natural, the magical, and the barbaric in ways which have served to define, by opposition or excited alliance, the operations of (usually male) creativity across a range of media: from drama, through opera, to film.[44]

Recent work on adaptation and appropriation has stressed creativity as a vital aspect of engagement with earlier literature: for Hutcheon, 'adapters are first interpreters and then creators', while Julie Sanders argues that 'it is usually at the very point of infidelity [to the original] that the most creative acts of adaptation and appropriation take place'.[45] For early modern authors, the fact that Medea's was such a well-known classical story paradoxically encouraged them to greater heights of invention: specifically, it drove them to consider the nature of their relationship with the classics, and how far they could and should deviate from the Greek and Latin Medeas they had encountered. These classical originals might well be familiar to their readers but, at the same time, translators like Wye Saltonstall and Zachary Catlin are keenly aware that some readers (particularly women) might not be able to compare Latin and English, and would be wholly reliant on the translator's text, a consideration which might endow the translator with a specific kind of responsibility to his readers. Alternatively, of course, readers might be unable to read Ovid or Seneca, but might know medieval versions of Medea's story, such as those provided by William Caxton and John Lydgate: as I shall show in Chapter 1, these are often radical revisionings of classical tradition, and themselves make use of intermediary authors. The sheer number and range of her literary incarnations meant that a reader might also have an awareness of Medea and her crimes that is not rooted in any one text: her wickedness might be what Thomas M. Greene terms 'a topos that conventional repetition has removed from the purview of any one author or work'.[46] What is certain is that, where a figure like Medea is concerned, authors are aware that they may be presenting her to what Hutcheon terms the 'unknowing' reader, or, alternatively, to a reader who is intimately familiar with the details of her story, able to appreciate where and how an author deviates either from a specific source (what Gérard Genette would term the 'hypotext'), or from received wisdom about Medea.[47]

Speaking of the medieval idea of historical writing, and medieval authors' use of specific and familiar topoi in their histories, Ruth Morse suggests that

> [A]s soon as writers become aware that they are repeating a unit which has appeared before, their interpretation becomes self-conscious, because it expects readers to compare it to another. Such units can be recognized across genre boundaries, and it is important to remember that this recognition and comparison was part of the pleasure of reading. There is something inescapably intertextual in this kind of reading, where the alert interpreter is constantly on the lookout for what it is he is supposed to be reminded of, and in which texts he has seen it before.[48]

Though Morse's study concerns itself with the Middle Ages, and specifically with medieval ideas of history and historical truth, her articulation of the roles of the reader and author here is extremely useful. Elsewhere, Morse sees classical literature as 'suggesting – but not compelling – varieties of creation and interpretation' for medieval authors.[49] Precisely because medieval writers like Chaucer, Gower, Lydgate and Caxton had written the stories of Medea and the Golden Fleece before them, and because of the resurgence of interest in classical culture that was central to the Renaissance, authors in the sixteenth and seventeenth centuries were far more concerned than their medieval counterparts with the need to experiment with the classical legacy that they had inherited, to rewrite and reinterpret rather than repeat. A study of Medea in the period thus also becomes a study of classical reception and of debates about the division between the medieval and the early modern, about imitation and adaptation, as early modern authors, dissatisfied with the Medea they had inherited from the classics and from medieval literature, sought to reshape her story and make it relevant to the concerns of their own age.

As Morse's first observation also suggests, however, the reader, or 'alert interpreter', as well as the author, has work to do, when they encounter Medea rewritten for the sixteenth and seventeenth centuries. In his study of allusion in Roman poetry, Stephen Hinds points to the potential for 'a non-inert reading of a commonplace'.[50] Such a reading is more than repetitive, and, moreover, represents a challenge for the engaged reader. The complexity, controversy and excitement of Medea's story lent itself naturally to such engaged and educative readings, in early modern England, as today. For example, as I shall show in Chapter 4, the Restoration burlesquers of Ovid relished the possibility that their readers might already know the original Latin of Hypsipyle's and Medea's epistles, or (even better) the relatively accurate and straight-faced *Heroides* compiled by Jacob Tonson, and introduced by John Dryden, which had appeared in 1680. While the burlesqued translations might be enjoyed by a reader with no prior knowledge of Ovid's Medea, or of the Dryden-Tonson Ovid, such knowledge adds an extra enjoyment to the experience of reading, demanding what Hutcheon calls a process of 'interpretive doubling, a conceptual flipping back and forth' between source text and adaptation.[51]

To give a different, and perhaps even less subtle, example of the potential for a reader to *interpret* an author's use of Medea, in the quotation that began this introduction (and that also introduced his own tragic poem about Didaco and Violenta), Thomas Achelley may insist that there is nothing to be gained in recycling such stories, but, despite his specific rejection of Medea's example in his dedication, he is driven to include her in his tale, to underscore Violenta's hideous and uncontrolled violence against Didaco. As much as the more bloodthirsty of his readers may relish being reminded of the damage a woman can wreak on the male body (either the body of Medea's brother Apsyrtus, mentioned in Achelley's dedication, or that of the faithless Didaco), however, Achelley is keen to warn and chastise as well as thrill, and he does this by asking his readers to interpret what he has set before them correctly. Having dealt with Violenta's crime and punishment, he goes on to explain to his female readers in particular how such a terrible, Medea-like woman should be read:

> You Ladies all whose weeping eyes
> This hystorie peruse:
> At rarenes of this monstrous fact
> No marveyle though ye muse.
> But as the splendant blasting lampe,
> Doth never burn so bright:
> As when a darkesome shade doth seeme
> For to eclipse his ligh[t]
> So you, deere dames whose vertuous minds,
> Abandon all such wayes:
> By contrarie of this foule facte,
> Deserve immortal prayse. (Fiii^r)

Achelley argues that his female readers should 'No marveyle though ye muse', and that through this musing they should engage in what Hinds might call a 'non-inert reading' of Violenta's example, interpreting her in such a way that they feel all the more secure in their own goodness. He suggests in the dedication to his poem that there are no lessons to be learnt from the stories of women like Medea, but, in retaining the comparison between his foreign anti-heroine and the classical murderess, he implies a connection between the reading of classical figures and the gleaning of moral messages, that was even more clearly communicated in the works of contemporaries who turned to Medea, such as Richard Robinson.

Achelley's brief references to Medea, in his introduction and once again in the body of his poem, also provide an opportunity to define the scope of this study further. Brief references or allusions to earlier texts are, for the most part, excluded from recent work on adaptation and appropriation, for example by Hutcheon and Sanders. Many such brief mentions and allusions are included here, however, alongside more sustained engagements (such as the translations addressed in Chapter 2) because, while they may sometimes be little more than part of a catalogue, with Medea simply another example of a wicked or abandoned woman, often even a fleeting reference to Medea can potentially reshape the text in question, or suggest that it can be viewed in a new and different light. A good example of this is Jessica's misguided invoking of Medea's rejuvenation of Aeson, as she prepares to elope in *The Merchant of Venice* (discussed at more length in Chapter 4). Shakespeare knew, of course, that this generous act of Medea's would be swiftly outweighed by acts of murder and cruelty, and he knew that some of his audience would appreciate this too, even if Jessica cannot: even the most fleeting reference to Medea thus colours the work for the knowing reader, suggesting a troubling movement towards tragedy.[52] Despite Jessica's focus on the rejuvenation, early modern authors, like modern day film directors or playwrights, realised that the most exhilarating aspect of Medea's story was not her love for Jason, or her assistance in his quest, but her magical, violent and murderous powers, those qualities that make her a protagonist in her own story rather than merely a 'helper-maiden' of the kind familiar from medieval romance, and they consistently nod towards this power, even if, like Shakespeare, they do so only via a brief reference, and rely on the reader or audience to appreciate its full import.

Like Achelley, medieval authors seem unable to ignore Medea, but at the same time they cannot unapologetically celebrate her destructive power. As I shall demonstrate in Chapter 1, English authors including Chaucer, Gower, Lydgate and Caxton grappled enthusiastically with the challenge to male authority represented by Medea, and, usually by romanticising her or strategically truncating her story, they sought as keenly as their Renaissance successors to subdue the threat she represented to the patriarchally controlled institutions of marriage and kingdom. Medieval English strategies for dealing with Medea's power differ significantly from the typical early modern approach, which was far more willing to embrace her criminality and violence, but I argue that these works provide an important lens through which to view the more adventurous handlings of the sixteenth and seventeenth centuries, and contribute to an understanding of how the medieval Medea becomes early modern.

Chapter 2 examines the most important printed English translations of classical works that retold Medea's story, including translations of Seneca's *Medea* (by John Studley, 1566, and Edward Sherburne, 1648),

Ovid's *Metamorphoses* (by Arthur Golding, 1567, and George Sandys, 1626 and 1632), his *Tristia* (by Thomas Churchyard, 1572, Wye Saltonstall, 1633, and Zachary Catlin, 1639) and his *Heroides* (by George Turberville, 1567, Wye Saltonstall, 1636, John Sherburne, 1639, and John Dryden and others, 1680). Particular attention is paid to the ways in which these texts do more than just translate Medea, and in fact direct their readers' interpretation of her threat, through prefaces, notes and marginal glosses, and often, by augmenting, truncating or directly contradicting their classical sources. The chapter also considers how translations of Medea evolved across the period, and how they reconciled the seemingly contradictory demands of classical and early modern translation theory, remaining true to the spirit of their originals while also building on what they found in Seneca and Ovid.

In sixteenth- and seventeenth-century English literature, Medea's most natural home was in tragic writing, whether this took the form of drama, poetry or prose, and these uses form the basis for Chapter 3. Breitenberg notes that, in modern Hollywood, a powerful woman is usually unsettling to the male community because of her aggressive sexuality, and that 'more often than not, the female protagonist is punished for her transgression: she functions as the scapegoat whose degradation restores the normative order'.[53] As this chapter will show, if we shift its focus from female sexuality to violence, Breitenberg's point may be applied to early modern representations of Medea, in both print (poetry and prose) and drama. The chapter argues that while Medea was often chosen as a deliberately provocative and titillating example in tragedy (particularly when she is invoked by female characters), it is also possible to discern a clear interest in reshaping her power and punishing the Renaissance Medea, in order to caution or instruct the reader or audience member, and restore some sense of 'normative order' to male and female audiences and readers alike.

Chapter 4 examines the ways in which Medea's alarming power is incorporated into comic works, whether these are plays, prose tales or poems (e.g., the burlesqued translations of Ovid that appeared in the Restoration). One comic approach to Medea's power, discernible in the prose works of Robert Greene, is to joke at the expense of the reader or character who is insufficiently engaged or informed, who does not understand the full import of her story, and so invokes her glibly or foolishly.[54] Occupying a space somewhere between Hutcheon's 'knowing' and 'unknowing' readers, such a figure knows something of Medea's story, but not quite enough, and thus becomes a figure of fun through their misreading. In comic and tragicomic drama, meanwhile, such as

Shakespeare's *The Merchant of Venice* and *The Tempest*, or James Shirley's *The Schoole of Complement*, Medea's power is used to cast doubt on happy endings and particularly romantic unions, destabilising them even as they are apparently achieved. Here, her story is used 'to mark the dark shadows of alternative possible plots beneath an unfolding comedy', as Colin Burrow puts it in the course of noting Ovidian influence on another of Shakespeare's comedies, *A Midsummer Night's Dream*.[55] Later in the period, Medea's power is itself belittled, parodied and made into a source of black comedy, in the works of Matthew Stevenson (*The Wits Paraphras'd*, 1680) and Alexander Radcliffe (*Ovid Travestie*, 1680). Comic uses of Medea's power in the period are unsurprisingly rare, but I argue that in many ways they are the most intriguing of all, demonstrating as they do the early modern author's refusal to remain tied to their classical models, and relying on a finely tuned balance between a reader's knowledge of the classics and their willingness to accept that even the bloodiest myths were mutable and could be adapted to an unexpected genre of writing.

In my final chapter, I show how Medea's power was appropriated and made to serve English monarchical interest, as it was applied to both historical and contemporary events. Recent adaptation theory has disputed the tendency to see the revisiting and reworking of older stories as a conservative act: modern adaptations of myths for stage or screen might depart radically from their sources, often with political intent, and even in early modern England a figure like Lucrece or Philomela might be used as a way of voicing protest or dissent from the status quo.[56] Moreover, in her work on exemplarity and early modern political writing, Susan Wiseman has warned that even well-known examples from classical or biblical literature might be used unpredictably: 'the identification of a repertoire of examples that put women into politics does not mean that exemplarity and examples worked in a stable way'.[57] Medea's notoriously horrible crimes, which are so disproportionate to the wrongs she has suffered, and which are not balanced with any suggestion of punishment, however, meant that by and large English authors shied away from using her in a politically radical way. More commonly, she is used to demonstrate the horrors of disobedience and rebellion, made into Greenblatt's 'Other', against which early modern monarchists or conformists could define themselves. Terrible though her power may be, a focus on Medea's violence and her terrifying disregard for order allows politically minded authors to achieve a perverse kind of security through use of the Colchian sorceress, either by punishing their politically dangerous Medea-figures or by urging their readers to shun her example, and see the benefits of obedience and conformity.

Of course, such divisions do not attempt to suggest that each early modern manifestation of Medea fits neatly into one genre or category of literature. For example, Thomas Heywood's treatment of her legend in the mythological drama *The Brazen Age* (1613) is clearly indebted both to his own earlier epic poem, *Troia Britanica* (1609), which features Jason and Medea in Canto 7, and to medieval English approaches to her myth. This debt is apparent in the play's focus on Medea's passionate love for Jason; in Heywood's decision to abandon her story as the pair leave Colchis and in his use of the myth to introduce the first sack of Troy by Hercules, who has been slighted by King Laomedon. *The Brazen Age* also incorporates more recent material from early modern translation and adaptation, however: from Golding's *Metamorphoses* (1567) he takes Medea's boast that she can 'Darken the Sunne at noone, call from their graues / Ghosts long since dead' (p. 214), while her reference to 'the elues of Hils, of Brookes, of Groues, / Of standing lakes' (p. 215) takes its cue from Prospero's words in *The Tempest* (and/or from Shakespeare's source, Medea's words in Golding's poem).[58] Moreover, Heywood embellishes his version of the story with the intrigue and deceit that was typical of Jacobean tragedy: Medea's father passes her a secret note, demanding that she bring about Jason's downfall, but is double-crossed by his daughter, and meanwhile a Machiavellian Jason has his own agenda, confiding in the audience:

I have obseru'd Medea
Retort upon me many an amorous looke,
Of which I'le studdy to make prosperous use. (p. 212)

There is even room for black comedy in Heywood's strange mixture, in the form of the doomed Apsyrtus' cheeky and innuendo-laden retorts to his sister. When she asks for his discretion regarding her meeting with Jason, her brother, who is shortly to die at her hand, responds, 'Do you take me to be a woman, to tell all I see, and blab all I know, I that am in hope one day to lie with a woman, will once lie for a woman, Sister I saw you not' (p. 215).

Heywood's play also demonstrates a dramatist's appreciation for the spectacle inherent in Medea's story, with one stage direction instructing: 'Two fiery Buls are discovered, the Fleece hanging over them, and the dragon sleeping beneath them: Medea with strange fiery-workes, hangs above in the Aire in the strange habite of a Conjuresse' (p. 217). This brief account of Medea's appearance in *The Brazen Age* demonstrates that one appeal of Medea's story was clearly the opportunity it afforded

Heywood to combine the familiarity of medieval Troy-legends with the popularity of Elizabethan translation, and the innovations of early modern drama. This careful combination, of the novel and the comfortingly familiar, is one that appears again and again, in whatever genre Medea finds herself. For Horace, Medea's power and will are central to her representation, and must not be altered: he advises, 'See to it that Medea is fierce and indomitable'.[59] However, he also cautions against overly literal or 'slavish' use of old stories, in terms that would become particularly influential in the Restoration, when authors like John Dryden came to formulate theories of English classical translation.[60] Early modern authors were keenly aware of the pressure to imitate effectively, to look back to classical authorities, while rejuvenating these old stories and making them relevant to the specific concerns of their Renaissance and Restoration readers. The spectre of Medea's murderous power means that she is seldom less than 'fierce' in early modern English writing, whatever the genre. Indeed, authors of the period keenly appreciated the entertaining and didactic potential of her power, electing to dwell on it as their medieval predecessors did not. However, they also chose to balance it with punishment or repentance, thereby both innovating and making their Medeas something less than the 'indomitable' figure Horace recommends. Raising questions about the control of women, how controversial literature could be made relevant and appealing to its audience, and how the classics should be adapted, and encapsulating the most alarming early modern taboos about witchcraft and child-killing, Medea represents a peculiar challenge for early modern authors. Hers is a challenge that they accepted with alacrity, however, determined to appropriate her magical, violent power and turn it to their own ends, both for the profit and the delight of early modern England.

1
Medieval Medea

In the English literature of the Middle Ages, Medea is often deprived of the opportunity to demonstrate her considerable and alarming powers to the full. In Book 5 of John Gower's *Confessio Amantis*, the figure of Amans assures the Confessor, 'I have herde it ofte seie / Hou Jason tok the flees aweie / Fro Colchos' (5.4231–3).[1] Medea's crucial role is unmentioned here, and although earlier in the poem Gower has described her magic, and the crimes she was willing to commit for Jason, it is not her ability or her ruthlessness but her unrequited love for Jason that is stressed as her story closes, in terms which clearly disempower Medea and give Jason the upper hand. Such a description is typical of the medieval English approach to Medea, which on the whole sought to elide or undercut her power wherever possible, despite medieval authors' knowledge of powerful classical and continental Medeas. English authors such as Chaucer, Gower, Lydgate and Caxton gleaned their knowledge of Medea not only from Ovid but also from continental sources, such as Guido delle Colonne's *Historia Destructionis Troiae*, Boccaccio's *De Claris Mulieribus* and *De Genealogia Deorum Gentilium Libri* and Raoul Lefèvre's *Histoire de Jason*, as well as from late antique and medieval mythographies and commentaries.[2] What is most noticeable, however, is the extent to which these English authors attempt to contain Medea's power, by either ignoring it altogether or describing it in highly circumscribed ways.

Continental Medea

There was a thriving tradition in the Middle Ages whereby continental authors in particular sought to allegorise or rationalise Medea's story, particularly as they found it in the *Metamorphoses*. Also significant for

English medieval authors who sought to represent Medea, however, were two early continental accounts of Jason's quest for the Fleece and of the assistance he received from a love-struck Medea. These were Benoît de Sainte-Maure's Old French poem the *Roman de Troie* (*c*.1160) and a Latin prose adaptation by Guido delle Colonne, the *Historia Destructionis Troiae* (1287). Although Guido's work takes Benoît's as its model, the two are significantly different, and in fact may be said to exemplify the two most common English approaches to the problem of Medea's power: the romanticising impulse and the misogynistic attack.

As its title suggests, Benoît's *Roman de Troie* sees the Argonautic voyage, and Jason's love affair with Medea, as a precursor to the first sack of Troy by the Argonauts, and to the eventual Greek defeat of Priam's city, as a result of Paris' rape of Helen. The poem as a whole owes a clear debt to Ovid, and also to the *De Excidio Troia Historia*, a sixth-century Latin work by Dares the Phrygian, which was believed in the Middle Ages to be an eyewitness account of the Trojan War.[3] Benoît is primarily interested in Medea as a woman who is undeniably magical and powerful, but who is utterly overthrown by the strength of her own feelings for Jason. In this account, Medea is struck by love for Jason immediately, and suffers the physical changes medieval readers would expect from a romance heroine – going red and white, hot and cold as she looks at him. Benoît observes that when she sees the Argonauts, Medea, 'que d'amor esprent, / S'en vient a eus mout vergondose' (who burned with love, / came to them very modestly) (1.1308–9).[4] Equally, an account of Medea's magical abilities finishes with a reference to her beauty: 'el païs ne el regné / N'aveit dame de sa beauté' (There was nobody of her beauty in the country or kingdom) (1.1247–8).

Unlike some subsequent authors, who attempt to rewrite the quest for the Fleece as a wholly male achievement, Benoît recognises and acknowledges the part Medea has to play. Though he provides a lengthy account of Jason's success in his tasks (which is contained in the *Metamorphoses*), Medea's role is also underscored by their long conversation which precedes the tasks, and which is absent from the *Metamorphoses* (there, Medea speaks only to herself, to debate the wisdom of saving Jason). Barbara Nolan has shown how Benoît builds on his sources, both Ovid and Dares (who does not mention Medea at all) to create a sense of the intimacy between Jason and Medea, and indeed between Medea and the reader: as Nolan points out, the reader is invited into Medea's bedchamber, as she wrestles with her desire for Jason.[5] During their subsequent night together, Medea describes in detail what Jason must do to overcome his obstacles, and gives him a ring and magic potion to ensure success. Here, Benoît takes his inspiration from the *Metamorphoses* and *Heroides*, both in his account of Jason's tasks and in the very clear sense that Jason owes his success to Medea, something she angrily stresses in *Heroides* 12.[6]

Benoît's interest in emphasising Medea's role in the conquest of the Fleece might seem to reflect an interest in her power. After Jason's triumph, however, Benoît abruptly cuts short the story, blaming Dares (whose *De Excidio Troia Historia* does not say a word about Medea) in his disingenuous observation 'Ne Daires plus n'en voust escrire, / Ne Beneeiz pas ne l'alonge' (As Dares does not wish to write any longer, so Benoît will not elaborate) (1.2064–5). Though the pair return to Iolcos in triumph, Benoît does not describe the killing of Apsyrtus or Pelias, or the rejuvenation of Aeson, and refers only obliquely to Medea's final revenge, which, as Morse shows, he ascribes to 'The gods' rather than to Medea herself.[7] His determined ignoring of the grisly events he would have found amply referenced in the *Heroides* and *Metamorphoses* is noticeable and notable. The elision of Medea's crimes, instantly obvious to those of his readers who might have recourse to Ovid, is problematic, betraying Benoît's desire to construct a Medea who is powerful but essentially and predominantly a romance heroine, a woman whose power serves male interests in a productive way, and who is intended above all to demonstrate the pitfalls of what Nolan calls 'young, foolish love'.[8]

This version of the story was popular in its own right, and spawned several prose redactions. The enduring legacy of the *Roman*, particularly with regard to the presentation of Medea, however, is its impact on the Latin work of Guido delle Colonne.[9] Despite his emphasis on Medea's sensitivity and his refusal to dwell on the most negative aspects of her classical characterisation, such as her violence and anger, Benoît's account ironically provides the model for one of the most concerted attacks on Medea in the Middle Ages, Guido's deeply misogynistic *Historia Destructionis Troiae*, completed in 1287.[10] The *Historia* is a Latin translation of a prose redaction of Benoît's work (though it does not advertise itself as such, claiming instead to draw directly on Dares). It is a translation with significant additions and alterations, however, for though he follows the basic outline of the story that he inherits from Benoît, Guido makes critical and often virulently misogynistic additions to Benoît's observations on Medea's power and abilities, and her love for Jason. For example, while Benoît suggested an intimate and passionate relationship between Jason and Medea, Guido makes this far more explicit and characterises Medea as in control and sexually insatiable, in ways that would be deeply alarming for the male medieval reader:

> Medea licet sui uoti satisfactionem impleuerit per uiriles amplexus et optatos actus uenereos a Iasone, propterea non euanuit scintilla cupidinis in eadem; immo per expertos actos postea grauiora concepit incendia quam per facinus ante commissum. (p. 25)

> [A]lthough Medea enjoyed the satisfaction of her wishes through the manly embraces and longed for acts of love by Jason, still the spark of lust did not die down in her; on the contrary, when the acts were finished, she conceived a more intense passion than she had before the thing was done. (3.117–21)[11]

Crucially, Guido also extends his criticism of Medea into an attack on all women, as he criticises her willingness to deceive her father (and herself) over the nature of her desire for Jason:

> Omnium enim mulierum semper est moris ut cum inhonesto desiderio uirum aliquem appetunt, sub alicuius honestatis uelamine suas excusationes intendant. (p. 18)

> For it is always the custom of women, that when they yearn for some man with immodest desire, they veil their excuses under some sort of modesty. (2.294–6)

Guido's inspiration for these lines may be the *Metamorphoses*, in which Medea wonders whether she is deluding herself as to the nature of her relationship with Jason, as she ponders whether to help him: 'coniugiumne putas speciosaque nomina culpae / inponis, Medea, tuae?' (But do you deem it marriage, Medea, and do you give fair-seeming names to your fault?) (7.69–70).[12] In Guido's rendering, the answer is supplied: Medea clearly deludes herself that her desire for Jason is blameless. Her ability to follow the wrong course of action here makes her peculiarly alarming and worthy of a criticism that can be conveniently extended to medieval women.

Similarly, just as he makes it clear that her sexual desire for Jason is a flaw in Medea's character and one which should be condemned, Guido seeks to undermine the magical power that Benoît has suggested and which he finds so threatening. After including Benoît's description of Medea's powers, Guido feels driven to include a lengthy explanation of how Medea could not really have enjoyed the power over God and nature that Benoît ascribes to her. Guido attributes such stories to 'fabularis Sulmonensis Ouidius' (p. 16) ('that storytelling Ovid of Sulmo') (2.206–7), and later he points out that Medea ultimately proves unable to foresee her own undoing:

> Sed certum est astronomie iudicia super incerto firmata, de quo manifestum exemplum potenter et patenter in te elicitur, que tibi prouidere per ea nullatenus potuisti … In quibus nullus deprehenditur futurorum effectus, nisi a casu forte contingat, cum solius Dei sit, in cuius manu sunt posita scire tempora temporum et momenta. (pp. 24–5)

> It is certain the judgements of astronomy are based upon uncertainty, of which the manifest example is most powerfully and plainly seen in you, who were in no way able to see into the future through astronomy … In these things no effect of the future is to be discovered, unless perhaps it is touched upon by chance, since it is of God alone, in whose hand is the knowledge of times and the moments of times. (3.103–11)

Like Benoît, Guido ends his account of Medea once the pair leave Colchis, observing of her: 'Sane diceris peruenisse in Thesaliam, ubi per Thesalum Iasonem, ciuibus inueneranda Thesalicis, occulta nece post multa detestanda discrimina uitam legeris finiuisse' (p. 32) (You are said to have arrived in Thessaly where, on account of Thessalian Jason you are described as having finished your life with an obscure death, despised by the Thessalian citizens, after many detestable adventures) (3.379–82). Guido is far more keen than Benoît to characterise Medea as alarming, to linger on her unseemly desire for Jason and hint at the crimes she goes on to commit (which are not, as they are in Benoît's poem, ascribed to the gods). Guido sees nothing to commend in Medea's abilities, however, and as a result he either questions the very existence of such power, or else turns it into an attack on women. These are two approaches that would retain their popularity into the sixteenth and seventeenth centuries, even as later versions of Medea's story became more widely read in England than the *Historia Destructionis Troiae*.

Medea in allegorical and moralising tradition

If Medea's story was turned to the ends of romance and misogynistic criticism by Benoît and Guido, equally important are those uses of her which reflect another abiding interest of medieval writers: the tradition of summarising or allegorising classical authors, particularly Ovid. Medea had featured in late antique and early medieval mythographies, such as the works of the Vatican Mythographers, Hyginus' *Fabulae* and Fulgentius' *Mythologiae*. In these works, her criminal power is described: for example, the second Vatican mythographer expands on the work of the first, which had described the murder of Glauce, and the attempted murder of Theseus, by explaining that Medea fled Corinth 'suis Iasonisque natis interemtis' (having killed the sons that belonged to her and to Jason) (138.35).[13] The *Fabulae*, attributed uncertainly to the first-century AD Roman writer Hyginus, describes Medea's killing of Pelias, Creusa and her sons, although, like Apollonius Rhodius' earlier epic the *Argonautica*, it attributes the killing of Medea's brother Apsyrtus (here an adult) to Jason.[14] In the *Metamorphoses*, medieval authors would have found similar accounts of her violence and cruelty, but unlike the Vatican Mythographers and Hyginus, who give matter-of-fact descriptions of Medea's abilities and crimes, writers who allegorise the poem often undermine her role, despite the compelling power they found in Ovid. For example, John of Garland's mid-thirteenth-century commentary on the poem, the *Integumenta Ovidii*, picks up on Ovid's description of her as 'spolia altera' (another spoil) (7.157). He notes, 'Auratum vellus Medeam dicimus ipsam. / Auro preda fuit hec speciosa magis' (We speak of Medea herself as the golden fleece. She was a prize more splendid than gold) (297–8).[15] As Kathryn L. McKinley notes, 'Here Garland represents Medea as a glittering prize, a type of faint praise suggesting Jason's perception of her as a useful means to his own ends.'[16] Medea's power is acknowledged, albeit doubtfully: McKinley points out that 'Garland goes on to attribute all of Jason's victories to Medea and her *ars*, however unreliable such skill may be in the end.'[17] Such qualified praise of Medea, as a 'glittering prize', foreshadows later medieval accounts which focus reductively on those attributes (beauty, grace, charm) that make her an attractive partner for Jason, as well as those that rewrite the quest into a paean of praise for Jason (such as Raoul Lefèvre's *Histoire de Jason*), discussed later in this chapter. Similarly, McKinley shows how commentaries on and summaries of the *Metamorphoses* by Arnulf of Orléans (*Allegoriae*, c.1175), Giovanni del Virgilio (*Allegorie Librorum Ovidii Metamorphoseos*, 1322–3) and Pierre Bersuire (*Ovidius moralizatus*, 1362) manage to sideline Medea, despite the pivotal part she plays in Book 7: in particular, they do not allow her the impressive oratorical power she enjoys in the *Metamorphoses*.[18]

However, medieval responses to the *Metamorphoses* could document Medea's powers more enthusiastically, and even read them positively.

The early fourteenth-century poem the *Ovide moralisé* attempts to make Christian sense of the power Medea wields. McDonald notes that in the poem, 'The sorceress is explicitly identified with Christ who, by means of his prodigious powers, guaranteed the salvation, and thus the rejuvenation, of all mankind.'[19] She points out that, as this surprising identification would suggest, the poet 'consistently offers a positive reading of the enchantress'.[20] Medea is described in terms familiar to any reader of Benoît's *Roman*: she is 'Bele pucele et simple et sage' (A beautiful maiden, innocent and wise) (7.295).[21] More inventively, the poet goes on to read in even Medea's worst crimes (which Benoît tactfully skates over) a positive message for the Christian reader: Medea's dismemberment of Apsyrtus is compared to Christ's willingness to suffer to absolve mankind's sins (7.808–20), while Creusa, Medea's love rival and an innocent victim of her jealous rage, is explained as a malign force, come to earth to mislead mankind 'Par sa fraude et par sa fallace' (by her fraud and falsehood) (7.1649).[22] In the fifteenth century, the *Ovide moralisé en prose* follows the fourteenth-century verse version, explaining that Medea should be understood as 'la beneoiste Vierge Marie' (p. 209) ('the blessed Virgin Mary') when she rejuvenates Aeson, while Creusa is representative of the power of the Antichrist, and thus deservedly destroyed.[23] Bersuire's redaction of the *Metamorphoses*, which was printed in the early sixteenth century and known in England, where it was attributed to Thomas Whalleys, however, interprets her more negatively. She might be Jason's helpmate, a physical manifestation of 'sapientiam cunctis artibus eruditam' (erudite knowledge of all arts) (VII. Fol. LIIII), or a hellish force, whose example should encourage parents to exercise control over their children and men to choose their wives carefully.[24] McDonald shows that while Bersuire interprets Medea positively on occasion, for example by comparing her rejuvenation of Aeson to the power of 'the preacher who enchants the congregation in order to provide them with moral renewal', in the main Bersuire's handling of Medea is 'extensively and resoundingly damning'.[25]

This medieval interest in interpreting or explaining Medea, and attaching an inventive moral to her story rather than just obediently repeating it, survives into some early modern mythographies and dictionaries. For example, while Thomas Elyot's 1542 English dictionary, *Bibliotheca Eliotae*, describes her simply as 'wyfe unto Jason, a wytche and a cruelle woman', Natale Conti's 1567 *Mythologiae*, discussed in my introduction, provided a far more extensive account and analysis of Medea's crimes, and argued, crucially, that the story of such a wicked woman must be interpreted correctly, since 'the ancients used this myth to teach us something about decency and integrity' (490).[26] In turn, seventeenth-century reference works might respond to this interpreting and moralising tradition more factually, rationalising and explaining Medea's magical power in ways that diminish her skills and make those who believe in her mythical abilities ridiculous. For example, both the lexicographer Thomas Blount and the physician Thomas Browne draw on the ancient mythographer Palaephatus to explain that, rather than rejuvenating Aeson, Medea simply dyed his hair black, and that any magical ability that has been ascribed to her is the result of misunderstanding or false report.[27]

Medea can also be found in the catalogues of well-known women that were so popular in the period, and here she is most often used critically, as one might expect, or else as an example of a woman abandoned by her cruel lover.[28] In Giovanni Boccaccio's *De Claris Mulieribus*, for example, she is described as 'the cruellest example of ancient treachery', who will stop at nothing to achieve her desires; and he recounts the killings of Pelias, Apsyrtus and her children. Medea is far from innocent here: though he describes her being reunited with Jason, and restoring her father Aeëtes to his kingdom, he notes that her own 'virginal honour', her father's reign and her brother's life were all irrevocably harmed by her desire for Jason, what he calls 'the shamelessness of her eyes'.[29] It is also worth noting that, even as he criticises her vocally, Boccaccio simultaneously seeks ways to reduce her power. As Janet Cowen notes,

> Boccaccio offers a naturalistic explanation of all her strange feats: she helped Jason to win the Fleece by causing a war to break out among her father's people as a distraction; Aeson was so happy at his son's return that he 'seemed' to regain his youth; she 'armed' the daughters of Pelias against their father.[30]

This combination, of disapproval at her crimes and scepticism regarding the extent of Medea's abilities, would surface in later English works, for example John Lydgate's *Troy Book*. In contrast, Christine de Pizan includes Medea in her response to Boccaccio, *The Book of the City of Ladies*, which sees her represent Medea less critically, attempting to preserve the sense of her skill and learning, while pitying her as one who 'loved Jason with a too great and too constant love' (II.56.1, p. 189).[31] Christine employs 'understatement', to use Cowen's term, in an effort to exonerate Medea, and, while her love for Jason is stressed, 'the results of [this love] are tactfully generalized', as they are not in Boccaccio's more critical collection.[32]

These medieval poems, prose texts, redactions and commentaries would have familiarised English authors with the most alarming aspects of Medea's power: her magic (demonstrated by her control over nature and her rejuvenation of Aeson) and her murders, of her brother Apsyrtus, of Jason's uncle Pelias, of his new wife Creusa and father-in-law Creon, and finally of her own children. They also suggest various strategies for dealing with Medea's power, which are apparent in medieval English versions of the story, and often survive into the sixteenth and seventeenth centuries. For example, Guido's misogyny influences John Lydgate's disapproving representation of Medea, and in turn Lydgate paves the way for sixteenth- and seventeenth-century English writers such as Richard Robinson or Geoffrey Fenton to hold Medea, or the Medea-like woman, up as an example of all that was wrong with the sex. Equally, the medieval allegorising instinct – the idea that Medea is actually, and comfortingly, something other than a terrifying and murderous witch, and that the test is to interpret her fiction correctly – exerts a clear influence on later mythographers such as Conti and on authors of reference works such as Blount and Browne, but may also be discerned in monumental early modern works such as George Sandys's annotated translation of the *Metamorphoses* (1626, 1632), which goes to great pains to explain and rationalise virtually every aspect of the story. At the same time, though, while they share a common discomfort with Medea's resistance to male control, and her deviation from feminine and Christian norms, medieval and early modern English authors also approach the problem of Medea's power in crucially different ways. In this chapter, I argue that the favoured English medieval approach is to ignore or rationalise Medea's power, or weaken her by stressing her love for Jason, and that it is not until the end of the fifteenth century that Caxton's *History of Jason* (itself a translation of a continental work by Raoul Lefèvre) makes a concerted effort to confront Medea's magic and violence, in ways that foreshadowed more usual sixteenth- and seventeenth-century approaches to her power.

Medea in medieval English literature

As she is excluded from Amans' pronouncement on Jason's successful conquest of the Fleece in Book 5 of *Confessio Amantis*, Medea is frequently noticeable only by her absence in English medieval texts, though these might still find space for the exploits of Jason and the Argonauts. For example, the author of the fourteenth-century English poem *The Seege or Batayle of Troy* follows Dares the Phrygian not only in his reference to the Argonautic voyage but also in his exclusion of Medea.[33] Similarly, the twelfth-century Latin poem *De Bello Troiano*, by the English cleric Joseph of Exeter, which very clearly advertises its debt to Dares, finds room for a brief mention of the Argonauts and the Fleece, but no space to record Medea's role.[34] In contrast, texts that modelled themselves on Benoît or Guido do include Medea, and they might even choose to augment their sources with more extensive reference to Ovid, in order to emphasise her abilities. Thus the composer of the late fourteenth-century alliterative poem *The Destruction of Troy*, one of the earliest English accounts of Medea, notes the rejuvenation of Aeson, explaining 'Ovid openly in Eydos tellus / How Medea the maiden made hym all new' (1.123–4).[35]

Despite this apparent determination to go beyond Guido, his principal source, in his representation of Medea's power, however, elsewhere the author is keen to play down her threat. After his account of Medea's troubling magical powers, where Guido invokes Pseudo-Dionysius the Areopagite to explain how only God can affect nature in this way, the poet connects the implausibility of the story not just to the Christian faith of his readers but also to Medea's gender, declaring: 'Hit ys lelly not like, ne oure belefe askys / Þat suche ferlies shuld fall in a frale woman' (1.420–1). For the poet, it is important that Medea is a 'frale woman', and he also judiciously revises Guido to exclude or soften references to her troubling and deceitful desire for Jason. For example, on Jason's return from the tasks, the poet describes how Medea 'Kyst hym full curtesly' (975), while Guido notes both Medea's desire and her decision to feign modesty she does not feel: 'Cui, si licuisset, in aspectu multorum multa per oscula blandimenta dedisset, et rege mandante iuxta Iasonem quasi pudibunda consedit' (p. 31) (if she could have, she would have given him the pleasant reward of many kisses in the sight of all these people, yet at the command of the king she sat next to Jason *as if* full of shyness) (3.360–2, emphasis my own). The alliterative poet makes no mention of Medea's future crimes, and, like Guido, he notes that Jason leaves her behind when he goes to besiege Troy with Hercules. Later English authors, most notably Lydgate, were comfortable with Guido's strategy of emphasising Medea's power in order to attack it (and, through Medea, to attack the spectre of the Medea-like woman). For this author, though, a preferable strategy is to emphasise the weakness of Medea's gender, and quietly ignore the alarming private desires detailed by Guido, as well as the 'detestable crimes' to which the thirteenth-century author had alluded.

Other authors also adopt this approach of diminishing Medea's power, though they may hint heavily at what they are leaving out, as Guido had done when he concluded Medea's story. Nicky Hallett notes that 'Chaucer's women come to their medieval readers ready-clad, as to their hapless writer, ready-written'.[36] This observation could, of course, be applied to any of the medieval authors discussed in this chapter: they have all inherited Medea from earlier texts or authorities. While she may be 'ready-written', however, this does not preclude authors from reshaping or experimenting with the Medea they found in their sources, and none do this as enthusiastically as Chaucer, in his brief address to her myth in the *Legend of Good Women*. The modern reader might expect Medea to be rewritten, in the hands of this most innovative and adaptive of medieval poets, but it is the way that he alters her that has proved troublesome, for feminist critics in particular. This is because what Chaucer excises utterly from the *Heroides*, his Ovidian source, is Medea's anger with Jason, her references to her past crimes and her grim hints of what is to come. In so doing, it seems that Chaucer deprives his anti-heroine of all her terrible and compelling agency, rendering her merely a helpless figure abandoned by Jason.

The most famous crime that Chaucer leaves out of the 'Legend of Medea' is, of course, her murder of her two children, motivated by Jason's cruelty and their fatal resemblance to their father. It is true that neither the *Heroides* nor Guido's *Historia,* both of which Chaucer cites as sources, actually tell the story of the murders. Additionally, in their notes to the poem, A. S. G. Edwards and M. C. E. Shaner attractively suggest that Chaucer's reference to the 'Argonautycon' (line 1457) may betray first-hand knowledge of Valerius Flaccus' Latin *Argonautica*,[37] which does not portray the murders of the children and presents a Medea whose weakened, romanticised character seems reflected in the 'Legend of Medea'.[38] Nevertheless, despite his (perhaps deliberate) references to texts that do not present the murders, Chaucer was aware of Medea's final and most notorious crime, mentioning it in the *Book of the Duchess* and in the 'Man of Law's Prologue' (where it is used, tellingly, as an example of the kind of legendary tale that Chaucer has told before).[39] In eliding the murders here, and in making Medea far less alarming than many of her continental predecessors (most obviously Boccaccio's Medea), Chaucer also elides the most famous example of her action and agency. Thus Chaucer seems to suggest that a woman's 'goodness' is linked to her passivity and suffering at the hands of men: a suggestion that has proved endlessly troublesome for critics.[40] It is important to note, too, that

Chaucer does not just omit the murders: the rejuvenation of Aeson, the killing of Pelias and Apsyrtus, and Medea's magical powers are all determinedly excised (and all of these, except for the rejuvenation, are mentioned in Guido and/or Ovid, the sources Chaucer specifically chooses to cite).

In the poem, which is a third-person narrative account of Jason's adventures (rather than a letter written by Medea, in the tradition of the *Heroides*) Medea outlines the dangers Jason will face, as she does in Guido, but her help is described in deliberately vague terms:

Tho gan this Medea to hym declare
The peril of this cas from poynt to poynt,
And of his batayle, and in what disjoynt
He mote stonde, of which no creature
Save only she ne myghte his lyf assure. (1629–33)

Medea is portrayed as a woman who is only able to help Jason not because of her magic but because of her knowledge of her country, and of the safeguards her father has placed on the Fleece. Though Chaucer mentions briefly that Jason succeeds through 'the sleyghte of hire enchauntement' (1650), and thus he does make some reference to Medea's ability exceeding Jason's, Carolyn Dinshaw finds that Jason's victory demonstrates his greater control: it is 'masculine appropriation of feminine story, or feminine wit and knowledge'.[41] Chaucer's Medea is not criticised as is Guido's, but this is because all agency, threatening and helpful, is undermined or excluded: for example, while Guido may criticise Medea's intemperate lust, and her conniving to satisfy it, here Jason is the protagonist, arriving in Colchis determined 'To don with gentil women his delyt' (1587).

Cowen notes that Medea's story, in its many incarnations, 'provides a particularly apt example of a story shaped to divergent ends within the classical and medieval texts which recount it'.[42] While it may seem disappointingly reductive, Chaucer's brief rendering of her might in fact be carefully shaped to such 'divergent ends'. The *Legend of Good Women* has been read as a satiric attack on the very idea of 'good women', a poem that seeks to demonstrate 'just what women are *really* like', as Suzanne C. Hagedorn puts it. However, she suggests that, actually, 'the target of the parody in the *Legend of Good Women* is not women themselves, but forms of literary representation by (male) poets and the courtly ideology that makes the idealization of women into an end in itself'.[43] Similarly, Lisa J. Kiser finds the *Legend of Good Women* to be a successful experiment at the expense of this established medieval literary tradition of cataloguing women, arguing that 'Chaucer means for us to recognize and appreciate his dextrous (and very funny) avoidance of narrative material that might contradict the legendary's commissioned goal – to tell of "good women"'.[44] Chaucer may, as Kiser suggests, expect his readers to recognise that he is not telling them the full story in his presentation of a passive and abandoned Medea, who is worthy of inclusion in a legendary. Equally, when, at the legend's close, he gives his readers a brief taste of Medea's reproachful letter to Jason, at lines 1670–9, he may expect some of these readers to appreciate the irony of a reference to Ovid's poem (which gives a full account of Medea's first crimes and hints at the murders of the children) in the context of his own abbreviated and sanitised retelling. He may also be playing a joke at the expense of others, who did not know the classical poems, and who would not therefore realise how selectively he was reading his Ovid here. However, whether Chaucer intends ironic subversion of the practice of classical adaptation, a sly commentary on the wisdom of relying on textual authorities, or on the possibility of finding a good woman; or whether he is attempting merely to show how any woman, however bad, can suffer as a result of male actions, his decision to end Medea's story with Jason's abandonment of her (instead of, for example, at the point that she and Jason elope) still disempowers Medea as she appears in this text, and makes a mockery even of the limited ability that Chaucer has allowed her to display.

If Chaucer attempts to weaken Medea (either straightforwardly or ironically) in his emphasis on her abandonment and distress, and by excluding direct mention of her well-known crimes, his contemporary John Gower aims at a similarly sympathetic rendering, but one that also engages, far more directly than the *Legend of Good Women*, with the danger that Medea typically poses to men and kingdoms. In *Confessio Amantis*, the Confessor criticises Jason for flouting his promise of faithfulness, while portraying Medea as relatively blameless, and Gower appears particularly keen to build on his sources (including Ovid, Benoît and Guido) in his portrayal of Medea's distress. For example, she has behaved in a transgressive way by offering to help Jason win the Fleece in exchange for marriage, but when Medea has laid out her terms and explained the tasks Jason faces,

> Sche fell, as sche that was thurgh nome
> With love, and so fer overcome,
> That al hir world on him sche sette. (5.3635–7)

Medea is 'overcome', and already pinning 'al hir world' on the response of a relative stranger. Morse finds her portrayal here inherently disempowering, and sees Gower as using 'the clichés of romance … in order to push Medea towards a certain kind of heroine'.[45] If Gower does respond enthusiastically to the literary taste of the fourteenth century, and to the models provided by his classical and medieval predecessors, however, his romanticising impulse does not come, as Chaucer's seems to, at the expense of Medea's character, and her magical power is not sacrificed to Gower's romantic agenda. Absent are both Guido's misogynistic interpolations and the attempts apparent in the *Historia*, in the *Legend of Good Women* and in the alliterative *Destruction of Troy* to downplay Medea's powers, through outright elision of them, or through reference to God's greater power or to her gender. That Gower uses his Guido very differently from Chaucer is apparent in Gower's observation that, having offered Jason her help, Medea

> … gan fro point to point enforme
> Of his bataile and al the forme
> Which … he scholde finde there. (5.3501–3)

In Guido and Gower, what follows is a detailed description, by Medea, of the dangers Jason will face. In Chaucer, Medea tells him of his peril, but with no reference to the specific tasks.

Gower describes her power and accomplishments in detail, but, like Chaucer, he also attempts to render Medea a sympathetic character. Thus, a significant omission from Gower's poem is Guido's scathing observation that Medea attempts to gratify her lust by pretending to herself that she desires marriage. Meanwhile, a significant addition is the exclamation Medea makes to herself as she watches Jason from her tower: 'Sche preide, and seide, "O, god him spede, / The kniht which hath mi maidenhiede!"' (5.3739–40). While these words may make Medea more sympathetic than she is in Guido, because they demonstrate the risk Medea has taken in committing herself to Jason sexually, however, it is difficult to escape the conclusion that she is sympathetic because help-less and that, in sleeping with Jason and giving him the secrets of how to obtain the Fleece, she finds herself at his mercy. Gower certainly does not shy away from presenting a capable Medea who, despite her fears for Jason, orchestrates his success. After his triumph, however, Jason makes no mention or acknowledgment of the help he has received from Medea. Remaining constrained by her gender, she wants to congratulate Jason with a kiss, 'Bot schame tornede hire agayn' (5.3790), and instead she displaces her feelings of happiness onto her female companion, in the privacy of her chamber: 'And sche for joie hire Maide kiste' (5.3800). This detail stems from the *Metamorphoses*: Ovid notes, 'tu quoque victorem conplecti, barbara, velles: / obstitit incepto pudor' (You also, barbarian maiden, would gladly have embraced the victor; your modesty stood in the way) (7.144–5).[46] Colchis is a masculine community, and, despite her acknowledged assistance, Medea finds herself on its outskirts, able neither to praise nor to be praised. Once Jason has succeeded with her help, Medea is reduced to an object, another prize he has won, as she is in the *Metamorphoses*, and in John of Garland's thirteenth-century commentary: the narrator observes, 'Jason to Grece with his preie / Goth thurgh the See the rihte weie' (5.3927–8), and, despite Medea's undoubted abilities, the balance of power between them seems to have shifted back in his favour.

Gower's account also differs from Chaucer's, and even from the far more critical *Historia Destructionis Troiae*, in that it recounts some (though not all) of Medea's crimes and transgressive acts of magic, those parts of her Ovidian story at which Chaucer only hints. After the pair leave Colchis (with no account of the murder of Apsyrtus), Jason requests that Medea rejuvenate his father. Gower's account draws heavily on the *Metamorphoses* in his description of Medea's making the potion, her search for her ingredients, and even Medea's appearance – the way she runs wild and speaks in strange tongues:

> ... tho sche ran so up and doun,
> Sche made many a wonder soun,
> Somtime lich unto the cock,
> Sometime unto the Laverock,
> Sometime kacleth as a Hen,
> Somtime speketh as don the men:
> And riht so as hir jargoun strangeth,
> In sondri wise hir forme changeth,
> Sche semeth faie and no womman;
> For with the craftes that sche can
> Sche was, as who seith, a goddesse,
> And what hir liste, more or lesse,
> Sche dede, in bokes as we finde. (5.4097–109)

Ovid describes Medea thus:

> egreditur tectis vestes induta recinctas,
> nuda pedem, nudos umeris infusa capillos,

fertque vagos mediae per muta silentia noctis
incomitata gradus: homines volucresque ferasque
solverat alta quies, nullo cum murmure saepes,
inmotaeque silent frondes, silet umidus aer,
sidera sola micant; ad quae sua bracchia tendens
ter se convertit, ter sumptis flumine crinem
inroravit aquis ternisque ululatibus ora (7.182–90)

[Medea] went forth from her house clad in flowing robes, barefoot,
her hair unadorned and streaming down her shoulders; and all
alone she wandered out into the deep stillness of midnight. Men,
birds, and beasts were sunk in profound repose; there was no sound
in the hedgerow; the leaves hung mute and motionless; the dewy
air was still. Only the stars twinkled. Stretching up her arms to
these, she turned thrice about, thrice sprinkled water caught up
from a flowing stream upon her head and thrice gave tongue in
wailing cries.

Gower adds to this with an extended potion-making scene that is a
confusion of running and squawking, featuring a Medea who 'kacleth
as a Hen', and is, inevitably, reduced in the reader's eyes by such
domesticating touches. Indeed, despite the obvious reliance on the
impressive Ovidian Medea of the *Metamorphoses*, Morse points out
that here 'There is still no sense that Medea is powerful in and of
herself.'[47] Gower tells us that 'what hir liste, more or lesse, / Sche
dede' (5.4108–9), but just as this 'more or lesse' destabilises what, in
the reader's mind, would seem to be Medea's independence, later the
reader is told that she performs her impressive rites, and assists Jason
as she does, because of the hold that he (reassuringly for the masculine
community) maintains over her:

Lo, what mihte eny man devise,
A womman schewe in eny wise
Mor hertly love in every stede,
Than Medea to Jason dede?
Ferst sche made him the flees to winne,
And after that fro kiththe and kinne
With gret tresor with him sche stal,
And to his fader forth withal
His Elde hath torned into youthe,
Which thing non other woman couthe. (5.4175–84)

Here, Medea's abilities translate very clearly into Jason's accomplishments, and Gower emphasises the power not of Medea but of the love that compels her to act for Jason. In the 'Legend of Medea', Chaucer makes a similar point when he concludes:

> This is the mede of lovynge and guerdoun
> That Medea receyved of Jasoun
> Ryght for hire trouthe and for hire kyndenesse,
> That lovede hym beter than hireself, I gesse. (1662–5)

Gower, like Chaucer, emphasises Medea's devotion to Jason, but at first it seems that his Medea will not react to abandonment with the help-lessness of her Chaucerian counterpart: she poisons Creusa, kills her children and then rises 'Unto Pallas the Court above' (5.4219) before Jason can touch her. As he has done previously with his observation that all her evil deeds were done for love of Jason, however, here Gower uses Jason's hold over her to undermine Medea. She ends her appearance in the poem in the afterlife (not identified as Christian Heaven), 'Wher as sche pleigneth upon love' (5.4220), free from the threat of Jason's revenge, but apparently as powerless over her circumstances as is her deserted husband. The word 'pleigneth' is significant here: in his work on early modern female complaint, John Kerrigan has pointed out that the (male-authored) female speaker of Elizabethan complaint poetry will often be blameless yet suffering, possessed of 'a special kind of vitality, dependent on weakness'.[48] Gower, unusually, describes Medea's crimes, but finally, and despite this, the only power she has is this same power of the Elizabethan heroine: the ability to complain, lament her suffering for love, and display her own weakness for the approval of the reader. In this way, Gower foreshadows Elizabethan determination to suggest both some punishment for Medea and a sense of her regret, both because of her crimes and because of the gender which reduces her, finally, to a complaining subject.

Some effort to make Medea appear both active and sympathetic can also be discerned in the anonymous, *c.*1400, poem the *Laud Troy Book*.[49] The author cites Guido and Dares as his sources, but goes on to deviate from Guido in his presentation of Medea, if not in the narrative as a whole. Like Guido, he is writing a very obviously male-oriented quest narrative: much room is given to Pelias' challenge to his nephew Jason, to the Argonauts' arrival in Colchis and to the already familiar descriptions of the perils Jason must face. Noticeably absent, however, are Guido's misogynistic attacks on Medea, with which he embellished his rendering of Benoît. After his enumeration of Medea's skills, for example, the *Laud* poet exclaims

> In al the world was no man
> So kunnyng of wit and wisdam –
> As seyn these autours and these clerkes
> As was Medee in here werkes. (637–40)[50]

He pointedly ignores whatever writings of 'these clerkes' do not please him, however, presumably in an effort to make Medea a more appealing character, rather than one reflective of the distasteful 'reality' of women (the role Guido assigned her). He leaves out Guido's references to Medea's lustful and deceptive nature, and in fact in some ways makes her a far more powerful character than she is in the Latin text. Dorothy Kempe points out that 'The English writer does not profess to he [sic] more than a "gestour", consequently he is at less pains to give verisimilitude to his tale.'[51] Predictably, this has an impact on his representation of Medea's magic: unlike Guido and Lydgate (who relies on his Latin source far more closely), the *Laud* author does not feel the need to explain it away. Most noticeably, as Jason prepares for the tasks, Medea 'an-oynted alle his body' (919) with her protective ointment, where usually Jason does this himself. Later, too, the passive description of Medea helplessly watching Jason from her tower is left out, and the *Laud* poet notes:

> The tydynges thorow the Cete is ronne
> Many a man come him to see,
> Ther he was set by dame Medee. (1118–20)

The pair leave Colchis in triumph and, like Guido's work, the narrative quickly switches to an account of the first fall of Troy, with no mention of Medea's later crimes.

The *Laud Troy Book* constitutes a minor but interesting example of how the medieval Medea may be presented as both powerful and sympathetic (though her main virtue, as always, is her willingness to bend her extraordinary powers to Jason's advantage, and the poet does not attempt a rehabilitation of her crimes). More importantly, it is an example of how medieval writers read their sources (even the magisterial Guido) critically, and rewrote them selectively. McDonald argues that Medea benefits from what she calls 'The process of vernacularisation', noting that as a result of this process, which saw works translated into their country's vernacular, 'women become members of both the implied and real audiences, and there is a clearly evident shift towards an accommodation of their interests'.[52] As far as Medea is concerned, McDonald finds the vernacular to be 'a medium in which we generally find a sympathetic portrait of her', and cites Gower, Chaucer, the *Ovide moralisé* and the *Laud Troy Book* as such sympathetic vernacular renderings, with John Lydgate's misogynistic attacks on her constituting a surprising exception.[53] Certainly, this vernacularisation meant that more women could have read Medea's story, and this may have resulted in less damning assessments of her. If a work is written in English, however, it does not necessarily follow that Medea is to be pitied or sympathised with, and male authors may also have sought to play up Medea's transgressive folly, as a way of educating and cautioning their female readership: in the sixteenth and seventeenth centuries, English accounts of Medea are usually highly unsympathetic, and might specifically highlight her behaviour as an example to be shunned by the female reader. The *Laud Troy Book* is a surprisingly positive account of Medea's early career, while Gower does seem willing to present Medea sympathetically (though in the process she must be reduced, in various ways, from the terrifying Ovidian sorceress). Chaucer's 'Legend of Medea' complicates its own sympathy, however, and it is also important to appreciate the extent to which authors such as the alliterative poet and the *Laud* poet feel driven to ignore key episodes, in their attempts to write a sympathetic Medea. Fourteenth- and fifteenth-century English writers, and their continental counterparts, were just as alarmed by Medea's magic and desire for Jason as was Guido, and thus while vernacular accounts may tone down his most stinging misogynistic tirades, it does not necessarily follow that they represent Medea with approval.

Medea and misogyny in Lydgate: the *Troy Book* and the *Fall of Princes*

If Chaucer, Gower and the *Laud* poet present a Medea whose magic and murderous power must be somehow undermined, or else quietly ignored, fifteenth-century English authors appear increasingly eager to leave such unsatisfactory solutions behind them, and, in the renderings of Caxton and Lydgate in particular, the choice to represent the worst and most active elements of Medea's behaviour, and to make her utterly unsympathetic as a consequence, is clearly apparent.

   In his presentation of Medea, John Lydgate augments his reading of Guido, Boccaccio and Laurent de Premierfait with Ovid's *Heroides* and

Metamorphoses, and this often results in extensive embellishment. For example, in his account of her story in the lengthy narrative poem the *Troy Book* (1420), which is based on the *Historia Destructionis Troiae*, he extends Guido's observation that Medea was 'virgo nimium speciosa' (an extremely beautiful maiden) (2.175, p. 15):

> ... Medea with hir rosene hewe,
> And with freschenes of þe lyle white
> So entermedled of kynde be delite,
> Þat Nature made in hir face sprede
> So egally þe white with þe rede,
> Þat þe medelyng, in conclusioun,
> So was ennewed by proporcioun,
> Þat finally excesse was þer noon,
> Of never nouþer; for bothe two in oon
> So Ioyned wer, longe to endure,
> By thempres þat callyd is Nature. (1.1578–88)[54]

Lydgate's extension of his source to describe Medea's beauty is in keeping with the copious nature of his poem, but he also wants to reflect unfavourably on her character through his description of her physical appearance. The deceptive nature of her beauty, and the extent to which it does not reflect her later actions, is stressed by the deliberately ironic observation that in the perfect blending of red and white in Medea's complexion, 'excesse was þer noon' (1585) – the reader who knows something of Medea before coming to the *Troy Book* could scarcely avoid reflecting that the same cannot be said of her temperament. After his descriptions of Medea's deceptive and transgressive desire for Jason, and of feminine inconstancy, he declares, 'Þus liketh Guydo of wommen for tendite' (1.2097), and claims, 'My purpos is nat hem to done offence' (1.2104). In fact, though, Lydgate includes Guido's interpolations on feminine inconstancy and changeability at every opportunity, and often extends them into the bargain, even as he presents himself as a 'hapless' author to use Nicky Hallett's description of Chaucer. For example, Lydgate sees Medea's adorning herself as being not just a typical feminine trait, as Guido does, but as an indication of her attempts to disguise her true character from the oblivious Jason, noting 'Fer al þe foule schal covertly be wried, / Þat no defaute outward be espied' (1.1813–14).

At some points, Lydgate's changes make Medea seem more of a victim: his account of how Medea is torn between Love and Shame is greatly extended from Guido, and she is described as confounded and led astray by 'Fortune with hir double face' (1.2251) and 'þe whirlyng of hir whele aboute' (1.2253). Later too, Lydgate draws on Ovid in his account of the couple's night together, as Guido had done, but seems to regard Medea's decision to sleep with Jason with far more sympathy, surmising, 'And ȝet sche ment nat but honeste; / As I suppose, sche wende have ben his wyfe' (1.2940–1). Ultimately, though, Lydgate's adherence to Guido means that he abandons Medea abruptly (although he does mention the murders of the children and points his readers in the direction of texts such as the *Metamorphoses* and *Heroides*, which give a fuller account of her crimes). His reliance on the *Historia* is such that, though he sometimes plays down Medea's threat by emphasising her own helplessness or honest delusion, she remains a troublesome incarnation of female desire and disobedience, and an attractive target for criticism.

Lydgate's second extensive account of Medea, in the poem *The Fall of Princes*, is another adaptation, this time of Laurent de Premierfait's *Des Cas des Nobles Hommes et Femmes*, itself an expansion of Boccaccio's *De Casibus Virorum Illustrium*.[55] Where Laurent expands the brief mentions he has found in Boccaccio to give a fuller account of Medea's story, Lydgate often adds a misogynistic note of judgement, as he had done frequently in his rendering of Guido's Latin into English in the *Troy Book*. For example, Laurent's Medea is simply described as 'la cruele femme' (the cruel woman) (1.7.5, p. 127)[56] when she kills her sons, whereas Lydgate's Medea does so 'Withoute routhe or womanli pite' (1.2346).[57] Similarly, in Laurent's rendering she flees to Aegeus when she has been rejected by Jason, and in Lydgate's the reader is told that she plots there 'void off shame & dreede' (1.2363). In Lydgate's translation of his source, Medea's gender is repeatedly linked to her threat, as it has been in the *Troy Book*: like other women she is deceptive and vain, but she also specifically deviates from accepted feminine behaviour or reactions, displaying no acceptable or expected emotions such as shame or pity. Accordingly, even though Medea is reconciled with Jason at the end of the account, her lack of regret for her crimes means that it is scarcely an uncomplicated example of a disobedient woman being returned her rightfully subservient role. Other accounts that describe Jason taking her back (for example Justin's *Epitome of the Philippic History of Pompeius Trogus,* translated by Arthur Golding and printed in 1564, or Lefèvre's *Histoire de Jason*, translated by Caxton and printed in 1477) emphasise his control, and his pity for Medea, while in *De Claris Mulieribus* Boccaccio had described the reunion, but offered no explanation for it.

Laurent notes that when her treachery was discerned by Aegeus, Medea left and was reunited with Jason 'par une maniere incogneue' (by uncertain means) (1.7.5, p. 127). In the *Fall of Princes*, Medea's agency, and her manipulative threat, are emphasised further. Lydgate notes:

> Whan that she sauh hir purpos most odible
> Be kyng Egeus fulli was espied,
> She hath hir herte & wittis newe applied,
> As in ther bookis poetis han compiled,
> A-geyn to Jason to be reconciled. (1.2376–80)

Lydgate acknowledges that poets do not mention how they are reconciled, and hypothesises 'it were bi incantacioun' (1.2391).[58]

As he has done in the *Troy Book*, Lydgate later mounts an unconvincing defence of women, opining, 'It is no resoun tatwiten women all, / Thouh on or too whilom dede faile' (1.6646–7). His suggestion that Medea uses her 'wittis' to manipulate Jason, and to achieve her own ends, however, underlines the way that her story functions as a troubling example to medieval men of the deceptive and destructive powers that women might conceal. This approach, also popular among sixteenth- and seventeenth-century authors, had the added appeal that it gave authors licence to dwell on, rather than ignore, the most exciting aspects of the classical story, Medea's magic and criminality, and allowed them both to titillate and to educate their audiences, through their criticism of her behaviour. Later in the fifteenth century, William Caxton, the final medieval English author to engage at length with Medea's story, follows his source, Lefèvre's *Histoire de Jason*, in emphasising all that was most horrifying in her myth, but, unlike Lydgate's *Fall of Princes*, his *History of Jason* balances Medea's criminality with the comforting suggestion that, when they are eventually reconciled, it is Jason who has the upper hand.

Mastering Medea in Caxton

If Lydgate turned de Premierfait's adaptation of Boccaccio to his own didactic and misogynist ends, Caxton's prose narrative the *History of Jason* is a far more faithful translation of another French text, the *Histoire de Jason* of Raoul Lefèvre. Like Lydgate's *Fall of Princes*, this is a male-focused narrative, though here Lefèvre's primary aim is to excuse male folly rather than to underline the consequences of male failure to control daughters or wives, as Lydgate does. By the time he publishes the translated *History* in 1477, Caxton has already demonstrated his interest in the story: in the *Recuyell of the Historyes of Troye* (c.1473–4), he notes that 'Jason by the lernyng and Industrie of med[e]a conquered the sheep with the flees of gold whiche he bare with hym in to grece', and in 1480 he would produce a version of Ovid's *Metamorphoses*, based on a French prose redaction.[59] In the *History of Jason*, while 'folowyng myn auctor as nygh as I can or may not chaungyng the sentence. ne presuming to adde ne mynusshe ony thing otherwise than myne auctor hath made in Frensshe' (p. 1),[60] Caxton gives a far longer account of the story than he had done previously, and one that is particularly interested in the sensational aspects of Medea's myth. Rather than just being intended to entertain, the work's sensationalism also carries with it an instructive message, and in the prologue to the work, Lefèvre underscores the way that male interests underpin the narrative that is to follow. He notes that Philippe, Duke of Burgundy, has established a chivalric Order of the Golden Fleece, and claims that Jason came to him in a dream, complaining about his previous representations as a faithless seducer. Jason charges his author to clear his name (and, in so doing, to make Philippe's Order appear more impressive). Predictably, as this evidence of linked male self-interest would suggest, in their efforts to redeem Jason, Caxton and Lefèvre emphasise not only the negative aspects of Medea's character but also, finally and instructively, the extent to which she is reassuringly subject to the male rule that informs and motivates the narrative.[61]

Jason is presented very sympathetically, and the text's chivalric interests are clear from the outset. While he goes on several initial adventures with Hercules, the emphasis is always on his heroic (and unassisted) achievements, such as his defence of Mirro, Queen of Oliferne, who is being troubled by the attentions of the King of Sklavonye. Mirro is a hugely significant addition to the story. In some ways she echoes the 'romanticised' Medea presented by Benoît and his redactors: for example, she and Jason lie in bed separately, each tormented by thoughts of the other, as Medea and Jason do in the *Roman*. In other respects, however, she is very different from Medea. They meet when Jason comes to her aid, and Mirro loves him for his bravery, while Medea takes advantage of his helplessness. He triumphs over fantastic opponents with no help from Mirro: rather, it his adversaries who need help. Crucially too, their romance is very different from that of Jason and Medea. They speak openly (in contrast to Jason's furtive conversations with Medea) and Mirro is alarmed by his attention, rather than welcoming it as Medea does: Caxton tells his reader 'Jason began to beholde her so ardantly that she was ashamed how wel that she as wyse & discrete helde honeste manere' (p. 37). Jason is presented very positively: strong where he has traditionally been characterised as weak, he is able to make his suit to Mirro openly, and, crucially for the medieval author, the 'correct' balance of power between the sexes is preserved. In contrast, the Ovidian Medea's skill and the forthright manner in which she offers Jason her assistance in return for marriage always carry the risk that he will appear the weaker of the two partners.

Lefèvre and following him Caxton, however, face predictable problems in their desire to recount the whole 'Histoire' of Jason. Caxton describes Jason's encounters with both Hypsipyle and Medea, and must make his hero appear temporarily weaker than these women, and unable to stand up to them, in order to explain the necessity of Jason's abandonment of Mirro (the parallels with the medieval tendency to render Medea sympathetic, because powerless, are obvious). Jason attempts to resist Hypsipyle, but is eventually overcome by her charms, and, after Medea has heard of his quest for the Fleece, she lays out her terms in a far more uncompromising fashion than she has done in other English texts, telling him bluntly that he has no choice but to forsake Mirro, since 'if I be cause of sauacion of your lyf. as to the regarde of me I wil enjoye you allone with out ony other' (p. 123). Jason has very little choice here, and later he is further absolved from charges of wilful inconstancy, as Medea's nurse bewitches Jason's bed, and he is forced to fall in love with her and abandon Mirro. This kind of female control over male romantic destiny would be deeply alarming for the male reader, who is clearly intended to sympathise with Jason's predicament. As I shall show in subsequent chapters, this idea of a woman as enjoying unnatural power over a man, and thereby reversing the natural order, in a process that Frances Dolan has termed 'inverse coverture', meant that Medea's story provoked a particular and real anxiety among male authors through the early modern period.[62] Like Gower and Caxton before them, those working in the sixteenth and seventeenth centuries were presented with the problem of how to represent but finally overturn the troubling control that she wields over Jason.

As the tale progresses, it seems that Jason's only power, in relation to Medea, is worryingly reactive. For example, after her murder of Pelias, he rejects her furiously, and marries Creusa. Medea feigns submissiveness, telling him 'syn it is your plaisir that it so be. hit muste nedes be that it plese me. And so be it alway that youre plaisirs ben fulfillid' (p. 174). However, in an apparent echo of Seneca, she then asks him (rather than Creon) for her extra day in Corinth, promising to perform a trick for the couple's wedding. She conjures four dragons and appears to Jason and Creusa with one of her sons, and 'toke him by the two legges & by the force of her armes Rente him in two pieces. & in that poynt cast him in the plater to fore Jason and Creusa' (p. 175). Medea's power here is horrifying (the description is deliberately more graphic than the brief factual accounts of the murders that have gone before, in the works of Ovid or Boccaccio). The strength she gleans from her utter disregard for human mores is emphasised as Jason curses her, telling her he would kill her, if only she were a man, and she replies, 'Certes my dere love knowe ye for trouth that I had lever see all the world deye. thenne I knewe that ye shold have habitacion with ony other woman thenne with me' (p. 176).

Medea's abhorrent behaviour is compelling, even thrilling (particularly when read in the context of earlier, less adventurous English accounts). However it is also intended to direct the reader's understanding of Jason. In his work on the early modern use of classical exemplars, Timothy Hampton has stressed the importance of consistency: in order to successfully fulfil his 'ideological function', the classical exemplar must be wholly and entirely admirable.[63] Clearly, Lefèvre and then Caxton invert this idea: in order to excite readerly sympathy and even admiration for Jason, their Medea must be made as bad as she can possibly be. Thus the grisly horror of the infanticide is exaggerated, and, in its wake, Caxton continues with his attempts to absolve Jason from blame, stressing his lack of control over Medea's boundless wickedness. Finally, though, if the *History* is to succeed in its stated aim of demonstrating Jason's heroism, both Medea's magic and her insatiable appetite for violence must be curbed, as a result of her overriding love for him. After Medea has slaughtered her second son, and Mirro has been deliberately killed at the order of Jason's father Aeson, Jason and Medea meet for the final time. Medea repents her sins, and swears subservience to Jason: 'And thenne she sware to him & auowed that she sholde never medle more with sortes ne enchantements ne none other malefices ne of ony thing but first he sholde have the cognoissaunce and knowlech' (p. 198).[64] Following the remarkably conservative end of their story, they return to Colchis and restore Aeëtes to the throne, and 'had many fayr children to gyder that regned after hem of whome I have founde none historie or sentence' (p. 198). Finally, Caxton adds briefly to his source, by giving an account of Boccaccio's handling of the pair in his *Genealogia*, and by noting that Jason is frequently criticised for abandoning Medea, 'but in this present boke ye may see the evydent causes why he so dyd' (p. 199).[65] Lefèvre, and following him Caxton, deliberately and repeatedly emphasises Medea's power as earlier medieval writers do not, building on his Ovidian sources to stress her ruthless control over Jason and the bloody horror of her crimes. Finally and effectively, however, he undercuts Medea's power, through her unclassical rejection of her magic, and her promise to submit utterly to Jason. It is paradoxically by stressing Medea's capacity for evil throughout the narrative that the work is able first to exonerate Jason from blame, and even, finally, to suggest him as more powerful than Medea, because of her final repentance and the ultimate submission of such a terrible power to Jason's male control.

Because the English text does not depart significantly from its original, McDonald argues that:

> In general, we cannot credit Caxton with contributing in any serious way to the medieval history of Medea. What he does do, however, is to make Lefèvre's interpretation of Medea available to an English reading public, and in doing so, he provides a channel for the transmission of these Burgundian ideas to England.[66]

Of chief importance for writers of the English Renaissance was the demonstration, in Caxton's *History*, that Medea's violence and evildoing might be exaggerated (rather than diminished as they are in Chaucer's *Legend of Good Women*), and that this exaggeration might be both entertaining and perversely instructive for male and female readers, who are encouraged to see in Medea an example to be resisted, even while the story is relished. It may not make a significant contribution to a bilingual reader's understanding of Medea, because it does not build extensively enough on Lefèvre's French. Its focus on not only gruesome violence but also the eventual repentance of Medea, however, means that *The History of Jason* is the medieval English version of Medea's story that most clearly anticipates the dominant early modern English approach, which saw Medea as a horrifying figure to be marvelled at, and then comfortingly mastered, usually by torture and death as well as repentance.

Caxton's return to Medea's story, in his version of the *Metamorphoses*, approaches her power in a less contentious way.[67] Here, Caxton probably made use of a prose redaction of the *Ovide moralisé*, such as the one printed by Colard Mansion in 1484, rather than translating directly from Ovid.[68] Certainly, his debts to medieval models are apparent: unlike Ovid's poem, the relevant book of Caxton's *Metamorphoses*, like the *History of Jason*, begins by describing Pelias' suspicion of his nephew, and his hope that Jason will die in the course of the quest for the Golden Fleece. Also present in Caxton's version, but absent from the Ovidian original, is a brief account of Jason's landing in Lemnos: Caxton, like Chaucer, describes how Jason woos Hypsipyle with promises of fidelity, 'but soone he had forgote her' (Cap 2°). Then, the narrative moves into more familiar Ovidian territory, while retaining details given by medieval authors such as Lydgate: Medea is tormented not only by her love for Jason on his arrival in Colchis but also by her own doubts; and, when he wins the Fleece with her assistance, it is her shame that prevents her from congratulating him publically. Caxton describes the dismemberment of Apsyrtus, the rejuvenation of Aeson and the killing of Pelias, but he shies noticeably away from the extremes of violence recounted by the *History of Jason*. Betrayed by Jason for Creusa, Medea exclaims, 'evyl and meschaunce come to me, but yf I ende not and termyne not their love' (Cap 8°), but the killing of the children is not described in the horribly graphic detail of the *History*. Similarly, while Caxton describes the grief of Aeëtes on the discovery of his son's body, Medea does not brandish her brother's head at her father as she does in the *History*, and her wickedness is not underscored, as it is in the earlier text, by reference to the horror of Hercules, Jason and the other Argonauts.

This particular omission, of Jason and the Argonauts' shocked reaction, points to the reason for the later text's different attitude towards Medea. Caxton's *Metamorphoses* does not have the rehabilitation of Jason as its *raison d'être*, and accordingly he does not blacken Medea's name at every turn, by exaggerating her wrongdoing and repeating the new crimes invented by Lefèvre. At the same time, though, if it does not participate in the same character assassination of Medea as the *History of Jason* does, its debt to the medieval moralisations of Ovid meant that Caxton's *Metamorphoses* does not entirely subvert what was also the traditional medieval English approach of presenting Medea as passive and suffering rather than active and unpunished. This Medea, like her Ovidian counterpart, is not bent to Jason's will and made to reconcile with him, and moreover, as she does in the *Metamorphoses*, she escapes punishment at the hands of Aegeus, after a thwarted attempt to kill Theseus. However, her power is crucially compromised in the middle of the narrative, as Caxton pauses at the killing of Apsyrtus, to provide an allegorical reading, or, as he puts it in the Table, 'sense hystoryal for the ffable precedent'. He explains, 'Alle this is thystorye only of the flies of golde. Medea was the flies of gold that was so enclosed ...

that no man myghte have her w[i]t[h]out her counseyl and consente' (Cap 4°). Here, as she was in John of Garland's mid-thirteenth-century commentary on Ovid's poem, Medea is read as the Fleece itself, the golden prize awarded to Jason as a result of his feats. Caxton tells his readers that many noble knights have died in pursuit of Medea, 'ffor ayenst her wyll they wolde have had her away from her fader Oethes'. However, she falls in love with Jason, and he 'by her conseyl ravysshed her'. The unsatisfactory nature of this interpretation of Medea is suggested by the fact that it is included in the middle of the story, at Cap 4°, and that Caxton ventures no suggestions as to how Medea's later murderous career, and defiance of Jason's wishes, could be read in accordance with this explanation. This version of Medea's story is, as I have argued, far less of an endorsement of Jason than the *History*: Caxton presents Jason as 'so debonair, so humble and so amiable and so ful of good maners', and yet also acknowledges that 'ayenst love he hade lytil loyalt[i]e' (Cap 1°). Accordingly, it is not so necessary that this Medea is made to submit so comprehensively to male will, and she is allowed a voice and a magical and violent power that many of her fourteenth- and fifteenth-century predecessors are not. Evident in the intrusion of the allegorical reading, however, and in its explanation of Medea as a desirable object to be conquered, with her consent but because of Jason's manifold virtues, is the compulsion, irresistible to the English medieval writer, to reign in and subjugate the threat Medea represents, whether this is done at the beginning, middle or end of her tale.

These medieval approaches to Medea could be suggestive for later authors. The romanticised Medea of Chaucer and Gower, fatally weakened by her love for Jason and helpless in the face of his abandonment, is echoed to a certain extent in John Studley's translation of Seneca's *Medea* (1566), in George Whetstone's 'Pitious Complaint of Medea' (1576), and in Elizabethan translations of Ovid's *Heroides* and *Metamorphoses*. What early modern authors took more enthusiastically from their medieval predecessors (particularly the allegorisers, and Lydgate and Caxton), however, was the idea that Medea's power could be stressed, rather than ignored, if it was also rationalised and made less marvellous, or if Medea was represented as an exaggeration of feminine wickedness, perversely entertaining and also instructive. At the same time, the early modern period saw an explosion of interest in classical texts, and in adaptations not of vernacular Medeas, but of their Ovidian and Senecan originals. Like their medieval predecessors, early modern translators might represent their sources faithfully, or they might claim to do so, while making small but significant alterations. Equally, they might shun the idea of close or literal translation, and, even as they claim to represent classical texts in English, they might create new, and newly valuable, portraits of Medea. What is still apparent, too, in these translations from Latin, is the abiding interest in connecting Medea with an alarming sexual, violent or supernatural power, but a power that must be negotiated or explained, as it is not in the classical works of Ovid and Seneca.

2
Translating Medea

Euripides' *Medea* was printed in Florence in 1496, and Tanya Pollard notes eighteen editions of the Greek play in the sixteenth century: by the seventeenth century, English references to the Greek tragedy become more frequent, though Seneca's and Ovid's versions of Medea's story are more usually cited.[1] Despite an increased knowledge of the text, however, Euripides' tragedy does not appear to have attracted the attention of sixteenth- and seventeenth-century translators working in English, although in 1544 George Buchanan, one-time tutor of Mary Queen of Scots, had produced a Latin version, described by H. B. Charlton as 'almost a word-for-word translation' of the ancient Greek.[2] In contrast, English translations of Seneca's *Medea* appeared in print twice in the period, first by John Studley (1566, and reprinted in 1581 as part of Thomas Newton's *Seneca His Tenne Tragedies*) and then by Edward Sherburne (1648), and Ovid was extensively rendered into English.[3]

This chapter will discuss how the Ovidian Medea was translated in the early modern period, in two versions of the *Metamorphoses* (by Arthur Golding, 1567, and George Sandys, 1626), three versions of the *Tristia* (by Thomas Churchyard, 1572, Wye Saltonstall, 1633, and Zachary Catlin, 1639) and four versions of the *Heroides* (by George Turberville, 1567, Wye Saltonstall, 1636, John Sherburne, 1639, and John Dryden and others, 1680). Before this, it will consider how early modern knowledge of Medea (and particularly of her infanticide) was demonstrated and augmented by the two printed translations of Seneca's *Medea*, by Studley and Sherburne. I shall show how the translators' focus was on demonstrating Medea's power, but also undercutting or exploiting it, by means of paratexts, or by translation that was highly subjective, and either quietly or unashamedly misrepresentative of Ovid's and

Seneca's Latin. Linda Hutcheon has pointed out that 'Adapting across cultures is not simply a matter of translating words',[4] and Chapter 1 has shown how Guido had altered Benoît in accordance with his own tastes, and Lydgate in turn had altered Guido, both later authors claiming all the while to do nothing more or less than translate their source text. Similarly, translators who tackled the Greek or (more usually) the Latin Medea in the sixteenth and seventeenth centuries might do so with scant regard for the sanctity of their classical sources, and might expand, annotate or truncate these source texts as they saw fit, and with the early modern reader firmly in mind.

Early modern Seneca

Though there is little concrete evidence for a knowledge of Seneca's *Medea* among medieval English authors, despite Lydgate's misleading reference to the tragedy, Charlton notes twelve separate continental editions of the complete Senecan tragedies that had been printed by 1500,[5] and although Seneca may never have intended it for performance, the Latin tragedy had some stage history in England in the sixteenth century, apparently being performed at Cambridge in the early 1560s.[6] Whatever he had read or seen of the Senecan *Medea*, however, what is most striking about John Studley's early Elizabethan translation is his refusal to feel bound by his original, a refusal that has often attracted the disapproval of critics. Even before his significant alterations of content are considered, Studley's deviation from the Latin dramatist's direct and pithy style is inescapable: for G. K. Hunter, Studley and his fellow Elizabethan translators of Seneca are 'totally incapable of sharpness or compression', and the *Medea* is no exception.[7] Studley's translation as a whole is much longer than the original, and the most noticeable aspect of his style is his fondness for incongruous colloquialism and expansion: for example, Seneca's Medea asks Jove to strike her down with 'fulmen' (537) ([a] thunderbolt), while Studley's demands 'thumps of thwacking boltes' (1620).[8]

Elsewhere, though, the changes Studley make impact on Medea's representation, rather than merely serving to lengthen the play and (perhaps) to raise a smile in the modern reader that Studley presumably did not intend. The translator admits to cutting the first chorus of the play, 'because in it I sawe nothyng but an heape of prophane storyes, and names of prophane Idoles' (86–7), and, as this highly self-conscious, domesticating alteration of his original would suggest, the changes he makes are immediately apparent and focused on making his play relevant and palatable to an Elizabethan audience.[9] Frequently, Studley plays up the horror and gore that Seneca's play suggests: for example, when his Medea plots against her children's lives in Act 1, with far more bloodthirsty specificity than Seneca's heroine, who only hints, at this stage, that her revenge may come to encompass her children. Elsewhere, though, his changes are very often geared towards weakening Medea, just as medieval vernacular versions of her myth had focused on her emotional attachment to Jason: indeed, Frederick Kiefer argues that the Elizabethan translations of Seneca's plays have 'a distinctly medieval flavor'.[10] In Seneca's tragedy, the first chorus congratulates Jason for having escaped the wild Medea, and emphasises her unpredictability and dangerous otherness. Studley's new chorus rather pities Medea for her credulous love, in a way that foreshadows later Elizabethan uses of the suffering Medea, to caution overly trustful female readers against the wiles of men. Studley's chorus remarks:

> The shafte that flew from Cupids golden bowe,
> With fethers so hath dymd her daseld eyes,
> That can not see to shun the waye of woe. (361–3).

Here, what is stressed is Medea's inability to perceive and avoid the self-serving deception of Jason. The accounts of Euripides and Seneca, relying as they do so heavily on Medea's speech and her version of events, make it unclear whether Jason ever really loved Medea. Studley has drawn his own conclusions, and Jason is characterised as a flattering seducer rather than an eager young bridegroom. The chorus exclaims,

> Woe Jason, woe to thee most wretched man,
> Or rather wretche Medea woe to thee,
> Woe to the one that thus dyssemble can,
> Woe to the other that trayned so myght be. (389–92)

As such lines make clear, Studley's chorus takes on a far more obviously prophetic role than Seneca's, signposting Medea's misfortune (in her unwise trusting of a man who will abandon her) and her lack of power over him (as the audience is aware she cannot change his mind). In Act 3, Jason observes Medea's approach, and notes,

> And loe on me when ons she kaste
> the beames of glauncinge eie,
> Full blythe she leapes, she jumps for joye,

in fittes she ginnes to frye.
Depe deadlie blackish hate she seemes
in out warde brow to beare,
And whollye in her frownynge face
doth glutting grefe appeare. (1350–7)

Seneca has 'atque ecce, viso memet exiluit, furit, / fert odia prae se: totus in vultu est dolor' (And look, as she sees me she leaps up, becomes furious, shows her hatred; all her resentment is in her face) (445–6). Inspired by Ovid, Studley's lines recall the passionate affair recounted in the *Metamorphoses*, and his Jason describes Medea's happiness at seeing her beloved, and her grief at his betrayal, as well as the anger that the Senecan original foregrounds so powerfully, and that Studley exaggerates even further. At points, Studley has clearly drawn on his knowledge of Ovid to emphasise Medea's role in Jason's story: for example, in his translation of Medea's exchange with her Nurse in Act 2, he expands on Seneca's often brief and oblique references to the tasks Jason performed to win the Fleece (and which were described in the *Metamorphoses*), for the benefit of those readers who were not familiar with Medea's story. In the main, though, he is keen to play up the sense that Medea has lost her power over Jason, and even over her own emotions, which she seems far less able to control in the Elizabethan translation.[11]

The Elizabethan Medea's comparative lack of power over her situation in Corinth is also hinted at elsewhere: in Act 2, Studley expands Medea's appeal to Creon, simultaneously (and typically) bringing his readers up to speed on events which have preceded the Senecan tragedy, and compromising the imperious force of the Senecan Medea's demand that Jason be exiled from Corinth alongside her. In Seneca, Medea asks,

... si placet, damna ream;
sed redde crimen. sum nocens, fateor, Creo;
talem sciebas esse, cum genua attigi
fidemque supplex praesidis dextrae peti. (245–8)

If you so determine, condemn the accused – but give back her crime! I am guilty, I admit it, Creo: you knew me to be so, when I touched your knees in supplication and sought the promise of protection given by your hand.

In Studley's translation, Medea is more of a supplicant, more willing to acknowledge her ongoing remorse and lack of control over her situation:

It lyeth *Creon* in thy hande,
if thus it lyketh thee,
Condemne my gyltye gohste to death;
But render fyrste to mee,
My fault that forced me offende,
Then *Creon* graunt I thys,
Receavyng *Jason* (cause of cryme)
I gyltye dyd amysse. (878–85)

Medea's use of supplicating phrases like 'It lyeth *Creon* in thy hande', her repetition of 'gyltye' to refer to herself and her suggestion that she was 'forced' to sin, all demonstrate how the Elizabethan heroine emphasises Creon's power and simultaneously plays down her own. On the one hand, this supplicating attitude allows her to fool him into acceding to her request for more time in Corinth all the more easily. On the other hand, though, the same attitude allows Studley to satisfy the Elizabethan expectation that criminals (and particularly erring women) should recognise and regret their transgression against established order: an expectation that is very clearly apparent in the tragic uses of Medea discussed in the next chapter, where the didactic potential of her crimes is a crucial element of her story.

Creon himself is not able to exact punishment on Medea for the crimes that she readily admits, but this sense of Studley negotiating Medea's power, making her appear more helpless in an attempt to neutralise her threat, is still seen, very obviously, in his treatment of the final lines of the tragedy. In the Preface to his 1581 edition of translations from Seneca, the *Tenne Tragedies*, which included Studley's *Medea*, Thomas Newton defends Seneca against the objections of 'squeymish Areopagites' (A3ᵛ) (i.e., judges) who complain at his presentation of vice. Newton argues that while Seneca may represent wickedness,

I doubt whether there bee any amonge all the Catalogue of Heathen wryters, that with more gravity of Philosophicall sentences ... beateth down sinne, loose lyfe, dissolute dealinge, and unbrydled sensuality: or that more sensibly, pithily, and bytingly layeth downe the guerdon of filthy lust, cloaked dissimulation & odious treachery. (A3ᵛ–A4ʳ)[12]

Of course, Medea's escape at the end of the Senecan tragedy casts serious doubt on this pronouncement, and the Elizabethan need to represent sin and also its consequences is demonstrated as Studley once again steps in, this time to give his expectant Elizabethan readers some sense not only of her guilt but also of the punishment Medea might face for her crimes. Instead of the Senecan characterisation of Medea as negating the existence of divine power, that is contained in Jason's famous declaration 'testare nullos esse, qua veheris, deos' (bear witness where you ride that there are no gods) (1027), Studley has him say, 'Beare wytnesse grace of God is none / in place of thy repayre' (2889–2890). Fiona Macintosh, in common with other modern readers, sees this change as being in line with Studley's 'Christianized world-view',[13] and Studley's insistence that the grace and power of God (not 'gods') does exist, but that Medea is simply excluded from it demonstrates the dissatisfaction that the Elizabethan author felt with the classical Medea's famous escape. Indeed, this dissatisfaction extends to other early modern plays featuring unrepentant anti-heroes: Gordon Braden notes that the anonymous English drama *Nero* ends with an apparent homage to these Christianised lines, as the messenger proclaims,

> Thus great bad men above them finde a rod:
> People depart, and say there is a God. (5.3.152–3)[14]

Moreover, he points out that the early modern instinct to punish characters who escape censure in Seneca's tragedies can also be discerned in other Elizabethan translations of the dramatist's works: 'Renaissance adapters of *Thyestes* almost instinctively add some ode or speech at the end of the play to supply some more confident prospect for Atreus' downfall.'[15] Meanwhile Kiefer quotes the addition that Alexander Neville makes to the end of his Elizabethan translation of Seneca's *Oedipus*, in which the Messenger cautions his audience:

> Beware betimes, by him beware,
> I speak unto you all:
> Learne Justice, truth, and feare of God
> By his unhappy fall.[16]

Similarly, here Studley's Jason exercises a moral judgement on Medea that extends beyond the world of the play, making her seem, if not a weak character, certainly a less powerful one, who must seek a place of 'repayre' rather than going wherever she pleases. As Miola puts it,

> Seneca's Medea continues on as living testimony to the disorder of the world, as an embodiment of an evil so potent as to nullify divine power and presence; Studley's Medea is simply a spectacular sinner, one who infects her surroundings and lives without God's grace.[17]

Studley's translation, like other sixteenth-century English translations of the classics, has struggled to attract modern admirers, because of its infidelity to its original and because of its poetic form, characterised by Braden as 'numbing fourteener verse'.[18] In her edition of the translation E. M. Spearing argues that 'Contemporary references show that these tragedies were highly esteemed', but acknowledges that 'It is difficult to determine exactly how much of this influence was exerted by the plays in their Latin original, and how much through the medium of the translations of Studley and his companions.'[19] Spearing posits that Newton's publication of the collected translations 'undoubtedly' contributed to Elizabethan interest in Seneca: '[a]nd probably their influence was much greater than any examination merely of parallel passages in them and in Elizabethan plays would lead us to suspect.'[20] In contrast, Braden points out that while Golding's influence on Elizabethan literature (and particularly on Shakespeare) has been extensively discussed and convincingly proven, the same cannot be said of the Elizabethan translations of Seneca.[21] In fact, the influence that Senecan tragedy, in the original or in translation, exerted over Shakespeare and his fellow dramatists has been hotly debated. The Senecan *Medea* was referenced and quoted in the sixteenth and seventeenth centuries, despite (or because of) its controversial content. For example, in the series of sermons *The Devills Banket* (1614), Thomas Adams defends gory classical tragedies, including Seneca's *Oedipus* and *Thyestes* and 'the bleeding Bankets of the *Medea's*' (p. 42), arguing that such spectacles will encourage Christians to avoid sin.[22] More generally, critics such as Miola and M. L. Stapleton follow J. W. Cunliffe's ground-breaking nineteenth-century study, in identifying echoes of Senecan tragedy in Elizabethan and Shakespearean drama, particularly in revenge tragedy. Others, however, such as Peter Ure, G. K. Hunter and Howard Baker, are far more reluctant to acknowledge Senecan influence.[23] Ure concedes that Seneca 'may have contributed a ghost, a sensation, or a bloody hand here and there' to Elizabethan drama, while Baker dismisses the theory of Senecan influence on Elizabethan tragedy as a 'blighting critical fiction', and argues that typical or familiar tragic features such as the chorus and the use of ghosts and messengers are more properly attributed either to medieval *de casibus* tragedy or to the medieval mystery plays.[24]

It is notable that despite some seventeenth-century quotation of the tragedy, scholars who argue (convincingly) for a Senecan influence on early modern dramatists do not focus their arguments on *Medea*, and the tragedy is excluded from a list of five – the *Troades*, *Phaedra*, *Thyestes*, *Agamemnon* and *Hercules Furens* – which Miola sees as having a particular presence in Shakespeare's plays.[25] Equally difficult to determine is the issue of how far the early modern translations themselves (rather than the Latin versions) influenced authors who appear to make use of Seneca. Certainly, where echoes of *Medea* have been noted in Renaissance drama, it seems that in almost every case the author is using the Latin play, rather than Studley's translation. For example, Cunliffe suggests a Senecan influence on John Marston's comedy *Antonio and Mellida* (*c*.1599) in the lines of the disguised Duke Andrugio: 'Fortune my fortunes, not my mind, shall shake' (3.1.63).[26] The Senecan Medea exclaims, 'Fortuna opes auferre, non animum potest' (Fortune can take away my wealth, but not my spirit) (176) but in Studley she remarks:

> Full well may fortu[n]es weltyng whele
> to beggynge brynge my state,
> As for my worthy corage that
> she never shall abate. (645–8)

Elsewhere, Andrugio declares, 'Fortune fears valour, presseth cowardice' (4.2.29), and here Marston is clearly echoing the Senecan line 'Fortuna fortes metuit, ignavos premit' (Fortune fears the brave, but crushes cowards) (159).[27] By contrast, Studley has

> The valiant harte dame Fortune yet
> durst never harme wyth wronge
> But dreading dastards downe she drives. (583–5)[28]

In both cases, the dramatist adapts pithy Senecan phrasing, rather than Studley's lengthier reflections on Fortune, which are clearly influenced by medieval *de casibus* tragedy, in their personification of Fortune and their focus on her wheel. Even Thomas Hughes's *The Misfortunes of Arthur* (1587), the play that makes the clearest use of some version of the

Medea, sticks plainly to the Senecan rather than the Elizabethan version as it recounts the betrayal of King Arthur by Mordred. For example, in an example of the stichomythia so typical of Senecan tragedy, the classical Medea shoots down her Nurse's suggestion that she might fear the forces of Creon, with an oblique reference to her defeat of her father's earth-born soldiers in Colchis:

NUTRIX: Non metuis arma?
MEDEA: Sint licet terra edita. (169)

NURSE: You do not fear arms?
MEDEA: Not even if sprung from the earth.

Cunliffe proposes an exchange between Gawain and Mordred as evidence of the influence of *Medea*:

GAWAIN: And feare you not so strange and uncouth warres?
MORDRED: No, were they warres that grew from out the ground. (2.3)[29]

Hughes has lost the snap and crackle of the Senecan dialogue, and yet it becomes abundantly clear that he was using the Latin tragedy, when Studley's attempt is considered:

NURSE: Can not the deadly vyolence
          of weapons make the feare?
MEDEA: No though suche grislye laddes they were
          as whilom dyd appeare,
          That bred of gargell dragons teethe
          in holow gapyng ground,
          When mutually in blody fyght
          eche other dyd confounde. (617–24)

Studley's constant insistence on expanding Seneca's brief references to Medea's past crimes with embellishing details from Ovid's *Metamorphoses* and *Heroides* would doubtless be helpful to the reader encountering her for the first time, but when they adapt lines from the tragedy other early modern authors consistently seem to have had the Latin, not the Elizabethan translation, beside them, and used this as their point of reference. Indeed, J. L. Simmons suggests that, far from admiring Studley's translation, Marston (whose dramatic works echo the classical *Medea* repeatedly) parodies its final lines at the end of his revenge tragedy

Antonio's Revenge (*c*.1599), the sequel to *Antonio and Mellida*, when the revengers Antonio and Pandulpho turn to monasticism in repentance for their killing of the treacherous Piero, and vow to 'live enclosed' until 'dread power calls / Our souls' appearance' (5.3.33–4).[30]

Though Simmons sees parody in this recollection of Studley's *Medea*, however, and while it is true that early modern English dramatists prefer the language of Seneca's *Medea*, where the character herself is concerned, they lean away from Seneca, and towards Studley's weakened Medea. As I shall show in Chapter 3, where Elizabethan and Jacobean authors of drama, prose and poetry include Medea-like figures in their tragedies, they follow the models provided to them by Studley, or by *de casibus* tragedy, in that an evildoer who is compared to Medea is not allowed to escape and glory in the successful achievement of her (or his) bloody ambitions, as is the classical Medea. For example, though Reuben A. Brower argues that 'Shakespeare seems to have made very little if any use of the translations in Newton's edition', Miola sees Lady Macbeth, Shakespeare's most obviously Medea-like woman, as inhabiting 'the providentially ordered world of the translator', as opposed to the Senecan world which allows Medea to escape without even the suggestion of punishment, and, similarly, Inga-Stina Ewbank has explored the apparent echoes of Studley's translation, rather than the Senecan original, in Lady Macbeth's disavowal of her femininity and her threats of infanticide.[31] Studley's *Medea* is obviously not a faithful representation of his Latin original (though importantly he makes sure his reader is fully aware of this). Accordingly, his Medea is not quite Seneca's, is not the ruthlessly angry woman whose focus is all on what she can achieve in the one day before she escapes in triumph to the heavens. Between Seneca and Studley, medieval versions of the story such as those discussed in Chapter 1 have intervened, versions that stress Medea's love and suffering, and Jason's betrayal. The Renaissance Medea has become far more vulnerable than her classical ancestor, but society's expectations of crime and punishment as they might be represented in drama have also shifted. While she can be as bloodthirsty as any Elizabethan revenger, Studley also strives to make his Medea accountable, as Elizabethans felt themselves to be, to some higher power, or to her own feelings of guilt and regret: and this sense of accountability, if not Studley's language, was highly attractive to early modern authors.

English readers had to wait almost a century for another printed English rendering of *Medea*, and, when it appeared, it was a translation of a very different kind. Edward Sherburne translated Seneca's *Medea* into English in 1648, and though the unsigned prefatory address to the reader allies it to a freer style of adaptation, stating that the work 'is not by him stil'd a *Translation,* but a *Paraphrase'* (A2ᵛ),³² in fact it sticks far more closely than Studley's to its Latin original. The most significant alterations are Sherburne's extensive explanatory notes, and within the text itself the occasional elucidation of a confusing reference, or conversely a deviation from Seneca's words to display his own classical knowledge.³³ For example, in the 1701 edition, when Medea demands the return of her dowry, Sherburne takes it upon himself to add an explanation for his readers (and this kind of footnoted addition does seem to argue that they are readers rather than audience members):

> The Nuptiall Dowre, among the Antients, was the most certain Argument of Matrimony ... Nor (unless in the case of Adultery) by Laws of the *Athenians,* could a repudiated Wife be debar'd from receiving the benefit of it. (E3ʳ)³⁴

Occasionally, Sherburne's editorial decisions reduce Medea's account-ability for the crimes she will commit, for example by rendering her mad: Seneca describes the Medea of Act 3 as exhibiting the signs 'furoris ... lymphati' (of frenzied rage) (line 386), while Sherburne translates this in both editions as 'Lymphatick Rage' (C3ᵛ), and goes on to describe sufferers of this condition as 'dispossest of their Sences', either because of the anger of 'some Nymph or wat'ry Deietie' or else because of a 'superfluitie of the Brains Moisture' (G3ʳ). Most interest-ing among his additions is his alteration of Jason's final lines, between the first edition of the translation and the second, which appeared in 1701 and was reprinted in 1702. In 1648, Sherburne's Jason closes the play by exclaiming, 'Goe, mount the skies; and by thy flight declare, / (If thou unpunish'd go'st) no Gods there are' (E3ᵛ). Here, the deviation from the Latin, and the addition of the caveat '(If thou unpunish'd go'st)' suggests to Sherburne's readers the possibility, however slight that Medea might be held accountable for her crimes, a hint entirely absent from Seneca's tragedy, but added to Studley's, which had suggested that Medea was excluded from God's grace. In the 1701 version, however, this final line had become the more accurate 'Go, thro' the high Ætherial Stages post, / And shew there are no Gods where'er thou go'st' (G8ᵛ). The alteration of Jason's final words demonstrates Sherburne's evolving attitude to translating his contentious heroine, and linked to this a new desire to reflect closely the Senecan Jason's questioning of the gods' very existence, in the light of Medea's evil.³⁵

Hunter argues that Sherburne's translation is 'much more competent and readable' than its Elizabethan predecessor, and it was also lauded by his contemporaries.[36] A. F.'s commendatory verse to the 1648 translation praises Sherburne for winning Seneca new admirers, just as Seneca had increased Medea's notoriety, writing, 'He spreads *her Infamy*, and thou *his Praise*' (A3^v).

Thomas Stanley's verse, in the same edition, seems to contrast Studley's and Sherburne's efforts, stating, 'Though change of Tongues stolne praise to some afford, / Thy version hath not borrowed, but restor'd' (A3^r). Notwithstanding this praise of his approach, however, Sherburne's attitude to translation continued to evolve, and in 'A Brief Discourse Concerning Translation', in the preface to the 1701 edition of his Senecan tragedies, Sherburne rejects the term 'paraphrase', which had been attached to the 1648 *Medea*, and insists that what he aims at is

> not curtail'd or diminish'd by a partial Version, nor lengthened out or augmented by a preposterous Paraphrase; but the genuine Sense of *Seneca* in these Tragedies intelligibly delivered, by a close Adherence to his Words as far as the Propriety of Language may fairly admit; in Expressions not unpoetical, and Numbers not unmusical. But representing, as in a Glass, his just Lineaments and Features, his true Air and Mien, in his own Native Colours, unfarded with adulterate Paint, and keeping up (at least aiming so to do) his distinguishing Character: in a word, rendring him entire, and like. Which are the things a Translator should chiefly, if not solely attend. (c3^v–c4^r)

Robert Cummings has termed Sherburne 'the last of the early modern literalist translators',[37] and Sherburne's antipathy to what his new preface terms 'preposterous Paraphrase' is indicative of changing attitudes to translation in the last half of the seventeenth century. The period saw first a growth in popularity of paraphrastic translation, or translation that was neither too literal nor too free (the method lauded by John Dryden in his *Preface to Ovid's Epistles*) and then a backlash against the method, which was criticised for being too unfaithful.[38] The suspicion of paraphrase is clearly reflected in the 1701 *Medea*'s more accurate rendering of Jason's final lines. Moreover, this small but significant alteration might point to a burgeoning authorial willingness to celebrate, rather than quash, Medea's final triumph. In 1648, Thomas Stanley's commendatory poem had presented Medea as being somehow bested by the very act of translation, proclaiming to Sherburne 'thou ... her Revenge hast robb'd of halfe its Pride, / To see it selfe, thus by it selfe out-vy'd' (A3^r). By 1701, however, Sherburne has moved further away from his Elizabethan predecessor and from paraphrastic translation, and, as a result, his new eighteenth-century Medea is allowed to escape without caveat. No further translations of Seneca's *Medea* are printed during the seventeenth century, but surveying sixteenth- and seventeenth-century translations of the Ovidian Medea (as she appeared in the *Metamorphoses, Tristia* and *Heroides*) also amply demonstrates the period's shifting and evolving attitudes, both to Medea and to the practice of classical translation.

Early modern *Metamorphoses*

Lorna Hardwick points to the importance of the reader's experience, 'both actual and imagined', to adapters of earlier stories, and if a concern with the reader's understanding and moral instruction lies at the heart of the alterations both Studley and Sherburne made to Seneca, the same is true of many early modern translations of the Ovidian Medea.[39] While Studley's influence on early modern writing is uncertain, the first Elizabethan translation of the *Metamorphoses*, by Arthur Golding, which appeared the following year, was immediately popular and influential: as Jonathan Bate puts it, 'If Shakespeare and his contemporaries owed their intimacy with Ovidian rhetoric to the grammar schools, their easy familiarity with Ovidian narrative was as much due to Golding.'[40] Studley proudly explains to his readers that he has altered Seneca in order to bring his tragedy in line with Elizabethan tastes, and Golding also has his eye firmly on his audience, and immediately foregrounds the way in which he expects the Elizabethan male reader to receive and understand Ovid's myths, in his address to his patron, the Earl of Leicester. The *Epistle to Leicester* clearly lays out the lessons the reader can expect to learn from his English rendering of Ovid's Medea:

The *good* success of Jason in the land of Colchos and
The doings of Medea since, do give to understand
That nothing is so hard but pain and travail do it win,
For fortune ever favoureth such as boldly do begin;
That women both in helping and in hurting have no match
When they to either bend their wits; and how that for to catch
An honest meaner under fair pretence of friendship is
An easy matter. Also there is warning given of this:
That men should never hastily give ear to fugitives,
Nor into hands of sorcerers commit their state or lives.
It shows in fine, of stepmothers the deadly hate in part,
And vengeance most unnatural that was in mother's heart. (143–54).[41]

Here, before the translation proper has even begun, Golding's focus on male achievement, Jason's 'good success', is clear. Like Chaucer and Caxton before him, he emphasises Jason's contribution to his own triumph, thereby downplaying Medea's role and reducing her to ancillary behaviour, 'helping' or 'hurting' Jason's hopes. Just as the Elizabethan translation of Seneca can seem medieval in its emphasis on Fortune, and on Medea's suffering, Lee T. Pearcy points out that, throughout his translation of the *Metamorphoses*, Golding works with 'the medieval tradition of Ovidian interpretation … He looks back to *Ovide moralisé* as much as he looks ahead to the Ovid of the next generation'.[42] Golding is interested in creating an Ovid that is useful and relevant to his Elizabethan readers, but he does this by looking back to medieval allegorical interpretation and encouraging male readers in particular to interpret what appears to be an alarming tale of an unrestrained woman, for their own edification and instruction.

In 1564, Golding had produced a faithful English translation of the Roman historian Justin's *Epitome of the Philippic History of Pompeius Trogus*. This history had very little interest in presenting a transgressive Medea: it does not connect her with the Argonautic voyage, makes no mention of the killing of Pelias or her children, and refers to her enmity towards Theseus, and the death of her brother Apsyrtus, without implicating her in any wrongdoing.[43] The *Metamorphoses* presents a Medea who is often highly threatening and ruthlessly violent, and her power here poses Golding many more problems than it did in the *Epitome*. To overcome this difficulty, the translator employs a dual strategy that has the effect of either undermining Medea's power or else emphasising it and appropriating it for his own instructive purposes, despite the fact that, as Braden notes, in Golding's translation 'the moralization is almost all in the two prefaces, and Ovid himself is remarkably unaltered'.[44]

Golding stresses the horror of Medea's crimes to increase the entertaining and the didactic potential of her story, while also suggesting, more subtly than either his medieval forebears or Studley, that Medea is comfortingly weakened by her love for Jason. So he expands on Ovid's brief reference to Medea concocting a potion that includes 'strigis infamis' (the uncanny screech-owl) (7.269)[45] into

> … a witch a cursèd odious wight
> Which in the likeness of an owl abroad a-nights did fly,
> And infants in their cradles change or suck them that they die. (7.350–2)

This bloodthirsty addition interpolates material from the *Fasti*, and also from notes by Jacob Micyllus, in the 1543 reprint of Raphael

Regius's annotated fifteenth-century edition of the poem. It is intended to appeal to the sixteenth century's fascination with macabre stories of witchcraft and the occult, specifically here with the classical figure of the child-killing *strix*, a witch that could transform into an owl.[46] In the Regius-Micyllus commentary on Book 7, the reader is told:

> Vulgus aute[m] putat striges non esse aves, sed vetulas, quae se veneficio quodam in aves co[n]vertunt, infantsq[ue] dormie[n]tes aggrediuntur, ac eorum sanguine[m] ita exsugu[n]t, ut aut mortui inveniantur in cunis, aut diu vivere no[n] possint. (p. 158)[47]

> But the common people think that screech-owls are not birds but old women who change themselves into birds through some sorcery and attack sleeping children and suck out their blood in such a way that either they are found dead in their cradles or they cannot live long.[48]

In a discussion of Robert Graves's translation of Suetonius (1957), and of the 'domesticating' translation that he elsewhere argues was dominant in the early modern period, Lawrence Venuti notes that such translation may involve 'not merely the insertion of explanatory phrases, but the inscription of the foreign text with values that are not only anachronistic and ethnocentric, but dominant in the receiving culture'.[49] Golding domesticates, as he translates, reflecting the slippage between the figure of the witch and the child-killer that was so familiar in the sixteenth century, in order to increase readerly horror, which could then be displaced onto Medea herself.[50]

Elsewhere, Golding suggests that, in her excesses, Medea is not quite a person: Raphael Lyne argues that, in Golding's translation, 'Even minor changes help the reader towards a clear moral perception of the action described', suggesting that through additions such as descriptions of Medea as 'babling' and crying out 'ful bitterly', her concocting of potions in Golding's translation is made to appear an 'angry, incoherent, inhuman act'.[51] Later, too, when Ovid very briefly describes the murders of her children, Golding is at pains to stress the repugnant and inhuman nature of Medea's crimes, adding a line to the Latin to describe her as 'Not like a mother but a beast bereaving them of life' (7.504). In the *Epistle to Leicester*, Golding tells his readers that in the poem they will find 'double recompence with pleasure and with gain':

> With pleasure, for variety and strangeness of the things;
> With gain, for good instruction which the understanding brings.
> (544–6)

As these lines suggest, it is in Golding's interest to augment his translation to exaggerate the most alarming aspects of Medea's character and actions, as such subtle changes allow him to appeal to his readership, with 'variety' and 'strangeness', and also to instruct them, indirectly, about the horror of witches and child-killers.

Other changes, however, argue an attempt on Golding's part to make the Ovidian Medea more akin to the weakened woman represented by medieval authors such as Chaucer. Thus, in Ovid's *Metamorphoses*, the reader is told that Medea was impressed by Jason when he came to plead with her because he was more beautiful than usual: 'et casu solito formosior Aesone natus / illa luce fuit: posses ignoscere amanti' (It chanced that the son of Aeson was more beautiful than usual that day: you could pardon her for loving him) (7.84–5). In Golding's rendering, this assessment is far more obviously Medea's, and subjective:

> And, as it chancèd, far more fair and beautiful of face
> *She thought him* then than ever erst. But sure it doth behove
> Hir judgement should be borne withal *because she was in love*. (7.120–2,
> emphasis my own)

On the one hand, Ovid's Medea is the more powerless here: his Jason unarguably *was* more attractive than usual, and perhaps could not have been resisted by anyone. On the other hand, Golding's sense that Medea's attraction to Jason is subjective, and personal to her, weakens her by isolating her, and allying her to the earlier Medeas created by authors like Chaucer, who are reduced to suffering victims of Jason's seductive powers.

Earlier, subtle additions have betrayed Golding's sense that Medea's desire for Jason is unwise, and may be actively detrimental to her. Golding's Medea addresses herself as 'Unhappy wench' (7.20), and describes her love as 'this uncouth heat' (7.20) and 'an uncouth malady' (7.23). Ovid has merely 'conceptas … flammas' (these flames that you feel) (7.17) and 'nova vis' (some strange power) (7.19), and the repeated use of 'uncouth' (meaning strange or unknown) underscores the sense that Golding's Medea, like Studley's, never truly has control over her own feelings for Jason. Madeleine Forey has shown that later, when Golding translates Medea's invocation to Hecate, his small alterations mean that Medea subjects herself to the goddess more fully than her Ovidian predecessor, and Forey suggests that 'Golding's Medea seems more aware that, without aid, she is powerless'.[52] Golding's alterations of his original are far more subtle than Studley's, and yet they too transform Medea's power, often suggesting a weakness that was comforting to the Elizabethan male reader. At the same time, some of Golding's alterations emphasise her magic and brutality (for example when he embellishes Ovid's mention of the *strix*, or describes Medea as 'Not like a mother but a beast' when she kills her children) to cater to perverse Elizabethan interest in witchcraft, while simultaneously turning the reader away from such an unprofitable path.

Golding's *Metamorphoses* was followed some sixty years later by the complete translation of George Sandys, which first appeared in 1626, and was published again, this time with extensive explanatory notes, in 1632. Stuart Gillespie sees this and similar translations, accompanied by prefaces and notes and adorned with illustrations, as being 'designed to become cultural monuments',[53] and certainly the translation was admired by contemporary authors, as Golding's had been, and was recommended for use in schools by Charles Hoole, in *A New Discovery of the Old Art of Teaching Schoole* (published 1661).[54] Golding's epistles to Leicester and to the reader had explained how his translation should be used and interpreted by the reader, and Sandys too is keenly aware of his readership. For Liz Oakley-Brown, Sandys's translation (1632), dedicated to King Charles I, is 'the epitome of a conservative text', and one which 'embodies a complex translation of the court by the court, upholding and promoting an ideology of subjection and rule through notions of harmony and moderation'.[55] Indeed, the work is conservative both as a translation and as an endorsement of Stuart ideology. Sandys dispenses with Golding's colloquial touches: for example, he translates Medea's exclamation 'accingere et omnem / pelle moram' (7.47–8) as 'goe on; delay decline' (Cc5ᵛ),[56] while Golding has Medea tell herself, 'Step to it out of hand' (7.65). Like Golding, though, Sandys for the most part confines his additions and expansions to the paratextual material: here the notes that accompanied the 1632 edition.[57] These additions, far more extensive than Golding's epistles to Leicester and to the reader, serve Sandys's conservative purpose in their undermining of Medea's destabilising magical power. For example, Lyne notes that Golding added an explanation of Hecate's story into his passage on Medea, and that he did this because 'for the sixteenth-century translator ... it is important to clarify that witchcraft (with all its connotations) is involved'.[58] Sandys approaches this purported magical power in a different way, not turning it to his own ends to entertain and horrify the reader, but questioning it, to the extent that Rubin sees Sandys not as stressing the real danger of witchcraft but as exhibiting 'compassion for disturbed and deluded women' in his portrayal of witches in the

Metamorphoses.[59] Sandys's scepticism towards witchcraft is demonstrated in his notes to Medea's boasting of her powers over nature:

> But these wonders, and the rest here rehearsed, were not effected by the vertue of words, or skill of Medea; but rather by wicked Angels, who seeme to subject themselves, the better to delude, to the art of the Inchantresse. (Ff3ᵛ–Ff4ʳ)

Here and elsewhere, Sandys suggests that it is a power greater than Medea that actually affects nature: that of 'wicked Angels', which fool Medea into thinking she possesses 'the art of the Inchantresse'. It was an important tenet of early modern witchcraft belief that the Devil was thought to be in control of witches, who either did his bidding or were fooled by him into believing their own abilities: either way, they were not really empowered.[60] This idea that Medea is deluded, rather than truly powerful, is also apparent in Sandys's annotation to his description of Medea's concocting her potion and, specifically, of her inclusion of the *strix* in her brew. Golding had embellished Ovid's mention of the screech-owl with sensationalising reference to child-murder, and Sandys also quotes the *Fasti* in his notes on this point. He is then quick to qualify the hideous anecdote, however, noting that while some believe that witches can transform in this way:

> diverse wise Judges have admonished, that men should not give too rash a beleife to the confessions of Witches, nor yet to the evidence which is brought against them: because witches themselves are imaginative, beleeving ofttimes that they doe, what indeed they doe not; withall the vulgar are credulous in this kinde, too prone to impute meere accidents, and naturall operations, to the power of Witch-craft. (Ggʳ)[61]

Sandys's Caroline readers would be well used to hearing scandalous reports from witchcraft trials of 'the confessions of Witches', and the supposed evidence of their crimes, and here the translator's sceptical notes lump Medea in with exploited or delusional seventeenth-century women who do not possess magical powers, however fervently they may believe this.

Even when Medea is not shown to be personally deluded as to her own power, Sandys shows how accounts of her achievements have become garbled and far-fetched in the reporting. In his notes on Jason's conquest of the Fleece, he explains carefully how each of the apparently supernatural obstacles he overcomes should be understood. The fire-breathing bulls are:

> a garrison of mercenary souldiers of Taurica (called therefore Bulls) ... who in regard of their robustious bodies, and fierce dispositions, were said to have hornes of iron, hoofes of brasse, horribly to bellow, and throw flames from their nostrills. Hether Medea conducting the Argonautes by night, and calling to the watch in the Taurican language to open the gates unto the daughter of the King, by that pollicy brought them in. (Ff2ᵛ–Ff3ʳ)

The defeat of the earth-born men represents Jason's ability to stir up discord between soldiers, while Medea's bewitching of the dragon should be understood as 'Draco the priest of Mars, and keeper of the treasure, being corrupted with hopes, and charming perswasions' (Ff3ʳ). Here, Sandys draws on the annotations that George Sabinus had made to the poem, which in turn make use of the rationalising classical account of Diodorus Siculus, who had been at pains to describe how the supernatural elements of Medea's legend should be understood figuratively, rather than literally.[62] In his annotations, Sabinus tells his readers that 'Tauros ignem efflantes Diodorus Siculus scribit Æëtae regis custodes fuisse' (Diodorus Siculus writes that the fire-breathing bulls were the guards of King Aeëtes) (p. 227), and, similarly, his commentary is the source for Sandys's explanation of the fire-breathing dragon as a priest:

> Unde non dubium est & Draconem fuisse primarium quem piam virum & principem apud Colchos, cuius nomen Poëtae simili modo ad animantis fabulam traduxerunt. (p. 227)[63]

> From this there is no doubt that Dracon was important and a pious man and a leader in Colchis, whose name the poets had transferred in a similar way, to a tale of a beast.[64]

Sandys also references the ancient geographer Strabo's suggestion that the Argonauts went to Colchis to find not the Golden Fleece but gold mines, and proposes that the obstacles Jason faced 'may allude to the rocks, straights, quick-sands, and other hazards in their perilous passage ... neither is it improbable that in the search of those mines they incountred with wild beasts and serpents, the inhabitants of such rough and unfrequented places' (Ff3ʳ). In all cases, the move away from the supernatural towards the rationalising serves to diminish Medea's power over Jason and his quest, and shifts the focus of praise back to Jason as intrepid adventurer, just as Golding's introduction of the tale had opened with an emphasis on his 'good success' (143).

Having supplied practical explanations for many of the tale's wonders, and recast Medea as a woman deluded by Satan and his wicked angels into believing her own power, Sandys sets the seal on his sceptical revision of Medea's story when he includes mention of the tradition that reads Jason as representing medicine, 'not for the body, but the mindes diseases', while Medea is 'counsell'. Sandys explains that counsel assists medicine, but is 'otherwise of itself unusefull' (Ff3ʳ). Through this reading, the success is all really Jason's ability to control his emotions:

> So that Jason, assisted by Medea, suppresseth anger; imbosom'd conflicts, and restlesse envy (furious Bulls, intestine warres, and sleeplesse serpents) with all the turbulent passions of the soule, and subjects them to his reason: by which he obtaineth the Golden fleece, and returnes with honour into his country. (Ff3ʳ)

This interpretation of Medea as 'counsell' was given by Conti in his *Mythologiae*, and repeated by Thomas Heywood in his mayoral pageant *Londini Status Pacatus, or Londons Peaceable Estate* (1639) another work which appropriates Medea's power to endorse and reflect male achievement, there in the shape of the new mayor of London, Henry Garway.[65] The assertion of the power of patriarchal rule in Sandys's notes is then underscored by the translator's mention of Philippe of Burgundy's establishment of the Order of the Golden Fleece. This medieval order of knights had been celebrated by Caxton's fifteenth-century *History of Jason* (1477), his translation of Raoul Lefèvre's *Histoire*, in which a horrifying Medea is satisfyingly subdued and mastered by Jason, who is thus made to appear admirable and a more fitting figurehead for the order. The rationalising instinct of Sandys's notes is thus clearly geared towards the subtle diminishing of Medea's power and influence, and the concurrent celebration of male success and conquest of new worlds, in ways that feed into the translator's larger project, to celebrate Stuart kingship.

Sandys clearly takes pains to show how the wonders he describes should be correctly interpreted, and Richard F. Hardin sees Sandys's commentary as 'evidence of the allegorical Ovid's continuing dominance in the early seventeenth century', and finds that 'the commentaries suggest that Sandys read Ovid much as any medieval *grammaticus* would'.[66] In contrast, Pearcy argues that 'Far from being a late flowering of the allegorical interpretation, his Ovid showed how ancient myths could be compatible with the new desire to know divine truth as directly as possible.'[67] In fact, Sandys, like Golding, treads a fine line between looking back to the medieval tradition, and making his Ovid relevant to early modern readers.[68] In the preface to the 1626 edition, Sandys describes his translation as 'Sprung from the stocke of the ancient Romanes, but bred in the New-world' (a2ʳ),[69] and Lyne notes that, in the 1632 edition, Sandys's notes are geared towards giving his commentary a flavour of his travels, while at the same time ridiculing any readerly belief in magical or occult powers. Lyne argues that: 'The idea of the New World as a world of marvels is actually satirized here – it can accommodate all kinds of semi-human degeneracy, but looking to it for fantastic benefits is made to look foolish.'[70] Liz Oakley-Brown notes Sandys's 'effacement of Ovidian violence' in his translation, and has shown that, elsewhere in the poem, the very form of the translation, particularly his use of the heroic couplet, can dilute the horror of the Ovidian text.[71] What captures his interest in Medea's story, however, is not violence but magic, a supernatural control over men and beasts that the conservative Caroline translator cannot allow her to wield, knowing as he does the terrible consequences it has for the kingdoms of Aeëtes, Pelias and Creon. Sandys's preface to the reader asserted that he has added notes to his translation, because 'it should be the principall end in publishing of Books, to inform the understanding, direct the will, and temper the affections' (no sig.). Sandys found in Ovid's tale of Medea a strangeness and a foreignness that accorded with his own interest in discovery and exploration. In the rationalizing explanations of Sabinus, Regius and Micyllus, and in his own combining of conservative translation with sceptical, rationalizing notes, however, he simultaneously discovered a way to play down the most alarming aspects of the magical power he found in the *Metamorphoses*, and make his Medea a source of instruction and reassurance for his readers, throughout the seventeenth century.[72]

Early modern *Tristia*

Studley's version of the Senecan *Medea*, and the *Metamorphoses* of Golding and Sandys demonstrate how the translator may augment or alter his source text's representation of Medea's power in ways that are intended to instruct his readers about natural phenomena, or the power of God, or the folly of belief in the supernatural. However, such instruction was not the only attraction her story held for the early modern translator. Elsewhere, Medea is translated in ways that are more intended to entertain an early modern readership, just as Golding hoped to titillate with his exaggerated description of Medea's magical powers, or Studley played up the bloodthirstiness he had found in Seneca. In 1572, the soldier and poet Thomas Churchyard translated Ovid's *Tristia* 3.9, which includes his most extended account of Medea's killing of her brother, and it was reprinted in 1580.[73] Ovid gives a matter-of-fact account of Medea's self-interested killing of Apsyrtus, accomplished as the Colchian forces bear down on the Argonauts:

> Forthwith while he in his ignorance feared no such attack she pierced his innocent side with the hard sword. Then she tore him limb from limb, scattering the fragments of his body throughout the fields so that they must be sought in many places. And to apprise her father she placed upon a lofty rock the pale hands and gory head. Thus was the sire delayed by his fresh grief, lingering, while he gathered those limbs, on a journey of sorrow. (3.9.25–32)[74]

Churchyard exaggerates the graphic nature of Apsyrtus' slaughter, and the reaction of Medea's father, in ways which foreshadow later grisly Elizabethan fictionalisations of Medea's story, such as that found in his friend Richard Robinson's *Rewarde of Wickednesse*. The translation reads:

> Hee all unwares and dreading nought, her cancred cruell spight,
> Into his side her bloudy sword, she thrust with raging might.
> Her blade pluckt backe from gored syde, she rent with ruthfull wound,
> And members minste in peeces small, she cast about the ground.
> ...
> With wayling new her aged syre, for this did make delay,
> And sob[b]ing sore the fleshe tooke up, she safely scapt away. (D^r)[75]

In his translation of Seneca's *Medea*, Studley had indulged in similarly bloodthirsty exaggeration of his source, in his expansion of Medea's declaration that she will kill her children:

> Then at the Alters of the Gods
> my chyldren shal be slayne,
> With crimsen coulourd blood of babes harte,
> their alters wil I staine.

Through livers, lounges, the lightes &
through every gut and gall,
For vengeau[n]ce break away perforce,
and spare no blood at all. (283–90)

In contrast, in his 1633 translation of the *Tristia*, which was frequently
reprinted through the Restoration, Wye Saltonstall dispenses both with
Churchyard's fourteeners, and with much of his melodrama: Medea
turns to her brother,

And with a sword she ran him through the side,
Who little thought by her hand to have dy'd.
Then teares his Limbes in peeces, and on the ground,
She scatters them, so that they may be found
In many places ...
And while that horrid sight did stop her father,
He stayd his course those scatterd limbes to gather. (E6ᵛ)[76]

Saltonstall's more matter-of-fact translation was closely followed by that
of Zachary Catlin, in 1639. In his preface, Catlin claims that he was not
aware of Saltonstall's earlier effort until he was halfway through his own
attempt, but decided to carry on with the project, imagining a reader
who is able to compare the two translations:

yet I thought better to perfit what I had begun then to desist and give
over in the midst, hoping that the intelligent Reader upon aequall
survey, will not thinke either my labour or his owne altogether
fruitlesse. (A4ʳ)[77]

Catlin argues that his fidelity to Ovid means that his translation holds
attractions for both those readers who are approaching the *Tristia* without knowledge of Latin and those who know the original:

To them that can swim without bladders, this translation will not
onely bring delight, but if they please with the matter to observe the
propriety of both the tongues, it may *Miscere utile dulci,* bring them
in delight and profit both. (A3ᵛ)

Accordingly, like Saltonstall he sticks more closely to the Latin than his
Elizabethan predecessor Churchyard, and Medea's killing of Apsyrtus is

described without much embellishment, beyond some exaggeration of the child's innocence:

Forthwith, whilst he, poore soule did nothing feare,
Her bloody sword his ha[r]melesse brest doth teare.
And with his mangled limbs she strowes the ground,
That being disperst, they might be slowly found. (E^v)

Just as Edward Sherburne's *Medea* would be a more faithful and literal translation than Studley's, the two later versions of the *Tristia* are far closer to the Latin than their Elizabethan counterpart, and their treatment of Medea's fratricide reflects a move away from sensational Elizabethan engagement with the classics, suggesting instead an interest in relatively faithful translation of the body of the text, that is also discernible in Sandys's *Metamorphoses* (which does not deviate far from Ovid's Latin in its account of Medea, despite the addition of extensive notes) and in Caroline versions of the *Heroides*. Indeed, when dealing with translations of the *Heroides*, as with the *Metamorphoses*, the *Tristia* and Seneca's *Medea*, it is possible to compare melodramatic Elizabethan handlings of Medea, concerned with gore, sensation and the punishment of sin, with the more measured mid-seventeenth-century translations of the same Latin works, which reflect a growing concern with the expectations of the translator's readership, with the responsibility he bears to these readers, and with the choices he makes, in rendering Ovid's Medea in English.

Early modern *Heroides*

Recent criticism of the *Heroides* has argued for a reading of Ovid's heroines as somehow independent from the poet, and possessed of their own powerful voices: for example, Laurel Fulkerson suggests that Hypsipyle and Medea are finely attuned to one another, as letter-writers and heroines.[78] In the sixteenth and seventeenth centuries, however, male-authored translations of the letters of Hypsipyle and Medea, participating in what Elizabeth D. Harvey terms 'transvestite ventriloquism', the male adoption and adaptation of a female voice, sought to undercut Medea's power, and to present her as subject not only to the poet but also to the translator who could manipulate and shape what he had found in the Latin.[79]

George Turberville's translation of the *Heroides* appeared in the same year as Golding's *Metamorphoses*, in 1567, and includes the so-called

'Sabinus' epistles, responses to the Ovidian letters of Phyllis, Oenone and Penelope, from Demophoon, Paris and Ulysess.[80] Like Golding, Turberville is fond of colloquialism, but does not stray markedly from his Latin original in his translations of Hypsipyle's and Medea's epistles, with one dramatic exception. The minor changes he makes to Hypsipyle's letter are geared to making Medea appear more alien: she is described as 'that beast' (Evi[r]), and she and Jason are condemned as 'you beastly folkes' (Evii[r])[81] rather than being termed 'nuptaque virque' (6.164) (wife and husband).[82] Turberville's Hypsipyle sees Jason and Medea's union as invalid, remarking: 'Some furie fell with bloodshot eyes / did frame this cankred spight' (Eiii[r]), while, in Ovid, Hypsipyle applies this image more clearly to herself and to her marriage to Jason: 'at mihi nec Iuno, nec Hymen, sed tristis Erinys / praetulit infaustas sanguinolenta faces' (And yet neither Juno nor Hymen, but gloomy Erinys, stained with blood, carried before me the unhallowed torch) (6.45–6).

Patricia B. Phillippy has noted that Turberville's 1560s Ovid is 'unique in its lack of moralizing gloss': she argues that Turberville's goal is to entertain his male readers, and so he eschews the opportunity to provide heavy-handed didactic interpretation of his original.[83] Nevertheless, while the arguments to Turberville's epistles do not criticise his transgressive women as we might expect, his Hypsipyle aims to attack Medea in a more outspoken way than her Ovidian predecessor, something that is made clear as her letter draws to a close, by the most obvious change that Turberville makes to his original. Turberville's Hypsipyle hopes that Medea will 'banisht begge / hir bread with dish and clap', and then startlingly wishes that she might kill herself:

> When Sea and Lande she hath
> Consumde, up to the skie,
> Let her goe rangle lyke a Rogue
> and by selfe slaughter die (Evii[r])

Ovid's *Heroides* has no reference to begging for food or to suicide, and instead Hypsipyle wishes 'cum mare, cum terras consumpserit, aera temptet; / erret inops, exspes, caede cruenta sua!' (When she shall have no hope more of refuge by the sea or by the land, let her make trial of the air; let her wander, destitute, bereft of hope, stained red with the blood of her murders!) (6.161–2).[84] In numerous sixteenth-century editions of Ovid, however, 'caede cruenta sua' is glossed with the explanation 'idest quae seipsam interficiat' (that is (to say) she kills herself), the notes being attributed to the fifteenth-century cleric Ubertino da

Crescentino.[85] Here, as Golding had done with his addition of the description of the *strix*, Turberville seems to take his cue from Ubertino's frequently reprinted notes, and apparently uses them to make an addition to the text itself. Like Studley's augmenting of Jason's final lines in his *Medea*, the addition of the suggestion of suicide is intended to portray Medea as subject to some kind of higher power, even if it is only that of her own guilty conscience. As I shall show in Chapter 3, this instinct to punish a Medea-figure by having her commit suicide, or be executed, was to become highly popular in tragic works that invoked her story.[86]

Moreover, while they contain a suggestion of punishment that would be attractive to Turberville's reader, the Elizabethan Hypsipyle's disgusted closing words also demonstrate a clear desire to distance herself from her rival Medea. Diane Purkiss has shown how accounts of female testimony at early modern witchcraft trials can highlight a particularly female alarm at the figure of the witch: 'For women, a witch was a figure who could be read against and within her own social identity as housewife and mother.'[87] The Hypsipyle who condemns Medea so absolutely in 1567 is, of course, a male creation, rather than a real woman testifying at a trial, and yet the venom she turns on her rival can thus be read as reflecting a dual anxiety about Medea, one that is experienced simultaneously by both male translator and female character, and is resolved in these final lines by the translator having his character emphasise her wish for Medea's punishment and her own difference from the witch.[88] Certainly, the significance of Turberville's addition to his original is suggested by the fact that by the last decades of the seventeenth century, over a hundred years after the translation first appeared, English translators of Hypsipyle's epistle, including Elkanah Settle and the burlesquer Matthew Stevenson, continued to include her wish for Medea's suicide. This is despite the fact that it is not mentioned either in the Latin poem itself or in the sparse notes of more up-to-date Restoration editions of Ovid's Latin, such as the 1670 version of Borchard Cnipping, which had appeared ten years before Settle's or Stevenson's translations.[89] Turberville's has been termed a 'pedestrian translation'[90] of Ovid, and, like Golding, he does not usually stray far from the Latin. This conservative bent means that his favouring of the commentator's notes, and his deviation from Ovid's actual text, however, is all the more significant at this point, indicative of the threat that Elizabethan authors saw in Medea, and their corresponding desire to contain this threat by somehow punishing her behaviour, even if the punishment is only hoped for, rather than certain.[91]

In Medea's epistle, Turberville continues to foreground female sexual reputation in ways that again suggest a woman's determination to distinguish herself from her rival: as Medea 'playde a harlots caste' (Evi^r) in Hypsipyle's epistle and is described as a 'Drabbe' (Evi^r) and 'the Harlot' (Evi^v), Medea describes her own love rival Creusa as a 'strumpet' (Ki^r). If Medea criticises Creusa in terms that suggest sexual impropriety, equally significant is Medea's desire to show how, as a faithful wife, she suffers as a result of her devotion to the philandering Jason. In Ovid, Medea reflects, 'facti fortasse pigebit – / et piget infido consuluisse viro' (Mayhap I shall repent me of what I do – but I repent me, too, of regard for a faithless husband's good.) (12.209–10). In his tragedy Studley's first chorus had pitied Medea for her misplaced faith in Jason, and Turberville's Medea ends her letter not by wondering if she will regret her future crimes but by admitting that she has been weakened by her foolish love for Jason:

And then perhaps he shall repent his deede,
As I lament, I gave a faythlesse man
Such credit, and beléevde the words he spake. (Kii^r)

Such an admission owes something to the weakened Medea represented by authors such as Chaucer and Gower, and reflected in Studley's translation of Seneca, which held Medea up not only as an example of wickedness but of undue credulity. Medea's Elizabethan epistle reads more as an Elizabethan complaint poem than does the classical letter, in large part because of this final emphasis on her misplaced faith and her current sorrow, and the reader is left to reflect that this Medea seems far more likely than her furious classical counterpart to take her own life, as Turberville's Hypsipyle had cruelly hoped.

Turberville's *Heroides*, like the *Metamorphoses* of Golding and Sandys, was a popular and frequently reprinted translation.[92] While Golding's and Sandys's Ovids were the only complete translations of the *Metamorphoses* into English in the sixteenth and seventeenth centuries, to be followed by multi-authored translations such as that produced by Samuel Garth (1717), however, the *Heroides* were far more frequently attempted in English. Turberville's Elizabethan translation was followed by two Caroline versions, by Wye Saltonstall (translator of the *Tristia*) in 1636 and by John Sherburne (brother of Edward, who would translate Seneca's *Medea*) in 1639. When he translated the *Tristia*, Zachary Catlin had felt bound to acknowledge the existence of Saltonstall's contemporaneous version and, here again, translations of the *Heroides* demonstrate authors engaging in conversation with one another's works in ways that the English translations of the *Metamorphoses* and Seneca's play (which were separated from one another by many decades) do not.

Sherburne's version of the *Heroides* makes clear use of Turberville's Elizabethan translation, while also aiming to distance itself from Saltonstall's earlier effort. He declares in his preface that there are too many books now in print, but that he has been driven to produce his translation, 'the worke having a long time lain by me', by 'an humble, and modest hope, of rectifying the wrongs our Author hath sustained through the rude attempts of a too-too busie pen' (A4ʳ).[93] This seems a jibe at Saltonstall, a prolific translator of both classical and medieval works, who had already produced English versions of both Ovid's *Tristia* and his *Ex Ponto*. Sherburne goes on to use his preface to set out his own approach to translation, promising his readers a faithful rendering of Ovid's Latin. He gives his readers clear instruction as to what they should seek for in a translation:

> I am not ignorant of a sort of curious ones, that looke for wonders from a translation: when indeed they ought rather to checke, and limit their expectation: far different is the case with one who in his course exspatiates at randome, and with another, who is forc't to tread the steps of a fore-runner. (A4ʳ)

Sherburne tells his readers that, while his commitment to faithful translation might seem to stymie him, they will find much to enjoy in his effort, if they approach it 'without prejudicate, and peremptorie opinions':

> they may herein meet with a strictnesse (such as is requisite) in the words, and a respective care towards the meaning of our Author; a sweetnesse too, as much as could conveniently be attained, having throughout observed a verse for verse traduction. (A4ᵛ)

Reading Sherburne's preface, the reader could be forgiven for assuming that, while his will be a very close translation of the Latin, Saltonstall's might be a far freer interpretation of Ovid. In fact, Sherburne's debt not to his Ovidian original but to Turberville's Elizabethan version is revealed as he retains Hypsipyle's wish that Medea will commit suicide, something that Saltonstall does not include. Moreover, despite Sherburne's apparent antipathy to the earlier effort, and his insistence that his is the only properly faithful translation, Saltonstall's is also a close translation of the matter of the epistles of Hypsipyle and Medea, albeit one that is, as Timothy Raylor notes, 'a clumsy, long-winded affair' rendered into 'bourgeois idiom'.[94] Saltonstall's effort is dedicated to 'the Vertuous Ladies and Gentlewomen of England', and he tells these women that the epistles are 'chiefly translated for your sakes' (A3ʳ), since they are less likely than men to be familiar with the Latin original:

> Since this booke of Ovids, which most Gentlemen could reade before in Latine, is for your sakes come forth in English, it doth at first addresse it selfe as a Suiter, to wooe your acceptance, that it may kisse your hands, and afterward have the lines thereof in reading sweetned by the odour of your breath. (A4ʳ)[95]

Saltonstall's flattery here is highly reminiscent of that found in Elizabethan works of fiction, such as George Pettie's *A Petite Pallace of Pettie His Pleasure* (1576), which specifically court female readers in similarly flirtatious tones. Susan Wiseman argues that Saltonstall's text, in its privileging of the female reader, simultaneously engages with the 'moral problem' of 'women readers being required to manage the desiring and transgressive nature of Ovid's heroines put before them so vividly by Ovid's language'.[96]

Despite Saltonstall's claims, in these epistles, however, the only acknowledgement of the female readership he foregrounds in his prefatory address is first, perhaps, their focus on female sexual misdemeanour – Hypsipyle calls Medea 'A barbarous Harlot' (D2ᵛ) and a 'Succubus' (D4ʳ), and insists 'I was no Whore' (D2ʳ) – and, second, and paradoxically, a slight softening of the ruthless anger of both women. Saltonstall's Hypsipyle hopes that Medea will lose Jason and be left 'a widow with two children' (D4ʳ), but does not hope that any harm may befall Medea's sons, while his Medea describes the gods' knowledge of 'my wrongs, my sorrowes, and my injury', and predicts that she will 'act e're long some Tragick part' (F8ʳ). In contrast, Sherburne's Medea exclaims to Jason 'Where rage shall lead, I'le follow, & it may be / Thou mayst lament, as I, t'have trusted thee' (Eʳ). He retains not only Turberville's reference to Medea's suicide but also other details from the Elizabethan translation: both refer to the 'crackling scales' (Sherburne, D11ʳ, Turberville, Jviiᵛ) of the dragon that guards the Fleece, as Saltonstall does not, and in Sherburne's translation the argument to Medea's epistle, which describes her as 'complaining, suing and menacing' Jason (D9ᵛ), echoes Turberville's, while Saltonstall's argument is quite different, spending longer on Medea's killing of Pelias and describing her as 'expostulating with him of his ingratitude, and [threatening] speedy revenge' (F4ʳ).

In their prefaces, Saltonstall and Sherburne demonstrate a clear concern with the readership of their poems and with the expectations that such readers might have, either of Ovid in general or of translation in the 1630s. This concern, with how to translate the classics, and for whom, only gathers force as the seventeenth century progresses. Harold Love has suggested that increased enthusiasm for the production, reading and buying of classical translations in the period 1670–1700 may be the result of an increase in literacy but a decline in the knowledge of Greek and Latin necessary to read the classics in their original languages.[97] Certainly, interest in the *Heroides* in translation continued into the Restoration: Harriette Andreadis notes that Saltonstall's *Heroides* went through 'at least' six editions to 1671, while Raylor counts eleven by 1695.[98] Moreover, while there are no new translations of Seneca's *Medea* printed in English in the seventeenth century after Sherburne's of 1648, and no new seventeenth-century versions of the complete *Metamorphoses* after Sandys's of 1632, the epistles were also translated afresh in the period, most famously in Jacob Tonson's hugely popular edition of *Ovid's Epistles* (1680), which was introduced by John Dryden, and included translations by Dryden himself, Elkanah Settle, Nahum Tate and Aphra Behn.[99]

While previous translations of Ovid's *Heroides*, *Tristia* and *Metamorphoses* had been single-authored, the *Epistles* drew together the work of many different translators and was, as Stuart Gillespie puts it, 'a new type of work in terms of variety, modernity, and quality'.[100] Arguably the most famous and modernising aspect of the Dryden-Tonson Ovid is its preface, in which Dryden lays out his project of translation and rejects the efforts of many of his predecessors, arguing that translation should neither be too close nor too loose, but that the ideal method of translation is by paraphrase (the same term used by the anonymous address to the reader that had prefaced Sherburne's 1648 *Medea*). Nevertheless, despite Dryden's insistence that he is doing something new, Garth Tissol notes that 'All the contributors, Dryden included, make much use of earlier versions of the *Epistles*', and he identifies Saltonstall's 1636 translation, and Sherburne's 1639 effort, as having had a particular influence over the 1680 collection.[101] So Elkanah Settle, translator of Hypsipyle's epistle, again plays with the threat of female sexuality, as Saltonstall had done in his emphasis on female sexual virtue, or lack thereof: his Hypsipyle demands of Jason, 'How can you doat on such Infernal Charms, / And sleep securely in a Syrens Arms?' (M7ᵛ).[102] In Ovid the 'Infernal Charms' and description of Medea as a 'Syren' are both absent, and Hypsipyle merely asks, 'Hanc potes amplecti thalamoque relictus in uno / inpavidus somno nocte silente frui?' (A woman like this can you embrace? Can you be left in the same chamber with her and not feel fear, and enjoy the slumber of the silent night?) (6.95–6). Settle also emphasises the threat that Medea's assistance poses to Jason's fame, while in Saltonstall's translation the focus was on loss of female reputation, through the repetition of terms like 'whore' and 'strumpet'. In Ovid, Hypsipyle warns her errant husband that 'aliquis Peliae de partibus acta venenis / inputat' (someone of the partisans of Pelias imputes your deeds to her poisons) (6.101–2) and spreads this rumour among the people, while Settle's Hypsipyle puts things far more bluntly:

Though your great Deeds, and no less Race you boast,
Linkt to that Fiend your sullied Fame is lost.
Nay by the censuring World 'tis justly thought;
Your Conquests by her Sorceries were wrought; (M7ᵛ)

Tissol calls Settle's epistle 'vigorously coarse', and suggests that it belies Dryden's famous insistence in his preface that the translation (and its source material) are essentially modest and suitable to be read 'by Matrons, without a blush' (A7ᵛ).[103] Settle, unlike Saltonstall, however, usually directs his readers' attention away from the sexual element of Medea's threat, despite his exaggeration of Hypsipyle's warning to Jason.[104] Instead, his vocabulary frequently emphasises Medea's barbarism, in terms that make her seem scarcely human: in Ovid, Hypsipyle wishes 'illa sibi a Tanai Scythiaeque paludibus udae / quaerat et a ripa Phasidos usque virum!' (Let her seek for herself a husband – from the Tanais, from the marshes of watery Scythia, even from the shores of Phasis!) (6.107–8). Settle's Hypsipyle combines the wish with vicious xenophobic insult: 'Let some wild *Scythian* her loath'd bed possess, / A Mistress only fit for Savages' (M7ᵛ). Medea is 'th'hunted Monster' (Nᵛ), and a 'loath'd Hag' (Nʳ), and like Turberville and Sherburne before him, Settle has Hypsipyle hope 'let her attempt the skies, / Till in despair by her own hand she dies' (Nᵛ). In 1667, Dryden's reworking (with William Davenant) of *The Tempest*, entitled *The Enchanted Island*, had made racist and misogynistic sport of the barbarism and unrestrained sexuality of Sycorax, who is a pallid echo of the far more Medea-like Shakespearean Sycorax.[105] Here, Settle's translation indulges in the same kind of exaggeration of Medea's racial otherness, and the effect, again, is that Medea is dehumanised and sidelined as a result of her difference from the dominating culture, whether this is Hypsipyle's home of Lemnos, or Corinth, the city from which Medea is banished in her final humiliation at Jason's hands.

Nahum Tate's translation of Medea's epistle in the same collection is more faithful, but although he tends to condense Ovid's Latin in his English (for example in his description of the tasks Jason faced) the translator does make slight alterations to bring Medea's crimes to his readers' attention: where Ovid's Medea makes oblique reference to her murder of her brother, exclaiming, 'quod facere ausa mea est, non audet scribere dextra' (Of the deed my right hand was bold enough to do, it is not bold enough to write) (12.115), Tate's heroine laments, 'This hand that tore the Infant in our Flight, / What then it dar'd to Act, dreads now to Write' (N5ᵛ). This Restoration Medea's willingness to confess her sins is further demonstrated, as the Ovidian Medea writes to Jason that they both deserve to die, he for his deception of her and she for her 'credulitatis' (trustfulness) (12.120). In contrast, Tate's Medea laments, 'we shou'd have dy'd; / For falsehood Thou, and I for Parricide' (N5ᵛ). The classical Medea does not kill her father Aeëtes (though she does kill Jason's uncle and his father-in-law), and here the exaggeration of the collateral damage caused by Medea's flight from Colchis may be due to Tate's preference for a version of the Latin text that reads 'crudelitatis' rather than 'credulitatis'.¹⁰⁶ It also echoes an earlier alteration, in which Tate's Medea describes not just leaving her mother and sister but also bringing about their deaths as she flees with Jason: 'My tender Mother in my Absence dies, / And at her Feet my breathless Sister lies' (N5ᵛ).

While Settle's translation of Hypsipyle's epistle had imagined Medea as a terrifying manifestation of racial otherness, and one whose ruthlessness extends even to herself, Tate emphasises her guilty conscience by having her exaggerate the extent of her crimes. He simultaneously endows Medea with more power than her classical counterpart (over the lives of her father, mother and sister) and less, weakening her by the addition of an unclassical sympathy for those whose lives she has so affected, something which in turn excites pity for Medea herself. In his tragedy *The Enchanted Lovers* (1678) Tate had included a powerful sorceress, Ragusa, who is specifically credited with the powers of the classical Medea. His heroine, though, was the unnamed queen of Syracuse, who was disgraced by a sexual relationship outside marriage and died, repenting, as her city fell to invaders. Restoration tragedy was fascinated by the sexual, physical and emotional suffering of its heroines, and, as I shall show in Chapter 3, this fascination extends even to women compared to Medea, who might be dealt with far more sympathetically than they were in Elizabethan and Jacobean tragedy. Thus, while Settle's translation of Hypsipyle's epistle responds to prurient Restoration interest in the racial and sexual Other, Tate's foreshadows the common affective approach to Medea in eighteenth-century tragedy, in which she is often to be pitied, rather than condemned, for her crimes.

It is worth restating here that, whether or not they make it explicitly clear, as Saltonstall's preface to the *Heroides* does, many of these translations imagined at least some of their readers as having an insufficient grasp of Latin to enjoy the originals. For example, in the preface to the 1566 translation of Seneca's *Medea*, John Studley explains that he translated the play 'For the pleasure of the learned, and the profyte of the unlearned by reading of it in theyr native language' (71–4). In his work on parody and imitation in the Restoration and eighteenth century, Howard Weinbrot has argued that 'most pure translation was meant for the mere English reader and did not include knowledge of the original as one of its legitimate pleasures'.[107] However, as Gillespie points out, '[f]or readers with good Latin or Greek, a translation could become a kind of commentary on its original, generating at the highest artistic pitch a complex intertextual play'.[108] In the preface to his *Tristia*, Zachary Catlin had expressed the hope that his translation would be used by such readers, those who did not need the help of his translation, and could 'swim without Bladders', as well as by those who were not fluent in Latin. Translators were keenly aware of both kinds of reader, and of the influence that their translations of Medea could wield. Studley's preface to *Medea* draws his reader's attention to some (though not all) of the points at which he has chosen to deviate from his original. At the same time, translators like Golding and Turberville make silent additions to their poems, augmenting them with material from commentators and earlier editors, and making their own judgements on Medea as they do so. In their own ways, translations of the classical Medea plainly had the potential to direct their readers' understanding and appropriate and manipulate her power, just as more original compositions might. Moreover, the translators' two influential approaches to Medea's power – the instinct to exaggerate it for sensational and admonitory effect, and (often simultaneously) to undercut it by suggesting her regret, suffering and punishment – are plainly apparent in the treatments of Medea in tragic drama, prose and poetry, the genre that will form the focus of Chapter 3.

3
Tragic Medea

If the English translators of Medea's story often found themselves compelled to alter or to augment classical accounts of her crimes, to cater to the tastes and expectations of their early modern readers, those authors who chose to present more original Medeas clearly felt a similar pressure. Given the brutal nature of her story, it is unsurprising that the most common rewritings of Medea, whether in prose, verse or drama, were tragic, and yet even such accounts, which often mimicked Caxton's medieval *History of Jason* in that they emphasised the most sensational, violent and gory elements of her story, also sought to undermine Medea's power or punish her, in a way that classical accounts do not.

In the preface to his late seventeenth-century drama *Phaeton, Or The Fatal Divorce* (1698), a tragedy that takes the Euripidean story of Jason and Medea and transposes it onto two other mythological characters, Phaeton and Althea, Charles Gildon engages robustly with the earlier classical incarnations of Medea's myth, despite his decision to rename his characters.[1] In his preface, he is scathing in his assessment of the 'abominable' Senecan Medea, quoting Jason's final lines in the original Latin, and terming the play's ending 'very odd, and impious' (B4ᵛ, B2ᵛ). He claims not to have read Euripides' tragedy until his work was half-completed, and though he declares that the work gave him 'extraordinary pleasure' (Bᵛ), he confesses to deviating from Euripides' heroine in his presentation of Althea, because even the ancient Greek dramatist's relatively sympathetic version of Medea would be fundamentally unsatisfactory to his late seventeenth-century English audience:

> First I was Apprehensive, that *Medea*, as *Euripides* presents her, wou'd shock *us*. When we hear of her tearing her Brother to pieces, and the[n] *murdering* her own Children, contrary to all the Dictates of

Humanity and *Mother-hood*, we shou'd have been too impatient for her Punishment, to have expected the *happy Event* of her barbarous Revenge; nay, perhaps, not have allow'd the Character within the Compass of Nature; or at least decreed it more unfit for the Stage, than the Cruelties of *Nero*. Monsters in Nature not affording those just Lessons a Poet ought to teach his Hearers. But we shou'd with the extreamest Indignation have seen her (as Mr *Dryden* observes) at last furnish'd with a Flying Chariot to escape her just Punishment. (B^v)[2]

Here, Gildon succinctly details some of the main problems that Medea posed for the early modern tragedian: her crimes are terrible, perhaps too terrible for presentation on the stage; Medea is implausibly allowed to escape on her chariot; and, as a result of this, the audience is left impotently demanding a punishment that never arrives. Julie Sanders has argued that what she calls 'appropriation' (as opposed to adaptation) may involve 'a wholesale rethinking of the terms of the original', and, in this preface, the dramatist acknowledges both his use of Euripides and those elements of the Greek tragedy that he found unsatisfactory, and which must, therefore, be altered in his version.[3] In his reworking of the tragedy, Gildon aims to address all three of the objections to the original that he has identified, and in doing so he creates a Medea-figure who is not only significantly weakened but also more sympathetic.

Most problematic for Gildon is Medea's child-killing, and the monstrosity that, he suggests, means she cannot satisfactorily be used to teach 'those just Lessons a Poet ought to teach his Hearers'. Fiona Macintosh notes that, in the eighteenth century, 'the English playwrights used every conceivable means to avoid presenting Medea as a deliberate infanticide', a dramatic pattern that mirrors the fall in real convictions after 1700 for women who killed their children.[4] A growing sympathy for the infanticidal woman meant that eighteenth-century (married) women who killed their children were far more likely than their seventeenth-century counterparts to be found not guilty, because they were thought to be gripped by temporary insanity when they committed their crimes.[5] Gildon's work is certainly an early dramatic example of this instinct to excuse, rather than condemn, a Medea-figure, by means of rewriting her myth, and his late seventeenth-century drama anticipates the eighteenth-century fashion for the more affective Medea, as well as developments in eighteenth-century legal thinking about the status of infanticides. In his preface, he acknowledges his attempts 'to render her Revenge as involuntary an Act as possibly I cou'd' (B2^r), for the satisfaction of his audience, and argues that it might have been possible for the audience to empathise with a deliberate infanticide, driven to the crime by 'the Natural Effect of those Passions every one finds in himself' (B2^r). The audience is encouraged to feel sympathy for Gildon's Medea-figure, Althea, since during the first two acts of the play she is oblivious to the shifting affections of Phaeton, who is urged by his friend Epaphus and mother Clymene to abandon Althea for a more diplomatically astute match with Lybia. When Althea discovers she is betrayed, she reacts with the grief of the Euripidean Medea, exclaiming:

> Ah! me!—Alas!—Undone, undone! forsaken!—
> Weep, weep fond Eyes! dissolve, dissolve in Tears!
> You let the fatal Mischiefs in!—Oh! woe!
> Oh! Misery! Oh! Ruin! (C3^v)[6]

Althea's thoughts turn, inevitably, to revenge, but where Euripides' Medea concludes, eventually, that she must kill her children as well as her rival, Althea exacts revenge only on Phaeton's new bride, Lybia, killing her by means of a poisoned robe and crown, as Medea dispatched her rival Glauce. Crucially, and despite Gildon's debt to the Euripidean version of the tragedy (which was perhaps the first to make Medea an infanticide), Althea is absolved of blame for this most terrible crime, and her children are actually killed by the citizens, in revenge for the killing of Lybia. This is an allusion to the lesser-known story, referenced by the ancient historians Aelian and Pausanias, and mentioned by Edward Sherburne in the notes that accompanied his translation of Seneca (1648), which held that the Corinthians slaughtered Medea's children, and then sought to blame her.[7]

Maddened to hear of the deaths of her children, Althea attempts to stab herself, before dying as a result of a scratch from her own poisoned blade. In his portrayal of a pitiful, suffering Althea, who enjoys little command over her own destiny (even Lybia's poisoned robe is given to her by Juno), who is cleared of infanticide, and who is defeated by her own grief, rather than escaping triumphant, Gildon is according with what would become the eighteenth-century taste for representing Medea. He is deviating markedly from sixteenth- and seventeenth-century preference, however, in attempting to excite pity for his Medea-figure rather than simply revulsion. Lybia's death, brought about by Althea, is certainly gruesome, the details of Epaphus' description closely echoing the Messenger's report in Euripides' tragedy,[8] but Gildon is more concerned than Euripides with exciting pity and empathy for Althea: for example, by making the audience aware of Phaeton's love for Lybia from the very start, but keeping this knowledge from Althea until much later. Most importantly, though, he does not confront his audience with Medea's killing of her children, an act that he maintains his audience would find too shocking, despite the fact that Euripides handles it with greater sensitivity than Seneca (for example by having Medea speak tenderly of her children and express a tormented reluctance to kill them). Earlier English dramatists, in contrast, were far more eager than Gildon to exploit their knowledge of the worst of Medea's crimes. Like him, though, they acknowledge the thorniest of the problems surrounding Medea: her triumphant escape from punishment. John Kerrigan summarises the views of the seventeenth-century French dramatist Pierre Corneille, author of *Médée* (1635) thus: in tragedy 'It is not witnessing the punishment of wickedness which deters us from evil deeds, but seeing its ugliness finely displayed.'⁹ Gildon had elected not to show, or even to suggest, the pinnacle of Medea's wickedness, her killing of her children. For Corneille, meanwhile, the display of wickedness is edifying enough, without the addition of punishment. In contrast, for English authors of sixteenth- and seventeenth-century tragic works, influenced not only by classical criticism but also by medieval *de casibus* tragedy, there is only one trajectory appropriate for Medea, or for figures like Medea, and her terrible crimes (up to and including infanticide) can be stressed and even exaggerated, as long as they are balanced, comfortingly, by unclassical punishments or expressions of guilt and repentance.

Nevertheless, even if Medea's violence was artistically justifiable, as an example *in malum*, English writers retained certain reservations about it. Horace had famously insisted that 'Medea must not butcher her children in the presence of the audience', and early modern English dramatists were similarly reluctant to stage the infanticide, as is demonstrated by Gildon's decision to have the act reported.¹⁰ Sixteenth- and seventeenth-century tragedy was not confined to drama, however, and tragic tales were also told in prose collections and long complaint poems. Such forms of tragedy might actually be more appealing to early modern authors, as prose and verse do not pose the same problems about whether, or how, to stage the worst of Medea's crimes. Moreover, tragic tales intended for a print readership held the additional appeal that they avoided the problem of staging infanticide while, paradoxically, allowing more detailed and grisly description of Medea's atrocities. It is thus unsurprising that early modern English writers turned first to print – to prose and to narrative verse – in their efforts to explore and (sometimes) to curtail Medea's terrible power.

Elizabethan prose and verse

In one of the most gruesome tales from Geoffrey Fenton's collection of prose tragedies, *Certaine Tragicall Discourses* (1567), which was translated from the Italian of Matteo Bandello, via the French tale of François de Belleforest, the reader is introduced to the infanticidal Italian anti-heroine Pandora. Abandoned by her lover Parthonope, the pregnant Pandora induces a miscarriage and then kills the child, in order to be revenged on its father. Pandora is repeatedly termed a 'seconde Medea' (Fol. 62ʳ), with Fenton following Belleforest, who had added several references to the Colchian sorceress to Bandello's single description of Pandora as 'questa nuova Medea'.[11] Both the French and English Pandoras wish they had Medea's powers to exact revenge, and both kill the child after noting its resemblance to Parthonope (a likely reference to the Heroidean Medea's observation that her children look uncomfortably like Jason).[12] Here Bandello makes the story even gorier, however, and has Pandora exceed Medea by performing an even more taboo act, just as Caxton's Medea outdoes the violence that the classical Medea practises on the bodies of men and children. Like Caxton's Medea, Bandello's Pandora takes her son by the legs and tears him in half, but, as Fenton reluctantly admits to his fascinated readers in one of his customary additions, there is worse to come. Revealing a concern with his female readership that would come to characterise much Elizabethan prose fiction, Fenton, like Belleforest, insists that, in revealing the worst of Pandora's nature, he does a service to women, by making them appear better in comparison:

> because yᵉ vertue of honest & chast ladies shal shine the clearer, by the darke eclipse of such cómon enemyes of the whole sect *Femenyne*, I wil yet treat of the tyrany of this PANDORA who reserved thextreame pointe of her Jewishe creweltie until the last act of her tragedye, for marteringe the dead childe, and treadinge it under her fete, shée thrust her hande under his shorte rybbes, and taking out his hart, gnawed it (as a bych of HERCANIA) betwene her teth into littell morsels, saying that shee hoped one daye to provyde the like banquyt for PARTHONOPE, whiche shoulde confirme the quyet she felt in the present death and detestable execucion of his Image and likenes, and having her ha[n]d yet dyed with the blodd of this guiltles impe of nature, shée cold not be ryd of the importunat devil that possessed her, until she had brought yᵉ ryver of her rage unto thextreme brink of tyrannye, neyther could her harte be brought to appeasement so longe

as her eyes fed upon the viewe of the deade infant: Wherfore callinge in a great mastyphe cur, she gave him (by pecemeale) the members of her childe, an act suer of no lesse detestacion afore the hygh throne of God, then to be abhorred of all the world. (Fol. 77^v–78^r)

Fenton outdoes himself in this hair-raising description of Pandora gnawing on her child's heart, before feeding the infant to her dog, and he is able simultaneously to entertain and to warn against such behaviour, through his account of gruesome violence. In comparison to such examples, he tells his female readers, their goodness will be all the more apparent, or, as Helen Hackett pithily puts it, 'While claiming to present a deterrent example to women of the wages of sin, [he] succeeds in creating the thrills of a video nasty.'[13] Moreover, it was not just feminine sin that could be lovingly catalogued and then criticised by Fenton's narrative of Pandora.[14] Fenton's Protestantism is highlighted throughout his collection,[15] and here, in the face of such abhorrent cruelty, Fenton panders happily to Elizabethan horror of Catholic Europe, adding to Belleforest's outrage to emphasise Pandora's Italian background:

Ah las, have thytalyan mothers no other [t]ombes for their children, then to bury them in ye belly of a dogge? be these the teares wherewith they accompanye them into the shrouding shete? Is this the curtesy of Italye? or a creweltie derived of the barbarous nacion? (Fol. 78^r)

Here, Pandora's nationality is used to hint at her Catholicism, and Fenton simultaneously collapses any difference his readers might perceive between 'the curtesy of Italye', as he ironically terms it, and 'creweltie derived of the barbarous nacion'. The connection that might be made between jealous and murderous foreign women and the famously barbarian Medea was an attractive one to authors of sensational narrative throughout the period.[16] In the course of *Eliosto Libidinoso* (1606), a lengthy prose romance in the tradition of Robert Greene, which describes the incestuous passion of Eliosto and his mother, and their eventual discovery and execution, John Hind digresses at some length to include the tale of the Cyprian Gatesinea's murder of Dihnohin, carried out when he has left her for another woman, on the instruction of his father.[17] Tempting him into bed before stabbing him furiously, Gatesinea exclaims:

I will not die unrevenged as *Dido*, nor live discontent as *Medea*, who failed in the sexe, and therefore in the certaintie of her revenge ...

That said, she redoubled her bloody stroke, casting a steerne aspect on poore *Dihnohin,* which lay weltring in his blood. (M^r–M^v).[18]

Here, Gatesinea declares that she has outdone Medea, 'who failed in the sexe, and therefore in the certaintie of her revenge', because she has directed her murderous fury towards her husband, whereas Medea killed her rival Creusa. Gatesinea kills herself after committing the murder, and, though the double death reconciles the lovers' warring fathers, Hind, like Fenton before him, stresses the literal barbarism of Gatesinea's cruelty and lack of remorse:

What [r]emorceless Scythian, or savage Tartarian, nourished in the desarts beyond *Tanais,* could have beheld so ruthfull a spectacle, and not be pierced with compassion? Yet she, whose heart was more impenetrable than the adamant, seemd to triumph in his tragedy, loading his dying eares with reproachfull termes, and accusing him of disloyalty. (M^v)

Hind's peculiar digression onto the story of Gatesinea and Dihnohin emphasises the main story's focus on the destructive effects of transgressive passion: in foreign climes, desire is transformed all too easily into taboos such as incest, sexual jealousy and murder.

In his earlier work, Fenton stresses the Italian heritage of his Medea-figure, but, above all, Pandora is alarming and Medea-like as a monstrous mother, and her hideous crime speaks to male anxiety about women's child-bearing power.[19] Once again building on his sources, Fenton exploits this example of transgressive womanhood to encourage very different reactions and behaviour in his female readers. Having described Pandora's maid jumping up and down on her mistress's body, in an effort to produce a miscarriage, he remarks sagely,

Truelye I knowe that vertuous Ladyes (sprinkled wyth the dewe of pytie,) wyll not onelye tremble at the remembraunce of the inordinate crueltye of this cursed mother, but also open the conduits of their co[m]passions, weping on ye behalfe of the torment wherin unnaturally she plunged the innocent impe which nature had formed of the substance of her selfe. (Fol 76^r)

Here, Fenton claims a certainty ('I knowe') that more virtuous women than Pandora will interpret her example in the correct way, feeling horror at her cruelty, and pity for the 'innocent impe' she has punished so cruelly. Once the tale has reached its grisly climax, he makes this lesson all the more apparent, urging his readers 'let also the yong ladyes and lyttel girls learne to direct the cours of their youth by ye contrary of this example' (Fol. 78^v).

In encouraging his female readers to consider and be repelled by this crazed infanticide, who is repeatedly likened to Medea, Fenton leads the way for subsequent Elizabethan authors, many of whom are concerned with women's readerly experience of the Medea-figure and are at pains to stress that hers is an example to be shunned with horror.[20] In one way, though, Pandora is highly unusual as a sixteenth-century Medea-figure, in that there is a 'disturbing ambiguity' to the end of her tale, which sees her cover up her crime with apparent success.[21] Although Jonathan Gibson argues that Fenton's collection as a whole 'emphasizes repression and control' (particularly of women), here is an English Medea-figure who is not clearly punished either before or after death.[22] Fenton does stress, however, that the point of her tale is that such crimes cannot be hidden forever:

for ther is nothi[n]g co[m]mitted in secret, but in ye end it bursts out to a co[m]mo[n] brute, which our savior Christ affyrmeth by the mouthe of ye prophet sainge, y^t what so ever is done in the darkest corner of the house, shalbe published in ye end in open audience, And he who sekes most to conceile his faulte, is not onlye (by the permission of God) the first opner of the same, but also beares the badge of shame afore the face of ye world, and standes in daunger of grace in the presence of him from whom no secret canne bee hydde. (Fol. 78^v)

The Jacobean statute against infanticide of 1624 would make concealing the death of a child a crime, and, speaking of a particularly grisly 1677 infanticide case, Susan C. Staub notes that the infanticidal woman's concealment of her crime is seen as particularly damning: 'it is concealment, the fear of something unknown and hence uncontrollable, that indicts the woman'.[23] Fenton's text demonstrates that male fear of the hidden crimes of women (particularly infanticide) was reflected in literature long before the 1624 statute.[24] His solution is to lay such crimes open to the view and judgement of the *reader*, even if Pandora has, alarmingly, been able to keep them hidden from her peers. In reassuming control over Pandora's story, and broadcasting what she would wish to keep secret to a (presumably censorious) Elizabethan readership, Fenton thus takes steps towards undermining her power, participating in the same process that Frances Dolan sees at work in early modern accounts of public executions of women, whereby confession and repentance lay bare women's secrets and undercuts agency even as this agency is suggested.[25] In subsequent Elizabethan works, this censorious instinct would become far more pronounced, and Pandora remains a rare Medea-figure indeed, in that she commits dreadful acts, but is not explicitly punished by and within the text she inhabits.

Fenton's infanticidal Pandora is identified as Italian and, by extension, Catholic, and yet Medea's example could also be used to increase alarm about the Catholic (and maternal) threat even nearer to home. Moreover, just as Fenton presents Pandora's crimes for censure, even if she herself escapes punishment, one way of exorcising this murderous Catholic threat was to lay it open to the scrutiny of the early modern reader.[26] The anonymous pamphlet *A Pittilesse Mother* (1616) describes the crime of the Englishwoman Margaret Vincent, who has been seduced into Catholicism by 'Popish perswasions' (B2ʳ), and is compared to 'a fierce and bloudy Medea' (A3ᵛ) as she kills her children, in the misguided belief that she is saving their souls.[27] Although initially she remains steadfast in her conviction that she has done the right thing, at last Margaret is persuaded to repent, before her execution. The pamphlet acknowledges that Margaret was misled by the Devil, and, despite the fact that it records her murders, it simultaneously urges reading gentlewomen to 'Forgive and forget her' (B2ʳ), since her crimes have been redressed with repentance (and, presumably, because she was motivated not by jealous rage but by maternal concern).[28] However, it ends with a stern warning to the 'Countrymen of England' (B2ʳ), to appreciate the dangers posed by 'that dangerous sect' (B2ʳ) of Catholicism: the spectre of Medea has been raised and associated with infanticide and Roman influence, before being comfortably quashed and turned into a lesson for both men and women to learn from and resist.

Margaret's example notwithstanding, 'real' or 'historical' early modern infanticides like Vincent (as opposed to those represented in drama or prose fiction) are seldom compared to Medea, perhaps because, as Frances Dolan and Keith Wrightson have demonstrated, early modern infanticidal women, like those accused of witchcraft, were typically unmarried, and of low social and economic status, and they often acted out of concern for their children, or the desire to conceal an illegitimate birth, rather than fury.[29] The reluctance to identify real infanticidal women as Medea-figures may also spring from the growing early modern interest, identified by Randall Martin, in mitigating the crimes even of self-confessed female murderers, who are excused (and simultaneously weakened) by the author's decision to stress (for example) the injuries and cruelties they suffered at the hands of their husbands. A comparison with Medea would clearly impede such efforts to provide mitigating circumstances for real-life women, because her dreadful crimes were at least as memorable as her suffering, and far outweighed what Jason had done to her. As Martin has noted, however, while such women might use the scaffold to repent their crimes, 'active defiance was not unusual either'. Such defiance might seem to conveniently ally real murderous women to the Euripidean or Senecan Medea, but it was simultaneously unsatisfactory for the authors who wished to use such women as admonitory examples of repentant suffering, and so again a comparison with Medea is not in the best interests of the documenting author.[30] Fictional criminal women did not need to be treated with the same sympathy as their real counterparts, and their defiance was far easier to control and subdue, and so it is these women who are far more commonly likened to Medea.

At the same time, even if real criminals were seldom likened to Medea, authors continued to see the lessons taught by their fictional Medea-figures as directly relevant to the early modern reader. In his second published work, the long dream-vision poem, *The Rewarde of Wickednesse* (1574), printed seven years after Fenton's grisly tale of Pandora, Richard Robinson, servant to the Earl of Shrewsbury, uses Medea herself (rather than a figure who is likened to Medea), and makes the horror of her crimes relevant to both male and female readers, and particularly to English Protestants. The poem sees the persona of the author recount a dream in which, accompanied by the figure of Morpheus, he travels into the Underworld, where he meets a variety of classical and medieval sinners, including Helen of Troy and Pope Alexander VI. The episode in which Medea appears is entitled '*The rewarde of* Medea *for hir* wicked actes, and false deceyving of hir father, sleying of hir children and hir owne Brother, and working by inchauntment. This historie is merveylous tragicall, and a good example for Women' (F2ᵛ). Since, as this heading makes clear, he claims to be providing a cautionary example against female wickedness, Robinson is predictably keen to represent Medea's crimes and her transgressive behaviour to their fullest extent, just as Fenton refused to deny his readers any detail of Pandora's hideous crimes.[31] For example, Robinson's Medea tells Morpheus and the figure of the poet how she killed her brother Apsyrtus, an emphasis which Robinson may owe to his friend Thomas Churchyard's grisly description of the fratricide in his 1572 *Tristia*. Here, though, it is Medea who is given a voice to confess her own violence:

I kilde my Brother, his armes and legges I cast
Throughout the fielde whereas my Father rid,

Which when my Father sawe, so ill betide,
and knewe his sonne thus martyrred for to bée:
With woefull cheare to get them uppe straight hide,
togeather (alas) eache chopped péece layde hée. (F4^r)

While she is allowed to voice her crimes, however, Robinson's Medea is never allowed to rejoice in her wickedness as the Senecan and Euripidean Medeas do, and is clearly rewritten in accordance with Elizabethan values. Thus, in the course of a lengthy complaint, and in a curious patchwork of classical and Christian references, she acknowledges her magical power as less than that of the Christian God, as well as less than that of Jove:

O that witches and Conjurers knew so well as I,
of Joves mightie doome that doth in heaven sitte,
Then woulde they mende, if they had grace or witte,
To serve the Lorde woulde set theyr whole delight:
And disobedient children woulde their follye flitte,
assuredly the Lorde at length doth smite. (G^v)

Medieval authors like Lydgate, feeling bound to present Medea's crimes as they were recounted by earlier authors like Guido delle Colonne, shy away from suggesting that divine punishment awaits her in this way (although they may well have found the idea attractive), preferring instead to add Christian elements to her story by, for example, echoing Guido's doubt that she could really enjoy power over nature. Robinson's Medea is rewritten far more radically, and made to speak about the consequences of challenging male control through sin, whether it be adultery, disobedience or murder.[32] Most notably, Medea's part in the poem concludes with a focus on her grisly and enduring punishment in the afterlife. The narrator goes on to dwell at length on her torture in the Underworld, describing how, as she practised witchcraft in life, it is witches who torment her in death:

Innumerable of Witches, out of theyr Cabbins rose,
with screming scrikes, they yelded loude and hye.
Hote Pitche and Brimstone, eache one on other throse,
A hell it selfe, mée thought it was to sée.

Eache one in hande, begrypte a Butchers knife,
the blades in fleshe on everye side they hide:
The throate, the Guttes, or nexte to ridde the life,
the mortall woundes they make on every side. (G2^r)[33]

Here, in additions to the classical tale which focus on Medea's suffering in alarming detail, Robinson has Medea experience physical wounds, where usually she practises violence on the male bodies of her children, of Pelias and of Apsyrtus. In hell, in contrast, it is Medea's body which is bleeding, feminised and made subject to another's control.[34] Robinson's graphic and horribly inventive description of Medea's punishment, and the voice he gives her with which to acknowledge her own guilt, may owe a debt to Studley's translation of Seneca's *Medea*, published eight years previously. In one of Studley's characteristically gruesome expansions of a Senecan passage, Medea is made to indulge in a bizarre and masochistic fantasy about the kind of punishment Creon might exact upon her. Seneca's Medea addresses Jason and exclaims,

> cruentis paelicem poenis premat
> regalis ira, vinculis oneret manus,
> clausamque saxo noctis aeternae obruat. (462–4)

> Let the king's anger crush your mistress with bloody tortures, burden my hands with chains and bury me in a stony prison of unending night.

Studley, typically, goes further, not least in the strange suggestion that Creon might exact Medea's punishment personally:

> Let *Creon* in hys pryncely ruffe
> lay to his heavye handes,
> To whyp an whore, in torments sharp,
> wyth iron gyves, and bandes
> Let her be chaynd, in hydiouse hole
> of nyght for aye her locke:
> Let her be cloyed wyth pestryng payse
> of restless rowlyng rocke. (1408–15)

Having imagined such elaborately alliterative torments for herself, Studley's Medea admits, 'Yet lesse than I deserved have, / In all thys shall I fynde' (1416–17), leaving the reader to wonder what penalty could possibly be sufficient. Like Studley, Robinson aims to titillate as much as to teach in the passages that detail her punishment, in the tradition of early modern murder ballads which catered to 'the ghoulish thrill of *someone else's* suffering'.[35] Frances Dolan suggests that such ballads, penned in the voice of a murderous woman and describing her crime and punishment, can 'engage the singer or auditor in both identification with and alienation from the woman's voice; they invite her to share the woman's guilt as well as to observe her punishment from a distance'.[36]

Robinson's presentation of Medea operates along very similar lines: we hear not only her voice but also her remorse; her crimes are balanced with their just deserts; and the reader (particularly the female reader) is invited to marvel at Medea's wrongdoing and applaud her punishment, but is also encouraged to see themselves in her. Having described Medea's gruesome suffering, Robinson warns:

You witches all take heede, you see how God rewardes:
And what appoynted is your meede, that divelish actes regardes.
Leave of your invocation, your crosings and your charmes:
(Alas) it is abomination, and doth increase your harmes. (G3^r)

Robinson's use of Medea is finely attuned to Elizabethan fear of witchcraft and Catholicism, as one might expect from a work written, as its author explains, while he was employed to guard Mary Queen of Scots, then under house arrest at the estate of the Earl of Shrewsbury. While the didactic and Protestant nature of Robinson's project means that he describes Medea's evildoing meticulously, however, this does not mean she has any power remaining: he deliberately (and very unusually) presents a dead Medea, speaking from the afterlife, and the threat she once posed the male community, and to her own immediate and extended family, is referenced only to stress how she has been brought down by God and subjected to deserved punishment. J. A. Sharpe argues that through their confessions on the scaffold, early modern criminals were 'willing central participants in a theatre of punishment, which offered not merely a spectacle, but also a reinforcement of certain values ... they were helping to assert the legitimacy of the power which had brought them to their sad end'.[37] While reading the confession of a real criminal, brought to justice in their own time and country, would provide a clear salutary message for the early modern English reader, the confession and punishment of such a famous classical villain might, in its own way, prove just as instructive. Indeed, Sharpe shows that the early modern criminal was not expected simply to atone for one particular crime, but was encouraged to acknowledge and repent of 'a whole catalogue of wrongdoing', just as Robinson's Medea does.[38] In his verdict, Robinson advises that parents ensure their daughters read only 'godlie bookes' (G3^r), and he has rewritten his classical model into the kind of edifying, cautionary and god-fearing text he recommends, but one that, like Fenton's work, uses Medea to thrill as well as chastise, and simultaneously exploits both the sensational and the didactic appeal of her story.

The interest in exploring how Medea might be punished or contained extended, predictably, into punishment of women who are like Medea: this kind of Medea-figure was introduced by Fenton, whose Pandora is not Medea herself, but is far more explicitly and frequently likened to the sorceress than Bandello's original. Like Fenton, Thomas Achelley exaggerated and expanded on the mention of Medea he found in his source tale, of Violenta's terrible revenge on her lover Didaco. The tale was another of Bandello's, his forty-second, and was also found in the first volume of William Painter's *Palace of Pleasure* (1566), and in the *Histoires Tragiques* of Pierre Boiastuau.[39] In his introduction to the long narrative poem *The Tragicall Historie of Didaco and Violenta* (1576), Achelley initially refuses to speak of 'the furious tirannie of the boocherly Medea', terming it irrelevant to his readers, and its recounting 'a loste labour' (Aii^r). Despite his professed resistance to pagan tales, however, Achelley adds frequent mythological references to what he had found in Painter and Boiastuau, including a lengthy subplot in which Venus orders her son Cupid to afflict the resistant Didaco with love for Violenta. Predictably, though, after Didaco has wooed her with promises of marriage, he follows Jason's example, leaving Violenta for a more suitable woman. Employing a comparison much loved by forsaken Elizabethan heroines, Violenta exclaims that Didaco has proved himself a 'perjurd Jason' (Dviiii^v) in his faithlessness, and she is likened to 'vile Medea fell' (Fi^r) as she butchers her sleeping lover with the help of her maid Janique, cuts out his eyes, heart and tongue, and hurls his butchered corpse out of the window. Achelley's preface demonstrates that despite his professed disdain of Medea's story, he cannot resist building on Painter's and Boiastuau's single references to her, in his story of a murderous foreign woman.[40] Importantly, though, like his source authors, while he indulges in the sensational violence that a reference to Medea heralds, Achelley also *undermines* the threat that such a reference suggests, because he is at pains to demonstrate the consequences of such unbridled revenge. Violenta confesses her crime, but, unlike the Senecan and Ovidian Medeas, she cannot escape punishment, and the poem ends with her calm confession, and execution by beheading. Like Robinson's Medea, she thus conforms to the model of behaviour that Elizabethan society expected of their murderers, and finally, like Robinson before him, Achelley uses her story to caution his female readers, as well as to thrill them.[41]

The desire to caution and to educate women by using Medea's story could be fulfilled without an author needing to resort to bloody and sensational violence: in his miscellaneous collection of verse and prose tales, *The Rocke of Regard* (1576), George Whetstone includes the poem 'The Pitious Complaint of Medea, Forsaken of Jason, Lively Bewraying the Slipperie Hold in Sugred Words', in which the sorceress complains that her magic cannot help her to win back Jason, and reflects that 'harmelesse Ladies' are too often the victims of flattery, or 'sugred woordes' (p. 76).[42] She makes no explicit mention of her crimes and, like Chaucer's Medea, she is contained not by being punished but by being weakened and made more passive. Even the fact that she is given a voice does not grant her power, for as Kerrigan notes in his work on 'female' complaint in the period (which was usually, of course, male-authored): 'the rhetoric of abandonment seems feminine, while wooing belongs to men'.[43] While Robinson's complaining Medea, who had appeared two years earlier, recalls (albeit with a posthumous regret) the violent action she took while alive, Whetstone's Medea is denied the traditional terrifying reaction to Jason's rejection, and given only empty words, 'the rhetoric of abandonment', as consolation. Kerrigan points to the fact that most 'plaintful women' of the Tudor period are characterised not as active wrongdoers but rather as 'victims of guile and frailty', who 'tug at the heart-strings in a way that a Richard III cannot'.[44] More Richard III than innocent ingénue, Medea was not a figure who tugged at Elizabethan or Jacobean heart-strings (though she would do so with far more success in the eighteenth and nineteenth centuries). Whetstone's use of her notwithstanding, the more popular approach to Medea in early modern tragic narrative was that employed by Robinson, Hind and Achelley, in which an author dwells in loving and graphic detail on the violence of his Medea-figure, before demonstrating her punishment, in order to be seen to make titillating horror into some kind of moral message. It is this instinct, to use Medea to horrify and simultaneously to educate, which also came to define Medea's brief appearances in early modern English stage tragedy.

Tragic drama

The dramatic instinct to punish a Medea-like woman, while also exhibiting perverse delight in her crimes, is at its most obvious in William Alabaster's Latin tragedy *Roxana* (*c*.1592–5), which was staged at Cambridge University in the 1590s. The text was pirated and printed in 1632, and, apparently in response to this, Alabaster released his own printed version in the same year. There also exists an anonymous English manuscript translation, which may have been composed at around the same time by Alabaster himself.[45] The play concerns the villainous Atossa's revenge not only on Oromasdes, the husband who has wronged her, but also on her love-rival, the virtuous Roxana, who is tortured, forced to kill her children, and who then kills herself. Since the play was staged (i.e., it was not a closet drama, which was written to be read or recited) it is unsurprising that Alabaster opts not to show the children's deaths. By way of compensation to his audience, however, Alabaster has Atossa force Oromasdes to listen to the gruesome details of the slaughter, exclaiming,

> O had'st you heard their heart strings how they crack'd
> When they were strayned, or seene their livers squeez'd
> Betwixt my fingers! O what a screekeing song
> The sobbing hearts sung to their funeralls.
> Thou saw'st not how when scorcht with heate of fire
> The bloudy goare dropt from their trembling joints,
> And livers panted still upon the spitts;
> Nor didst thou see the night owles flye
> About the house and with their gripeing clawes
> Tare from the spittes the skorched reeking hearts. (1660–9)[46]

Atossa's horribly evocative word-choice and use of sibilance ('squeez'd', 'screekeing', 'sobbing', 'skorched') is intensely disturbing, her exultant recollection of the children's torture and death combining with the audience's imagining of the scene to produce something far more horrific than anything the play could have staged. Euripides' tragedy (translated into Latin by George Buchanan, and printed in 1544) had described the horrifying offstage death of Creon's daughter, Glauce, at similarly grisly length, but the terrifying effect is heightened here, as it is the deaths of children that Atossa describes, and with relish rather than the Euripidean messenger's horror. The delight she takes in punishing Oromasdes by making his children suffer means that she outstrips even the more brutal Senecan Medea, and earlier, in a deliberate appropriation of Medea's incantations (described in *Metamorphoses* 7.192–209 and 262–74, and in Seneca, 731–9), she boasts that her power is the greater, because she has acted without the help of magic:

> You fleeteing gales, and whirling blasts of wind
> Which through each quarter of the world

> More swift then posts doe carrie messages
> When as you hover over Hesperia
> Remember that you tell Medaea this
> That I have done, and bid her not be proud
> For that poore peice of mischeife that she wrought
> On Jasons sons, in wreake of Jasons wrongs.
> Say that Atossa hath outstrip't her farre,
> And yet Atossa will out strip herselfe.
> I have not now, as erst Medea did,
> Us'd magicke spells, or charms of Thessalie,
> Nor mingled any venemous dragons gall
> And temper'd it with ghastly screechowles blood,
> Nor gathered poysonous hearbs, whose deadly juyce
> Mix't with the ashes of a deadmans tomb
> Worke such effects of death, nor called the moone
> From out her spheare to further mine attempts.
> What I have done, t'is I alone have done;
> The prayse of all this feate belongs to me:
> From foorth the plenteous storehouse of my breast
> It all proceeds, whatever hath bene done. (1344–65)

Binns notes that 'Atossa sees herself consciously acting like a character in a Senecan tragedy',[47] and the references to Medea (whether
Ovidian or Senecan) are repeated and insistent, and recall the way
Demetrius and Chiron, in Shakespeare's *Titus Andronicus*, are shown to
outdo the Ovidian Tereus in their rape and mutilation of Lavinia, the
play's Philomela-figure. Despite the force of her declaration of power,
Alabaster cannot leave his Medea-figure unpunished, however, and so
Atossa is poisoned by her husband, and dies declaring that she is happy
to perish, having achieved victory over her enemies. In her final speech,
Atossa, like Violenta, declares her crimes willingly, and steels herself to
endure the torments of famous classical sinners:

> Guilty, judge Minos, I confesse I was
> The author and the actor of those villanies.
> Bessus was guilteles, for he but brought to me
> The harlot and her bratts, I murdered them:
> And I will onely bide those punishmentes
> Which all my former villanies deserve.
> Aye justice will something my torments ease
> But justice still denies all hope of ease.

Well then perforce I must and will indure them.
Let Tantalius, Ixion, Belides,
Let Sisyphus and all the hellish rout
Resigne their taskes and torments unto me,
All these I will endure, what will you more? (1741–53)[48]

The rhetoric is powerful and defiant, particularly Atossa's insistence that she is the sole guilty party (and not her lover Bessus, who delivered Roxana and the children), and that she will take on the tortures suffered by 'all the hellish rout' of classical sinners. At the same time, though, this is very far from the Senecan Medea's exultant escape, despite the clearly Senecan flavour of much of the action. Inevitably, Atossa, like Violenta, must be punished for her likeness to Medea, and, though she welcomes death and punishment, the fact that she must suffer in this way means that she does not enjoy final control, just as Robinson's Medea cannot escape the hellish and eternal tortures waiting for her in the Underworld.

Like Achelley and Fenton in particular, Alabaster delights in the gruesome imaginative freedom granted to him by the portrayal of a woman who is like Medea, and a mention of her name seems to spark a kind of competition of torture and blood-letting among Elizabethan authors. Importantly, though, the classical sorceress herself is not part of Alabaster's play, and, in fact, she appeared on the English stage infrequently, and was only very rarely given a speaking part.[49] In Thomas Norton and Thomas Sackville's earlier play *Gorboduc* (1561, printed 1565), a tragedy set in ancient Britain, and performed at the Inns of Court and later before Elizabeth, Medea is included as part of a dumbshow, which foreshadows the queen Videna's furious revenge on her son Porrex, for his murder of his brother Ferrex. After news has come of Ferrex's murder, Medea appears at the beginning of Act 4, where she is driven across the stage by the Furies, and accompanied by other classical murderers including Tantalus, Ino and Althea, with the stage directions noting of their appearance: 'hereby was signified the unnaturall Murders to followe' (Cv^r).[50] Here, fascinatingly, Medea's story is tied to Britain's history, where previously she was insistently associated with the foreign (e.g. Fenton's Italian Pandora) or the barbarian (e.g. Hind's Gatesinea, who is likened to the Scythian or Tartar for her cruelty). Gorboduc, king of Britain and representative of a monarchic and restrained (if misguided) power, acts within the law in an attempt to punish his younger son, but the banishment he proposes in response to Porrex's crime stands in stark contrast to the violence of Videna's killing of her son, which is foreshadowed by the appearance of Medea, and reported by the nurse Marcella.[51] The Medea story is used here to highlight feminine unpredictability and revenge, and Norton and Sackville emphasise how the fabric of the State, as well as the family, may be torn apart by such unrestrained action, as well as by Gorboduc's fatal decision to split his sons' inheritance.[52] Indeed, when Porrex's story was added to John Higgins's 1574 edition of *The Mirror for Magistrates*, a compendium of Elizabethan tragic verse that recounted the falls of great men and women, Porrex compares both himself and his mother to Medea, himself for fratricide and his mother for killing of a son, and accepts that they both sinned grievously, not least because their combined actions 'ended *Brutus* line' (Fol. 73ʳ).[53]

In Sackville and Norton's tragedy, Gorboduc and Videna are quickly killed by their subjects, in retaliation for the murder of Porrex. While the king's secretary, Eubulus, is allowed to end Act 5 of *Gorboduc* by looking forward to the eventual restoration of a lawful monarch, the play's climax is a series of gloomy prognostications about the civil disorder and suffering that Britain will endure, as a result of the king's determination to divide his kingdom between his sons, the princes' willingness to listen to flatterers, and the queen's bloodthirsty fury.[54] At the same time, however, the fact that Videna is killed by her outraged subjects after her murder of Porrex (and, indeed, that her punishment extends to encompass the husband who could not keep her adequately under control) is a testament to the Renaissance insistence on containing such destabilising women: an insistence that seems particularly daring coming, as it does, early in the reign of Queen Elizabeth.[55] Medea is driven across the Elizabethan stage by the Furies, while Videna is punished like the Renaissance Medea-figures of Robinson or Achelley, and, like Achelley's Violenta, she is shown to be subject to human control, and particularly human justice, rather than to the divine retribution presented by Robinson: a comforting suggestion, perhaps, that sinners can be held to account by man as well as God.[56]

Medea's story is again associated with that of ancient Britain in *Locrine* (1594, printed 1595), an anonymous tragedy which drew on chronicle history (such as Geoffrey of Monmouth's *Historia Regum Britanniae*) and reshaped this into entertainment and instruction for its Elizabethan audience. Again, Medea features in a dumbshow, and heralds female revenge, this time the revenge of the wronged Guendoline on her faithless husband Locrine, who has abandoned her for Estrild. At the beginning of Act 5, Medea is led in by Ate, Greek goddess of folly, and is shown killing Creusa and, in a departure from classical legend, Jason. Ate then notes the similarity between Medea and Guendoline, for the benefit of the audience:

> *Medea* seeing *Jason* leave her love,
> And choose the daughter of the *Thebane* king,
> Went to her divellish charmes to worke revenge,
> And raising up the triple *Hecate*,
> With all the rout of the condemned fiends,
> Framed a garland by her magick skill,
> With which she wrought *Jason* and *Creons* ill.
> So *Guendoline* seeing her selfe misus'd,
> And *Humbers* paramour possesse her place,
> Flies to the dukedome of *Cornubia*,
> And with her brother stout *Thrasimachus*,
> Gathering a power of Cornish souldiers,
> Gives battaile to her husband and his hoste,
> Nigh to the river of great *Mertia*,
> The chances of this dismall massacre,
> That which insueth shortly will unfold. (H4ᵛ–H5ʳ)⁵⁷

The use of Medea's story is in line with the play's consistent use of classical examples, and yet, unlike the outspoken Videna of *Gorboduc*, Guendoline seems to have little in common with her vengeful fore-bear: as Ate herself notes, Medea calls on her 'divellish charmes' and her affinity with Hecate to exact revenge, while Guendoline must rely on the military strength of her brother, 'stout Thrasimachus'. When she learns of Locrine's betrayal, Guendoline's words are, perhaps delib-erately, a pale imitation of the Senecan Medea's furious appeal to the gods, which Alabaster's Atossa appropriated far more fiercely:

> You gentle winds that with your modest blasts,
> Passe through the circuit of the heavenly vault,
> Enter the clouds unto the throne of *Jove*,
> And beare my praiers to his all hearing eares,
> For *Locrine* hath forsaken *Guendoline*,
> And learne to love proud *Humbers* concubine.
> You happie sprites that in the concave skie
> With pleasant joy, enjoy your sweetest love,
> Shead foorth those teares with me, which then you shed
> Whe[n] first you wood your ladies to your wils,

Those teares are fittest for my wofull case,
Since *Locrine* shunnes my nothing pleasant face. (I3ʳ)

Guendoline speaks to elements and supernatural forces that are 'modest', 'gentle', 'happie' and 'pleasant', and asks the spirits she addresses to share in her tears at Locrine's betrayal: while the entreaty to the supernatural seems modelled on Medea's address to the gods at the beginning of Act 1 of Seneca's play, in her weakness Guendoline appears far closer to the powerless and thus sympathetic women whom Kerrigan identifies as typical of Elizabethan complaint.[58] Persuaded by her brother that Locrine must die, Guendoline becomes more bloodthirsty as the final act progresses, and specifically hopes to revenge herself on Locrine's illegitimate daughter Sabren, demanding:

Find me yoong *Sabren, Locrines* only joy,
That I may glut my mind with lukewarme blood,
Swiftly distilling from the bastards brest ... (K3ʳ)

Nevertheless, although she has begun, with such pronouncements, to move closer to the murderous model provided by Medea in the dumbshow, unlike Pandora, Violenta, Atossa and Videna, Guendoline is deprived of her revenge by the hasty suicides of Locrine, Estrild and Sabren. Contenting herself with ordering an ignominious burial for her love-rival, Guendoline survives the play's conclusion, precisely because her failure to exact revenge means that she is fundamentally different from Medea, despite Ate's insistence on their similarity.[59]

In such tragedies, the brief appearances of Medea are predictive of violence, and suggest a disorder that will be allowed to intrude on the world of the play, and spiral excitingly out of control for the entertainment of the audience, before being quashed. Videna is killed as she deserves, and Guendoline's fantasies of revenge are thwarted. At the end of *Locrine*, Ate appears again, this time with a pointed message for the Elizabethan audience:

And as a woman was the onely cause
That civill discord was then stirred up,
So let us pray for that renowned mayd,
That eight and thirtie yeares the scepter swayd,
In quiet peace and sweet felicitie,
And every wight that seekes her [grievous?] smart,
wold that this sword wer pierced in his hart. (K4ᵛ)

The decision to blame Estrild for the upheaval of the play is a curiously unjust one, and, as it was with *Gorboduc*, it is tempting to see *Locrine* as consciously underlining the trouble that ungoverned women may cause, as a way of registering doubt about female rule. At the same time, Dermot Cavanagh has suggested of *Gorboduc* that the play's disorder is used to 'admonitory effect', to encourage Elizabethan audiences to appreciate 'the benefit deriving from Elizabeth's accession', and, through Ate's final address, *Locrine*'s audience is encouraged to appreciate that many women may be Medea-like, may provoke or exacerbate disorder through their sexual desire, their own desirability, or their untempered passions, but that Elizabeth, 'that renowned mayd', is clearly and importantly unlike Medea.[60] Here, a tragic use of Medea reflects how she is used in other genres of early modern writing, for, as I shall argue in Chapter 5, political or politicised plays, poems and prose works, particularly those produced at times of instability or crisis, could invoke Medea as symbolic of a threat to order and to monarchy that has been comfortingly dispelled.[61]

Cathy Shrank has noted the capacity of 'nondramatic dialogue' to direct the reader's understanding in ways that drama cannot, suggesting that the nondramatic form 'allows the author to keep a firmer grip on the reader's interpretation'.[62] This is certainly apparent in Achelley's and Robinson's uses of Medea, in that their prefaces, headings and interjections clearly direct the reader towards a particular, disapproving attitude towards the texts' murderous women. Dramatists who employ Medea may be less heavy-handed, preferring to keep her confined to the outskirts of drama, rather than granting her centre-stage, and not presenting their audiences with her example in such a direct and didactic way as Elizabethan authors of prose or verse. Nevertheless, inescapably present in drama, as in prose and verse, is the same sense that, thrilling as she is, Medea, or a Medea-figure, must be held accountable somehow, if not by Christian or pagan deities then by the judgement and condemnation of a patriarchal society. Shakespeare is no exception to this rule, and, though he seldom refers to her directly, his tragedies flirt with the exciting potential of the destructive and vengeful Medea-figure, before showing how such a woman can be reduced and put reassuringly in her place.

Shakespeare's tragic Medea

Echoes of Medea can be discerned in two of Shakespeare's most alarming anti-heroines, Tamora and Lady Macbeth. However, the first of these seems initially to be very far from the classical sorceress, who slaughters her young children in cold blood. Tamora's first appearance in *Titus Andronicus* is as a supplicant, begging for the life of her son Alarbus, and the first apparent allusion to Medea's story comes as Lucius demands Alarbus' murder and dismemberment:

> Give us the proudest prisoner of the Goths,
> That we may hew his limbs and on a pile
> *Ad manes fratrum* sacrifice his flesh
> Before this earthy prison of their bones,
> That so the shadows be not unappeased,
> Nor we disturbed with prodigies on earth. (1.1.96–101)

The idea of committing murder to appease the shades of the dead, and particularly the use of the phrase *Ad manes fratrum*, recall the Senecan Medea's vision of her dead and dismembered brother Apsyrtus, a vision which drives her on to kill her sons:

> mihi me relinque et utere hac, frater, manu
> quae strinxit ensem. victima manes tuos
> placamus ista. (969–71)

> Leave me to myself, and act, brother, through this hand that has drawn the sword. With this sacrifice I placate your shade.

When Alarbus is killed despite her impassioned protests, Tamora is not Medea, but is almost a Jason-figure, powerless to stop the slaughter of her son. However, like Medea, Tamora is then very quickly revealed as a threat to patriarchal security. In her introduction to the play, Katharine Eisaman Maus notes,

> In a world in which women are treated as the sexual property of their male relatives, "good" women like Lavinia seem destined for passivity and victimization. One acquires power in such circumstances by refusing to play by the rules.[63]

In her foreignness and particularly in her desire for bloody revenge on the male ruling community she sees as having wronged her, Tamora is an echo of Medea. She is described by Lucius as a 'tiger' (5.3.194), an epithet applied to Medea in both Golding's *Metamorphoses* and Studley's *Medea*, and the gruesome death and dismemberment of her sons may also be intended to recall Medea's killing of Apsyrtus, as well as other Ovidian tales of mutilation.[64]

For all her monstrous behaviour towards innocents such as Lavinia, however, Tamora is in essence far less of a transgressive threat than the Colchian witch. As she relies on Saturninus for her position of power in Rome, so she relies on Demetrius and Chiron to wreak revenge on Lavinia and Bassianus. In contrast, Medea's young sons carry her poisoned gifts to Creusa, but are ignorant of her plans, and play no active part in the grisly death of Creon and his daughter, which is entirely masterminded by Medea. The essential difference between Tamora and Medea is brought home forcibly in the play's conclusion. While Medea kills and dismembers her own children, Tamora is horrified to hear of her sons' brutal murder at the hands of Titus. She herself is quickly and unceremoniously killed, and in the play's final scene Lucius commands her corpse's undignified expulsion from the city. Robert S. Miola notes that in his Restoration adaptation of the tragedy, Edward Ravenscroft goes far further in drawing parallels between Tamora and Medea, principally by making Tamora an infanticide.[65] At the climax of this later play, the dying Tamora warns Aaron, 'Moor, speak not a word against my honour / To save the world' (H3ᵛ).[66] To save their child, however, Aaron reveals his affair with Tamora, and Tamora then feigns an interest in her only surviving son, before brutally dispatching him:

> TAMORA: I have now no other Son, and shou'd
> Be kind to it in Death, let it approach me then,
> [The Child is brought to the Empress, she Stabs it].
> That I may leave with it my parting Kiss. —
> Dye thou off-spring of that Blab-tongu'd Moor. (H4ʳ)

In some ways, the survival of Tamora's and Aaron's child, the off-spring of a Goth and a Moor, and his reception into Rome, would be more alarming for an early modern audience than his death at the hands of the barbarian Tamora. Ravenscroft's decision to make Tamora an infanticide renders her far more like Medea, however, and as his audience would expect, Tamora is killed after her final terrible crime, just as Ravenscroft's Aaron (who outdoes his Shakespearean counterpart in his vow to eat the child's corpse) is swiftly burnt to death on stage.[67]

The shocking addition of the onstage infanticide in Ravenscroft's play emphasises how Shakespeare's Tamora, by contrast, ends the play distanced from Medea, in that her infant son survives, rather than being slaughtered at his mother's hands to spite his father.[68] Still, whether similarities to Medea are reduced or amplified at the conclusion of the two plays, in both, Tamora herself must die, if the society she leaves behind is to have any hope of survival or improvement. Rather than ascending, and transcending, triumphantly, as Medea can by virtue of her divine connections, in both tragedies the Medea-figure is literally and figuratively excluded from the male society which she sought to destroy, but which will attempt regeneration in her absence. At the same time, though, the intrusion of this Medea-figure has been inherently alarming and destabilising, even if she is defeated as the audiences of both plays would expect. David Willbern points to Marcus' desire, in Shakespeare's play, to

> … knit again
> This scattered corn into one mutual sheaf,
> These broken limbs again into one body. (5.3.69–71)

He sees in this a reference to the myth of Pelops, but it also recalls the killing and dismemberment of Apsyrtus, an association which would suggest that hopes of regeneration and restoration are futile.[69] Liz Oakley-Brown, meanwhile, suggests that Shakespeare's tragedy resists closure, ending, as it began, with slaughter: perhaps the enduring legacy of the Medea-like woman is bloody destruction and disruption, and the unclassical death of such a figure cannot entirely neutralise the threat she represents, however satisfying such a death might be, in the eyes of Elizabethan or Restoration audiences.[70]

If *Titus'* themes of bloody revenge by women, the slaughter of innocents and the fall of dynasties all seem to echo Medea's story, the same is true of *Macbeth*, and here the supernatural elements added by the Weird Sisters suggest the influence of the Ovidian or Senecan Medea even more compellingly. Lady Macbeth's ruthlessness is often seen as echoing that of the Senecan Medea, particularly given that both women regard femininity as incompatible with their bloody plots, and call on supernatural forces to help them overcome any lingering mercy in their souls. Lady Macbeth asks,

> Come, you spirits
> That tend on mortal thoughts, unsex me here,
> And fill me from the crown to the toe top-full
> Of direst cruelty. (1.5.38–41)

In Studley's translation and expansion of Seneca's tragedy, which Inga-Stina Ewbank notes is rhetorically more similar to Lady Macbeth's speech than the original Latin,[71] Medea demands of herself:

If anye lustye lyfe as yet
within thy soule do reste,
If ought of auncient corage styll
doe dwell within my breste,
Exile all folysh female feare,
and pytye from thy mynde,
And as thuntamed Tygers use
to rage and rave unkynde,
that haunt the crokyng combrus caves
and clumpred frosen clives,
And craggy rockes of *Caucasus*,
whose bytter colde depryves
The soyle of all inhabytours,
permit to lodge and rest,
Such salvage brutysh tyranny
within thy brasen breste. (291–306)

Lady Macbeth's hints at her capacity for infanticide also ally her to Medea, who kills not only her own children but also her young brother. Though she can promise and hint at terrible deeds, however, like Tamora, and unlike Medea, Lady Macbeth cannot commit murder herself in the play, instead relying on her husband to carry out the necessary slaughters: as Colin Burrow suggests, she 'is trying to turn herself into a British Medea, but she is not quite succeeding'.[72] Like Tamora's, her plot to triumph over her enemies is unsuccessful, and she commits suicide offstage, thus realising the fate that George Turberville's Hypsipyle wished for her rival, in a tantalising hint at Shakespeare's knowledge of the popular Elizabethan translation. In fact, Miola argues that Shakespeare's use of Medea at first serves to make Lady Macbeth appear more powerful, before ultimately demonstrating that she falls short of the classical sorceress, who triumphs where Lady Macbeth is overcome by her own guilt: 'Seneca's Medea provides initially a paradigm of passionate atrocity for Lady Macbeth and then a revealing counterpoint to her deterioration.'[73]

Macbeth himself is also shown to be both like and unlike Medea. Stephen Greenblatt describes his sense of guilt and self-loathing in terms that underscore his moral weakness, and seem deliberately evocative of Medea's famous pronouncement in *Metamorphoses* 7.20–1, 'video meliora proboque, / deteriora sequor' (I see the better [course] and approve it, but I follow the worse). Greenblatt notes of Macbeth:

> Far more than any other of Shakespeare's villains ... Macbeth is fully aware of the wickedness of his deeds and is tormented by this awareness. Endowed with a clear-eyed grasp of the difference between good and evil, he chooses evil, even though the choice horrifies and sickens him.[74]

Of course, in the *Metamorphoses*, Medea agonises over whether to love Jason: when it comes to murder, though, she is utterly ruthless in her determination, just as she is able to brush off any doubts in the Senecan tragedy as quickly as they occur to her. Thus Macbeth, like his wife, is at best a distorted reflection of the Senecan witch, despite Burrow's suggestion that 'Macbeth is more of a woman than his wife, and takes on the mantle of Medea'.[75] While Medea's atrocities (her killing of her brother, of Pelias, of Creon and Creusa) seem only to make her stronger, spurring her on to commit the final taboo of infanticide, the Macbeths' power, inextricably linked to status and court politics as Medea's is not, crumbles as the play's horrors accumulate, and they are unable to draw any real strength from supernatural forces, as can Medea.

Indeed, for Miola, the appearance of magic and necromantic skill in the play only serves to underscore how Lady Macbeth in particular is a pale imitation of Medea: speaking of the Weird Sisters, he notes:

> Shakespeare again practises transference, this time removing Medea's supernaturalism from his female protagonist, conferring it on non-human creatures, the black and midnight hags. So doing, he denies Lady Macbeth this moment of eerie self-actualization and transcendence; she remains intransigently human, subject to supernatural forces outside her control not master of them.[76]

The Weird Sisters wield a Medea-like magical power that Lady Macbeth does not, and they are not punished, as she is, by the play's close.[77] Even they can be seen as diminished by association with and comparison with Medea, however: in a scene which may have been interpolated into the play, and is often ascribed to Thomas Middleton, Hecate chides them angrily for becoming involved in Macbeth's affairs, pointing out:

> all you have done
> Hath been but for a wayward son,

Spiteful and wrathful, who, as others do,
Loves for his own ends, not for you. (3.5.10–13)[78]

Adelman sees this description of Macbeth as a 'wayward son' as suggestive of the witches' terrifying and terrifyingly maternal power over
Macbeth,[79] but another reading is possible, one that undermines their
power even as it is stressed, and allies them to weakened and suffering
incarnations of Medea. Macbeth is 'wayward', and 'Loves for his own
ends', and here Hecate seems to suggest that, like the Medeas of Ovid,
Chaucer and Whetstone, the Weird Sisters naively practise their magic,
to advance a selfish and self-centred man.

However they choose to use it, as Miola points out, the witches wield
a magical power that is denied to Lady Macbeth. The Jacobean statute
against witchcraft of 1604 was far stricter than the Elizabethan statute of
1563, but despite this suggestion that witchcraft was more of a concern
than ever in the first years of James's reign, Shakespeare's treatment
of the witches is not as punitive as might be expected.[80] For Harry Berger,
they are 'as comical as they are sinister', while Dolan points out that,
in English drama, the early modern witch is only usually allowed to
survive their play's ending if she is sidelined: the same sidelining that
Creon and Jason far less successfully attempt to impose on the Senecan
Medea in Corinth, with horrific consequences.[81] He may not kill his
witches, but in his sidelining of their power, and in his punishment of
Lady Macbeth, Shakespeare thus signals his departure from his Senecan
model, and an interest, shared by so many of his contemporaries, in creating and delighting in disorder, before taking the decision to exorcise
it: what Karin S. Coddon has termed 'the construction and containment
of subversion'.[82] Like Tamora in *Titus Andronicus*, Lady Macbeth and the
witches are alarming and deliberately Medea-like additions to *Macbeth*,
intended to delight and disturb the audience in equal measure with
their bloody and unfeminine ambition (in the case of Lady Macbeth)
and their eerie command of the supernatural forces that so fascinated
Jacobean audiences (in the case of the witches). Whatever the subversive
potential of their power, though, both Lady Macbeth and the witches
are, like Tamora, more subject to early modern mores and expectations
than they are similar to their Ovidian and Senecan forebears. In fact,
Shakespeare's move to silence or punish his Medea-figures (particularly
Tamora and Lady Macbeth) argues for his use of Elizabethan translations
of the *Heroides* (by George Turberville) and Seneca's *Medea* (by John
Studley), both of which, as I have shown in Chapter 2, demonstrate
the early modern need somehow to contain or to undermine Medea,

even as they describe her worst excesses.[83] *Macbeth* has been termed 'astonishingly male-oriented and misogynistic',[84] and a play that indulges in both 'the fantasy of a virtually absolute and destructive maternal power and the fantasy of absolute escape from this power', with the latter fantasy achieved, in part, via 'the radical exclusion of the female'.[85] If the play is thought of in these terms, it is no surprise first that it brings forth Medea-figures of more than one kind (both the ruthless murderer and the witch), and second, and crucially, that it punishes or silences these Medea-figures, particularly in response to their disturbing efforts to exert malign influence over the minds and bodies of men.

Shakespeare's Tamora and (in particular) Lady Macbeth might in some ways be closely allied to the classical Medea, but they are not permitted to commit her crimes in the course of Shakespeare's plays: only Young Clifford, in the second and third parts of *Henry VI*, is shown swearing to emulate Medea, and then doing so, in his killing of Rutland. Authors of tragic prose and poetry, though, had found in Medea's story inspiration for gory and lasciviously detailed accounts of violence against men or children, and their example is followed by Elizabethan tragedies such as *Roxana* (though such plays cannot stage the worst of their violence, and must describe it instead). For authors of sensational sixteenth- or seventeenth-century tragedy, Medea's story was useful and suggestive because it provided such a wealth of memorable and specific episodes of grisly violence, any of which could be adapted into their own plays. For Edward Ravenscroft, Restoration adapter of *Titus Andronicus*, the infanticide was what stuck in his mind, while in Henry Chettle's melodramatic revenge tragedy *Hoffman, or the Revenge for a Father* (c.1602, printed 1631), much is made of the burning or poisoned crown that Medea traditionally uses to murder Creusa or Glauce.[86] Hoffman declares that his revenge on the enemies who have killed his pirate father will surpass that of 'Duke Jason's jealous wife' (1.3.382), and he gleefully murders the first of these foes, Prince Charles, with a burning iron crown, the same method as was used to dispose of his own father, before finally being condemned to die in the same way.[87] As he perishes in Act 1, Charles obligingly describes his own suffering in lascivious detail:

> ... I feel an Etna burn
> Within my brains, and all my body else
> Is like a hill of ice; all these Belgic seas
> That now surround us cannot quench this flame.
> Death like a tyrant seizeth me unawares;

My sinews shrink like leaves parched with the sun;
My blood dissolves, nerves and tendons fail;
Each part's disjointed, and my breath expires;
Mount soul to heaven, my body burns in fire. (1.2.212–20)

Such gruesome flourishes seem to echo the horribly exaggerated description of suffering that (for example) Studley's Medea eagerly forecasts for her rival, Creusa:

Her stewing brest, her sethyng vaines,
let fervent fyer freate
And force her rosted pynyg lymmes,
to droppe and melte awaye. (2406–9)

This fascination with the grisly and sensational potential of Medea's legend, the way that her violence might be echoed to thrill and horrify an audience, is typical of Elizabethan and Jacobean tragedies which recall her myth, whether these were dramas, poems or prose tales. From the middle of the seventeenth century, however, it is possible to discern the beginnings of what would become the focus of many eighteenth-century dramatic versions of Medea's story.[88] This is an instinct to emphasise the worst of her crimes, but often, too, to direct the audience's attention towards pity or empathy, either for Medea or for her victims, rather than towards the bloodthirsty expectation of vengeance and punishment.

Late seventeenth-century tragedy

In the middle of the century, Robert Baron's closet drama, *Mirza* (c.1647–55), demonstrates how one minor episode from Medea's story may be used to indulge the growing seventeenth-century taste for affect or pity in its drama.[89] The young Persian princess Fatima looks at a painting of Medea's flight from Colchis, and demands of her nurse 'Why do's this woman look so angry here?'(C^r).[90] Medea's father Aeëtes is clearly also meant to be depicted, for her older brother Soffia asks, 'What ailes that old man so to weep? I can't / Indure to see a man weep it showes cowardly' (C^r). However, unlike her brother, Fatima is greatly affected by both the nurse's explanation of Medea's killing of her brother and the old King's distress. She exclaims,

I hate all cruelty so perfectly:
Yet could I bear a part with that old man,

And weep as fast as he; so infectious
Is a just sorrow, chiefly in old persons. (Cʳ)

In contrast to Soffia, Fatima sees Aeëtes' grief as enjoyably 'infectious' and, though she protests that she could not bear to see the story acted, she relishes its sentimentality in painted form, telling her mother and nursemaid,

This piece shall be
My m[e]lancholly study, and sad Tutor.
When I have either cause or will to weep,
Ile take up this, and sit, and think, I see
The tender boy stretcht out his hands unto me
For help, and sigh, because I cannot rescue him.
Then think again, the old man calls out to me
To help him gather up his sons limbs; and weep
Because I cannot. (Cᵛ)

Medea's slaughter of her brother teaches Fatima how to 'weep', to display the feminising emotion and pity that Soffia finds so troubling in a king, but which was increasingly popularised in late seventeenth-century tragedy. Baron's use of Medea's story echoes her appearances in Elizabethan and Jacobean tragedy, in that a mention of Medea foreshadows violence: here the murder of the seven-year-old Fatima herself, at the hands of her maddened father Mirza. Fatima's enthusiasm for sentimentalising the story, and emphasising her own vicarious grief, however, also represents a break with Elizabethan and Jacobean tragic representations and a move towards a more affective use of Medea's story. This movement is particularly pronounced in Baron's treatment of the murderous father. Having regained his senses and realised his crime, and subsequently drunk poison, Fatima's father Mirza suffers a thoroughly expected (and hugely protracted) death, but there is not the sense of punishment well deserved that is so discernible in Elizabethan and Jacobean tragedies: rather, suicide is the only option that remains for Mirza, in the wake of such an act. Mirza sadly tells his wife Nymphadora, 'I know th' art angry with me for the losse / Of *FATYMA*', but she replies that she is 'Not angry sir, but grieved' (L4ʳ). Mirza then assures her:

Come I have sent the child t' a place fit for her,
A sacred place of rest, worthy her goodnesse,
This world was not, it was her Hell and mine;

And I am following her; I sent for thee
To take my last leave. (L4ʳ)

With these lines, Baron excites pity in his reader, while simultaneously ascribing to Mirza an altruistic motivation for infanticide, one that would become particularly prominent in nineteenth-century dramatisations of Medea's myth.[91] Like the anonymous pamphlet *A Pittilesse Mother* (1616), *Mirza* presents an early attempt to acknowledge Medea's killing of children (both her sons and her young brother), but to use these crimes to provoke pity, both for the murdered child and, more controversially, for the misguided parent.

Restoration theatre took up earlier tragedy's interest in Medea, and she could be treated in very similar ways, particularly in adaptations of earlier works, such as Ravenscroft's *Titus Andronicus* and Crowne's *The Misery of Civil War*, both of which exaggerate the horrors suggested by their sources, Shakespeare's *Titus Andronicus* and *Henry VI* plays, elaborating on the earlier dramas with, respectively, an onstage depiction of infanticide, and the suggestion of cannibalism. Elsewhere, a violent and particularly a foreign woman compared to Medea could often expect a similar fate to that meted out so enthusiastically by earlier authors and dramatists: in Henry Payne's *The Siege of Constantinople* (printed 1675), the murderous Calista is beheaded offstage, despite the failure of her plot to poison her love-rival Irene and Irene's friend Udoxia, and notwithstanding her plea that, like Medea's, her sins were motivated by love.[92] Also increasingly discernible in Restoration tragedy, however, is a new suggestion of sympathy for the Medea-figure. This sympathy is the logical extension of Robert Baron's suggestion, in *Mirza*, that descriptions of the deaths of Medea's victims (and indeed of a Medea-figure) could excite pity and compassion, rather than the horror of earlier renderings. It also accords with the late seventeenth-century taste for 'she-tragedy': Jean I. Marsden notes that

> Instead of horror, the tragedy of the 1680s emphasized pathos and perhaps most notably shifted its emphasis from the hero to heroine, usually a virtuous woman beleaguered and overwhelmed by sorrows.[93]

Unlikely as it may seem, given the ferociously vindictive stance that Elizabethan and Jacobean tragedy took on her crimes, even a figure like Medea could be reimagined to accord with this new literary fashion. In her survey of Medea on the eighteenth- and nineteenth-century stage,

Edith Hall has shown how the infanticide, in particular, was variously ameliorated or excused:

> The 18th century needed to deny that Medea killed her children, or to exculpate her by a fit of madness; the 19th century needed to change her motive from vindictive jealousy to maternal altruism.[94]

As we have seen, medieval treatments of Medea often negotiate the problem of her murders by ignoring them, and presenting her as a wronged romantic heroine. Far later, Gildon's *Phaeton* (1698) is both an early example of the increasingly sympathetic eighteenth-century attitude towards the Medea-figure and a demonstration of how a dramatist's adaptation of Euripides (rather than the more commonly used Seneca) can achieve this heightened sympathy. Earlier Restoration tragedy also demonstrates a new sympathy for the Medea-figure, although, like Gildon's Althea, such a figure will focus her anger on her love-rival rather than killing her own children. In Nathaniel Lee's *The Rival Queens* (1677), when a rejected Medea-figure kills, blame is displaced onto her husband, Alexander the Great, who has betrayed his second wife Statira by returning temporarily to his first, Roxana. Conspirators against Alexander take advantage of his lapse, and of the dramatic power of the Medea comparison, urging first Statira and then Roxana to emulate or to outdo the sorceress. For example, Roxana is told:

> Let not *Medea*'s dreadfull vengeance stand
> A pattern more, but draw your own so fierce,
> It may for ever be Original. (E2ʳ)[95]

Roxana, who is pregnant by Alexander at this point, does stab her rival to death, but she is banished, not executed as her Elizabethan and Jacobean forebears had been. Moreover, despite her pregnancy, there is no suggestion of the child-murder that earlier tragic authors had found to be almost a mandatory part of their use of Medea: in contrast, Roxana's pregnancy inspires her to spare her husband.

In her discussion of Charles Johnson's famous failure the *Tragedy of Medœa* (1730), Edith Hall points out that sentimental eighteenth-century dramatists might embellish their plays with 'explicit statements intended to guide the audience's reactions towards "humane" sympathy'. In Johnson's play, Hall notes, one example of such guidance comes when Creusa expresses the willingness and ability to sympathise with Medea.[96] Similarly, in Lee's play, the dying Statira tells her husband, 'spare

Roxana's life, / 'Twas Love of you that caus'd her give me death' (I[v]), and much of the blame is laid at Alexander's feet.[97] Unlike medieval English treatments of Medea, which very often ignored her crimes, Restoration authors do not shy away from the Medea-figure as murderer, and their association between Medea and 'dreadfull vengeance', as Lee puts it, is clearly indebted to the sixteenth- and early seventeenth-century accounts which saw Medea's cruelty and ruthlessness as crucial to her character. Unlike these earlier, bloodthirsty versions, however, tragedy of the late seventeenth century might choose to deal with its Medea-figures and their crimes in ways that do not necessarily include torture, execution or suicide. Such works might invite their audiences to react with pity and understanding, rather than with the disgust and righteous condemnation that earlier authors sought to excite. This movement towards affective drama, and towards sympathy for female characters, can, as Elizabeth Howe convincingly suggests, be closely linked to the rise of the female actress in the 1670s and 1680s.[98] Indeed, Marsden has noted how two of the most famous tragic actresses of the period, Elizabeth Barry and Anne Bracegirdle, brought a new depth of pathos to Lee's play, when they took on the roles of Roxana and Statira respectively.[99] In its treatment of Roxana, Lee's play contrasts markedly with a Restoration tragedy like Edward Ravenscroft's adaptation of *Titus Andronicus* (1687), in which the Medea-figure, Tamora, kills her child, and then is swiftly and predictably killed herself. *The Rival Queens* demonstrates the way in which some late seventeenth-century tragedy finds a new empathetic and affective potential in the Medea-figure as a wronged woman, and is able to accommodate her crimes with understanding, and in ways that look forward to eighteenth-century handlings, which might even be able to excuse the infanticide.

Introducing the 1701 edition of his translation of Seneca's *Medea*, Edward Sherburne acknowledges the contentious nature of his source material, but insists that 'the severest Tragedies (seen or read) may afford a kind of pleasurable Diversion' (A5[v]–A6[r]). The bloodthirsty entertainment value that authors perceived in Medea's story had been apparent from some of the earliest tragedies of the Elizabethan period. Moreover, as Sherburne's words suggest, such tragedies need not be staged, and could be read instead (and telling, rather than showing, arguably allowed authors greater scope for gory embellishment). Lee's play demonstrates, however, the extent to which the tragic representation of Medea had also evolved, and become more complex and challenging, in the century since Richard Robinson's brutal and self-righteous punishment of his anti-heroine, in his poem *The Rewarde of*

Wickednesse (1574). Although she appears infrequently on the stage throughout the period 1558–1688, the rise of tragic drama, and its willingness to reference Medea's well-known story, becomes increasingly important to this evolution of her representation. While some tragedies, such as Chettle's *Hoffman*, saw in a mention of Medea simply a cue to recreate her grisly and horrible violence, and inventive methods of torture and murder, others, such as *Gorboduc* and *Locrine*, had shown how the necessary containment of the wayward and alarming woman might bear lessons for Britain itself. Tragedies by Alabaster, Shakespeare and Ravenscroft, meanwhile, deliberately disturb their audiences and readers, even as they entertain, with the suggestion that the damage a Medea-like woman does to the fabric of state and society cannot easily be erased or repaired, even if she herself may be comfortingly disposed of. At the end of the century, some Restoration playwrights clearly saw a new potential in Medea as abandoned lover, a woman trapped and weakened by the cruelty of her partner: Lee's relatively sympathetic attitude to his betrayed Medea-figures, Statira and Roxana, is paralleled by an epilogue, which chides male playgoers for their heartless seduction of gullible actresses. More usually, though, authors of early modern tragedy, whether this took the form of prose, verse or drama, had very little interest in softening the brutality of the crimes committed by Medea, or by Medea-like women, against the bodies of men and children. Where they often undercut and negotiate her power is in their presentation of punishment for such women, of retribution and judgement either divine or worldly. Sixteenth- and seventeenth-century comic works might also seek to negotiate this power, though they did so, predictably, with a very different emphasis: in early modern parody, for example, Medea's power might be undermined by deliberate mockery, rather than by punishment. In other works of comic prose and drama, Medea's violence, so central to tragedy, may recede into the background. The memory of her tragic cruelty does not wholly disappear, however, and this memory is exploited by authors of comic and tragicomic works, used to add a fascinating sense of threat to even the happiest of endings.

4
Comic Medea

Particularly in the sixteenth and early seventeenth centuries, tragic representations of Medea's story, or of characters who are likened to her, plainly had a value for early modern authors, readers and audiences in that they were not merely entertaining but also didactic. The crimes of Medea, or of Medea-like women such as Atossa, Violenta and Videna, could be represented in verse, prose or drama, provided that such crimes were balanced by repentance and/or punishment. In his *Defence of Poesie* (published 1595), Philip Sidney had argued that poetry was preferable to history, since in a fictional work, 'if evil men come to the stage, they ever go out ... so manacled as they little animate folks to follow them' (p. 425).[1] In this way, tragic works could justify their representation of sin, by looking outward to reader or audience member (and often, where Medea is concerned, specifically to women), and suggesting that the representation provides the auditor with an example to shun. In the early modern period, authors of comic works, whether these were drama, prose or poetry, wrestled with the same problem of how to justify their works, and often they resolved the difficulty in a similar way, by pointing to the didactic and educative effect of what they wrote. In *The Governor* (1531), Sir Thomas Elyot argues that while the uninformed see comic dramas as 'doctrinal of ribaldry', in fact

> they be undoubtedly a picture or as it were a mirror of man's life, wherein evil is not taught but discovered; to the intent that men beholding the promptness of youth unto vice, the snares of harlots and bawds laid for young minds, the deceit of servants, the chances of fortune contrary to man's expectation, they being thereof warned may prepare themselves to resist or prevent occasion. (pp. 238–9)[2]

In *An Apology for Actors* (1612) Thomas Heywood follows Sidney's argument, in the *Defence of Poesie*, that comedy might be written with two different ends in mind, those of laughter and delight.[3] Heywood differentiates between kinds of theatrical comedy, but insists that it all has some instructive value:

> If a comedy, it is pleasantly contrived with merry accidents and intermixt with apt and witty jests to present before the prince at certain times of solemnity, or else merrily fitted to the stage. And what is then the subject of this harmless mirth? Either in the shape of a clown to show others their slovenly and unhandsome behaviour, that they may reform that simplicity in themselves which others make their sport, lest they happen to become the like subject of general scorn to an auditory; else it entreats of love, deriding foolish enamorates who spend their ages, their spirits, nay themselves, in the servile and ridiculous employment of their mistresses; and these are mingled with sportful accidents to recreate such as of themselves are wholly devoted to melancholy, which corrupts the blood, or to refresh such weary spirits as are tired with labor or study, to moderate the cares and heaviness of the mind, that they may return to their trades and faculties with more zeal and earnestness after some small, soft and pleasant retirement. (pp. 559–60)[4]

Authors in the sixteenth and seventeenth centuries were insistent that comedy, as well as tragedy, could instruct, and was therefore justifiable. As the quotation from Heywood's *Apology* might suggest, however, Medea's story did not lend itself readily to comic retelling, particularly on the stage. Heywood lists 'merry accidents', 'apt and witty jests', clowns and 'foolish enamorates' as among the typical features of comedy, and an early modern reader would fail to find any of the first three elements in her story. They would find the fourth element of Heywood's definition of comedy, 'servile and ridiculous employment' as a result of misguided love, manifested as purely tragic: Medea's loving willingness to assist Jason, which transforms into passionate hatred and rage once he has abandoned her.

Moreover, if the content of Medea's story might seem unsuited to comic treatment, particularly on the stage, then the same is true of the characters and their actions. In his *Compendium of Tragicomic Poetry* (1601), Giambattista Guarini, Italian author of *Il Pastor Fido*, and a vocal defender of the new genre of tragicomedy, had defined comedy as representing 'only private persons, with defects evoking laughter, mocks, sports, intrigues of little importance, covering but a short time and ending happily' (p. 514).[5] Similarly, Sidney argues that comedy, like tragedy, instructs its auditors by presenting them with characters who are imperfect: comedy is 'an imitation of the common errors of our life, which [the author] representeth in the most ridiculous and scornful sort that may be, so as it is impossible any beholder can be content to be such a one' (pp. 431–2). Moreover, comedy might provoke laughter, but this must be achieved in appropriate ways: 'the great fault, even in that point of laughter, and forbidden plainly by Aristotle,[6] is that they stir laughter in sinful things, which are rather execrable than ridiculous; or in miserable, which are rather to be pitied than scorned' (p. 452). When they are represented by Elizabethan and Jacobean writers, Medea's crimes typically plumb the depths of sin and encompass taboos such as witchcraft and infanticide in ways that make them seem very far from 'ridiculous'. In fact, by Sidney's definition Medea is doubly unsuited for comic treatment, since, as the previous chapters have shown, there is also a marked tendency in the Middle Ages to see Medea as pitiable rather than wicked (because cruelly treated by Jason) and this empathetic attitude to her might resurface in the late seventeenth and eighteenth centuries, even in tragedies which reference or represent her murders. Medea's story might be suited to various kinds of tragedy: medieval *de casibus* tragedy, such as Lydgate's *Fall of Princes*, Elizabethan and Jacobean revenge tragedy, or the affective 'she-tragedy' that comes to prominence in the eighteenth century, but has its roots in the seventeenth-century works of authors like Robert Baron and Nathaniel Lee. As these various definitions of comic drama suggest, however, Medea appears manifestly unsuited to comic treatment, because of her high status, the shocking nature of her crimes and the cruelty with which Jason treats her.

Nevertheless, Medea and her story could, on rare occasion, be used for comic effect, not only in drama but also in prose works, and in the burlesqued translations of Ovid that became popular in the Restoration. The most common comic approaches to Medea's power included incorporating brief references to her story in order to allow authorial joking at the expense of a naive reader (who may not understand that Medea is being used in singularly inappropriate ways) or else at the expense of a naive character, who misreads the classical character or context in a similar fashion. In sixteenth- and seventeenth-century drama, Medea is most commonly incorporated into tragicomedy, where she enables authors working in this pioneering new genre to incorporate tragedy's 'danger but not its death' (p. 511), as Guarini puts it in his famous definition. As this implies, although Medea could be used to *suggest* upset and disorder, her traditionally murderous and transgressive magical power is not allowed to overturn an apparently happy ending. Indeed, on occasion she may even bring a happy ending about, as she does in Robert Greene's comical history play *Alphonsus*, which takes advantage of Medea's association with what Susan Snyder terms 'magico-metamorphic strategies', those supernatural forces which Elizabethan and Jacobean drama so frequently harnessed to produce 'satisfying comic conclusions'.[7]

Although she is made a matchmaker in *Alphonsus*, however, Medea's notoriety means that the threat of a return to chaos and violence is disturbingly retained in Greene's comedy, as it is in the most famous example of this nuanced, tragicomic approach to Medea: Shakespeare's *The Tempest*, in which Medea's power is not itself presented comically, but is first invoked and then, crucially, rejected by Prospero, in the interests of the unity and conformity expected at the ending of a comedy or romance. At the beginning of Act 5, Prospero echoes Medea's Ovidian address to Hecate, to Night and to the Earth in a speech that is heavily reliant on Golding's translation of *Metamorphoses* 7.192–209, in order to boast of the alarming power he has enjoyed throughout the play, before rejecting it, breaking his staff and promising to destroy his books, in favour of reconciliation with his brother and acceptance back into society. Medea's power is renounced, but it has also been brought to the fore by Prospero, in ways that might superficially reassure the audience, while also unsettling them with the hinted potential for tragedy.

Finally, towards the end of the seventeenth century, the Restoration burlesquers of Ovid's *Heroides* take their cue from other, earlier irreverent treatments of classical mythology (such as Ben Jonson's crude and exuberant rewriting of Marlowe's *Hero and Leander* in *Bartholomew Fair*) or of Medea herself (for example James Shirley's tragicomic references to the death of Apsyrtus in several of his plays and masques). In their hands, Medea's witchcraft, her passion for Jason and her fury – all the things, in other words, that make her power so transgressive and terrifying – are undercut and made laughable, for example either by introducing deliberate and ridiculous anachronisms or by using intentionally coarse language. What is central to all these approaches is, once again, an authorial fascination with Medea's power, which is so compelling that authors allow its intrusion into an early modern genre to which it seems fundamentally unsuited.

Medea's comic intrusions into prose and drama are so remarkable precisely because they so clearly contradict what a reader or audience member would expect to feel, when confronted with her story: horror or pity, the two reactions explored in the tragic works that choose to incorporate her in some way, in the sixteenth and seventeenth centuries. In fact, this issue of expectation is key to comic representations of Medea in the period, in that, frequently, it is not Medea herself who is made comical but a character who does not understand the import of her story and uses it in an unknowingly reductive or otherwise inappropriate fashion. In Jonson's *The Alchemist*, for example, Sir Epicure Mammon provides an unwittingly comical alchemical reading of Medea's assistance in the conquest of the Fleece. He boasts to Surly:

> I have a piece of Jason's fleece too,
> Which was no other than a book of alchemy,
> Writ in large sheepskin, a good fat ram-vellum.
> Such was Pythagoras' thigh, Pandora's tub,
> And all that fable of Medea's charms,
> The manner of our work: the bulls, our furnace,
> Still breathing fire; our *argent-vive*, the Dragon;
> The dragon's teeth, mercury sublimate,
> That keeps the whiteness, hardness, and the biting;
> And they are gathered into Jason's helm,
> Th'alembic, and then sowed in Mars his field,
> And thence sublimed so often till they are fixed. (2.1.89–100)[8]

What Mammon presents as classical and alchemical learning is in fact nothing more than an avaricious obsession with gold, and while he swaggers as if his possession gives him control over the legend, in fact he has entirely misunderstood it, claiming that the obstacles to Jason's winning of the Fleece (bulls, the dragon, the men who spring from the dragon's teeth) are actually the means to obtain it. Throughout the scene, Mammon's misunderstanding of myth is a source of entertainment for Surly, as well as for the audience: he claims to have 'a treatise penned by Adam ... O'the philosopher's stone, and in High Dutch' (2.1.83–4), prompting an amused Surly to ask, 'Did Adam write, sir, in High Dutch?' (2.1.85). Mammon is a figure of fun here, not only because of the avarice that is coupled with an insistence that he will use his wealth for good but also because of his comical misreading of classical mythology. Gordon Campbell and Supriya Chaudhuri both point out that Renaissance alchemists, like their classical ancestors, believed that the quest for the Golden Fleece should be read as instructions to obtain gold from base metals.[9] Mammon boasts of possessing instructions that at least some of Jonson's contemporaries genuinely believed in, but because he is a ridiculous character his belief and his appropriation of Medea's story become themselves ridiculous. Margaret Healy notes Jonson's fondness for puncturing such pretensions to learning throughout his comic works:

> Time and again, Jonson's city comedies present demonic magic and its close associates alchemy and astrology ... as the product of delusions entertained only by madmen and fools motivated by greed, lust and thirst for power. At the mercy of his burlesquing pen, such activities seem impossible to take seriously.[10]

Mammon is mocked for his devotion to the false science of alchemy (and for the obvious greed which informs his desperate belief) and for his ludicrous misreading of Jason's quest, his insistence that the obstacles Aeëtes places in front of Jason can be read as various alchemical instruments. Mammon briefly mentions Medea's 'charms' as the equivalent of instructions on how to create gold: here, he takes the approach to Medea's power adopted by Chaucer's 'Legend of Medea' centuries before, in which Medea's assistance is deprived of any real magical power, and reduced merely to advice. Both authors, Jonson and Chaucer, pointedly ignore the tragic punishment that the intrepid adventurer Jason suffers at the hands of his far more skilled wife: both, though, would expect their readers to be aware of the second, darker half of the story. As I have discussed in Chapter 1, on the one hand, Chaucer's decision not to write of Medea's crimes but to slyly point his readers in the direction of Ovid's *Heroides* mocks the medieval catalogue tradition, its separation of historical or mythical figures into good or bad. Jonson, on the other hand, mocks Mammon, the insufficient reader or interpreter who jumps eagerly on the alchemical bandwagon offered to him and, like the stereotypical medieval cataloguer imagined by Chaucer, reads only what suits him into Medea's story. This idea, that a character can appear comically ridiculous in their failure to appreciate the whole of Medea's story (or to take appropriate lessons from it) appealed to authors of Elizabethan fictions, men like George Whetstone and Robert Greene, who were often hugely concerned with the reader's reception and interpretation of their works.

Misreading Medea in early modern prose fiction

If Jonson makes Mammon appear ridiculous (while simultaneously belittling Medea's legend) in his misreadings of Medea's magic, pioneers of Elizabethan prose fiction often do something similar with Medea's romantic disappointment at the hands of Jason. As Chapter 3 has shown, a brief allusion to Medea was a popular strategy for an author wishing to heighten the tragedy of his narrative: she is used in this way in George Pettie's tale of Progne and Philomela, part of his collection of short prose tales *A Petite Pallace of Pettie His Pleasure* (1576). Here, Progne underscores the wickedness of her husband Tereus, who has raped and mutilated her sister, by exclaiming: 'It is evident hée is ingendred of Jasons race, who disloyally forsooke Medea y^t made him win y^t golden [f]léece' (Fii^r). The strangely unfair comparison with Jason (who is faithless, but never commits Tereus' horrible crimes) is intended not just to critique Tereus but to foreshadow the brutal murder of his young son, committed by Progne. Medea could also be used to signpost forthcoming tragedy for the knowing reader if a tale's outcome is not murder but romantic disappointment and death: so in the tale of Scilla and Minos, also part of the collection, Pettie's Scilla, fated to be scorned by Minos and die in pursuit of his ship, fondly and mistakenly imagines that he will be delighted at her betrayal of her father Nisus, and will welcome her as a lover 'by the exa[m]ple of *Medea*, who betraied her father to *Jason*' (Giii^r).[11] As this latter example suggests, Elizabethan prose fiction, with its innovative focus on the early modern reader, both male and female, often makes a bad or insufficient reader into a literary character, and such a bad reader can be comical rather than tragic and fatally misguided, as is Scilla. Heroes and heroines created by prose authors return time and again to the same examples from the *Heroides* and *Metamorphoses*, appearing ridiculous, pompous and pitiful in their vain efforts to make classical authority and their selective or insufficient knowledge of Medea's story chime with their experience or expectations of romance.

George Whetstone, author of the collection of prose and poetry *The Rocke of Regard* (1576) recognised a tragic potential in Medea's story: as I have noted in Chapter 3, in 'The Pitious Complaint of Medea', he has her lament her suffering, and regret her faith in Jason. Whetstone is also aware of her less obvious comic potential, however, and wryly exploits it elsewhere in his collection, in the lengthy tale 'Inventions of P. Plasmos touching his hap and hard fortune'. The narrative alternates between Plasmos's story of betrayal and loss as he tells it and the 'Reporters admonition' which acts as a kind of gloss on Plasmos's narrative. Plasmos speaks fulsomely of his love Laymos but, in commenting on his praise, the Reporter foreshadows the betrayal and disappointment which is to follow:

[I]t seemeth his Lady *Laymos* that he so highly commended, was in very déede as fayre as *Flora*, as faithful as *Faustine*, as loving as *Layis*,

> as meeke as *Medea*, as honest as *Hellen*, as constant as *Cressed*, and
> as modest as *Maria Bianca*, and therefore worthie of estimation. (Pʳ)

Here, Whetstone's Reporter is included to provide another point of
view on the love affair, one that makes Plasmos appear ridiculous and,
simultaneously, to encourage the reader to think more carefully about
the implications of such classical comparisons: as Paul Salzman notes,
in his preface to the reader Whetstone acknowledges the possibility of
misreading or misunderstanding his examples, before dismissing those
who err thus by remarking that 'the folly is yours, & no fault in me'.[12]
Here, of course, the folly would be to miss the Reporter's irony, and
to believe that these are appropriate comparisons for one's beloved.
Laymos does not surpass these women in goodness: she is their equal,
and the damning alliteration that condemns (rather than commends)
her to be 'as meeke as *Medea*, as honest as *Hellen*, as constant as *Cressed'*
pokes fun at the hapless Plasmos, who cannot appreciate his lover's true
nature. Moreover, in its insistent and alliterative repetition of women's
names and their qualities, the passage makes sport of readers' and writers' fondness for such proof by example, which was to become ever
more popular via the euphuistic fictions of authors such as John Lyly
and Robert Greene in the 1580s.

Jason's betrayal of Medea was a favourite story of Greene's, and his
heroines knew it well. For example, in *Arbasto, The Anatomie of Fortune*
(printed 1584), the betrayed Myrania bellows curses at her faithless
lover Arbasto from her sickbed, in terms which echo the Senecan and
Ovidian Medea's denunciation of Jason's ingratitude. She specifically
names Medea as an example that she knows, and which should have
prompted her to take greater care:

> Was I the meanes to save thy life, & wilt thou wythout cause procure
> my death? have I forsaken my Countrey, betraied my father, and yet
> wilt thou kill me with discurtesie? O haplesse *Myrania*, could not
> *Medeas* mishap have made thee beware? (F4ᵛ)[13]

Here, as in Pettie's tale of Progne, the story that makes use of Medea
is tragic, with both the tale's heroines, Myrania and Doralicia, dying
of passionate grief because of Arbasto's fickleness, and Arbasto himself
losing his kingdom and going to live as a hermit. Elsewhere, Greene's
heroines might display their (selective) knowledge of Medea's story, but
persist in hoping for a positive outcome, in a way that could be read
as comic by the more knowledgeable reader. Speaking of complaints

written in the female voice, John Kerrigan argues that, 'even when non-parodic', such works have 'an unfocused comic air which needs dispersing by poets seeking pathos'.[14] If Greene seeks to amuse, rather than provoke pity, he will not disperse the 'comic air' of a complaining Elizabethan heroine invoking the hopeless love affair of a classical forebear but rather will seek to heighten this effect, for example by repetition. Mamillia and Publia, the two heroines of *Mamillia* (first printed 1580, extant version 1583), one of his earliest prose romances, make extensive complaint about their fears concerning the trustworthiness of Pharicles, and Mamillia repeatedly recalls Medea's credulity and Jason's faithlessness, each time hoping fondly for a different outcome where her own love affair is concerned. She even voices her fears directly to Pharicles (echoing the Ovidian Medea as she does so), telling him, 'Medea knew the best, and did followe the worst in choosing Jason: but I hope not to finde thee so wavering' (C4ᵛ).[15] This is a vain hope indeed, for as Katharine Wilson puts it, Mamillia 'has read all the right books and made all the wrong choices', and her knowledge of the Medea of the *Heroides* and *Metamorphoses* will not help her to avoid romantic disappointment.[16] The tale is not a tragedy, and so, like Jonson's Mammon, a more arrogant but similarly misguided reader of the classics, Mamillia can appear foolish as well as pitiful for her frustrating inability to apply her knowledge of Medea's story appropriately and her refusal to shun the faithless Pharicles, who continues to flit between the two women for the duration of the romance.

Caroline Lucas has noted that male authors of Elizabethan romance, including Greene, often purport to sympathise with women in their texts, while 'constructing a role for the woman reader which is marginalizing, trivializing and ultimately self-destructive'.[17] By making her repeatedly misinterpret or misuse Medea's story, Greene trivialises Mamillia as a female reader of classical tales, making her a figure of fun, and her reading becomes self-destructive (to use Lucas's term), even as she remains determined that things will turn out better for her than they did for Medea. Timothy Hampton's work on exemplarity in the Renaissance demonstrates that the early modern character or reader is constantly under pressure to read correctly, which means knowing and taking into account all aspects of an exemplar's story:

The reader who comes upon the name of a heroic ancient exemplar in a text has come upon a single sign which contains folded within it the entire history of the hero's deeds ... The task of the Renaissance reader who is well schooled in ancient history and poetry is to unpack those great deeds from the mere appearance of the name, recognising them as models by which to measure his own action in the world.[18]

As with great heroes, so with an anti-heroine: Greene's characters should be able to unpack the whole of her story from a mention of Medea's name, to appreciate, first, that she was betrayed by Jason and, second, that she took a terrible revenge that has no place in a romance, and so is scarcely a suitable example for a romance heroine to invoke. If characters cannot read or recall so perceptively, then Renaissance readers who are more able will smile at their folly (and will be entirely unsurprised by Pharicles' betrayal of both women). In this way, a comic approach to Medea is reflective of the enjoyment Linda Hutcheon has identified as central to an auditor's reception of an adaptation or appropriation: 'the doubled pleasure of the palimpsest', or the ability to recall the original story that lies behind the adaptive use and to appreciate their frictive interplay.[19] At the same time, Greene's knowing use of Medea to make sport of both the reading and the romantic hopes of Mamillia and Publia is revealing about the text's double standard where men and women are concerned. Katharine Wilson points out that both sexes are tasked with recalling and interpreting classical examples in this work: 'Mamillia is as intimately involved in rewriting exempla to her own advantage as Pharicles.'[20] While Mamillia is able to persuade herself that she will pursue her romantic desires without suffering as Medea did, Pharicles declares his determination to follow the example of Jason, in leaving one woman for another. Though the reader might also smile at his foolishness, and see impending disaster in his choice of example, however, Pharicles actually ends the second part of *Mamillia* triumphant, enjoying the love of Mamillia and an inheritance from the deceased Publia: as Wilson puts it, the two parts of Greene's *Mamillia* are 'a comically wish-fulfilling fantasy for his male readers'.[21] Of course, such a fantasy comes at the expense of his female characters, with Lucas arguing that Greene's narrator 'only appears to be on the side of women'.[22] Such a reading seems confirmed by the fact that Mamillia suffers for her repeated (and rather ridiculous) misinterpretation of Medea's story, while Pharicles does not face any penalty for glibly invoking Jason. It seems that in *Mamillia* only female characters are made laughable through their inability to read myth correctly, and, for the modern reader, Greene's joke might thus be harder to enjoy.

Greene frequently and enthusiastically upsets readerly expectation, just as he does by allowing Pharicles to escape scot-free: this occurs most famously at the climax of his later prose romance *Pandosto* (1588), the source for Shakespeare's *The Winter's Tale*, which sees the eponymous king kill himself, in regret at the way he has treated his wife Bellaria and his exiled daughter Fawnia. This unexpected tragic climax is sprung on the unwary reader, even as Fawnia is reconciled to her father, and celebrates her marriage to the prince Dorastus. At the same time, the reader of *Mamillia* expects tragedy, and perhaps even terrible revenge on Pharicles, when Medea's abandonment is mentioned, but is wrongfooted when this never materialises (though Pharicles does betray Mamillia, as the knowing reader would expect). Another clever example of Greene's comic exploitation of Medea's violent threat appears in the pamphlet *The Defence of Conny-catching* (1592). Greene's 'conny-catching' pamphlets were prose works, often taking the form of collections of short tales, that presented themselves as guides to the criminal underworld of early modern London. Frequently purporting to be written in the voices of pickpockets, thieves and scam-artists, they claimed to give the Elizabethan reader a means to understand, and thus avoid, the tricks and deceits employed by such figures, and they often portrayed the deserved downfall and punishment of their crooks and conmen. In a tale entitled 'A pleasant tale of an usurer', however, one such criminal, 'Cuthbert conny-catcher', attempts to defend his kind against the criticisms they have received from 'R. G.', and he does so by presenting the brutal but bizarrely comical punishment of those who practise far worse crimes. A young gentleman is tricked out of his lands by a usurer, but the gentleman's wife traps the villain, when he arrives to collect his ill-gotten gains, by offering him the chance to stick his head out of the window and admire the view:

> The Usurer mistrusting nothing, thrust out his craftie sconce, and the Gentlewoman shut to the windowe, and called her maids to helpe, where they bound and pinyond the caterpillers armes fast, and then stood he with his head into a backeyard, as if he had beene on a pillory, and struggle he durst not for stifling himselfe. When she had him thus at the vauntage, she got a couple of six peny nayles and a hammer, and went into the yard, hauing her children attending upon her, every one with a sharpe knife in theyr handes, and then comming to him with a sterne countenance, shee looked as Medea did when she attempted revenge against Jason. The Usurer seeing this tragedie, was afraid of his life, and cryed out, but in vaine, for her maydes made such a noyse, that his shriking could not be heard, whilest she nayled one ea[r]e fast to the windowe, and the other to the stanshel, then began she to use these words unto him. (B3ʳ)[23]

The image Greene creates, of the usurer trapped by his nailed ears, is both arresting and absurdly comic, even more so when the author tosses in a classical allusion that would sit far more comfortably in a tragedy. The reader is gleefully told by Cuthbert, the narrator, that the furious wife 'looked as Medea did when she attempted revenge against Jason'. The wife does not identify herself as Medea, and it is Cuthbert who draws the comparison, but the deliberate ambiguity of the following statement, that 'The Usurer seeing this tragedie, was afraid of his life', suggests the possibility that the usurer may have seen or read some version of the tragedy of Medea: if so, it is understandable that he fears for his safety in such a vulnerable position. The wife tells the usurer that since his wealth and position will not allow her to take legal action against him, she has taken it upon herself to exact revenge:

> I my selfe wil bee Justice, Judge, and Executioner: for as the Pillory belongs to such a villaine, so have I nayled thy eares and they shal be cut off to the perpetuall example of such purloining reprobates, and the executers shal bee these little infants, whose right without conscience or mercie thou so wrongfully deteinest. Looke on this old Churle litle babes, this is he that with his coossenage wil drive you to beg and want in your age, and at this instant brings your Father to all this present miserie, have no pittie uppon him, but you two cut off his eares, and thou (quoth she to the eldest) cut off his nose, and so be revenged on the villaine whatsoever fortune me for my labour. (B3ʳ)

Greene's heroine is Medea rewritten and comically inverted, a wife and mother who does not kill her children, but rather urges them on to violence, and does so not to punish her husband, but to safeguard his interests.[24] The frantic usurer confesses his deception of the gentleman, and is released, but not before the wife has invited her neighbours to come and make sport of him. When he is freed, his humiliation is compounded as it is made public knowledge:

> The next day it was bruted abroad, and came to the eares of the worshipful of the country, who sate in commission upon it, and found out the coossenage of the Usurer, so they praised the witte of the Gentlewoman, restored her husband to the land, and the old churle remained in discredit, and was a laughing stocke to all the country all his life after. (B3ᵛ)

Here, a wife who is explicitly compared to Medea for her bloody ruthlessness is not punished or even condemned, but instead admired for her daring stand against a hated authority figure, and the usurer is made the comic focus of the tale, not because he misinterprets or misapplies the story of Medea, as Jonson's Mammon and Greene's Mamillia do, but precisely because he knows it too well. His knowledge of who Medea is, and what a Medea-figure might do to a man in such a vulnerable condition, contributes to a terror that is, in the eyes of Cuthbert conny-catcher, both laughable and entirely well-deserved. The episode is fascinating as an example of the way in which brutal violence and laughter can co-exist in this type of tale, which recalls Chaucerian fabliaux such as 'The Miller's Tale'. To the usurer, his predicament is a 'tragedie', but the reader is clearly invited to laugh at his humiliation along with the townspeople, just as the auditor of 'The Miller's Tale' is expected to find the cuckolding and injury of John the carpenter amusing, rather than pitiable. In Greene's work, a heroine who has fallen on hard times, but who is nevertheless clever and resourceful, is able to triumph over a cruel authority figure, by appropriating the power of Medea's reputation to terrify him. Here, the triumph of the underdog recalls Medea's own use of her cunning and capacity for violence, to get the best of Creon, the king who wishes to expel her from Corinth, while the upset of economic hierarchy in the story, with the usurer's defeat, may have prompted Greene's upsetting of generic boundaries, by making Medea central to a comic tale of female revenge.

While Constance C. Relihan has pointed to 'the attempts of popular Elizabethan male writers to subdue and control the ever-present female Other', the Elizabethan fictions I have mentioned do not follow through on their use of Medea with the expected punishment for a woman who is Medea-like in her violence or disobedience, like the Elizabethan and Jacobean tragedies which invoked her.[25] Rather, these fictions, like Jonson's play, use her story as a comic and cautionary illustration of the dangers of too much or (usually) not enough knowledge of Medea's story, and in either case they make sport of their reading or interpreting characters, whether male or female. So Mamillia, who is like Medea only in her misplaced faith in Pharicles, is punished for her misapplication of Medea's story (not for murder), and her punishment is Pharicles' wholly predictable faithlessness, rather than the execution which typically awaited the Medea-like woman in tragedy. The clever wife of the conny-catching pamphlet, meanwhile, is Medea-like not because she commits murder but because the usurer imagines her to be so, and, while she comes out on top, he suffers deserved and comical terror, in part, at least, because of his overenthusiastic recollection of Medea's story.

This concern with how traditionally tragic examples might be read wrongly, and how this might be made comical, persists through the seventeenth century. The second book of the anonymous miscellany *The Academy of Pleasure* (1656) includes a brief dialogue entitled 'Two faithfull Lovers complement; each other meeting accidentally', in which a brief use of Medea owes much to the inappropriate classical allusions of naive Elizabethan lovers. Meeting her lover, the female speaker declares 'not Dido was more joyfull when Aeneas landed on the Carthaginian Shore than I am to meet thee thus happily' (p. 68). This is a singularly inauspicious example (and another that was used by Elizabethan authors like Greene to signpost a doomed relationship). However, her intended is a similarly poor reader of the classics, telling her,

> I shall be guided by thee, my Faire one, were the venture more perilous than that of Jason for the Golden Fleece, thou art my chaste Medea, and being armed with thy oraculous councell I shall not feare to force my way though opposed by millions of dangers. (p. 70)[26]

In the Elizabethan and Jacobean works of Greene and Jonson, the reader who is more knowledgeable than the character is rewarded, smiling at the naivety of Mamillia and Mammon, and at their inappropriate classical references. Here, in a compilation that promises on its title-page to teach its readers 'How to Retort, Quibble, Jest or Joke, and to return an ingenious Answer upon any occasion whatsoever', the author of the dialogue aims at a similar effect. Crucially, too, the compiler of the collection does not rely simply on the prior knowledge of his readers to discern that the reference to Medea is inappropriate, for later he includes 'a Dictionary of all the hard English words expounded', which includes classical characters, and defines Medea as 'the wife of *Jason*, for whose sake she betrayed her Countrey, slew her Brother, and lastly, her own Children' (p. 121).

In his work on mid-seventeenth-century printed miscellanies, Adam Smyth has shown how the printed notes that were sometimes included alongside the content might invite alternative readings of the text. Speaking of the mock-poem *The Innovation of Penelope to Ulysses*, by one James Smith, which was included in the collections *Wit and Drollery* (1656) and *Wit Restor'd* (1658), Smyth shows how the ostensibly serious notes that accompany the work collude with the burlesqued poem to mock other, more serious adapters: these notes are 'whispers in the ear of the reader which tell of the artifice of that being read'.[27] Of course, *The Academy of Pleasure* does not print its 'Dictionary' alongside the lovers' dialogue in note form, but even if the reader of the *Academy* approached the dialogue with little or no classical knowledge, if they find their way through to the 'Dictionary', its inclusion means that they cannot escape the joke implicit in the earlier piece, since they now have a fuller understanding of Medea's brutal and tragic legend than either of the hapless lovers who invoke her so blithely. Smyth points to the capacity for marginal notes to construct 'alternative dialogues' between text and notes, rather than simply 'set and limit readings'.[28] Here, the separation of the dialogue and the explanatory dictionary means that the reader who simply dips in and out of the work might form their own misguided ideas about what it means to love like Jason and Medea. In contrast, even if they had never previously heard of the couple, the more thorough and dedicated reader would be directed, via the dictionary, towards the correct (and comic) reading of the dialogue's misappropriation of the myth.

In these uses of Medea, the reader is of paramount importance, whether that reader appears within the text as a character, or is external to the text: it is the gap between their individual understanding of Medea's tale, and what it might mean, and the more generally known details of her legend (particularly, its tragic ending) that is used to provoke laughter. Elsewhere, though, and particularly in the comic or tragicomic drama of the period, authors felt the same pressure that the tragic playwrights did, to undercut and neutralise Medea's power, rather than to exploit it to joke at a reader's or character's expense. The punishment that was felt to be so appropriate to tragic handlings is not suitable here, though: in fact, Guarini had argued that 'Comedy ordinarily desires to give a prosperous end to its worst characters' (p. 527). Instead, comic dramatists might manage Medea by forcing her story of rupture and tragedy to contribute to happy endings, and to the restoration of the status quo. At the same time, though, even if her violence is not explicitly referenced, as it so frequently was in tragedy, including Medea in comedy (when she could so easily be excluded) inevitably introduces a troubling note of discomfort, just as it does when Greene's Mamillia, or the 'Two faithfull lovers', fondly compare their partners to either Jason or Medea. The romances of Whetstone's Plasmos and Greene's Mamillia end in heartbreak, as the readers would expect them to (although Greene does reunite Pharicles and Mamillia for the eventual sequel to his work, *The Triumphs of Pallas*). Comic or tragicomic drama of the period which incorporates Medea tends to end not with the dissolution of love affairs but with their ostensibly happy conclusions in marriage. Even so, however, tragedy and instability are hinted at, by the dramatists' choice to invoke this particular classical love affair, which is shot through with themes of filial disobedience, abandonment and the deaths of innocent children.

Medea in comedy and tragicomedy

As well as a suffering lover, Medea is, of course, a famous sorceress, and it is in this capacity that she can often feature in the comedy or tragicomedy of the period. The fear and suspicion that witchcraft aroused, in the sixteenth century in particular, might create the expectation that witches usually appeared in tragic drama. However, Frances Dolan has drawn attention to the paradox at the heart of the period's staging of the witch:

> [L]ate Tudor/early Stuart culture took witchcraft seriously enough to make it a criminal, capital offense. Yet, with the notable exception of *The Witch of Edmonton*, the stage overwhelmingly portrays witchcraft as trivial and humorous.[29]

H. W. Herrington suggests that the benign figure of the wise woman translated easily into comedy, and Dolan identifies Greene's Medea, in his self-proclaimed 'comicall history' *Alphonsus, King of Aragon* (c.1587–8) as an example of the benevolent power of the white witch.[30] As this would suggest, in order to stage her, Greene's comedy reshapes Medea substantially, making her into a facilitator of romance by means of magic, rather than a vengeful and rejected wife who uses her power to kill, and to escape triumphant after committing her crimes.

   Though Greene identifies the play as a comedy, the reality is not so simple, and the drama highlights its own peculiar blend of genres from the outset, in that it begins with Venus charging Calliope, the muse of epic poetry, to inspire scholars to tell the story of '*Alphonsus* warlike fame ... in the maner of a Comedie' (A4ᵛ).[31] Dubrow notes a work's title as one of the ways in which an author may set up what she terms a 'contract' with the reader, creating a specific set of expectations linked to the genre that has been named or referenced.[32] Greene's careful specifying of comedy, in his title and in Venus' lines, seems at odds with the play's bloodthirsty first half, which is clearly modelled on Marlowe's *Tamburlaine*, and which sees Alphonsus vowing to avenge the usurpation of his grandfather's throne, killing Flaminius, the current king of Aragon, and then setting his sights on the crown of the Turkish emperor Amuracke. Moreover, when Medea appears in Act 3, she does not seem to fit at all into a work that identifies itself so confidently as a comedy, for she is recognisable as the Ovidian sorceress, possessed of dark and alarming powers: specifically, she is able to raise the spirits of the dead (an ability Ovid's Medea claims in the *Metamorphoses*), summoning the shade of the prophet Calchas to predict Amuracke's fate.

Despite these alarming powers, however, Greene's figure is far more interested in helping others, without personal motive, than the classical Medea. Later in the play, when the Empress Fausta has been banished for her refusal to countenance a marriage between her enemy Alphonsus and her daughter Iphigina, Medea convinces mother and daughter to think again:

> Oh foolish Queene, what meant you by this talke?
> Those pratling speeches have undone you all.
> Do you disdaine to have that mighty Prince,
> I mean *Alphonsus*, counted for your sonne?
> I tell you *Fausta*, he is borne to be,
> The ruler of a mightie Monarchie:
> I must confesse the powers of *Amuracke*
> Be great; his confines stretch both far and neare,
> Yet are they not the third part of the lands,
> Which shall be ruled by *Alphonsus* hands,
> And yet you daine to call him sonne in law:
> But when you see his sharpe and cutting sword
> Piercing the heart of this your gallant gyrle,
> You'll curse the hour wherein you did denay
> To joyn *Alphonsus* with *Iphigina*. (E3ʳ–E3ᵛ)

Here, Medea is to be trusted, and her role is to warn against the potential violence of Alphonsus, rather than threatening bloodshed herself: it is through her counselling of Iphigina, Fausta and Amuracke that peace is achieved and, particularly, that the women's resistance to an advantageous marriage is dissipated.[33] Just as modern readers have frequently felt discomfited by Tamburlaine's brutal wooing of Zenocrate in Marlowe's play, however, here straightforward satisfaction with the match is also problematised, first by the ever-present threat of Alphonsus' violence, particularly against women: Medea warns that, if the proposed match does not come to pass, Fausta will watch Alphonsus 'piercing the heart of this your gallant gyrle' (E3ᵛ). Second, the uncertainty the audience feels about this match is only heightened by the presence of Medea herself: her own myth inevitably haunts Greene's *Comicall History*, and hints at the potentially tragic consequences of Iphigina's marriage to a foreign prince, against the wishes of her parents.

Medea's advice, and her ability to conjure visions which foretell the tragic outcome of the kingdom's continued opposition to Alphonsus, means that she eventually convinces Fausta of the benefits of the match. Iphigina, who had previously resisted Alphonsus' suit with contempt, accords with her mother's wishes, and Amuracke, who has repeatedly rejected Medea's counsel, is finally convinced to agree to the marriage, in the play's closing lines, by the princely birth of Alphonsus. However, while it is neat, and accords with Greene's identification of the play as a comedy, this ending remains difficult for the auditor to celebrate, because of Alphonsus' earlier brutality, and the reluctance of Iphigina and Fausta in particular to agree to the marriage. Any doubt such an auditor feels is only increased when Alphonsus compares his delight at winning his bride to Jason's joy 'when as he had obtaind, / The golden fleece by wise *Medeas* art' (I^v). This is an allusion that might initially seem a chivalrous acknowledgment of Medea's skill and assistance, but it also has the effect of disturbing the audience's satisfaction at the ending still further, leading them to conclude that, if Alphonsus really is like Jason, he may eventually come to regret the match. Dubrow points to what she calls 'authorial expectations' as shaping a reader's reaction to a text, suggesting 'what we know of the writer's previous work in that genre and of his general attitudes to tradition will shape the presuppositions with which we approach his work'.[34] As any reader of Ovid or Seneca would be well aware, Jason's conquest of the Fleece was only the first in a bloody chain of events, and, because of his fondness for the story, Greene's readers in particular would have learnt to associate a mention of Jason and Medea with the romantic disappointment of heroines, the upset of happy endings and the perils of a glib or selective reading, such as that which Alphonsus attempts here. Alphonsus' concluding nod towards a more familiar version of Medea's story, and his refusal to recognise the threat to himself that is implied by making Iphigina into a Medea-figure, epitomises the sense of danger that even a non-violent, helpful Medea, one who has apparently been radically altered, brings to comedy and to ostensibly happy endings.

Greene's decision to bring Medea onstage is highly unusual, particularly for a comedy. Such was the potency of her myth, however, that Medea's story could be used to compromise and unsettle comic or tragicomic drama even if she was only alluded to, or briefly mentioned. When he includes Medea in his comedies, Shakespeare also uses her to complicate tales of order restored and happy couplings achieved, tempering harmony with the memory of filial disobedience, betrayal and bloody revenge. In *Alphonsus*, Medea was used to counsel a young woman who was unwilling to accept the advantageous match that was offered to her. In *The Merchant of Venice*, Medea is naively invoked by Jessica as she prepares to elope with Lorenzo, against the wishes of her father. Jessica exclaims,

> ... In such a night
> Medea gathered the enchanted herbs
> That did renew old Aeson. (5.1.12–14)

Jessica is using Medea not as an example of a murderous revenger but as a lover who resisted paternal strictures (in Medea's case, those of her father Aeëtes) in order to pursue the object of her desire, and who aimed to keep him by rejuvenating his father. However, many in Shakespeare's audience would know well that Medea's devotion to Jason would end in the deaths of her children, and the destruction of Corinth. Even this particular episode is both evidence of Medea using her power benignly, to cure Jason's father, and a foreshadowing of a callous and brutal crime, her subsequent killing of his uncle Pelias by pretending to perform the same rite on him. Jonathan Bate argues that

> By activating Medea's destructive magic here, Shakespeare is contaminating a superficially lyrical interlude with a precursor text which is marked by bodily dismemberment that perhaps reawakens Shylock's demand for his pound of flesh ... What is more, the image of Medea gathering ingredients for her cauldron evokes a world of witchcraft akin to that of Shakespearian tragedy, not comedy.[35]

Elsewhere, Bassiano is compared to Jason, and Bate points out that these allusions to a faithless classical lover provoke the audience to question 'the future conduct of men'.[36] Perhaps, too, like Alphonsus' triumphant boasting at the conclusion of Greene's comedy, they invite Shakespeare's audience to consider the tragic consequences for a hero, if he proves himself too like his classical forebear. Like *The Alchemist*, *The Merchant of Venice* finds comedy in the misappropriation of classical allusion by insufficiently learned (or wilfully ignorant) characters. Here, though, unlike Mammon, Jessica is not ridiculous or risible, and, like the comparisons between Bassiano and Jason, her hopeful allusion to Medea's story worries the audience with the suggestion of tragedy far more than it makes them laugh. In *The Merchant of Venice*, the vital element of Medea's story is her disobedient desire for Jason, and the lengths to which she will go to achieve their marriage, as well as the betrayal and tragedy which follows, and which Jessica does not know of, or perhaps chooses to ignore. Elsewhere, it is once again Medea's magical power that Shakespeare incorporates into drama that ends happily. *The Tempest*, like both *The Merchant of Venice* and Greene's *Alphonsus*, is far from a straightforward comedy, however, and, in its blending of comic and tragic elements, is another drama that can be said to challenge an audience's idea of what comedy is, even as it ends with reconciliation and the promise of marriage.

Though it contains no direct mention of her name, Prospero's renunciation of his magical power in 5.1 of *The Tempest* represents Shakespeare's clearest and most famous engagement with Medea's story. He has the magician echo the Ovidian Medea when Prospero finally rejects his magic, frees Ariel, and is welcomed back into society at the play's close. Prospero declares,

> ... I have bedimmed
> The noontide sun, called forth the mutinous winds,
> And 'twixt the green sea and the azured vault
> Set roaring war – to the dread rattling thunder
> Have I given fire, and rifted Jove's stout oak
> With his own bolt; the strong-based promontory
> Have I made shake, and by the spurs plucked up
> The pine and cedar; graves at my command
> Have waked their sleepers, oped and let 'em forth
> By my so potent art. (5.1.41–50)

As has been frequently noted, Prospero's detailing of his power recalls Medea's boasts about her control over the natural world in *Metamorphoses* 7, here translated by Arthur Golding:

> I have compelled streams to run clean backward to their spring.
> By charms I make the calm seas rough, and make the rough seas
>   plain
> And cover all the sky with clouds and chase them thence again.
> By charms I raise and lay the winds, and burst the vipers jaw
> And from the bowels of the earth both stones and trees do draw.
> Whole woods and forests I remove; I make the mountains shake
> And even the earth itself to groan and fearfully to quake;
> I call up dead men from their graves; and thee, O lightsome moon,

I darken oft, though beaten brass abate thy peril soon.
Our sorcery dims the morning fair, and darks the sun at noon.
(268–77)[37]

Critics are now united in their acknowledgement of Shakespeare's use of both the Latin and the English versions of the *Metamorphoses*, but, as Jonathan Bate notes, Shakespeare's intentions are less clear: 'Were Jacobean audiences of *The Tempest* supposed to recognize the imitation and, if so, were they then supposed to reflect upon Prospero's art in relation to that of Ovid's Medea?'[38] Leonard Barkan ends his study of metamorphosis from Ovid to Shakespeare with a brief reading of this speech, and suggests that its importance lies in the comforting confirmation that Prospero and Medea are not the same: 'Prospero is a white magician and not an evil sorcerer like Medea; he is a father renewing the lives of his children rather than a child rejuvenating the father.'[39] Other critics, though, have seen Shakespeare's engagement with Medea's story as less clear-cut, and reflecting less positively on Prospero. There are two issues here: first, to what extent Shakespeare's audience could be expected to recognise the allusion to Medea and, second, what the allusion would suggest about Prospero, if it were recognised.

Frank Kermode, who sees a clear distinction between Prospero and Medea, suggests that part of Shakespeare's audience, at least, might recognise his use of Ovid, and the presentation of 'two opposed kinds of magic'.[40] Colin Burrow provides a close examination of what he terms the 'syntactic muting' of the Ovidian passage in Shakespeare's play and the elision of its more threatening elements, suggesting, 'The archaic magic and the vengeful impulses are both being written out – and many in Shakespeare's audience ... would hear that happening'.[41] In contrast, Charles and Michelle Martindale argue that 'educated members of the audience would recognise the presence of Ovid, but there is no question of any such complex interplay between the divergent meanings of the two texts as our more ingenious critics often suppose'.[42] I believe that Shakespeare did intend his audience (or at least some of them) to recognise Prospero's use of Medea's words, and also to reflect on the fact that Prospero is, at the play's climax, differentiating himself from the Colchian witch, who exults in the power that Prospero is choosing to reject: it is this differentiation, and the resultant quashing of Medea-like power, that is crucial to the happy resolution of the drama. At the same time, it is important to recognise that Shakespeare did not need to invoke Medea here at all and that, by doing so, he suggests uncomfortable truths about Prospero's own previously demonstrated capacity for dominance and cruelty: that is, his pre-existing similarity to the fearsome barbarian sorceress.[43] Throughout the play, Prospero has at points seemed troublingly close to Medea and to witches like her, particularly the alarming figure of the absent Sycorax, mother of Caliban.[44] Prospero himself is keen to stress how he (and his magic) are very different from Sycorax and hers. He describes Sycorax's exile to the island and her cruelty to his attendant spirit Ariel:

> This blue-eyed hag was hither brought with child,
> And here was left by th'sailors. Thou, my slave,
> As thou report'st thyself, was then her servant;
> And for thou wast a spirit too delicate
> To act her earthy and abhorred commands,
> Refusing her grand hests, she did confine thee
> By help of her more potent ministers,
> And in her most unmitigable rage,
> Into a cloven pine; within which rift
> Imprisoned thou didst painfully remain
> A dozen years, within which space she died
> And left thee there. (1.2.271–82)

Paradoxically Prospero's mention of Sycorax only emphasises their similarity, however, something that is stressed when he turns angrily on his servant, telling Ariel,

> If thou more murmur'st, I will rend an oak,
> And peg thee in his knotty entrails, till
> Thou hast howled away twelve winters. (1.2.296–9)

Here, in his threatening of Ariel, Prospero inadvertently collapses the apparent distinction between himself and Sycorax. His words also anticipate his famous allusion to Medea, in which he boasts that he has 'rifted Jove's stout oak' (5.1.45): here he threatens to imprison Ariel in an oak, rather than the pine used by Sycorax.[45] Prospero denigrates the absent Sycorax at every opportunity, but, as Diane Purkiss suggests, it is increasingly difficult to see Prospero as different from, and superior to, the witch:

> [T]he opposition that Prospero tries to make ... between himself and Sycorax is often too problematic to be sustained. It collapses so regularly that one must see these disintegrations as part of the play's strategy.[46]

Parallels have long been discerned between Sycorax and the Ovidian or Senecan Medea, and Bate has noted how Prospero's famous recantation speech also renders him akin to the classical sorceress, even as he rejects her power: 'The act of imitation here implies that all invocations of magical power are in some sense the same ... and therefore that Prospero and Medea are in some sense the same'.[47] Prospero thus seems doubly Medea-like, echoing her words, and, through his cruelty to Ariel, inadvertently revealing his own similarity to the Medea-like Sycorax.

However, in first invoking and then rejecting Medea's power, in 5.1, Prospero is signalling his desire to integrate back into society, as well as his recognition that he must reject his magic to achieve this. Medea's barbarity, her crimes and her final escape to the heavens all reflect the fact that her power is incompatible with human and early modern social mores. While tragic writing reflects this incompatibility in its punishment of Medea-like women, comedy or romance, genres concerned with what Daniel Vitkus terms 'forging bonds rather than breaking them',[48] must deal with Medea's power by rejecting it in favour of the conventionality, integration and conformity that the Colchian stands against (or by actually making Medea's power *serve* these conformist ends, as Greene's *Alphonsus* does). Indeed, if Prospero's similarity to Medea must be undermined, in order for the play to end happily, this is doubly true for his errant daughter Miranda. Lawrence Danson notes what he calls a 'comic feminization of authority' at the climax of this Shakespearean comedy and others, illustrated by the fact that 'Miranda chooses Ferdinand despite her father's feigned disapproval'.[49] However, it is crucial that any female subversion of authority that the play suggests is only allowed to extend so far. Prospero's disapproval is an act, and her father's eventual acceptance of her suitor means that Miranda, who has been identified as a Medea-figure by some critics because of her defiance of Prospero's wish that she shun Ferdinand, is never pushed to the murderous lengths of her classical forebear, who kills her brother and escapes Colchis to pursue her desires.[50] Medea's sorcery is an important and justly famous element of *The Tempest*, and it is invoked to suggest disturbing parallels between Medea and Prospero in particular, and between black and white magic, the barbarian outsider who kills her children and her brother, and the ostensibly benign magician who is reunited with both brother and child at the play's close. Her magic, recalled and rejected by Prospero, works with and against the comic and romantic resolutions of the play, simultaneously being subsumed by the play's move towards harmony and reconciliation, and acting as a disturbing reminder, as the play draws to a close, of the darker forces at work on the island.[51]

Shakespeare seldom names Medea: he does not do so in *The Tempest*, and although his use of her myth is beyond doubt, it is impossible to be certain that his audience would be able to recognise Shakespeare's adaptation of her words, and thus be in a position to reflect on the tragic potential that Shakespeare's play incorporates but does not realise. Medea's violent threat is far harder to miss in James Shirley's early Caroline comedy *The Schoole of Complement* (1625), and here again its purpose is to alarm and disconcert, though the play stops short of actual tragedy. Shirley would go on to work with the poet John Ogilby on his translations of the *Iliad* (1660) and *Odyssey* (1665), and his own dramatic works often demonstrate his interest in classical myth as a means to entertain and simultaneously unsettle his audience. Here, particularly horrifying aspects of Medea's myth are deliberately recalled, despite their being utterly unsuited to the genre of the work. In *The Schoole of Complement*, the despairing Infortunio tears up a letter that the object of his desire, Selina, has written to her future husband Rufaldo, and exclaims,

> This is *Medias* brother torne in pieces,
> And this the way where she with *Jason* flies ... (E^r)[52]

To the alarm of the servant Gorgon, Infortunio continues to address the pieces of the letter as if they were parts of Apsyrtus:

> GORGON: This?
> INFORTUNIO: And the hand beckens us
> To cry out murder.
> GORGON: Ile but hold it by the hand.
> INFORTUNIO: That's a leg o'th boy.
> GORGON: This sir, a leg, it shall goe with me then.
> INFORTUNIO: There, there 'tis, head and yellow curled locks,
> His eyes are full of teares, now they doe stare,
> To see where all his other members lye.
> GORGON: So I have all his quarters, Ile presently, sir, get poles for
> 'em, and hang 'em upon the Gates in their postures for you. (E^r)

Here, Infortunio runs mad, in a way that is reminiscent of, for example, the crazed reaction of Hieronimo to his son's murder, in Thomas Kyd's *The Spanish Tragedy*. Gorgon indulges Infortunio's insistence that the scraps of paper are the body parts of the dismembered Apsyrtus, and promises to display them on poles so that Infortunio, and others, can contemplate them: a reference to the practice of displaying traitors' heads on pikes in London. Left alone, Infortunio pursues his use of Medea's myth, and embarks on an insane soliloquy in which he imagines Selina and Rufaldo as Medea and Jason, and describes the fratricide, and the reaction of Medea's father Aeëtes, which would have been familiar to readers of Ovid's *Tristia*:

> But she and *Jason* are both slipt, and *Argos* is
> Sayling home to Greece, see how the waves
> Doe tosse the Vessell, and the windes conspire
> To dash it 'gainst a Rocke, it rides upon
> A watery mountaine, and is hid in cloudes,
> It cannot stay there, now, now, it tumbles,
> Three fatham beneath Hell, let 'em goe,
> Here comes the Father of *Medea* now,
> Calling in vaine unto the gods, and spies
> His Sonnes limbes throwne about, in stead of flowers,
> To his Daughters nuptials he does take 'em up,
> He knowes the face, and now he teares his haire,
> And raves, and cryes *Medea*, poore old man,
> Command a funerall pile for thy yong Childe,
> And lay the pretty limbs on, from whose ashes
> Shalt have another Sonne i'th shape of *Phoenix*.
> Shall I? excellent! Prepare a fire
> All of sweet wood for my sweet boy, a fire, a fire.
>
> *Exit* (E^r–E^v)

In his soliloquy, Infortunio dwells at unusual length on Medea's escape with Jason and her killing of her brother, and while his use of her myth would sit more comfortably in a bloody and classical revenge tragedy like *Titus Andronicus*, or in a tragedy geared towards exciting pity, like Robert Baron's *Mirza*, here it is bizarre and discomfiting. Gorgon is comical in his frantic efforts to appease Infortunio and gather together the scattered paper, but Infortunio himself seems, disturbingly, to relish his unclassical vision of Jason and Medea being wrecked in the *Argo*, and tumbling 'Three fatham beneath Hell'(E^v). On the one hand, just as *The Tempest* rejects Medea's magic, Shirley's use of Medea subsumes her violence into his chosen genre, in that Selina and Infortunio are eventually united without the need for such brutality, and the play ends with the apparent resolution of discord and with romantic harmony restored. On the other hand, Shirley's repeated uses of Medea's story, which are remarkable for their interest in the most violent aspects of her legend, must be intended to disturb the audience's complacency, and to suggest the potential for tragedy, particularly given that, like Greene's Alphonsus, Shirley's hero imagines his future bride as a Medea-figure. He identifies Rufaldo as a Jason-figure, but by the end of the play the ominously named Infortunio has replaced him as Selina's husband, thereby seeming to deliberately write himself a part in the grisly tragedy he had invoked, in his earlier jealous fury.

In other comic works, too, Shirley demonstrates his awareness of the flexibility of classical myth, and the extent to which its adaptation can allow darker and more tragic elements to intrude into even an apparently happy ending: in *The Constant Maid* (1640), for example, Playfair and his fiancée stage the wedding of Helen of Troy and Paris, as a way of tricking her uncle into witnessing and endorsing their real marriage ceremony. Their deception is successful, and the bride's tyrannical uncle accepts the match, but the classically educated audience member Shirley envisages would surely look more doubtfully on the outcome, given the deliberately inauspicious nature of the example. Like Greene's and Shakespeare's references to her in their drama, Shirley's use of Medea in *The Schoole of Complement* demonstrates a complex aspect of her appeal, one which sees her challenging the 'rules' of the genre she inhabits, importing the 'aesthetic and emotional discomfort' that Verna A. Foster argues is so typical of the popular genre of tragicomedy.[53] Medea, and her story, can be introduced into comedy to unsettle the auditor or reader with a hint at tragedy, and (particularly where romantic matches are involved) to suggest that endings might not be quite so happy as they seem, just as Jason's and Medea's love story did not end with their triumphant escape from Colchis.

Parodying Medea

Thus far, it has been possible to divide comic treatments of Medea into two groups. The first group is those, such as the prose works of Greene and Whetstone, or Jonson's *The Alchemist*, which play on characters' and readers' knowledge of her story, and make sport of those who might understand it insufficiently. The second group, comprising Greene's *Alphonsus*, Shakespeare's *The Merchant of Venice* and *The Tempest*, and Shirley's *The Schoole of Complement*, sees Medea's alarming reputation for sorcery, disobedience and murder casting an unsettling and tragic shadow over comic or happy endings, even if Medea herself sometimes seems to facilitate these endings (as she does in Greene's play). There can, of course, be overlap between the two groups: an audience might smile at Jessica's determined misreading of Medea's legend, in *The Merchant of Venice*, while simultaneously fearing for the tragic outcome to her love affair with Lorenzo, which her use of Medea's story suggests. Later, in Thomas Meriton's tragicomic closet drama *The Wandring Lover* (1658), the target of comedy is the classically knowledgeable reader outside the text, who might be fooled into anticipating tragedy by an unexpected use of Medea's name. Here, a conventional subplot, in which a merchant's daughter at first resists and then accords with her father's choice of suitor, seems as if it will be fatally destabilised, by the playwright's worrying decision to name his disobedient heroine Medea. By the end of the play, though, the knowing auditor, who complacently expects at least the suggestion of tragedy as soon as this name is mentioned, has been teased and then is deliberately disappointed, as Meriton's play contains few of the disturbing, quasi-tragic elements of *Alphonsus, The Tempest, The Merchant of Venice* or *The Schoole of Complement*.[54] In her work on early modern literary naming, Laurie Maguire (drawing on Jean Anouilh, and speaking of Helen of Troy) points out that 'when your name is Helen (in the sixteenth century at least) there is only one part you can play'.[55] Medea, as a name, might seem even more prescriptive than Helen, the behaviour of a character named as such even more predictable, because of the rarity of the name and the notoriety of the story it evokes. However, it is this apparent predictability that allows Meriton to upset his auditors' expectations, and to enjoy a joke at their expense, by having his Medea obediently acquiesce to her father's wishes, and do so exactly as she is told, without even the brief acknowledgement of her namesake's traditional role that Greene gave his audience, at the end of *Alphonsus*.

If these two related approaches, that of using Medea to hint at tragedy within a comedy and that of using her story to make sport of the practice of reading the classics, are dominant in the period, a third type of comic treatment of Medea's story can be discerned in the latter half of the seventeenth century. This is the instinct, particularly apparent in the burlesqued translations of Ovid which appeared in the Restoration, to make classical characters themselves (rather than those who read them insufficiently or wrongly) into figures of fun. Given the terrible nature of her story, this parodying treatment of Medea is perhaps the most surprising of all comic uses of her myth, and yet it is one that is informed by cultural change in the seventeenth century, just as more sympathetic treatments of Medea the infanticide, in the eighteenth and nineteenth centuries, have been linked to a greater empathy for the figure of the child-killing mother. Anthony Harris has shown that convictions for witchcraft decreased during James's reign, and suggests that

> The declining fear of witchcraft (rather than a loss of belief in its existence) is reflected in the drama of the post-1625 period. In contrast to the seriousness with which the subject was treated in nearly all the Jacobean works, it became increasingly a source of humour, particularly in the Restoration theatre.[56]

No longer seen as such a real threat to the lives and livelihoods of seventeenth-century people, witchcraft can be presented irreverently, and Medea made into a figure of fun, as she is not in earlier comedies (e.g., Greene's *Alphonsus*, which does not make sport of Medea, even if it reduces her to the status of matchmaker). In drama, so too in other forms of literature: for example, the burlesqued translations of Ovid's *Heroides* that became popular in the Restoration treat Medea with exultant disrespect, parodying her power in ways which reflect both a dismissive attitude to witchcraft and the burlesquers' determination to ridicule other, rival translations of Ovid.

Decades after he first employed her myth, in *The Schoole of Complement* (1625), James Shirley returned to Medea in *The Triumph of Beautie* (printed 1646), and in this second use it is possible to discern the movement towards a more parodic treatment of Medea, Jason and Apsyrtus, which would have been unthinkable to earlier English authors. Shirley's work is a masque, or kind of extravagant entertainment involving music, storytelling and song, which would often be performed at court in the reigns of James I and Charles I. The masque itself deals with the Trojan prince Paris' judgement of the goddesses Venus, Juno and Minerva, the contest which resulted in his rape of Helen and the outbreak of the Trojan War. Shirley's anti-masque, a shorter, often deliberately comic entertainment which might precede the masque, or (as in *The Triumph of Beautie*) be weaved between the acts, takes as its subject Medea's equally tragic story and, specifically, her flight with Jason after his conquest of the Fleece and her killing of her young brother.[57] This is the same episode that Shirley referenced at length in *The Schoole of Complement*, where it was used to incorporate the suggestion of tragedy into an otherwise conventional romantic comedy. Here, as its use in the anti-masque would suggest, the legend is not treated at all seriously. Shirley, clearly taking his cue from Shakespeare's *A Midsummer Night's Dream*, presents the futile efforts of a group of shepherds, led by Bottle and comprising others such as Crab, Clout and Toad-Stoole, to dramatise the conquest of the Fleece, in order to entertain Paris.[58] In Shirley's work, which was printed during the closure of the theatres, and was, as the 1646 title-page states, performed by a group of gentlemen 'at a private Recreation', comedy springs from the lowly origins of his shepherds, and their misunderstanding of the elevated classical tragedy they have chosen to enact.[59] In contrast, the educated elite of Shirley's audience would know it well, having access not only to Ovid's Latin but also to hugely popular English translations of Ovid's *Heroides*, by Turberville and Saltonstall (as well as to John Sherburne's less commercially successful effort), and of his *Metamorphoses*, by Golding and Sandys. In the course of this 'backstage drama' (to use Julie Sanders's useful term) Shirley's shepherds squabble over who gets to play the Golden Fleece, and make nonsensical suggestions such as excluding the role of Jason, or having Medea and the dragon guarding the Fleece played by the same performer.[60] Shirley's main debt for this clowning is clearly to the mechanicals' staging of the Ovidian tale of Pyramus and Thisbe, in Shakespeare's *A Midsummer Night's Dream*, but it is important that while Shakespeare also elected to render the story of a tragic woman (Thisbe) comical, through the bungling of his insufficient players, Shirley deliberately chooses a far more violent and contentious heroine, playing on his audience's knowledge of Medea's story, and testing the boundaries between comedy and tragedy even more daringly, by making such a terrible story into something so risible.

Here, the tragedy and comedy which Shirley blends in his anti-masque affect, and perhaps infect, one another. The shepherds' ludicrous squabbling obviously undermines the gravity, and tragedy, of Medea's story, which is mishandled by the kind of low characters more suited to comedy. At the same time, though, despite the fact that she does not appear, Shirley's choice of Medea as the focus of the shepherds' story introduces an element of darkness to the comedy that is absent from the mechanicals' production in *A Midsummer Night's Dream*, but springs from Medea's implied threat to men and kingdoms: she might die, but the Ovidian Thisbe is without a doubt far less alarming than Medea, and thus, arguably, less patently unsuitable for a comic treatment. This blending of comedy and tragedy recalls how the audience of *The Merchant of Venice*, or *The Tempest*, is unsettled by a mention of the sorceress, even if the threat she suggests can never be realised in comedy or romance. In fact, while Bate sees hints at the murder of Pelias in Jessica's mention of Aeson in *The Merchant of Venice*, Shirley goes much further, in that his comic anti-masque, like *The Schoole of Complement*, specifically mentions Medea's terrible violence, rather than simply alluding to her magical power, and relying on the audience's ability to understand the full import of the reference, as Shakespeare's play does. One of the company, Hob, worries he is too tall to play Medea's luckless brother Apsyrtus, but Bottle earnestly assures him that his height is irrelevant, since 'You must be cut a peeces, and have your limbs throwne about the waves' (A4ᵛ). There is no suggestion as to how this act of gruesome violence might be achieved in performance, and, perhaps to the disappointment of the audience, the shepherds' production never materialises, as the action shifts back to Paris' musings. The calculated use of Medea, though, has unsettled the audience, hinting at incipient tragedy, or tragedy that has been only narrowly averted, as Shakespeare's references do, in *The Tempest* and *The Merchant of Venice*. Classical characters themselves are not exactly mocked here, as they are in the Restoration burlesques: since the production never comes to pass, they are not manifested onstage, as Shakespeare's Pyramus and Thisbe are, and it is the shepherds who are the real target of laughter. What *The Triumph of Beautie* achieves, though, in its deliberate mishandling of such a notorious story, is a new way of thinking about Medea's story comically, one that embraces rather than elides the most notorious and exaggerated elements of her tale (such as her slaughter of her brother), and turns these to the service of the period's growing interest in tragicomedy and parody.

In the Restoration, other works, whether drama, poetry or prose, are even more explicit than Shirley's masque in their crude and comic undermining of Medea's power, and such works are particularly remarkable for their emphasis on the erotic or sexually transgressive elements of her story, which they use to entertain their readers and diminish Medea and her achievements, often while slyly purporting to educate their readers. For example, in his work of erotic prose fiction *Erotopolis, The Present State of Betty-Land* (1684), the Restoration wit Charles Cotton claims to teach his readers (while also poking fun at their reverential attitude to the classical past) by explaining Medea's rejuvenation of Aeson as an attempt to hush up the unsavoury truth:

> Aged *Aeson* was so improvident, as to get a Clap in his old Age, but his Daughter *Medea* so well sweat him in her *Cornelius*'s Tub, that she recovered him, which gave an occasion to the Poets to feign, that she boyl'd him so long till she renewed his Age. (B4ᵛ)⁶¹

Cotton's elaborately ridiculous and crude explanation of the 'truth' behind the rejuvenation pokes fun both at the myth and at other authors' attempts to rationalise or account for the enchantment: following the ancient author Palaephatus, it was often explained as evidence of Medea's use of hair dye, and Cotton takes an already trivialising explanation and makes it into an episode of grotesque and entertaining scurrility, with his reference to venereal disease.[62] This mockery of Medea's capabilities had surfaced before the Restoration, in Shirley's parodying of the dismemberment of her brother in *The Triumph of Beautie*, though there Medea and Apsyrtus themselves were noticeably absent, and it was the foolish players who were the real figures of fun. Here, in the more daring Restoration fiction, it is the classical characters themselves who are mocked, in ways which may be informed by the dramatic drop in prosecutions and executions of witches in the reign of Charles II, and a concurrent move away from seeing them as figures to be feared.[63]

Another way of belittling Medea's disturbing abilities is evident in *The Enchanted Island* (1667), Dryden and William Davenant's reworking of *The Tempest*. In this play, Sycorax, Shakespeare's absent Medea-figure, and a troubling reflection of Prospero, is revived, and made the sister of Caliban: however, she is deprived of the magical power of her Shakespearean and classical forebears. Sexually uninhibited and racially other, she is fondly and patronisingly described as 'My dear Blobber-lips' (3.3.12) by her lover Trincalo, who later tells another casta-way, Stephano, how he found her having sex with Caliban: 'an hour ago under an Elder-tree, upon a sweet Bed of Nettles, singing Tory, Rory, and Ranthum, Scantum, with her own natural Brother' (4.2.106–9).[64] Stripped of Medea's magic, despite being the offspring of a witch and the Devil, and made instead into a crudely sexualised figure of fun, Sycorax is a comically and troublingly diminished echo of Shakespeare's Medea-figure, one who enjoys almost no control over her situation, for as Trincalo tells Stephano, 'to tell thee true, I marry'd her to be a great man and so forth' (4.2.111–12). While Jason almost always takes Medea with him when he leaves Colchis, Trincalo cruelly dismisses Sycorax, as he prepares to leave the island, telling her 'You are partly Fish and may swim after me' (5.2.252–3). She can only watch as her lover sails away, however, and like the abandoned Medeas created by Chaucer ('The Legend of Medea') and George Whetstone ('The Pitious Complaint of Medea'), she is shown to be helpless despite his cruel suggestion of her ability. Dryden and Davenant have brought onstage the Medea-figure that Shakespeare only hints at, but in so doing they have stripped her of all her power and rendered her ridiculous. There is magic present on Dryden and Davenant's isle, but it is not Medea's, and the two Restoration playwrights bring forth a distorted Medea-figure in order to demonstrate her impo-tence and to make reductive sport of her racial and sexual difference.

Moreover, the playwrights' determination to exclude Medea from the play is underscored by their decision to cut Prospero's renunciation of his powers, which, in its troubling allusion to the sorceress's magic, constituted Shakespeare's most extensive engagement with Medea's story, and which is, as a result, probably the best-known early modern reference to the Colchian sorceress today. Dryden and Davenant do retain a veiled allusion to Medea's skill, from Act 5 of Shakespeare's play. Gonzalo, seeing Sycorax and Caliban, takes over the Shakespearean Sebastian's question to Antonio, and asks Prospero, 'But pray, Sir, what are those mishapen Creatures?' (5.2.223). In reply, the Restoration Prospero, like his Jacobean predecessor, alludes to the magical powers enjoyed by the Ovidian Medea and witches like her, telling Gonzalo,

> Their Mother was a Witch, and one so strong
> She would controul the Moon, make Flows
> And Ebbs, and deal in her command without
> Her power. (5.2.224–7)

In both versions of *The Tempest*, this pronouncement may recall Medea's story, but it is less than a ringing endorsement of Sycorax's ability: as Kermode points out, the words 'without / Her power' can be interpreted variously, and might imply that Shakespeare's Sycorax, like other seventeenth-century witches, does not enjoy autonomous power, instead relying on 'diabolical agents'.[65] What is most important, though, is that in the Restoration adaptation Prospero does not make his final veiled allusion to Medea, as he does at the beginning of Shakespeare's Act 5, and he rejects the use of magic without recalling such a contentious example of rebellion and resistance to kingly authority.[66] In their cutting of Prospero's renunciation speech, Dryden and Davenant exclude the final Shakespearean hints at the magician's disturbing similarity to Medea, preferring, in their reductive portrayal of Sycorax, to parody those facets of Medea's character (the barbarian and the desiring woman) which were more commonly represented as terrifying and alarming, in early modern tragedy or translation.

Nowhere is the instinct to debase Medea more apparent than in the two Restoration burlesques of Ovid's *Heroides* 6, Hypsipyle's epistle to Jason, by Alexander Radcliffe and Matthew Stevenson. Such parodies of the classics have not always been admired: Douglas Bush dismisses them as 'tawdry stuff', and divides them into 'dull and obscene, and merely dull'.[67] More recently, however, burlesques of the *Heroides* in particular have attracted more positive attention, in part at least because of their fascinating relation to earlier translations.⁶⁸ The three Restoration collections that burlesque the *Heroides* in this way are the anonymous *Ovidius Exulans, or Ovid Travestie* (1673), which includes only the letters of Dido, Laodamia, Hero, Leander and Penelope; *The Wits Paraphras'd, or, Paraphrase upon paraphrase in a burlesque on the several late translations of Ovids Epistles* (1680, attributed to Matthew Stevenson); and *Ovid Travestie*, produced by Alexander Radcliffe in 1680, and in 1681 issued once again, under the title *Ovid Travestie, A Burlesque Upon Ovids Epistles. The Second Edition, Enlarged With Ten Epistles Never Before Printed*. Susan Wiseman points out that when the *Heroides* are adapted or translated in early modern England the reader is often encouraged to read 'outside the text to the immediate, and often political, world of its interpreters'.⁶⁹ The burlesquers of Hypsipyle's epistle sought to entertain not only by undermining and parodying the power of Medea herself, as Shirley begins to do, but also by delighted anachronism, situating their burlesqued heroines firmly in a seventeenth-century English context, and all the while engaging combatively with one another, or with the Dryden-Tonson collection of 1680 (discussed in Chapter 2), one of the most popular and ambitious translation projects of the period.

Stevenson's *The Wits Paraphras'd* uses its title to remind his readers of Dryden's discourse on translation, in his 'Preface to Ovid's Epistles' (in which the Laureate famously identified paraphrase as the ideal mode of translation). Moreover, Stevenson's 'Preface to Ovid's Epistles' (which in its very title apes Dryden's preface to the Dryden-Tonson Ovid) very clearly acknowledges the earlier collection, in which Ovid was 'so Elegantly Translated by the most Eminent wits of the Times' (A5ʳ). This apparent admiration soon gives way to thinly disguised jibes, with Stevenson professing wonder

> that so many able Workmen should joyn their Shreds and Thrums together, to dress him up in a Buffoons Coat, when I really conceit (and I question not but there are more Fools in the World of my Opinion) that I in my own simple naked shape, come nearer the Original than the best on 'em. (A5ᵛ–A6ʳ)⁷⁰

As Wiseman observes, such a mockery of the patchwork approach to translating Ovid is clearly a reference to the miscellaneous nature of the earlier, multi-authored translation.⁷¹ Stevenson's words also betray a desire to joke at the expense of the unknowing reader, however, to see how far he can push his burlesque, which claims to be a 'simple naked shape', or more accurate and perfect version of Ovid, before the 'Fools' of his readership

152 Early Modern Medea

begin to suspect that his is not, despite his claims, the most faithful edition of Ovid available. Here, the sport with the idea of the reader recalls Robert Greene's and Thomas Meriton's deliberate and playful confounding of audience expectation, in their dramatising of benign or obedient Medeas. Similarly, Radcliffe's *Ovid Travestie* responds to earlier efforts to translate Ovid: but this time, Stevenson's burlesque is the target, rather than the Dryden-Tonson Ovid, and Stevenson is accounted 'an unlucky Pretender to Poetry' (3^v), who is urged to 'consider, and follow any other Employment, more agreeable with his Genius (if he have any) then that of Poetry'(2^r).[72] Clearly irritated by the appearance of a rival, Radcliffe takes issue, line by line, with virtually the whole of Stevenson's preface, and such a close response encourages, and virtually urges, the reader to make a decision as to the winner of this competition in burlesque.[73]

Radcliffe's annoyance was almost certainly informed by the similarity of Stevenson's approach to parodying Ovid. Both Radcliffe and Stevenson are very clearly concerned with the experience of their Restoration readers, but they afford their female letter writers scant respect: indeed, Kerrigan suggests an unfounded male 'paranoia' about the supposed rise of female readers and writers as informing the derisive attacks of the burlesques.[74] Moreover, if one effect of what Kerrigan calls 'falsetto production', and what Elizabeth D. Harvey has termed 'transvestite ventriloquism', the appropriation of a female voice by a male author, is that the apparently female voice might be controlled in troubling ways by the male author, the Restoration burlesquers go further, in that neither grant Medea a letter at all, ignoring *Heroides* 12.[75] In both collections, though, Hypsipyle is made to rail at Jason and about Medea, in coarse and earthy language which betrays Radcliffe's and Stevenson's delight in bringing both dignified classical women low. In Stevenson's earlier collection, a workmanlike argument to the epistle (lifted in its entirety from Elkanah Settle's translation in the Dryden-Tonson collection) quickly gives way to deliberate colloquialism and scurrility. Stevenson's Hypsipyle complains that Jason has humiliated her by forcing her to rely on others for news of his voyage, and exclaims,

> Yet I cou'd cease my jealous grunting,
> Cou'd I but say you are my Bunting.
> But ah! That hope is vain! A Witch
> Has got my *Bunting* by the Breech. — (G3^v)[76]

Stevenson follows the narrative of the Ovidian epistle, but at every point he is keen to diminish what he has found in Settle's translation.

Kerrigan rightly notes the burlesquers' misogynistic interest in feminine bodily functions and the ways in which these are 'violently reinscribed and produced as evidence against female nature', but here, Jason's bodily responses are similarly foregrounded and made into sport.[77] For example, Settle's Hypsipyle scornfully recalls Jason's feigned grief at leaving her: ''Twixt sighs and Tears, thro' those false gales did pour / These falser shours, till grief could speak no more' (M6ᵛ); and in Stevenson's hands Jason's distance from the ideal hero is underlined and his emasculating inability to control his bodily reactions parodied, as Hypsipyle recalls how he 'bubbles at the Snout, and maunders, / As if your Nose had got the Glaunders' (G5ʳ).[78]

Also apparent is both burlesquers' interest in entertaining their readers by adding salacious details about Medea's witchcraft, her barbarism, and, linked to both, her demanding and transgressive sexuality: in this, the burlesques recall the uncomfortable misogynistic and racist attitudes to Sycorax in Dryden and Davenant's *The Enchanted Island*. In his version of Hypsipyle's epistle, Settle's Medea was a 'Barbarian Harlot' (M7ʳ), a close translation of Ovid's 'barbara paelex' (6.81), but to Stevenson's Hypsipyle she is a 'lewd *Barbarian* Strumpet' (G5ᵛ) and a 'Trallop' (G6ʳ). Along with wishing for Medea's suicide, Hypsipyle imagines taking a specifically sexualised revenge on her rival, exclaiming, 'I shou'd have riv'd the Witches Placket' (G7ʳ): that is, torn her apron, where apron is suggestive of female sexual organs.[79] In Radcliffe's even more explicit offering, Medea is a 'nasty Quean' (C3ʳ), and

> A Witch, a Bitch, in whom the Devil dwells,
> Whose Face is Made of Grease and Wall-nut-Shells.
> ... A plaguy Jade, who curses Night and Noon,
> And houls, and heaves her Arse against the Moon. (C3ʳ–C3ᵛ)

We have seen, in Chapter 2, that earlier translators were keen to emphasise Medea's barbarism, and Radcliffe goes further, emphasising not just Medea's dark complexion (elsewhere she is 'a Bacon-visag'd Gipsey' and a 'Tawny-Trull' with 'course black Skin', C2ʳ, C2ᵛ, Dʳ), but also the transgressive sexuality (particularly, the charge of sexual congress with the Devil) that was so associated with witchcraft in the early modern imagination, and turning this into a ridiculous and deliberately debasing parody.[80] Radcliffe's Medea is an amalgamation of all the very worst taboos of witchcraft, including cannibalism (Hypsipyle cannot leave her children safely with Medea, since 'it is ten to one, the Hag would eat 'em', C4ʳ) and bestiality (Hypsipyle speculates that 'Her Children have been gotten in a Bog / By some large pintled Wolf, or mastive Dog' (C4ʳ),[81] and imagines Jason and 'the hell-born Toad / Engendring in a Tree that's near the Road' (C4ᵛ). Like Stevenson's, Radcliffe's Hypsipyle fantasises a sexualised punishment for Medea, one that seems to culminate in Jason's being forced to eat her sexual organs:

> And, for your Fire-brand there, that loathsome Hag,
> I would contrive the greatest Pain and Plague:
> Her Nose being slit, to make her look more grim,
> Like a *Spred-Eagle* on her Face should seem:[82]
> Her coarse black Skin should from her Flesh be rent;
> I'd run a Spit into her Fundament;
> And stake her to the ground; and when I'd don't,
> I'd cut both Lips from her insatiate ... [83]
> And, Jason, this thy Punishment should be,
> Thou shouldst eat those, so oft have swallow'd thee. (C4ᵛ–Dʳ)

To a modern reader, this is eye-watering stuff, and it is easy to see why critics such as Bush have passed over such parodies rapidly. However, that the epistle is supposed to be in equal parts horrifying and amusing is suggested by its climax: to the damning final couplet 'May she be burnt to Cinders as a Witch, / And you be hang'd for loving of the Bitch' (Dʳ), Radcliffe adds the postscript 'Yours, as you have us'd her, HYPSIPYLE. For John Jason, to be left at his house, in a hollow Tree, between Barnet and St. Albans' (Dʳ). Such references to contemporary life are not unusual in translations of the period, and in both versions of Hypsipyle's epistle they are intended to provoke laughter through bathos, and also, perhaps, to comment satirically on the sexual immorality and violence of Radcliffe's and Stevenson's own age.[84] Stevenson's collection attacks the political convictions of the many Tory contributors to *Ovid's Epistles* (such as Dryden and Aphra Behn), having his Hypsipyle remind Jason that she came with 'a Dowry / Enough for any filching *Tory*' (G6ᵛ). Radcliffe's parody is dated 'From So-hoe Fields, Feb. 27. 1670/80' (Cᵛ), and the argument of the epistle describes Jason as 'a quondam Foot-man', engaged not in the quest for the Golden Fleece, but in a foot race 'from Barnet to St. Albans', which he won with the unfair assistance of Medea, 'a Gipsey, and Strouler in those Parts' (Cʳ). The fury of Radcliffe's Hypsipyle seems at times almost to jump off the page, and she goes further than previous English incarnations (who have wished for Medea's suicide), instead hoping that both Medea and Jason are executed, Medea by the traditional witch's punishment of being burned alive. Consistently, though, horror and comedy are made to co-exist, by touches such as the deliberately bathetic explanation of how 'John Jason' should receive his letter. All parties are enthusiastically diminished by these burlesques, and the precarious balance between exaggerating Medea's barbarism, her sexuality and her diabolical magic, on the one hand, and rewriting Ovid's tale as a sordid contemporary love triangle, on the other hand, is an unsustainable one, and means that the suggestion of tragedy and threat inevitably, and deliberately, collapses into ridicule.

C. S. Lewis argues that 'The pleasure of myth depends hardly at all on such usual narrative attractions as suspense or surprise. Even at a first hearing it is felt to be inevitable', but both Stevenson's and Radcliffe's parodic rewritings rely on surprise, and particularly on the distance between the reader's expectation of the myth and what they are presented with here.[85] So a reader who knows Settle's contribution to the Dryden-Tonson collection will enjoy Stevenson's sly response to it, while one with even the most basic knowledge of Medea's story will appreciate the deliberately jarring movement in Radcliffe's contribution, between the famous classical story and the mundane, provincial and present-day setting with which he frames it. Dubrow points out that parody should not be regarded as entirely at odds with its chosen genre, but rather as working within a genre in the same way as an imitation.[86] Stevenson's and Radcliffe's versions of Ovid are translations of a sort, and they clearly (if irreverently) participate in the period's debate over how best to translate the classics, implying, mockingly, that a close, accurate translation of Latin into English is neither necessary nor as interesting as what they present. Simultaneously, they also represent the climax of another Renaissance movement: the tradition of treating Medea's story, her magic and sometimes even her crimes, with a deliberate irreverence, in order to entertain, mislead or shock knowing or unknowing readers.

Edith Hall notes a vogue for comic dramatic entertainments featuring Medea in the nineteenth century, including James Robinson Planché's *The Golden Fleece; or, Jason in Colchis and Medea in Corinth* (1845) and *Jason and Medea: A Ramble after a Colchian* (1878), and argues that the comic as well as the tragic Medea could be relevant to nineteenth-century thinking about, or legislation on, divorce, infanticide and the rights of women, if Medea's plight prompts an audience to reflect on Jason's unreasonable behaviour as a husband.[87] As this chapter has shown, earlier authors also saw some kind of comic potential in Medea's story. This does not mean that they necessarily shy away from the more contentious and violent aspects of her legend: in fact, they might often go out of their way to include references to her magical power, her aggressive pursuit of Jason, his abandonment of her, and her terrible revenge, despite the fact that none of these sit comfortably in comedy. In fact, if Renaissance tragedy in particular employs Medea precisely as we might expect, as symbolic of disorder and destruction that is punished, as the classical witch's crimes are not, comic uses of Medea might do the opposite, challenging the reader's perception of what is appropriate in such a genre, and destabilising or questioning happy endings even as they are represented. In their enthusiasm for the experience of reading (apparent in the prose works), and their engagement with generic instability (the comic and tragicomic drama) and with contemporary debates on translation (the burlesques), all these works can be said to be finely attuned to the literary developments of their own time. In the final chapter, I shall explore how Medea's controversial career was used to shed light on far more pressing concerns, both religious and political, in sixteenth- and seventeenth-century England.

5
Political Medea

In writing that was somehow concerned with England's present or historical politics, Medea's threat, which is rooted in her magic, her foreignness and her ruthless violence, was often appropriated to teach lessons to the monarch or the country about the damage that an untempered will can wreak on the body politic. Introducing the 1701 edition of his translations of Seneca's tragedies, which comprised *Medea* (first printed 1648), *Phaedra and Hippolytus* (i.e., *Hippolytus*) and *Troades*, Edward Sherburne suggests,

> [I]n the order they lie exposed to view, they seem to offer this Political Lesson, that the hidden Malice of revengeful (though seemingly reconcil'd) Enemies, together with the flagitious, unbridled Lusts of dissolute Princes, have been the Ruin of most flourishing Kingdoms (A7ʳ)

Here, Medea's threat is that of 'hidden Malice', which contains the potential to destroy kingdoms, just as Medea betrayed her father, killed Pelias and razed Creon's Corinthian palace.

Sherburne was not alone in finding contemporary political applications for Medea's myth. Sometimes, her power could be acknowledged and then tamed, made benign and bent to the service of male rule, as it is in the mayoral pageants by Thomas Heywood and Anthony Munday, produced in the first decades of the seventeenth century. The attraction of Medea's legend sprang from her association with the Golden Fleece, which in turn appealed because these pageants were produced under the auspices of the Drapers' Company: so in Munday's *The Triumphs of the Golden Fleece* (1623), written to commemorate the instalment of Martin Lumley as Mayor of London, Medea remains silent, but Munday describes her handing over the Fleece 'in regard of her affection to the

DRAPERS Companie, to whom she gave it freely' (34–5).[1] In his earlier pageant *Metropolis Coronata* (1615), which celebrated the investiture of John Jolles as Mayor, Medea's 'powerfull charmes' (122) are acknowledged, but it is the potential of Jacobean men that is really lauded, with the shade of London's first Mayor, Henry Fitz-Alwine, telling Jolles,

> You are our Jason, Londons glorie,
> Now going to fetch that fleece of Fame,
> That ever must renowne your name. (129–31)[2]

Such pronouncements recall the sidelining of Medea's achievement in Book 5 of Gower's fourteenth-century *Confessio Amantis*, in which Amans can only remember the part Jason played in the conquest of the Fleece. In fact, though, neither Medea nor Jason, nor even the Fleece, are really the focus here, for, as Tracey Hill points out:

> Although the whole of *Metropolis Coronata* is founded on the myth of Jason and the Argonauts, Munday makes it clear that the immediate pretext for the myth's use – celebrating the traditions of the Drapers' Company – is much more significant as well as more historically valid than such pagan narratives.[3]

In Heywood's *Londini Status Pacatus* (1639), again produced for the Drapers' Company, to mark the investiture of Henry Garway, Medea is allowed to speak (after she has been explained as representing 'Counsell'), but she does so with almost no reference to her traditional bloody story, instead describing 'the worth of golden wooll', and by extension 'The rich Commerce and noblenesse of your Trade' (348, 366, 398).[4]

The mayoral pageants make use of Medea in ways that are simultaneously unusual and conservative: she is not demonised, instead being welcomed into the celebrations that mark a new period in London's politics, but at the same time she is somehow muted, being made to endorse the status quo and male power, in ways that jar with her more familiar attitude of resistance. More commonly, when Medea is used politically, it is her worst and most terrifying traits that are exaggerated, for didactic or admonitory effect. Her monstrous femininity allowed Edmund Spenser and Thomas Wilson to confront their doubts about female rule and women's dominance over male bodies, while, for Shakespeare and Drayton, embellishing accounts of England's tumultuous medieval history with reference to Medea's cruelty, witchcraft and deception makes Elizabethan England seem more secure in comparison.

Moreover, as Peter Elmer notes, by the seventeenth century 'Catholicism and witchcraft had long gone hand in hand in the mental outlook of Protestant Englishmen',[5] and this association, coupled with what such Englishmen saw as the Catholic Church's inappropriate promotion of female power, meant that for authors including John Vicars and Henry Burton Medea was a natural example to invoke when they wished to underscore the threat posed by Rome to the security of Jacobean or Caroline rule.[6] Finally, after the Civil Wars and regicide, in the works of a writer like John Crowne, Medea's rending of bodies is used to warn not England's monarch but the country's subjects about the danger of attempting ill-considered reform and the comparative security offered by conformity and obedience: for, as Morse notes, crimes like her vicious killing and dismemberment of her brother are suggestive of 'the dis-jointing of the patriarchal family and state'.[7] Medea is useful to such writers as a witch, a foreigner, and a violent rebel who refuses to accord with established patriarchal authority, and her power is appropriated by Tudor and Stuart authors, and used to confront England's monarchy and subjects alike with dire warnings about the dangers of untempered will and the terrible consequences of rebellion.

Medea, Elizabeth and Mary Queen of Scots

In Seneca's *Medea*, King Creon confronts Medea, who is refusing to accept Jason's betrayal and new marriage, and leave Corinth quietly. He tells her that she, not Jason, must bear all the responsibility for the murders of her brother and Jason's uncle Pelias, and the betrayal of her father, and accuses her of combining 'feminea ... nequitia, ad audendum omnia, / robur virile est, nulla famae memoria' (a woman's evil willingness to dare anything, along with a man's strength, and no thought of reputation) (267–8). In the words of the Elizabethan translator John Studley, Medea combines 'shamelesse womans wilie braine / and manly stomack stoute' (942–3), lines which, in their focus on ability and identity that is simultaneously masculine and feminine, seem a tantalising foreshadowing of Elizabeth's 1588 pronouncement to English troops at Tilbury, who were preparing for an assault by the Spanish Armada, that she had 'the body ... of a weak and feble woman' but 'the harte and stomack of a kinge'.[8] As Chapter 3 has shown, much of the interest and censorious comment that Medea's story attracted from early modern authors centred not only around her deviation from the accepted norms of femininity but also, paradoxically, around the terrifying idea that any woman had the potential for Medea-like behaviour.[9] Because she was

such a contentious example, comparisons between Medea and female
figures usually occur in fiction, and authors like Geoffrey Fenton and
Thomas Achelley are often at pains to stress their anti-heroines' foreignness, their essential difference from early modern English women,
who should (these authors argue) draw comfort from their distance
from Medea, while remaining wary of their own potential to follow her
example. Given Medea's notorious reputation, it seems highly unlikely
that Elizabeth could have wished to draw on the sorceress's example to
emphasise that her own abilities transcend her gender.[10] Nevertheless,
on occasion a real woman could be compared to Medea, if an author is
particularly desirous to demonstrate either her troubling control over
men and male bodies or her wickedness. M. L. Stapleton notes that in
1 Henry VI, in his representation of Joan la Pucelle, Shakespeare 'echoes,
parodies and imitates' Studley's Elizabethan version of the Senecan anti-
heroine.[11] Others look more daringly to the present, however, and the
central importance of Medea's gender, and the connection that Creon
perceives between her femininity and her ruthless will meant that, for
some, the parallels between the Colchian sorceress and the most politically significant women in Elizabethan England were too compelling
to ignore.[12]

Both Mihoko Suzuki and Bart van Es note Edmund Spenser's growing
unease with the Elizabethan regime, between the publication of the first
three books of the *Faerie Queene* in 1590 and the second three in 1596.[13]
Medea is briefly mentioned in both halves of the poem, and the second
mention of her, in Book 5, seems to reflect Spenser's growing discomfort
with women's control over men, where in the first half of the poem
female power had been lauded. In his representation of the female
knight Britomart in Book 3, Spenser portrays a female character who is
simultaneously strong and chaste, and uses classical mythology – here,
specifically, the story of the fall of Troy – to reinforce Britomart's virtue,
by contrasting her with Paridell, another descendant of the Trojans.[14]
He has his knights, Paridell and Britomart, retell their own versions of
the fall of Troy and of their common Trojan ancestors: but Britomart,
unlike the manipulative Paridell or the object of his lust, the dissatisfied
wife Hellenore, is able to resist the sexual adventures that these histories
seem to suggest. In his rewriting of the famous Trojan story of adulter-
ous desire, which culminates first in Paridell's seduction of Hellenore
and then in her abandonment, Spenser reinforces a message about the
destructive nature of lust that he had suggested in Book 2, through use
of the equally famous myth of Jason and Medea. Here, at 2.12.44–5, he
linked Medea's desire for Jason to its terrible consequences, describing

not only her love for Jason but also her killing of Creusa and of her own children and brother, depicted on the gateway to the sorceress Acrasia's Bower of Bliss:

> Her mighty charmes, her furious louing fitt,
> His goodly conquest of the golden fleece,
> His falsed fayth, and loue too lightly flitt,
> The wondred *Argo*, which in venturous peece
> First through the *Euxine* seas bore all the flowr of *Greece*.
>
> Ye might haue seene the frothy billowes fry
> Vnder the ship, as thorough them she went,
> That seemd the waues were into yuory,
> Or yuory into the waues were sent;
> And otherwhere the snowy substaunce sprent
> With vermell, like the boyes blood therein shed,
> A piteous spectacle did represent,
> And otherwhiles with gold besprinkeled;
> Yt seemd thenchaunted flame, which did *Creusa* wed.[15]

As the repeated references to ivory suggest, this is a dangerous and potentially misleading vision of how sexual desire and conquest, and chivalric success in a quest, may be linked.[16] The ekphrasis – the poetic description of the carved artwork – moves deftly between the positive and negative associations of both lovers, not only Medea's 'mighty charmes' but also her 'furious louing fitt', not only Jason's 'goodly conquest' but also his 'falsed fayth'. Finally, though, the tragedy of their ill-fated union is alluded to, in Spenser's description of ivory waves sprinkled with 'vermell' (the red of Apsyrtus' blood, or possibly that of Medea's sons) and gold (simultaneously suggestive of the wedding torches that were used to celebrate Creusa's marriage to Jason and the enchanted fire that would consume her so horribly).[17] Earlier in Book 2, Spenser's hero Guyon had met Amavia, wife of the dead Mortdant, and learned that the knight had perished as a result of a curse placed on him by Acrasia, his deserted lover. Syrithe Pugh points out that 'the quick and fatal action of Acrasia's curse' and 'its particular application to her former lover's wife' suggest an echo of Medea's story, and the connection between the classical and Spenserian sorceresses is made inescapably clear by the time Spenser describes the pictorial representation of the myth, at the climax of Book 2.[18] While it might, on a very superficial level, seem a triumphant vision of the 'wondred Argo' traversing the

sea with 'all the flowr of Greece' on board, the bloody associations of
Medea's story, and particularly the fatal inability of either Medea or
Jason to display temperance (the central virtue of Book 2) mean that
this depiction should serve as a pointed caution to Guyon as he enters
the Bower, just as Paridell's story about his ancestor's conquest of Helen
is a model for Britomart to consider and reject.

In the first half of the poem, then, Spenser had clearly associated
Medea's story with tragedy and the potential downfall of chivalric or
imperial ambition (represented in Book 2 by Guyon), while in Book 3,
he had demonstrated Britomart's ability to recall and interpret myth
correctly, in ways that strengthen her commitment to the key knightly
virtue of chastity. In Book 5, Britomart is brought to the fore again,
and in this second half of the poem Medea also re-enters. Once again,
though, as in Book 2, it is a male knight, Artegall, who must overcome
the threat Medea represents, and in fact his quashing of a Medea-like
woman is the means by which Artegall may rehabilitate his knightly
reputation, which has suffered not only through his humiliating impris-
onment by the sorceress Radigund but also by the fact that he has had
to rely on Britomart for rescue. In Book 5, having escaped Radigund,
Artegall encounters the murderous Souldan and his queen, Adicia.
Artegall and Prince Arthur defeat the Souldan, and, at 5.8.47, Spenser
repeats Thomas Achelley's 1576 epithet for the Colchian sorceress,
comparing Adicia, raging at her husband's death, to 'fell Medea', before
suggesting that in her anger with Artegall and with Samient, the maid
she hoped to take prisoner, she is even more terrifying:

> Like raging *Ino*, when with knife in hand
> She threw her husbands murdred infant out,
> Or fell *Medea*, when on *Colchicke* strand
> Her brothers bones she scattered all about;
> Or as that madding mother, mongst the rout
> Of *Bacchus* Priests her owne deare flesh did teare.
> Yet neither *Ino*, nor *Medea* stout,
> Nor all the *Moenades* so furious were,
> As this bold woman, when she saw that Damzell there. (5.8.47)

Here, Spenser uses classical women – not just Medea but also Ino and
Agave, who also killed their children, albeit while deceived or maddened –
to demonstrate the murderous rage of Adicia. While his use of Medea
emphasises the ferocious anger of the Souldan's wife, however, Spenser's
invocation of Medea simultaneously incorporates the suggestion that in

the *Faerie Queene* such powerful women can be contained and neutralised by men, even if their classical ancestors were not. Adicia's defeat and banishment by Artegall and her subsequent transformation into a wild beast underscore her own feral nature and, in contrast, demonstrate Artegall's triumphant return to normality and masculinity, after his humiliating encounter with Radigund and emasculating rescue by Britomart.

In fact, Artegall's defeat of this Medea-figure indirectly suggests his superiority to both Britomart and Radigund at this point in the poem, for both women have been likened to Medea, though less explicitly than the fearsome Adicia. Syrithe Pugh notes Spenser's apparent allusion to the Medea of *Metamorphoses* 7, in his description of Britomart's passionate and anxious desire for Artegall in Book 3. This same desire surfaces again in Book 5, where it is mirrored by Radigund's passion for Artegall, and descriptions of both women's desire in Book 5 are tantalisingly evocative of Medea's for Jason.[19] Suzuki reads in Radigund's control of her male knights 'anxiety concerning what is perceived as the necessary correlation between female ascendancy and male humiliation'.[20] Similarly, Medea's function in the *Faerie Queene* is to emphasise the terrible threat that powerful female figures like Acrasia and Adicia might wield over male knights such as Guyon and Artegall, whether this threat is both sexual and violent (as in the case of Acrasia, when Medea's fierce desire for Jason is highlighted by reference to the fratricide she commits to assist him) or simply violent (as it is with Adicia, when Spenser foregrounds both her infanticide and her hideous slaughter of Apsyrtus). Just as Radigund's hold over the poem's male knights is broken, however, the knights of the *Faerie Queene* (Guyon in Book 2, Artegall in Book 5) can either resist the charms of a Medea-like woman or subdue and tame her, as Jason could not. Artegall's vanquishing of Adicia restores normalcy after his capture by Radigund, who has been read as representative of both Elizabeth's cousin and rival Mary Queen of Scots and of the troubling control that Elizabeth herself wielded over even the private lives of her courtiers.[21] Britomart overcomes Radigund (and in the process quashes the alarmingly passionate, Medea-like tendencies in her own nature, becoming instead a 'chaste Penelope'), but, in order that his masculine pride might be salvaged, and the proper balance between the sexes restored, Artegall is allowed to go even further than her in acts of heroism, defeating a woman who is explicitly described as even worse than the child-killing Medea.[22]

In Adicia's overthrow, Book 5 of the *Faerie Queene* demonstrates that the defeat of a Medea-figure represents not just the triumph of masculinity in the shape of Artegall but also the overthrow of the Catholic threat that is so frequently foregrounded in Spenser's Protestant epic. Justin Kolb notes the longstanding association readers have perceived between Artegall's foe the Souldan and Philip of Spain, and between his defeat and the failure of the Spanish invasion in 1588, and, for Judith H. Anderson, the Souldan is 'the explicit historical threat' of the Armada, while Adicia represents 'the principle of wrong he has wed'.[23] Like another of the poem's anti-heroines, the witch Duessa, this distorted and horrible version of femininity is representative of the Roman Church, but like Duessa, and unlike the classical Medea, this Elizabethan version can be exposed and defeated. Other Protestant authors of the period make the connection between the classical sorceress and the Catholic threat to England far more apparent than does Spenser, by specifically likening Catholic enemies of England, such as Mary Queen of Scots, to Medea.[24] For example, at the end of George Buchanan's highly critical treatise *Ane Detectioun of the Duinges of Marie Quene of Scottes* (1571), Thomas Wilson adds an account of her alleged plotting against her husband, Lord Darnley, entitled *Ane oratioun, with declaration of evidence against Marie the Scotishe Quene quhairin is by necessarie argumentis plainely provit that sche was giltie and privie of the sayde murder.* The work also reproduces the Casket Letters, allegedly sent by Mary to her lover, the Earl of Bothwell.[25] In one, Mary frets that a rival might win him, like 'the second love of Jason'. Here, Mary could be Hypsipyle; that she is Medea, though, is suggested by her anxious retreat from the comparison: it is simply that

> [Y]e caus me to be sumquhat like unto hyr in any thing that touchis you, or that may preserve and keip you unto hir, to quhome onely ye appertaine: if it be sa that I may appropriate that quhilk is wonne through faythfull yea onely luffing of you, as I do and sall do all the dayes of my lyfe, for payne or evill that can cume thairof. (Uiii^(r–v))[26]

Mary does not wish to punish or torment Bothwell, but identifies with Medea's possessive desire to 'preserve and keip you unto hir, to quhome onely ye appertaine'.[27] In order to win his sympathy, Mary attempts to direct Bothwell towards a particular reading of Medea: one that saw her principally as a wronged wife, first infatuated by Jason, and willing to do anything for him, and then callously betrayed in favour of Creusa. Unfortunately for Mary, however, Wilson leapt eagerly on Mary's ill-advised comparison. He encourages Mary's opponents to see in her words parallels with the more familiar Medea, the murderous witch whose romantic frustration leads to horrifying crimes, and urges his readers not to be taken in by her dissembling, telling them: 'Call to mind that part of her Letters to *Bothwel*, quhairin sche maketh hir selfe Medea, that is, a woman that nouther in love nor in hatrit can kepe any meane' (Gii^r). While Mary apparently meant to emphasise her helplessness through a reference to Medea, Wilson sees this comparison as evidence that Mary conspired to poison her husband, Lord Darnley: 'Quhilk may easily be gatherit by hir letter quhairin she partly compareth hir selfe with Medea a bludy woman and a poysoning witch' (Kiii^r). As the apparent author of the letter, Mary compares herself to Medea to win sympathy from a single reader, Bothwell, but, as Cathy Shrank puts it, in doing so she 'sets herself up for misreading'.[28] Her words are twisted by Wilson, and presented to a wider, hostile Protestant readership as evidence that she possesses the power and guile of Medea the Euripidean, Ovidian and Senecan murderer. In fact, Shrank suggests that 'the casket letters are almost certainly the source for the frequent depiction of Mary as Medea', for example in ballads printed in Edinburgh in the 1560s by Robert Sempill.[29]

John D. Staines suggests that in Wilson's treatment of Mary, which insistently emphasises her deviant femininity, 'The political overtones of the allusion to Seneca's *Medea* and *Thyestes* are … neutralized by reducing Mary to a mad lover instead of a tyrant abusing her power.'[30] Here, Staines argues that it is Mary's status as an abandoned lover, rather than a ruler, which is central to Wilson's comparison of her to Medea. The suggestion that a use of Seneca's play might have political overtones (even if these are 'neutralised'), however, raises an interesting point about another way in which authors of politically charged works might have used the figure of Medea. In Seneca's tragedy, Creon is the tyrant, who abuses his power to attempt to expel Medea, and he is first warned over his high-handed behaviour by the sorceress, at line 196, and then meets a grisly end. It is possible, therefore, to envision an early modern writer using Medea as an example of how tyranny may be resisted, by allowing her to become a 'revolutionary symbol' or a 'freedom fighter', to borrow two phrases used by Marianne McDonald to describe twentieth-century incarnations of the sorceress.[31] Early modern authors who use Medea in politically charged works seem to be unable to bring themselves to characterise her positively, however, and to set her against a tyrannical Creon figure in this way. When her Senecan warning, 'Iniqua numquam regna perpetuo manent' (Unjust kingship never remains unbroken) (196), is used as a caution to tyrants, it is quoted only briefly, and the tyrant's opponents are not likened to Medea in their brave resistance.[32] As Staines suggests, what is emphasised here is Mary's identity as a lover, rather than a queen, and Medea is useful not as an opponent of tyranny but as a destructive, irrational and terrifying murderous force, who can underscore the threat of the uncontrolled Queen of Scots and emphasise why it is important that she is subdued.

Michael Drayton's Medea

The familiar association between Medea and violent lawlessness, including murder and even regicide, meant that Elizabethan and Jacobean writers might use Medea to endorse Elizabeth's and James's rule, by emphasising the turmoil of previous centuries before the establishment of the Tudor monarchy, or by alluding to more recent threats to law and order which had been comfortingly dispelled, with reference to Medea. Bart van Es has pointed out the risk that writers of history ran, if they engaged too directly with the current regime: 'An almost obsessive awareness of parallels haunted the writers and readers of history alike: not only did the "example" of the past justify the practice of history, alleged allusions to the present could also be its downfall.'[33] Where classical myth is blended with historical writing, with a view to reflecting on the current state of the nation, authors had to tread carefully, particularly when they chose to invoke a notorious woman like Medea who, in her disobedience to her father, her plotting against Creon and Aegeus, and her violence towards Jason's heirs, could seem directly opposed to the preservation of the integrity and security of kingdoms. The resultant preference, for praising the monarch at a remove, and relying on the perceptive reader to interpret, can be discerned in the Elizabethan and Jacobean works which emphasise royal achievements, and the virtues of Elizabethan and Jacobean England, by using Medea not to praise the current monarch but to criticise or question what was not Tudor or Stuart. Specifically, such uses often reflect on the various violent upheavals of medieval England, now comfortingly past, as a way of shedding positive light on Elizabethan and Jacobean government.

The verse of the Elizabethan poet Michael Drayton reflects a keen and longstanding interest in England's medieval history, and often aims to give a voice to minor or sidelined historical figures: not just kings and nobles but also the mistresses and favourites who helped to shape England's medieval monarchy. He also had a clear interest in Medea's story, particularly in its Ovidian and Senecan incarnations. One of Drayton's most famous works, *Englands Heroicall Epistles* (1597), was, as the name suggests, inspired by the *Heroides*, and constitutes a series of letters exchanged between pairs of historical lovers. This pairing of male and female letters meant that the collection also allowed Drayton to turn his hand to the popular genre of female complaint poetry, which was usually authored by men, because of women's inability or unwillingness to venture into print. In one of these male-authored 'female' letters, Drayton adapts Medea's words in *Metamorphoses* 7, and clearly also writes with the fiercely angry Medea of *Heroides* 12 firmly in mind. The Duchess of Gloucester, however, as she appears in Drayton's epistle, is very far from Medea, and Drayton's use of Medea's words only serves, perversely, to demonstrate how she is a weakened and more pitiable figure. In the letter, Elinor, Duchess of Gloucester, writes to her husband Humphrey, Duke of Gloucester, uncle and Protector of the young king, Henry VI. In his *Argument*, Drayton explains that Elinor (or Eleanor) 'Convicted was, with Sorcerers to conspire' (p. 215), and was accused of plotting to kill Henry.[34] Elinor's letter, written during her banishment to the Isle of Man, curses the queen, Margaret of Anjou, and, though she denies that she has used magic to bewitch Humphrey, she admits, 'To Magick once I did myself apply' (26), and wishes for such power to take vengeance on her enemies. In Elinor's letter Drayton echoes the Ovidian Medea's invocation of the gods, which was appropriated and imitated by authors including Shakespeare, in *The Tempest*. While he intends his reader to recall Medea's magic, however, Drayton is keen to temper Elinor's power, to make it hypothetical rather than real. Thus, although in the poem's opening lines she has confessed practising witchcraft, here Elinor denies it and merely wishes for the power to punish Margaret:

> They say, the *Druides* once liv'd in this Ile ...
> O, that their Spels to me they had resign'd,
> Wherewith they ray'sd and calm'd both Sea and Wind!
> And made the Moon pawse in her paled Sphere,
> Whilst her grim Dragons drew them through the Ayre:
> Their Hellish Power, to kill the Plow-mans Seed,
> Or to fore-speake whole Flocks, as they did feed;
> To nurse a damned Spirit with humane Bloud,
> To carry them through Earth, Ayre, Fire, and Floud:
> Had I this skill, that Time hath almost lost,
> How like a Goblin I would haunt her ghost? (125–38)

Danielle Clarke argues that there is an empowered feminine voice discernible in Drayton's epistles, and yet she notes that, when Drayton's historical women speak, 'they do so in exemplary ways, to the end of upholding and extending the social and political status quo'. Here, even as she ventriloquises Medea's words in her desire for revenge, Elinor comfortingly demonstrates that she does not have the same power.[35]

Drayton chooses to weaken the Duchess, to make her sympathetic and pitiable, and he achieves this, perversely, by having her wish to appropriate the powerful magic of Medea, while acknowledging that she falls far short of her classical model. Elsewhere, though, Drayton had experimented with the representation of historical figures who do possess Medea's power (though this could be figuratively rather than literally), and he had suggested the destabilising threat that this power might pose to England's monarchy. In the historical poem *Peirs Gaveston, Earle of Cornwall* (1593), Drayton looks back to the tumultuous reign of Edward II, and particularly to the King's sexual relationship with his favourite Gaveston, which had already been dramatised, earlier in Elizabeth's reign, by Christopher Marlowe. Using Medea's story, Drayton emphasises the danger posed by this relationship, by comparing the Earl's effect on the King to Medea's rejuvenation of Jason's father, Aeson. Gaveston reminisces:

> As when old-youthful *Eson* in his glass,
> Saw from his eyes the cheerfull lightning sprung,
> When as Art-spell *Medea* brought to pass,
> By hearbs and charms, againe to make him young,
> Thus stood King *Edward*, ravisht in the place,
> Fixing his eyes upon my lovely face. (1411–16)[36]

In his notes to the epistle of Edward's queen Isabel to her lover Roger Mortimer, in *Englands Heroicall Epistles*, Drayton mentions 'the effeminacie and luxurious wantonnesse of Gaveston, the Kings Minion; his Behaviour and Attire ever so Woman-like, to please the Eye of his lascivious Master' (p. 165).[37] It was rare for medieval or early modern men to be compared to Medea, but here the comparison between Medea's rejuvenating power and Gaveston's beauty seemed natural to Drayton, because of Gaveston's homosexuality and apparent effeminacy. In fact, Medea is a particularly apposite choice, for, in his notes to Isabel's epistle, Drayton observes that the queen's attacks on her husband's favourite centred on accusations of witchcraft: 'It was urged by the Queene and the Nobilitie, in the disgrace of Pierce Gaveston, that his Mother was convicted of Witch-craft, and burned for the same, and that Pierce had bewitched the King' (p. 165). In his complaint, Gaveston compares his seductive power with Medea's to convey the intensity of his relationship with the King, and his bewitching and rejuvenating effect on a man who ought to enjoy supreme authority.[38] Parallel to this, though, Drayton relies on his readers' knowledge of Medea's story, through which they will appreciate how destabilising such relationships are to the security of the kingdom: in Ovid's *Metamorphoses* 7, Medea's rejuvenation of Jason's father Aeson is balanced almost immediately with her callous murder of his uncle Pelias via the same method. In the classical tradition, Pelias is hostile to Jason, and his killing demonstrates Medea's devotion to her lover, as well as her cunning, but in the early modern period this crime is always referenced to highlight Medea's ruthlessness and her control over the naive or desperate (represented by Pelias' daughters, who misguidedly follow her instructions and stab their father to death) and also over masculinity and kingship, represented by Pelias.[39] Jonathan Bate has argued that when he has Jessica invoke the rejuvenation in *The Merchant of Venice*, Shakespeare expects classically educated members of his audience to appreciate the selectiveness of her reading, and to see Medea as an agent of destruction, as well as a woman who bravely follows her own desires and uses her magic to assist Jason.[40] Here, Drayton's use of this part of the myth is similarly weighted, and more directly politicised. Gaveston's comparison of his hold over the King to Medea's rejuvenating power thus bears a secondary message, one that he does not intend, about the destabilising danger that he posed for England because of his influence over Edward. In fact, in *Mortimeriados* (1596), Drayton again uses Medea, underlining how Edward's reign was under threat from all sides, by describing Queen Isabel plotting against her husband, in terms that are reminiscent of the description of Medea's concocting of poisons, given by the Nurse in Act 4 of Seneca's tragedy:

> For after going out with frenzied steps and reaching her inner sanctum of death, she pours out her entire resources, brings forth everything that even she has long feared, and deploys all her host of evils, occult, mysterious, hidden things … every plant that burgeons with deadly flowers, every kind of injurious sap that breeds in twisted roots the sources of harm: all these she handles. (675–719)

Drayton echoes and adapts the Nurse's description of Medea's solitary plotting against her husband, and her command of poisons, in his description of Isabel:

> Thus sits this great Enchauntresse in her Cell,
> Invironed with spyrit-commanding charmes,

Her body censed with most sacred smell,
With holy fiers her liqors now shee warmes,
Then with her sorcering instruments she armes.
And from her hearbs the powerfull juyce she wrong,
To make the poyson forcible and strong. (638–44)

At the beginning of Act 3, the Nurse had urged Medea, 'Stop, curb your anger, control your aggression!' (381), and begged her, 'Think how many dangers there are, if you persist. No one can attack the powerful in safety' (429–30). Like Medea, Isabel cannot be swayed from her course, and her dedication to wickedness is such that she ignores the risks she runs by plotting against a king in this way:

Reason might judge, doubts better might advise,
And as a woman, feare her hand have stayd,
Waying the strangnesse of the interprize,
The daunger well might have her sex dismayd,
Fortune, distrust, suspect, to be betrayed;
But when they leave of vertue to esteeme,
They greatly erre which thinke them as they seeme. (645–51)[41]

Isabel is Medea-like in that she is an 'Enchauntresse' who is shown gathering herbs and using 'sorcering instruments' to concoct 'poyson forcible and strong'. In their reflection that 'Reason might judge, doubts better might advise', were it not for the fact that Isabel has ceased 'vertue to esteeme', these lines also recall the Ovidian Medea's famous acknowledgment, in *Metamorphoses* 7.20–1, 'I see the better [course] and approve it, but I follow the worse', as well as the alarm of the Senecan Nurse. Drayton then makes the comparison with Medea specific, to show that an innocent appearance should not be trusted:

Medea pitifull in tender years,
Untill with *Jason* she would take her flight,
Then merciless her Brothers lymmes she teares,
Betrayes her Father, flyes away by night,
Nor Nations, Seas, nor daungers could affright;
Who dyed with heate, nor could abide the wind,
Now like a Tigar falls unto her kind. (659–65)

The danger posed to Edward's kingdom, by both his weakness for Gaveston and by Isabel's plotting, is made plain by Drayton's appropriation of Medea's magical and rejuvenating power and of her murderous will. Isabel's machinations are ultimately thwarted by Edward III, but not before her husband is deposed and killed, as Creon is outwitted by Medea, and then dies horribly. Drayton's use of Medea's myth thus might be read as subtly underscoring the security of Elizabeth's reign, security which seems to be implicitly linked to the Queen's reluctance to enter into marriage, or to succumb to harmful relationships as previous monarchs like Edward II had done with Gaveston and Isabel: as Louis A. Montrose puts it, Elizabeth's 'control of the realm was dependent upon her physical and symbolic control of her own body'.[42] At the same time, Elizabeth is strengthened by her distance from the model of malign and desiring femininity represented by Medea, and by the traitorous Isabel, who does not rule herself but plots in secret to bring down her husband. Drayton avoids blatant comparisons between Elizabeth and the Plantagenet monarchs, and his reader, like Spenser's, must read between the lines to appreciate what is being suggested about England's government, by an allusive use of Medea's mythical power, and, on a larger scale, by what Clarke terms Drayton's 'orientation of Ovid's interiorized, highly textualized narratives towards the public sphere, towards a grand narrative of history'.[43]

Medea and medieval disorder

Shakespeare's history plays might often seem to function as implicit endorsements of the Tudor regime: this is most apparent in the majestic spectacle of *Henry VIII*, or in Richmond's victory at the climax of *Richard III*. Philip Edwards acknowledges the twentieth-century reluctance to regard Shakespeare as 'the propagandist of Tudor autocracy', but argues that in his earlier history plays, the three parts of *Henry VI* and *Richard III*, 'there isn't a shadow of doubt that much of the energy of the sequence comes from a sense of progress, or better, of emergence, by which the English nation is seen coming from the dark of the Wars of the Roses into the light of the Tudor dynasty'.[44]

In the plays depicting the Wars of the Roses, Shakespeare presents England as torn apart by conflict and faction, and Medea's is an attractive myth to illustrate such rupture, rupture which in turn could emphasise the relative security of the eventual Tudor settlement. Michael Hattaway has argued that Henry VI's reign was 'a pattern of disorder, a mirror for Shakespeare's contemporaries of the disasters of the type of dynastic strife ... which could so easily have broken out upon the death of Elizabeth',[45] and, in the Henriad, Shakespeare compounds this vision of medieval chaos with one of his only direct mentions of

Medea. In *2 Henry VI*, Young Clifford is determined to avenge the killing of his father, and exclaims,

> Meet I an infant of the house of York,
> Into as many gobbets will I cut it
> As wild Medea young Absyrtus did. (5.3.57–9)

In *3 Henry VI* he fulfils this ambition, savagely killing the Duke of York's innocent young son Rutland. T. W. Baldwin has suggested that Shakespeare knew Ovid's *Tristia* (which details the murder of Apsyrtus at 3.9, and had been translated into English by Thomas Churchyard by the time Shakespeare came to write his play), while Starnes and Talbert argue that his emphasis on the child's youth points to Shakespeare's use of Cooper's *Thesaurus*, which repeatedly describes Apsyrtus (there Absyrtus) as 'yong' and a 'yong babe'.[46] In fact, another of Shakespeare's sources goes further, assigning a specific (and incorrect) age to Rutland. In his chronicle of the Wars of the Roses, printed in 1547, Edward Hall writes that Rutland was 'sca[r]ce of ye age of xii yeres' (Ggiii^r)[47] when he was killed. (In reality, he was seventeen.) Hall recounts the confrontation between Rutland and Clifford, and describes Clifford as worse even than the lion, 'a furious and an unreasonable beaste' (Ggiii^v), because of his refusal to show mercy to a much weaker opponent. Hall's manipulation of history, his assigning of such a tender age to Rutland, to heighten the pathos of his death, and his emphasis on Clifford's cruelty, combined with Shakespeare's likely knowledge of the *Tristia* and of vernacular works that detail the fratricide, such as Cooper's *Thesaurus*, apparently inspired the playwright to identify Rutland with Medea's young brother and Clifford not only with a lion but with the unambiguous and utterly abhorrent figure of the sorceress.

The playwright's exaggeration of historical truth, the calculated killing of such a young child, makes a clear impression on Shakespeare's characters, even in the midst of so much slaughter: in *Richard III*, the Yorkists' recollection of this past horror unites them against the unrepentant Lancastrian Queen Margaret.[48] Ronald S. Berman points to the growing sense across the Henriad and into *Richard III*, 'that blood relationships, the sacred obligations of the past, are inconveniences in the way of ambition'.[49] Medea kills her brother because of love for Jason, rather than ambition, but again the desires of the individual are put above either familial bonds or the security of her father's kingdom, an upsetting of the natural order that meant the fratricide seems to have resonated with particular significance for sixteenth- and seventeenth-century authors.

Hattaway argues that *2 Henry VI* 'did not slavishly endorse 'the Tudor Myth … If there is a grand design it is only dimly glimpsed'.[50] Certainly, the comparison between past disorder and Elizabethan good fortune is not made as explicit as it is in the anonymous tragedy *Locrine* (1595), which ends with a praise of Elizabeth, 'that renowned mayd, / That eight and thirtie yeares the scepter swayd, / In quiet peace and sweet felicitie' (K4ᵛ). By using Medea's fratricide to exaggerate the chaotic and indiscriminate cruelty that had apparently raged in England in the fifteenth century, however, Shakespeare exploits her violence to underline the horror of medieval civil war, and warn against civil unrest. Moreover, Clifford's inevitable death, once he has invoked Medea and emulated her in his killing of a child, means that one of Shakespeare's only direct references to Medea serves paradoxically to endorse those structures that guard against the child-murder, rebellion and king-killing she represents. Crucially, by punishing Clifford, Shakespeare's play can contain her subversive myth, and bring it to a dramatically satisfactory conclusion, as Ovid's *Tristia* or Seneca's *Medea* refuse to.[51]

If Medea's myth might be invoked in *2 Henry VI* to highlight the civil strife of England's historical past, as it had been (more overtly) in *Locrine*, it is moreover significant that here it is the fratricide specifically that is chosen to highlight the horrors of civil war. Caxton's medieval *History of Jason* had drawn attention to the way in which the killing of Apsyrtus destabilizes Aeëtes' kingdom, and the continued didactic potential of this particular episode in early modern England was also emphasized when it was employed by the Restoration playwright John Crowne. In his adaptation of Shakespeare's *2* and *3 Henry VI*, entitled *The Misery of Civil-War*, and printed in 1680, Young Clifford exclaims,

I'll kill *Plantagenet,* and all his Sons
That when he is dead he may not have a Son.
To bear him to the grave, as I my Father;
And so cut off his memory from the Earth,
Meet I but any Infants of his House,
Into as many gobbits will I cut 'em
As wild *Medea* did the young *Absyrtis,*
And I will starve my men that they may eat 'em,
And so let us about our several business. (p. 16)[52]

In a spirited discussion of how best to read and to respond to Greek myth in contemporary America, Page duBois has shown how conservative adapters of myth might appropriate alarming stories, such as that of Oedipus, but will sanitise them, stripping them of all that makes them most shocking (and interesting) in an attempt to make them serve appropriately instructive, moralising ends.[53] Shakespeare's and Crowne's use of Medea shows how early modern England might choose the opposite tactic, exaggerating the horrors of classical stories in order not only to thrill but also to tacitly recommend obedience and to condemn rebellion. Both plays use Medea to emphasise the dehumanising effect of war on individuals, as well as its terrible effect on the body politic. Thus, while Matthew H. Wikander argues that Crowne's play presents Young Clifford as 'a paragon of heroic virtue throughout', here the playwright outdoes the horror evoked by Shakespeare's use of Medea, as his Young Clifford vows that his men will eat the scattered 'gobbits' of dismembered children.[54] Crowne's play might thus become what Sanders (drawing on Gérard Genette) terms a 'hyper-hyper-text', self-consciously responding to both the Ovidian story of the dismemberment and (more immediately) to Shakespeare's treatment of it, and expanding on both to gruesome and admonitory effect.[55]

Alongside this use of sensational exaggeration to recommend obedience and harmony to his Restoration audience, Susan J. Owen points out that, elsewhere in the play, Crowne also depicts 'royalist atrocities', including murder and infanticide, but argues that 'this only serves to point up the universally corrupting effects of civil war'.[56] Of course, Crowne's increased emphasis on war as universal savagery is so significant because, despite his use of the medieval conflict, when this Clifford swears to emulate the cruelty of Medea and tear his enemies to pieces, Crowne's Restoration audience could scarcely avoid reflecting on the recent horrors of the English Civil Wars, and the very current upheavals of the Popish Plot and Exclusion Crisis.[57] Even in the midst of such crises, however, Crowne's audience are encouraged even more clearly than Shakespeare's to appreciate monarchic rule, by reflecting on the tripartite horror of Medea's exaggerated crimes, the Wars of the Roses and the recent Civil Wars. Sanders argues that 'adaptation[s] and appropriation[s]' of pre-existing stories 'are frequently, if not inevitably, political acts', and though she suggests that adaptation of a previously known story may often be read as an act of resistance (as, for example, in the case of postcolonial rewritings like Jean Rhys's *Wide Sargasso Sea*, her adaptation of *Jane Eyre*) early modern England often saw fit to rewrite Medea and her crimes to recommend obedience and conformity.[58] If Shakespeare only hints at his endorsement of the current monarchical order by his dramatisation of its medieval and mythical opposites, later seventeenth-century authors were far more explicit in their appropriation of Medea's power to serve conservative and conformist ends: or, as Wikander puts it, 'To the adapters, Shakespeare's Elizabethan mistrust of disorder reflected with insufficient clarity their own hatred of faction, and their country's more recent experience of civil war.'[59] Medea's exultant disregard for taboos such as murder (and particularly the murder of innocent children) was deeply alarming for early modern authors like Shakespeare and Crowne, but they deal with their horror not by ignoring such acts (as medieval authors like Chaucer frequently do) but by transforming them into a symbol of the anarchy and mayhem that has been subdued and put firmly in the past, but which could easily rise again, if England's subjects did not recognise and appreciate their own good fortune.

Authors writing in the reign of James I follow the example of their Elizabethan forebears, and use classical mythology to praise the current regime, specifically by using Medea to attack James's enemies, or else to demonstrate to their readers and audience members how the country's ruling families were riven with animosity during the Wars of the Roses. In another return to medieval history, the prose chronicle *The True and Wonderful History of Perkin Warbeck* (1618), the Calvinist pamphleteer and playwright Thomas Gainsford describes the hatred that Margaret, sister to the late Edward IV, bears towards Henry VII. This malice, which leads her to support the cause of the pretender, Perkin Warbeck, is illustrated with a quotation from a Latin translation of Euripides' *Medea*:

Praeterea nos sumus mulieres,
Ad bona quidem ineptissimae,
Malorum vero omnium effectrices sapientissimae. (F[v])[60]

These are a version of the Euripidean Medea's words 'women, though most helpless in doing good deeds / Are of every evil the cleverest of contrivers', and in Euripides' play Medea speaks them as she urges herself to resist Creon's efforts to expel her from Corinth, so that Jason may enjoy his new marriage.[61] Here, Gainsford uses a Latin version of Euripides to subtly endorse James's kingship, criticising old opponents of the Tudor and Stuart regimes such as Margaret by likening them to a destructive and terrifying woman. By recourse to the Euripidean Medea's words to describe Margaret, Gainsford presents her as a real and malevolent threat to Henry, just as the Euripidean Medea presented a danger to Creon's kingship that the king did not perceive until it was too late. The association between Medea and enemies of the monarchy is underlined as the Scottish king James IV, taken in by the charming and persuasive Warbeck, pledges his allegiance to his cause with a particularly peculiar reference to Medea, 'telling him plainly he would assist him, and what-ever he was, or intended to be, he should not repent him of his comming thither, & so concluding with a speech of *Medeas* to *Jason: Hinc amor, hinc timor est, ipsum timor auget amorem'* (K4ᵛ).⁶² James implicitly likens himself to the lovestruck Medea, through his ventriloquizing of her Ovidian words and, in so doing, he unwittingly suggests to the reader the folly of his support for Warbeck, for, of course, both Jason and Medea will live to regret their match. Here, the Latinate reader of Gainsford's work is encouraged to recognise a greater threat in the pretender's cause, through Gainsford's repeated use of Medea's inauspicious example, but correspondingly to perceive the greater shrewdness of the first Tudor king of England, who, in the figure of Perkin Warbeck, could recognise and defeat a threat that was missed by both his classical counterpart Creon and his fellow monarch James IV.

The same pattern, of comparing an enemy of the monarchy to Medea, before imagining their comforting defeat, was also used in politicised Caroline writing, in Thomas May's long historical poem *The Reign of Henry II* (1633) which was dedicated to Charles I. Here, the treacherous queen Elinor compares herself to Medea as she considers how she may inflict additional wounds on the unfaithful Henry II, over and above the murder of his lover Rosamond. She considers following Medea's example in killing his sons, before deciding she can wound him more deeply by turning them against him:

> Besides *Creusaes* death, *Medea* shed
> Her childrens blood before their fathers eyes.
> But I, in stead of those mad tragedies
> (In which my selfe with him should beare a part)
> Can by his children more torment his heart.
> Their deaths, perchance, (though murder'd) could not be
> So much his griefe as their impiety. (I4ᵛ)⁶³

In *Englands Heroicall Epistles*, the Elizabethan poet Michael Drayton had showed the Duchess of Gloucester wishing for Medea's power to revenge herself on her enemies, before acknowledging that she does not possess the necessary magical ability, despite the accusations of witchcraft that have been levelled against her. Here, Elinor also refuses to identify wholly with Medea, acknowledging that she too would suffer from her sons' deaths, and would 'beare a part' in the guilt for their murders. Predictably, too, once it has been suggested, any vestige of

Medea-like power is quashed by kingly authority, and May's readers are told that, though she did engineer Rosamond's death by forcing her to drink poison,

> Nought did the Queene by this dire slaughter gaine:
> But more her Lords displeasure aggravate;
> And now, when he return'd in prosperous state,
> This act was cause, together with that crime
> Of raising his unnaturall sonnes 'gainst him,
> That she so long in prison was detain'd,
> And, whilest he liv'd, her freedome never gain'd. (J8ʳ–J8ᵛ)[64]

For authors such as Drayton, Shakespeare, Gainsford and May, Medea was often most useful when her power was equated to a threat posed to medieval monarchy, whether this was the disruption of civil war, the spectre of wifely treachery or the claim of a pretender to the throne. Also crucial, though, was that this threat could be recollected and brought to the attention of audience or reader via a mention of Medea, before being reassuringly dispelled. Medea's violence and disregard for rule can thus function as both a warning and a comforting reflection on the security of present order, in ways which recall Greenblatt's theory about the importance of the horrifying 'Other' to the establishment of early modern identity and security. One such 'Other' in early modern England was the Catholic Church, and in sixteenth- and seventeenth-century polemic Medea is frequently identified not just with violence and disorder, but specifically with the danger of Roman Catholicism.

Medea and the threat of Rome

Though he set out to undermine rather than reinforce popular belief in witchcraft, in his famous and sceptical treatise *The Discoverie of Witchcraft* (1584), Reginald Scot had acknowledged that those suspected of the crime were often 'papists; or such as knowe no religion' (Ciiiiʳ).[65] Given this association, it is unsurprising that the famous classical witch Medea was also used in Elizabethan and Jacobean writing to emphasise threats to the security of the monarchy that were religious as well as political. Luc Racaut has shown how, in Catholic France in the run-up to the French Wars of Religion, it was Protestants who were demonised by 'blood libel', the charge of killing and even eating of children.[66] For English Protestants, in contrast, Medea's magical power and her blood-thirsty crimes made her a natural comparison for Catholics, but so too did her barbarism, particularly when relations between England and Catholic Europe were at their most fraught.[67]

As Edith Hall has noted, Euripides made the decision to transform Medea into a barbarian, and Ovid followed his example enthusiastically.[68] In *Heroides* 6, her epistle to Jason, Ovid's Hypsipyle dismisses Medea as a 'barbara paelex' (barbarian jade) (6.81), and in *Metamorphoses* 7 Medea herself advertises not only her difference from Jason but also the way in which this makes his culture superior. She tells herself 'nempe est mea barbara tellus' (indeed my native land is barbarous) (7.53), and convinces herself that she should leave Colchis for Iolcos: 'non magna reliquam / magna sequar' (I shall not be leaving great things, but going to great things) (7.55–6). This emphasis on Medea's barbarism, coupled with the popular association between the Catholic and the barbaric, and between Catholicism and witchcraft, meant that she was recalled by authors writing about the Catholic threat to England, at home and abroad.[69] For example, in the rabidly anti-Catholic poem *Mischeefes Mysterie: or, Treasons Master-peece*, written by Francis Herring, and translated into English by John Vicars and published in 1617, the translator describes the conspirator Guy Fawkes (a Catholic and a Spanish sympathiser) as possessing 'foule Medeas guile' (E^v) as he conceals kegs of gunpowder beneath the Houses of Parliament.[70] In his work on theatre in the last decade before the outbreak of the Civil Wars, Martin Butler points to Protestant fascination with what he calls 'the king-killing side of Catholicism', and Medea's killing of two kings, Pelias and Creon, combined with her foreignness and her capacity for destructive plotting (against Pelias, Jason, Creon, Theseus and her father Aeëtes) makes her a neat point of comparison for Fawkes, and an instantly recognisable symbol of what such authors saw as horrifying Catholic disregard for government and kingship.[71]

It is important to note that Vicars's two references to Medea, here and later in the poem, are his additions to Herring's Latin poem, the ironically titled *Pietas Pontificia*.[72] The 1610 translation of Herring's poem by 'A. P.' describes Fawkes as 'this hellish weed, / Night-walking goblin, master of his skill' (B5^r), and *Pietas Pontificia* itself terms him 'Ambulo nocturnus, fraudis scelerisq[ue]; Magister / Horribilis' (B^r),[73] but Vicars adds both the oddly feminising comparison with Medea and a description of Fawkes as not a man but a '*Furie* of hell fire' (E^r).[74] Proudly terming his poem 'translated, and very much dilated' on its title-page, and writing for a fiercely Protestant readership, still eager for horror stories about the Catholic threat more than a decade after the defeat of the Gunpowder Plot, Vicars uses the murderous Medea to underscore the danger that Catholicism, epitomised by Fawkes, had posed to the kingdom and to the very lives of the King, Prince Henry and Princess Elizabeth. He does this by adding Medea where she had not been previously, just as Crowne, Ovid and Seneca enthusiastically embellish the Medea they had found in their sources, whether Shakespeare or Euripides.[75] Like Gainsford and May after him, however, Vicars presents Medea to his readers only to deliberately undermine his own use of her threat and to provide reassurance for supporters of the current regime that Medea-figures are inevitably and comfortingly vanquished. Nowhere is this more apparent than in his final addition of Medea, in the second part of the poem, in which he describes how the '*Crow-pickt sculs*' (N[v]) of two of the conspirators, Catesby and Percy, were displayed in London as a warning against treachery. Vicars writes that they are justly punished

Who by *ambitious* and *pernicious* wayes,
The *Golden Fleece* thus hoped to obtaine:
Not by stout *Jasons* merit and just praise,
But by *Medaeas* sorceries: in vaine
They gap't to get their *golden-fleece* their prize,
This did they fondly in their hearts surmize. (N[v])

Here, Percy's and Catesby's fatal mistake was not just to plot against King James but to do so in ways that associate them with the occult and the feminine: they pursue success by use of 'Medaeas sorceries' rather than by 'stout *Jasons* merit'. For Vicars, the assistance that Medea gives Jason is repellent because, like Acrasia's and Radigund's control over men in the *Faerie Queene*, it is emasculating, as well as associated with witchcraft, and thus Catholicism. Vicars makes Jason representative of heroic masculine endeavour, the route to success which Percy and Catesby rejected to their cost, in their fatal association with the evil and Medea-like Fawkes.

When she surfaces in these works, Medea is associated with the foreign, the Catholic and the hellish: and yet when historical opponents of England, of monarchy or of Protestantism are likened to Medea they are never quite able to measure up to her abhorrent example. The Colchian sorceress succeeded in her plots to destroy Creon and Pelias, and to ruin Jason's hopes for a new life, but Henry VII, Elizabeth and James have been able to see off the threats to their rule represented by the pretender Warbeck, the Spanish Armada and the treacherous Guy Fawkes, and terrible though she is, a use of Medea thus becomes perversely comforting for the English Protestant reader. Through associating her with the presentation and defeat of such enemies, Elizabethan and Jacobean authors effectively declaw their references to Medea, titillating their readers with the suggestion of her threat, before reassuring them with the defeat of the alarming historical and political figures to which she is likened. As the seventeenth century progressed, however, internal threats to England's stability became ever more real, and Medea's violent resistance to authority is used increasingly to speak to pressing contemporary event, rather than to past threat or disruption in England.

Medea and the English Civil Wars

Medea had been a useful figure with which to attack Catholicism in the reigns of Elizabeth and James, and when Charles I succeeded his father anti-Catholic uses of Medea could become urgently focused on correcting the King's perceived sympathy for Rome and High Church practices. For example, in *The Baiting of the Pope's Bull* (1627) Henry Burton references the Senecan Medea's plea to King Creon, that she should be allowed to remain in Corinth for one extra day before accepting her exile, as he warns Charles of the danger posed to England by Pope Urban VIII's issuing of a 'breeve' in 1626. Addressing the King directly in the 'Epistle Dedicatorie', Burton warns him that the Pope is trying to turn his Catholic subjects against him, and pointedly reminds him, 'A *Breeve* was sent from the *Pope*, to prepare the way for the *Spanish Invasion* in 88. Another, for the *Gunpowder Treason*' (¶4r). In Seneca's tragedy, when she asks for an extra day in Corinth, Medea demands of the king, 'Quae fraus timeri tempore exiguo potest?' (What fear of treachery can there be in so brief a time?) (291), and Creon accedes to her request, despite the doubts revealed in his reply: 'Nullum ad nocendum tempus angustum est malis' (No time is too short for the wicked to do harm') (292). Burton connects Creon's naivety to Charles's toleration of the Pope, warning that the consequences of his indulgence may be just as dire:

> Popes yeares are as precious, as that day, which *Medea* begged of
> *King Creon* before her banishment, wherein her womanish malice
> so bestirred her selfe, that ... shee consumed the Kings house with
> fire, and made a cruell massacre of sundry Noble personages, yea
> most unnaturally even of her owne Sonnes. And what massacres
> may not this present Pope, the head of that Antichristian Beast,
> yea of that Babylonish woman, *drunke with the blood of the Saints*

atchieve in *three yeeres and a halfe*, the time which the Antichristian Church (though most absurdly) limiteth for Antichrists Tyrannie; for whose blood-thirstie crueltie, neyther the Kings owne house, no nor yet the Popes owne, though most *beloved Sonnes* can secure themselves. (pp. 72–3)[76]

Burton equates the Pope's power, deceit and wilful evil with Medea's, and her unfortunate children, killed so 'unnaturally' by their mother, to subjects of Charles and of the Pope himself, who may yet suffer for the monarch's indulgence, and because of the Pope's inability to restrain his 'blood-thirstie crueltie'. Through his use of such emotive comparisons, Burton demands that Charles take notice of his appeal. Moreover, the text also includes letters to the 'Christian Readers' (p. 5) and to 'those my Countriemen whom the Pope calleth his *Catholicke sonnes*' (p. 74), and these make clear that Burton's polemic also aims to influence a wider English readership, one that is potentially undecided about what he perceives as England's highly dangerous and foolhardy drift towards Rome.

The connection between Medea's violence and the perceived cruelty of the Roman Church continued to be pursued by opponents of Catholicism through the 1640s and 1650s. The Puritan preacher Thomas Ady begins his treatise *A Candle in the dark* (1655) by lamenting that innocent men and women are often executed for witchcraft: 'The Grand Errour of these latter Ages is ascribing power to Witches, and by foolish imagination of mens brains, without grounds in the Scriptures, wrongfull killing of the innocent under the name of Witches' (A3ʳ). He later quotes from the account of Medea's powers in *Metamorphoses* 7, and gives Hypsipyle's accusation in the *Heroides*, that Medea sticks pins in wax effigies of her enemies in order to bring harm upon them. Ady tells his readers that such fictional texts, which are no more than 'inventions and pastimes of Poets', inspire the Pope to new heights of cruelty:

These are the Popes Scriptures whereon he groundeth his groundless inventions to torment the Christian World, and upon these grounds being inventions and pastimes of Poets, hath he sent out Inquisitors in all places to torment; from thence is the *Spanish Inquisition*, which maketh search for Hereticks and Witches all as one ... under the name of Witches he melteth away every one that hath but a smell of the reformed Religion, and the world perceiveth it not, this is that Grand Witch, the Whore of *Rome*, the Pope and his train. (pp. 95–6)[77]

Here, Ady explains how the Pope manipulates famous literary incarnations of witches, such as Ovid's Medea, playing on popular fear of witchcraft, when in fact his real aim is to root out 'every one that hath but a smell of the reformed Religion'. It is the Pope, Ady asserts, who should really be feared as a witch, despite his attempts to use Medea to stir up fear of black magic.

Dagmar Freist has argued that 'Throughout early seventeenth-century England, negative images of women time and time again furnish political symbolism equating opponents with women's vices, and sexuality', while Frances Dolan has noted that, in the 1630s and 1640s, anxieties about Catholicism and the Court's and the royal couple's sympathy for Rome were often expressed as fear about unnatural female power over men.[78] As the country advanced towards civil war, the long-established connection between Medea's power and the horrors of a Catholic regime retained its pull over authors, and authors' fears could become specifically focused on her femininity. John Vicars's vituperative poetic account of the Gunpowder Plot, *Mischeefes Mysterie*, was reprinted in 1641, and in the same year there appeared a much shorter, anonymous poem, *Novembris monstrum, or, Rome brought to bed in England*.[79] This searing attack, composed to mark the anniversary of the Plot, uses Medea's infanticide, her clearest deviation from the norms of femininity and humanity, to communicate the breakdown in society that would follow a rise in the influence of the Catholic Church in England. The poet warns that under a Catholic regime a litany of horrors would follow:

[Yo]u'l see perhaps a sucking babe anon,
[w]hich smiling to the mothers Lullaby,
Hangs on her melting breast, and whilst it takes
The hony flowing from those milkie lakes,

[So] me fist, that's brawnd with frequent cruelly,
[Qu]ite spoyles the draught, snatching it fro[m] her breast,
[A]nd to compleate determin'd villany
[Forc]eth the Parent for to doe the rest.
Making her turne *Medea*, rend and scatter
The tender softnesse of that infant matter. (B3ʳ)[80]

Chapter 3 has considered Lady Macbeth as one of Shakespeare's Medea-figures, and this dire prediction recalls her declaration to her husband that she would stay true to a promise, however horrible its consequences:

> I have given suck, and know
> How tender 'tis to love the babe that milks me.
> I would, while it was smiling in my face,
> Have plucked my nipple from his boneless gums
> And dashed the brains out, had I so sworn
> As you have done to this. (1.7.54–9)

Another likely inspiration was Vicars's poem, which includes a similarly grisly prediction about the likely consequences of Catholic triumph in England:

> Then mercilesly should the infant tender,
> Be *lugg'd* and *tugg'd* from wofull mothers brest:
> And tost up into th'aire, on pikes so slender,
> Before the face of *parents* most opprest. (K^v)

Shakespeare's Lady Macbeth would willingly slaughter her infant, while Vicars's parents would be forced to watch: but it is the author of *Novembris monstrum* who adds the explicit reference to Medea to his horrifying description of a mother forced to turn on her own child. The full title of the poem claims that it was composed 'long since' and privately circulated, but was finally published in 1641 to commemorate England's 'great deliverance' from the Catholic threat of the Gunpowder Plot. Of course, as well as reflecting on a past, defeated threat, as John Vicars's *Mischeefes Mysterie* had done, its publication at this particularly sensitive time, like the reissue of Vicars's work, was also intended to stir up readerly feelings of disgust and hysteria against the Roman Church, and through its use of Medea's abhorrent example the poem amply demonstrates the explosive state of England's relationship with Rome throughout the 1640s.

In the wake of the regicide, too, and although persistent emphasis on past disruption and its defeat had failed to secure the monarchy, Royalist writers continued to turn not only to England's past but also to the goriest of classical stories, to express their horror and despair at events in England, and to plead for reason. In the conclusion to his investigation into Charles's execution, Fabian Philipps writes sadly that 'The blood of old *England* is let out by a greater witchcraft and cousenage then that of *Medea* when shee set *Pelias* daughters to let out his old blood that young might come in the place of it' (I^v).[81] Here, 'old England' seems diminished in the most horrifying way possible, its life-force utterly drained, as the kingly body of Pelias was fatally compromised by Medea's malign deception of his daughters. Philipps described his account of Charles's downfall as an 'impartiall enquiry', but the title of his work also identifies Charles as 'no man of blood: but a martyr for his people', and thus it is clear where his sympathies lie: it is the regicides who are compared to Medea, deceiving the English people as Medea knowingly and cruelly deceived Pelias' daughters into killing their father, and weakening the nation as Pelias was emasculated by the letting of his blood.

Peter Elmer has noted that, in the 1640s and 1650s, there was a move away from the use of witchcraft as 'a normative system of discourse which fostered unity and concord in the body politic'. Rather, as he has shown, the rhetoric of witchcraft was used by both Royalists and Parliamentarians, and became increasingly associated with 'division and schism' rather than functioning as an aberration which can, perversely, promote order.[82] Medea is something of an exception here: her killing and dismemberment of her brother Apsyrtus was used in sermons and treatises in the 1640s to plead, by contrast, for moderation and harmony.[83] Moreover, while both sides used the language of witchcraft, the specific example of Medea was not equally useful to Royalists and Parliamentarians. Although Seneca's Medea stands up to the tyrant Creon, she was not an attractive example for opponents of the monarchy in works printed between 1640 and 1660: her crimes are simply too great, and when she is used in politically charged prose, poetry or drama, Medea is far more likely to be employed by supporters of the Royalist cause, as a warning against rebellion.

For example, in about 1648, one anonymous ballad used the misplaced trust which Pelias' daughters placed in Medea, whom they believed would rejuvenate their father, to pour scorn on the Long Parliament. The author ridicules its attempts to repair the country's wounds:

> This most unexpiated sin,
> will sure your ruine be;
> And sincke you all for what hath bin,
> to hells profundity.
> *Medea* like to cure our ill,
> our age for to renew.
> You did our ancient order kill,
> and yet we want, a new. (p. 1)[84]

In his criticism, the author of this ballad, entitled *The Turne of time*, reads Medea's killing of Pelias as an example of the futility of destroying something in an attempt to renew or improve it, and it is not surprising that this particular aspect of Medea's power was popular among Royalists during the Civil Wars and Interregnum.[85] It is clear that Medea was useful to politically minded authors in sixteenth- and seventeenth-century England as a cautionary example: specifically, as someone who committed acts of great cruelty, and who was a famous witch (and therefore could naturally be compared with Catholic threats). Moreover, Stuart Clark and Peter Elmer have noted the early modern fondness for associating witchcraft with rebellion, through the frequent quotation of 1 Samuel 15.23, 'Rebellion is as the sin of witchcraft'.[86] Medea, of course, is not just a witch but a killer of kings (Pelias, Creon), a destroyer of kingdoms (Corinth) and a threat to heirs (Apsyrtus and Theseus, as well as her own sons). Her violence and her political centrality in Colchis and Corinth thus made her, in many ways, an even more attractive figure with which to condemn rebellion than the elderly, poor and disenfranchised woman who was the typical target of early modern witch-hunters. Given the sensationalised and emotive ways in which Vicars, Burton, Ady and the anonymous authors of *Novembris Monstrum* and *The Turne of Time* used Medea's story, it is to be expected that politicised Restoration approaches to Medea's myth continued to adapt and to appropriate her story to warn about the horrors of king-killing and faction.

Medea, regicide and restoration

Royalist or Tory writing in Charles II's reign can often be distinguished by a particular kind of soul-searching by writers who use Medea's story, which was full of the deaths and betrayals of kings, to confront their own mistakes, and acknowledge that the whole country must shoulder some responsibility for the upheaval of the 1640s and 1650s and, specifically, for the regicide.[87] For the preacher Henry Glover, speaking in 1663 on the anniversary of the King's execution, the regicides outdo Medea in wickedness:

> Had they with *Romulus* killed their own *brother*, or with *Oedipus* their own *father*; had they with *Medea* chopt their *children* in pieces, or kickt the child out of their *wives bellies* with *Nero*, or ript up their *Mothers bowels*, to see the place they lay in before they were born; all this had been a sort of *Piety* to what these Monsters did. (C^r)[88]

In 1662, Cimelgus Bonde's prose treatise *A Royal Apologie for King Charles the Martyr* compares the people of England to Medea, because of their potential to do great harm. He tells his readers:

> Yet we, because by our wicked plots and devices, we have got a numberless company, of those who like our selves, will do any thing for gain, think it a sin, if we do not perform any wickedness, which our power will assist us to effect. (p. 159)

Bonde then illustrates this point, that evil is always striving to outdo itself, by quoting some of the Senecan Medea's most famous lines, her insistence that, having betrayed her father and killed her brother and Pelias, she has not even begun to fulfil her true potential for violence:

> Tremenda caelo pariter, ac terris mala
> Mens intus agitat, vulnera, & caedem, & vagum
> Funus per artus. levia memoravi nimis;
> Haec virgo feci. (p. 159)[89]

These lines translate as:

> [E]vils fearful to heaven and earth alike, my mind stirs up within me: wounds and slaughter and death creeping from limb to limb. But these things I talk of are too slight: I did all this as a girl. (46–9)

Medea speaks them at the close of Act 1 of Seneca's tragedy, as she urges herself on to even greater wickedness than her previous killings of Apsyrtus and Pelias, and for the Latinate reader Bonde's use of this specific quotation is thus not just a condemnation of past sin but a potent warning that even greater atrocities may follow the regicide, unless the people of England can restrain themselves from compounding their past crimes, as Medea did not.

Similarly, in *The Regal Proto-Martyr*, a sermon published in 1672 but first preached early in the Restoration, John Allington begins by using a quotation from Seneca's *Medea* as his epigraph (A^r). The lines he chooses are Medea's pronouncement to Jason: 'cui prodest scelus, / is fecit' (he who gains by a crime, committed it) (500–1).[90] Here, Medea is telling Jason that he must take responsibility for the crimes she committed to assist him, and Allington's sermon argues that Charles was betrayed by supposed friends as well as his enemies. Moreover, the Senecan Medea's words to Jason do not simply imply that he should feel guilt and regret for allowing her to commit the crimes she has. Rather, because Jason has abandoned her, and will not accept, as she demands, that he is guilty of her murders by association, they herald a new determination in Medea, to commit even more terrible acts. She builds on her killing of one king (Pelias) with another (Creon), and destroys the future as well as the present of Corinth's monarchy, in her murders of Jason's children and his new bride. Jason does not listen to his wife, despite knowing of what she is capable, and he and his new family, and the kingdom of Corinth, all pay the price. Linda Hutcheon has pointed out that, in the adaptive process, 'Context conditions meaning', and, in the hands of guilt-ridden Restoration writers, Medea's avowal of her own cruel sense of purpose, or her pointed criticism of Jason, take on very topical and particular meanings, becoming stern messages for the Restoration subject.[91] Like Bonde, Allington uses Medea's murderous potential not only to castigate the country that colluded in the regicide but also to counsel England for the future, to urge the country to think about how such a terrifying and destructive force might be handled differently, if it reared its head a second time and threatened yet more evil.

If Tudors and Stuarts writing in the reigns of Elizabeth, James and Charles I had seemed preoccupied with England's medieval past, supporters of Charles II were equally unable to forget the much more recent turmoil of the Civil Wars.[92] In the last years of Charles's reign, concerns about further rebellion in England were particularly pressing, in part because of the burgeoning Exclusion Crisis, which was precipitated by the increasing likelihood that the Catholic Duke of York, James, would succeed his brother Charles II. The Duke of York's opponents preferred Charles's illegitimate but Protestant son, James, Duke of Monmouth, and attempted to have the King's brother barred from the succession. This was followed, in 1683, by the Rye House Plot, a conspiracy to assassinate both Charles and his brother. In such a climate, witchcraft was a popular touchstone for those who wanted to demonstrate the horrors of rebellion against the Crown: Peter Elmer has shown that witchcraft and its association with rebellion unsurprisingly retained its popularity as a subject for sermons preached between 1660 and 1688.[93] In the burlesque witchcraft poem *Canidia* (1683), a lengthy oration in the voice of a witch, probably composed by the Anglican clergyman Robert Dixon, the chief witch, Canidia, plays on this association between rebellion and witchcraft. She first boasts that she and her fellow witches outdo famous sorceresses like Medea, but then points out that, for all the witches' anarchic behaviour, 'There was never any Rebellion in Hell, / 'Tis beyond any Infernal Spell' (p. 158). She then adopts the same approach as Henry Glover had taken in his 1663 sermon, insisting that the regicides were far worse than any other evil:

The worst of Murderers that ever spoke,
Were they that hew'd down the *Royal Oak*.
Ne're shew your Faces above Ground more,
Hell dares trust you, no farther than the Door.
Now Rail at Witches, who'l believe you?
Had you more Kings to kill, 'twould never grieve you. (p. 159)[94]

Dixon's lengthy poem is often hard to take seriously, and deliberately so, but as it draws towards its close here it demonstrates how even a comic work can use the spectre of witchcraft seriously and politically, and that even a witch's voice can be used to counsel against disobedience.

Because of the terrible excesses of her crimes, and because of the specificity of her attacks on male, royal bodies and kingdoms, in the period 1660–88 a focus on Medea's destructive power paradoxically allows the promotion of unity, and enables supporters of Charles and James to confront and exorcise their own worst fears about rebellion in England and to praise the security and order that they hoped James's succession would bring. This chapter has demonstrated, however, the variety of opponents of the monarchy who were compared to Medea, and, as one last example demonstrates, it begins to seem that hers is a threat that can never be truly and permanently overcome. In 1686, when the Tory political theorist Nathaniel Johnston dedicates *The Excellence of Monarchical Government* to the new King, he also reflects on the upheaval of the last fifty years, with particular reference to the struggles that characterised the last years of Charles II's reign: even after the horrors of the 1640s, he writes, there remained '[a] strange Propensity, in Male-contents, tumultuous Petitioners, Associators, and daring Promotors of the Bill of Seclusion, to involve the Kingdom again in a Civil War' (a2^r). However, it is the author's opinion that James has weathered these storms successfully, and when he mentions Medea, his (ill-founded) hopes for a new political and religious security in England after 1685 mean that unlike (for example) John Crowne, author of *The Misery of Civil War*, Johnston does not feel compelled to play up the horrors of Medea's crimes. Rather, he explains how an effective monarch may effortlessly outdo her and neutralise the necromantic threat she represents: '*Medaea* never knew so many Balsamick Herbs to renew the old Age of *Jason*, as a prudent Prince doth Rules and Methods to cure all the Distempers of his Kingdom, preserve it in a perfect Health, or restore it when declining' (p. 95).[95] Johnston argues that, unlike Medea, a king can effect genuine and beneficial change, and renew where Medea would only destroy. For the modern reader, though, the certainty that James's reign was to be curtailed so shortly by the Glorious Revolution means that Johnston's comparison between James II and Medea does not retain the triumphalism he intends, becoming contaminated, instead, by knowledge of the subsequent story, both political and mythical. In a way, Johnston's reference represents the culmination of the sixteenth- and seventeenth-century tendency to politicise Medea by making her a threat that has been dispelled or overcome: here, James is Medea rewritten, as benevolent and even more powerful. The modern reader knows, however, that James is fated to become far more a Creon or a Pelias, a king defeated by what Edward Sherburne termed the 'hidden Malice of revengeful (though seemingly reconcil'd) Enemies': that is, those Medea-like threats to England's security that can, perhaps, only ever be temporarily quashed.

Medea's violent, persuasive and magical power is insistently present in the foregoing examples, but, in all cases, her power is recalled in order that it may be dispelled, and in turn may go some way towards exorcising the threat represented by Catholicism, by continental enemies of England, or by civil unrest. In what may be broadly termed political writing, whether this writing takes the form of drama, prose treatises, poetry or published sermons, Medea's terrifying magical power, or her power over male bodies, is perversely compelling for authors. Consistently, though, it is inventively and hopefully rewritten, to demonstrate the fatal consequences of disorder, to affirm support for England's monarchy, and to encourage the country's subjects towards the temperance, loyalty and obedience that the classical Medea had so memorably and determinedly resisted.

Conclusion

What is't the Muses javelin cannot pierce?
When heaven and hell are master'd by a verse,
The Laurel staffe sway'd by a learned hand
Carries more magick than that silver wand,
Heavens verger waves, then that Medea shook,
When Aeson from the scalding bath she took,
Hot as the youth she gave him, or the ram,
Which from the Caldron leap't a frisking lamb,
Such boundlesse power doth on numbers wait
Without a blasphemy they can create,
Nor have they fame and strength alone, but can
Surfet the unconfin'd desires of man,
With soul-transporting pleasure and content,
Not to be thought on without ravishment. (A8ᵛ)
(Joshua Poole, 'To the hopeful young Gentlemen, his
Schollers in that private School, at Hadley, Kept in
the house of Mr. Francis Atkinson', in *The English
Parnassus* (1657)).[1]

In these lines, included in the prefatory poem to the mid-seventeenth-century miscellany *The English Parnassus*, Joshua Poole describes Medea's power, and particularly her rejuvenation of Aeson, to demonstrate how literary creation is able to outdo even her famous efforts: 'The Laurel staffe sway'd by a learned hand' is more magical, and more transformative, than Medea's 'silver wand', and literary creation contains within it a 'boundlesse power' that is, moreover, morally commendable, 'Without a blasphemy', as Medea's is not. The collection, a compilation of verses from a wide range of sixteenth- and seventeenth-century poets, including

190

Spenser and Drayton, and arranged alphabetically by subject, returns to Medea several times, and she is an overwhelmingly negative example. Michael Drayton's lines in Henry II's epistle to Rosamond, part of *Englands Heroicall Epistles*, in which he compares Rosamond's beauty to Medea's rejuvenating power, are incorporated into the long poem 'Beautifull':

As if she swaid an Empire in her face,
Nature her self, did her own self admire,
As oft as she were pleased to attire
Her in her native lustre, and confess
Her dressing, was her chiefest comeliness,
Where every limb takes like a face,
One accent from whose lips the blood more warms,
Than all Medea's Exorcismes, and charms[.] (R6ᵛ)

Elsewhere, though, she is defined as 'Unchaste, cruel, charming, subtle, bloody, furious' (K3ʳ) and included in definitions of 'Poyson', 'Furious' and 'Witch'. Poole's miscellany thus reflects the period's interest in, and familiarity with, Medea's legend, and the variety of uses to which this legend was put. As the previous chapters have shown, early modern authors were compelled to address Medea's fascinating power, but they sought to appropriate or query this power in a number of ways, and far more adventurously than their medieval counterparts. In some ways, medieval ways of handling Medea's threat persisted into the sixteenth and seventeenth centuries: for example, in 'The Pitious Complaint of Medea' (1576), George Whetstone renders her emotional and weakened, while George Sandys's *Metamorphoses* represents an evolution of the medieval tendency to allegorise Medea's power, to explain her magic as a way of limiting it. Elsewhere, though, early modern authors adopt a different approach. Chapter 2 has shown how the new and flourishing Renaissance and Restoration interest in classical translation sought to negotiate the terrifying Medeas of Ovid and Seneca, by suggesting regret for her actions, or punishment for her crimes, but that translators might also exaggerate her witchcraft, her barbarism, or her unbridled sexuality to titillate their readers. Chapters 3 and 4 have demonstrated how Medea was enthusiastically punished by early modern authors of tragedy, while comedy of the period shies away from the worst of Medea's excesses, and turns her magical and rhetorical power to more conformist ends. At the same time, though, works like Shakespeare's *The Tempest* and Greene's *Alphonsus* use evocative references or allusions to Medea to cast doubt on the ostensibly happy endings they create, setting comedy and tragedy alongside one another in provocative ways that reflect the period's enthusiasm for tragicomedy. Chapter 5 has argued that politically charged fiction or polemic of the sixteenth and seventeenth centuries reaffirms conformity to the status quo through Medea's terrible story, not only by emphasising the savagery and violence of her powers, as tragic authors had done, but also by endowing this power with additional relevance to the political and religious turmoil of their own time and suggesting that the rebellious malice she represents might be overcome.

Women writing Medea

Clearly, the alarming threat that Medea's power represented could be mastered in a variety of ways, but equally noticeable from a brief survey of such examples is that the authors who choose to grapple with Medea's story in the period are overwhelmingly male: indeed, Poole's poem, with its dismissal of Medea's achievements as far less than those of poetry, is specifically addressed to an audience of young men. Of course, this absence of female-authored treatments of Medea is partly a result of women's reluctance or inability to write or to venture into print in the period, and Medea's story poses the additional difficulty of its classicism: as Wye Saltonstall had acknowledged in the preface to his translation of the *Heroides*, many female readers in the seventeenth century did not have the classical education necessary to read this story in the original Latin (or Greek, for Euripides' tragedy and Apollonius Rhodius' *Argonautica* were increasingly well known in the seventeenth century).[2] Despite a growing eagerness on the part of such translators to make her accessible to the female reader, however, Medea's story very obviously poses other problems for the female author: as an aggressively wayward woman, who could scarcely accord less with the approved female virtues of silence, chastity and obedience, hers is not a story that can be used to inspire or to encourage women, much less reassure male readers anxious about the implications of female authorship. In medieval France, Christine de Pizan had attempted a rehabilitation and defence of Medea, but it is unsurprisingly one that is severely compromised. She observes in *The Book of the City of Ladies* that Medea 'loved Jason with a too great and too constant love' (II.56.1, p. 189),[3] and in *The Epistle of Othea* recalls, 'in lewde love sche suffrid hir to be maistried, so þat sche sette hir herte upon Jason and yaf him worschip, bodi and goodes; for þe which aftirward he yaf hir a ful yvil reward' (LVIII, p. 72).[4] Christine's repeated returns to Medea's story, however, seem to suggest that though she wishes to construct a sympathetic woman, one who will refute the negative incarnations that have come before, she can only do this by weakening Medea.[5] Thus *The Book of the City of Ladies* makes mention of Medea's learning and command of drugs but *The Epistle of Othea* demonstrates the extent to which Medea, as a woman, has little essential power over Jason. In it, Christine notes that knights should repay favours done to them, but that Jason 'fayled of his feiþ [& loved anothir]', 'nat-wiþstandinge sche was [of] sovereyne beaute' (LIV, p. 66–7). Medea's femininity and beauty are emphasised, and Christine, like Chaucer, defends her by stressing that she is vulnerable to Jason's control over the situation.

In 'The Copy of a Letter, lately Written in Meeter, by a Yonge Gentilwoman to her Unconstant Lover', the first poem in a short collection by the same name, which was published in 1567, the English poet Isabella Whitney hints at female revenge and the tragic repercussions that Jason-like faithlessness may have, before stepping back from promising these. Like the Heroidean Hypsipyle and Medea, both of whom learn from another that they have lost Jason (Hypsipyle via an embarrassed messenger, who reports Jason's dalliance with Medea, Medea through her own child, who describes Jason's and Creusa's marriage procession), Whitney's female speaker hears second-hand that her lover intends to marry another woman. She chides him with a familiar litany of classical examples of male faithlessness: Theseus, Paris and Jason, who has exploited Medea's knowledge and skill to win the Fleece, and has used her sexually into the bargain:

> For when he by *MEDEAS* arte,
> had got the Fleece of Gold
> And also had of her that time,
> al kynd of things he wolde. (A3ʳ)[6]

The speaker's lover is urged not to follow the example of faithless classical men, and, having spent several quatrains describing the injustice of Jason's safe escape from Colchis, she warns him:

> And unto me a Troylus be,
> if not you may compare:
> With any of these persons that
> above expressed are. (A4ʳ)

Jason has been the most prominent of these abandoning men, and the reader is invited, by Whitney's words, to reflect on how the speaker's lover might share not only Jason's fickle nature but also his fate: that is, the deaths of his children and new wife at the hands of the old. Whitney's speaker denies the possibility of such revenge, assuring her lover, 'Wed whom you list, I am content, / your refuse for to be' (A4ʳ), but if Jason is insistently invoked as an example it is difficult (if not impossible) to forget Medea, particularly when the next quatrain sees Whitney's speaker reflect:

> It shall suffice me simple soule,
> of thee to be forsaken:
> And it may chance although not yet
> you wish you had me taken. (A4ʳ)

Such ominous lines scarcely constitute uncomplicated acceptance of the speaker's lot, and as the poem draws to a close the uneasy balance between good wishes for her lover's future and hints that he may come to regret his decision is maintained, through deliberately ambiguous quatrains that ostensibly praise his new lover, while hinting at the possibility that she is an unwise choice. For example, Whitney's speaker wishes:

> For she that shal so happy be,
> of thee to be elect:
> I wish her vertues to be such,
> she nede not be suspect. (A4ʳ)

Whitney's speaker never goes so far as to liken herself to Medea, and she prefers this kind of backhanded compliment to the insults that Hypsipyle and Medea use to describe their rivals, when they write to Jason. Nevertheless, the very fact that the poem presents itself as the epistolary complaint of an unfairly abandoned woman, along with the insistent references to Jason (who is paid far more attention than Paris or Theseus), means that the reader is invited to recall Medea's revenge, even if Whitney's speaker, tellingly, does not go so far as to threaten it herself. Like Robert Greene's *Mamillia*, and Chaucer's *Legend of Good Women*, Whitney's poem presents a Medea-figure who is ostensibly nothing more than an example of a woman suffering for love, but the reader who is already familiar with Medea is tantalized by the suggestion of revenge that Whitney cannot articulate, but that is not entirely quashed by her speaker's protestations of stoic acceptance.

The spectre of Medea's revenge on a husband who has abandoned her for another woman also haunts Elizabeth Cary's closet drama, *The*

Tragedy of Mariam (printed 1613), and here Herod's rejected first wife Doris does wish for revenge on her love-rival Mariam. Doris lacks the drive or ability to follow Medea's example and carry out her revenge, however, as (for example) William Alabaster's Roxana can. Doris' son Antipater specifically and eagerly suggests revenge on Mariam's children, that they are killed 'By poison's drink, or else by murderous knife' (2.3.61), and Doris herself recalls her appeal to supernatural powers for assistance in her revenge:

> Oft have I begged for vengeance for this fact,
> And with dejected knees, aspiring hands,
> Have prayed the highest power to enact
> The fall of her that on my trophy stands.
> Revenge I have according to my will,
> Yet where I wished this vengeance did not light.
> I wished it should high-hearted Mariam kill,
> But it against my whilom lord did fight. (2.3.33–40)[7]

Doris recognises the wrong she has suffered, and can appeal for restitution in powerful terms, but, unlike Medea, she cannot control vengeance, which has, she believes, been exacted not on Mariam but on Herod, Doris' 'whilom lord'. As the play's frequent comments on the danger of women's speech and public self-representation suggest, Cary is keenly aware of the potentially transgressive impact of her play,[8] but, like Whitney, she steps back from having a woman carry out acts of violence. Herod's sister Salome achieves her ends by manipulating her brother to dispose of her enemies, while Doris and Antipater can do nothing more than 'retire to grieve alone' (2.3.69), as a despondent Doris puts it.

At the very end of the seventeenth century, although women ventured more extensively and enthusiastically into print, this uncertainty over how they ought to handle Medea, and particularly the issue of her violent revenge, remained. Like male Restoration tragedians such as Nathaniel Lee, Mary Pix, author of *The False Friend* (1699), recognised the dramatic and pathetic potential of a comparison between Medea and a scorned woman. In her tragedy, Appamia is in love with her friend Emilius, and is horrified to learn that he has married Lovisa. She compares herself to Medea in her shift from love to hatred:

> What was't, but slighted Love, made *Medea*,
> Prove a Fury? doubtless her Breast was,

Once as soft, as Fond, as Innocent as mine;
As free from black Revenge, or Dire Mischiefs—
Rise ye Furies! Instead of Tresses, Deck me
With your Curling Snakes!—For
I will sting 'em all to Death! (C^v)^9

Pix dwells in affecting detail on Appamia's gradual realisation that Emilius loves another, and on her attempts to conceal her true feelings. Unlike Isabella Whitney's slighted heroine, or Cary's furious and rejected Doris, however, Appamia is more than able to take revenge and, like Medea, she focuses her anger on her love-rival, rather than on the man who has betrayed her. She concocts a poison that she tricks Emilius into administering to his new wife, and Lovisa re-enacts Creusa's gruesome death, which was described by a messenger in Seneca's and Euripides' tragedies, but which had been enthusiastically exploited for its sensational onstage potential by Henry Chettle, in his early seventeenth-century revenge tragedy *Hoffman*. The year before Pix's tragedy premiered, Charles Gildon's *Phaeton* had described the tormented death of Lybia (Phaeton's new wife, and the play's Creusa/ Glauce figure) at the hands of his Medea-figure, Althea, in horribly graphic detail. Epaphus describes the scene to Phaeton:

Scarce had she reach'd the door of her Apartment,
When from her Mouth a white, but horrid Foam,
Spread o're her lovely Face, her Eye-balls roll'd,
And wildly whirl[e]d about with dire Convulsions.
Silent she lay, or breath[e]d but piteous Sighs,
And piercing groans, till the first fit was over ...

No sooner to herself she came, but saw
The blazing Crown belch out a fiery Deluge,
That prey'd upon her Hair, her Head, her Face;
From whence her Flesh like melting Wax ran down,
Mingl[e]d with Fire and Blood. Mean while the Robe
With fatal Rage devour'd her fainting Limbs.

First starting up, she shook her flaming Hair:
From side to side she toss[e]d her burning Temples,
To dash the cleaving Gold from off her Head.
In vain, the more she shook, the more it fix'd, and burnt. (E3^v)

Similarly, as she is slowly killed by the poison, Pix's Lovisa describes her torments at length, thrilling the audience with the spectacle of revenge successfully realised:

> Give me way, I am all Consuming Flames.
> Unhand me. Let me Lanch my
> Veins yet Deeper! They are all on Fire!
> Blood cannot quench 'em! My Breath is
> Flakes of Fire! My Eyes like flaming
> Meteors Shoot! My Nerves, my Arteries,
> Like Shrivel'd Parchment shrink in Fire—
> I Burn; I Blaze; I Dye—Oh that I cou'd—
> For Death they say is Cold! (I^r)

Both are ultimately indebted to Euripides' tragedy, in which the messenger recounts:

> The color of her face changed, and she staggered back,
> She ran, and her legs trembled, and she only just
> Managed to reach a chair without falling flat down.
> An aged woman servant who, I take it, thought
> This was some seizure of Pan or another god,
> Cried out 'God bless us,' but that was before she saw
> The white foam breaking through her lips and her rolling
> The pupils of her eyes and her face all bloodless.
> ...
> She leapt up from the chair, and all on fire she ran,
> Shaking her hair now this way and now that, trying
> To hurl the diadem away; but fixedly
> The gold preserved its grip, and when she shook her hair,
> Then more and twice as fiercely the fire blazed out.
> Till, beaten by her fate, she fell down to the ground,
> Hard to be recognized except by a parent.
> Neither the setting of her eyes was plain to see,
> Nor the shapeliness of her face. From the top of
> Her head there oozed out blood and fire mixed together. (1168–99)

The horror of Pix's scene is heightened, almost unbearably, however, by the fact that it is staged, rather than described by a messenger. In the aftermath of this gruesome scene Appamia is, of course, apprehended, and though she is not killed onstage like other unruly women, such as Shakespeare's and Ravenscroft's Tamoras, her father the Viceroy remarks that it is proper that the law holds her to account. Her downfall thus works to reinforce the systems of justice and order that her revenge initially seemed to subvert, and her father's remarks suggest that the parents in Pix's audience, like the Elizabethan parents who read Richard Robinson's *Rewarde of Wickednesse*, have lessons to learn from allusions to Medea's story. Like Medea's father, Aeëtes, the Viceroy is defeated as both a father and a ruler, and has been unable to enforce lawfulness even in his daughter, a dual blow that recalls early modern connections between the patriarchal institutions of family and state.[10] In response to this double failure, he declares that he will

> for ever from the World retire
> Leaving this sad Truth behind: That Parents
> Shou'd not, beyond the hopes of Heaven
> Their Children Prize.
> *Nor Indulg'd Children dare to Disobey,*
> *Lest they are punish't such a dismal way.* (I2ᵛ)

Most important of all, however, is Appamia's own expression of regret, and her hope that watching women should heed the example provided by her punishment:

> Let me for ever
> Warn my Sex, and fright 'em from the thoughts of
> Black Revenge, from being by Violent Passions
> Sway'd. Murder! And am I the cause? Fall Mountains
> On this Guilty Head, and let me think no more. (I2ʳ)[11]

Pix can exploit the gory potential of Medea's story as enthusiastically as any of her male counterparts, but she must simultaneously justify both her use of such a transgressive example of womanhood and her own decision to venture onto the stage, in order to allay male anxiety. So the Prologue reassures the play's audience of its edifying intentions:

> Amongst Reformers of this Vitious Age,
> Who think it Duty to Refine the Stage:
> A Woman, to Contribute, does Intend,
> In Hopes a Moral Play your Lives will Mend. (A3ʳ)

In her work on early modern witchcraft trials, Diane Purkiss has suggested that female witnesses often felt a particular pressure to differentiate themselves from the kind of threatening woman represented by the witch, and in her play Pix demonstrates a similar instinct in a female play-wright, to show how a woman who emulates Medea's crimes may be on some level instructive to other women, precisely because of her difference from them.[12] Unlike Whitney and Cary, Pix presents a vengeful Medea, but her Appamia nonetheless accords with stereotypical misogy-nistic views of women's jealousy, cruelty and irrationality. Moreover, the play is at pains to step back from its own alarming example, not only by punishing Appamia but also by stressing that, unlike Medea, the playwright herself aims to reform rather than corrupt. On the one hand, critics have been disappointed by Pix's reluctance to present a confident female voice in her works and by her contrastive preference for according with male expectation: so Derek Hughes has termed her 'a slavish upholder of male authority'.[13] On the other hand, Marsden has argued that she should be seen as '[c]ognizant of contemporary tastes and willing to promote them within her drama': perhaps it is unfair to expect Pix to deviate from the example of male dramatists who have presented Medea-figures, simply because of her own gender.[14] Moreover, male authors who invoke Medea, such as Achelley or Edward Sherburne, might go to some lengths to defend the morality of their works (and Elizabethan authors in particular might stress her value as an example for women). They do not need to defend themselves, as authors, how-ever, in the same way that Pix does, against charges of immorality that relate specifically to their own sex. As such a contentious example, and one who might reflect unflatteringly, in the eyes of the early modern auditor, on the author herself, it is perhaps unsurprising that early mod-ern English women elected, on the whole, to steer clear of Medea and the violent threat that she posed, both to men and to other women.

Towards the eighteenth century

Pix's wholly predictable interest in making an example of her Medea-figure, and in exploiting but also limiting her sensational power, is also discernible in eighteenth-century translation. In the preface to his multi-authored translation of the *Metamorphoses* (1717), Samuel Garth praises the effort of George Sandys, whose work was the only com-plete English translation of Ovid's epic produced in the seventeenth century.[15] In particular, he commends the edifying lessons contained in the poem, noting that 'The Reader cannot fail of observing, how

many excellent Lessons of Morality *Ovid* has given us in the course of
his Fables' (p. xvi).[16] Despite his approval of the poem and Sandys's
notes, however, when he comes to discuss Medea Garth is driven to
build on Sandys, to see some further weakness in her that his Caroline
predecessor had not. Sandys had explained in his notes how women
who believe themselves to have magical powers are often themselves
deceived, and Garth insists that the classical Medea feels regret and guilt
for her crimes and experiences weakness even as she escapes punishment. In the preface, he explains the message readers should take from
a particularly notorious part of the legend, Medea's pitiless murder of
Pelias: 'From Medea's flying from Pelias's court; that th'offered Favours
of the Impious should always be suspected; and that they, who design to
make everyone fear them, are afraid of every one' (p. xviii). This wholly
unclassical sense of distress is reiterated in the translation of this book,
by Nahum Tate (who had previously contributed Medea's epistle to the
Dryden-Tonson *Ovid's Epistles*).[17] Where Ovid's 'Quod nisi pennatis ser-
pentibus isset in auras, / non exempta foret poenae' (But had she not
gone away through the air drawn by her winged dragons, she would
not have escaped punishment) (7.350–1) stresses the potential consequences of her crimes that Medea is able to evade so successfully, Tate's
more emotive description has her 'dreading the Revenge that must
ensue' (p. 230), the emotive 'dreading' and the idea that Medea 'must'
expect some payback for her crime working to ally her to the distressed
and guilt-ridden murderess of Pix's tragedy.

By the middle of the eighteenth century, in his adaptation of Seneca's
tragedy (printed 1761), Richard Glover could present Medea (rather
than a Medea-like woman) as simultaneously possessed of awesome
magic and unable to control her own fate: when she summons Hecate
for assistance, she is told:

Ere night's black wheels begin thy gloomy course
What thou dost love, shall perish by thy rage,
Nor thou be conscious, when the stroke is giv'n:
Then a despairing wand'rer must thou trace,
The paths of sorrow in remotest climes. (53)[18]

In 1698, in *Phaeton, Or the Fatal Divorce*, Charles Gildon had absolved
his Medea-figure, Althea, of infanticide, by having the citizens kill her
children. Here, Glover makes clear that she will not be innocent of the
act, but in some ways excites even greater pity for his heroine, in that
Medea is told that she will kill her children, but that she will do so

when she is not in control of her own actions. Her despair and isolation, described by Hecate and paraphrased from Hypsipyle's curse on Medea in *Heroides* 6, are all the more affecting, because she can do nothing to avoid her fate, and the tragedy is also heightened by Jason's more positive characterisation. He regrets his marriage to Creusa, wishes to be reunited with Medea and, even when he has learnt of her infanticide, blames Creon (who is a far crueller and more tyrannous figure than he is in the classical tragedies). Medea exclaims to him, 'Oh! Jason – Thou and I have once been happy! / What are we now?' (p. 91), and, rather than rejecting her in horror, Jason assures her, 'we may still be happy' (p. 91). While the Ovidian and Senecan Medea tells Jason that they both deserve the gods' punishment, here Jason asks the gods, 'Drop thy asswaging pity on her heart; / On me exhaust the quiver of thy vengeance' (p. 92). Finally, in the aftermath of the children's deaths, both Jason and Medea try to kill themselves, before Medea is borne away by her divine chariot, at the will of the gods rather than by her own choice, and Jason is urged by Juno's priestess, Theano, to return to Colchis and restore the country's fortunes. During the eighteenth and nineteenth centuries authorial interest in Medea as such a weakened and pitiable figure (rather than one who is abhorrent and deserving of punishment) gathered force. Finally, though, as much recent work on more modern Medeas has demonstrated, four centuries of evolving representations of the English Medea, from the sixteenth to the nineteenth, culminate in modern representations which are able to combine uncompromised power with authorial admiration. In the twentieth and twenty-first centuries, Medea's agency and disregard for patriarchal and normative authority might be facets of her character that are celebrated rather than punished or quashed, and she might appear sympathetic and even admirable, rather than pitiable.

The wealth of the foregoing examples demonstrates the flexibility of the early modern Medea, how she may be incorporated into a range of genres and handled with a variety of approaches (for example an author may choose whether to emphasise Medea's monstrosity and deserved punishment, or to excite pity for her by suggesting romantic suffering). Simultaneously, and paradoxically, though, there is a sense that early modern authors felt themselves perversely constrained by Medea: although undeniably fascinated by her power, they cannot and do not celebrate it as their classical forebears do. In early modern writing, suggests Wynne-Davies,

A choice of destinies awaits the egressive woman: if she may be reintroduced into the patriarchal value system, then she will be awarded an identity within that structure. But if her irregularities prove too virulent, too ingrained, then she must be ejected from the system altogether.[19]

Medea is, it could be said, ejected from patriarchal society in all the best-known classical versions of her story: in the works of Euripides, Seneca and Ovid she escapes pursuit by Jason, or by Aegeus, by means of magical powers and divine connections. The difference between the ejections of the classical and early modern Medea is, however, very clear: in the classical tradition, Medea is given control over her own escape, which is presented as a last successful evasion of attempts to impose patriarchal order upon her. Sixteenth- and seventeenth-century literature was both sterner and more imaginative in its literal and figurative expulsion of this highly irregular woman: as Garth's note to the *Metamorphoses* shows, even when she is granted her traditional and triumphant classical escape, this may be in some way negotiated and compromised. For early modern male authors in England, Medea was a well-known and thrilling example of disobedience, used to confront fears about Catholicism, witchcraft, unruly mothers and women more generally, civil discord and the destruction of kingdoms. The lessons that Medea holds for the early modern reader or audience may be taught through a wide variety of genres, and their applications are both domestic and national, focused on both family and state. In all cases, though, somehow controlling or expelling the power she represents is essential, for it is the process of imaginatively mastering Medea that allows male authors to indulge in a fantasy that simultaneously pleasurably invokes, and reassuringly quashes, her famous threats to order and to patriarchy.

Notes

Introduction

1. The longer title is *A most lamentable and Tragicall historie, conteyning the outragious and horrible tyrannie which a Spanishe gentlewoman named Violenta executed upon her lover Didaco because he espoused another beying first betrothed unto her* (London: 1576), STC (2nd edn) 1356.4. The tale was one of the tragic *novelle* of Matteo Bandello, and was translated into French by Pierre Boiastuau (or Boaistuau). For Bandello's version, see Matteo Bandello, *Opere*, ed. Francesco Flora, 2 vols (Milan: Arnoldo Mondadori, 1935), 1.496–508. For Boiastuau's, see Pierre Boiastuau, *Histoires Tragiques*, ed. Richard A. Carr (Paris: Librairie Honoré Champion, 1977), pp. 139–67.
2. William Shakespeare, *2 Henry VI, The Norton Shakespeare*, ed. Stephen Greenblatt et al. (New York: Norton, 1997), 5.3.59. Unless otherwise stated, all quotations from Shakespeare's works are from this edition. Edmund Spenser, *The Faerie Queene*, ed. A. C. Hamilton, 2nd edn, text ed. Hiroshi Yamashita and Toshiyuki Suzuki (Harlow: Pearson Longman, 2007), 5.8.47.
3. Jonathan Bate, *Shakespeare and Ovid* (Oxford: Clarendon Press, 1993), p. 155.
4. Euripides' play was translated into Latin by George Buchanan, and printed in 1544. See George Buchanan, *Tragedies*, ed. P. Sharratt and P. G. Walsh (Edinburgh: Scottish Academic Press, 1983).
5. Jason's promises to Medea and their flight are also detailed in Apollonius Rhodius' *Argonautica* (3rd century BC), a Greek epic that was then adapted into Latin by Valerius Flaccus, in the first century AD. See Apollonius Rhodius, *The Argonautica*, trans. and ed. Richard Hunter (Oxford: Clarendon Press, 1993), and Valerius Flaccus, *Argonautica*, trans. and ed. J. H Mozley (Cambridge, Mass.: Harvard University Press, 1934).
6. Quintilian quotes a tantalizing extract from the lost play: Medea demands 'servare potui: perdere an possim rogas?' (I had power to save, do you ask, have I power to destroy?). Quintilian, *The Orator's Education*, ed. and trans. Donald A. Russell, 5 vols, Loeb Classical Library (Cambridge, Mass.: Harvard University Press, 2001), vol. 3, 8.5.6. On the tragedy, see A. G. Nikolaidis, 'Some Observations on Ovid's Lost *Medea*', *Latomus* 44.2 (1985), pp. 383–7. Other lost versions of the Medea story are discussed by Howard Jacobson, *Ovid's 'Heroides'* (Princeton: Princeton University Press, 1974), pp. 109–10.
7. The plays are compared by Robin Sowerby, *The Classical Legacy in Renaissance Poetry* (London: Longman, 1994), pp. 75–82. See also Carolyn A. Durham, 'Medea: Hero or Heroine?', *Frontiers: A Journal of Women's Studies* 8.1 (1984), pp. 54–9; and Hanna M. Roisman, 'Medea's Vengeance', in David Stuttard (ed.), *Looking at Medea: Essays and a Translation of Euripides' Tragedy* (London: Bloomsbury, 2014), pp. 111–22 (120–2). Evelyn M. Spearing describes Seneca's heroine as 'almost a raving maniac ... in Seneca's play she awakens no sympathy, for she is nothing but a savage throughout, except perhaps in one interview with Jason'. Spearing complains of Seneca that 'he has

followed Euripides almost exactly in the construction of the plot, and yet has contrived to vulgarise and degrade the whole conception' (Evelyn M. Spearing, 'The Elizabethan "Tenne Tragedies" of Seneca', *MLR* 4.4 (1909), pp. 437–61 (456); see also Spearing, *The Elizabethan Translations of Seneca's Tragedies* (Cambridge: W. Heffer and Sons, 1912), pp. 8–9).

8. See Aristotle, 'On the Art of Poetry', in T. S. Dorsch (trans.), *Classical Literary Criticism* (Harmondsworth: Penguin, 1965), pp. 31–75 (73).

9. The second-century AD mythographer Apollodorus describes her reconciling with her father, and defeating his usurping brother Perses. He also briefly mentions her afterlife in the Elysian fields, as the consort of Achilles. The classical versions of the myth that were best known in the early modern period, however, resist this kind of closure. See Apollodorus, *The Library*, trans. J. G. Frazer, 2 vols, Loeb Classical Library (Cambridge, Mass.: Harvard University Press, 1921) 1.9.28, and 'Epitome' 5.5.

10. Lorna Hardwick, *Reception Studies* (Oxford: Oxford University Press, 2003), p. 14.

11. Although in his edition of Seneca's *Medea*, H. M. Hine notes of the infanticide 'it is disputed whether the innovation was [Euripides'], or occurred earlier in a *Medea* by the tragedian Neophron' (Seneca, *Medea*, trans. H. M. Hine (Warminster: Aris and Phillips, 2000), p. 13).

12. Edith Hall, *Inventing the Barbarian: Greek Self-Definition through Tragedy* (Oxford: Clarendon Press, 1989, repr. 2004), pp. 35, 203.

13. On Seneca's use of *Heroides* 6 and 12, see Christopher Trinacty, 'Seneca's Heroides: Elegy in Seneca's *Medea*', *Classical Journal* 103.1 (2007), pp. 63–78.

14. Spearing, 'Elizabethan "Tenne Tragedies"', pp. 456–7. Medea has certainly reached this conclusion in the first act of John Studley's Elizabethan translation, in which Medea's language is far more gruesome and brutal: Seneca leaves the question of whether she has decided that the children must die by this point rather more ambiguous.

15. In his *Bibliotheca Historica*, the first-century BC Greek historian Diodorus Siculus explains how many of Medea's most famous feats should not be understood literally. For example, according to Diodorus, when Medea allegedly helped Jason subdue the fire-breathing bulls that guarded the Golden Fleece, she really won round a race of men known as the Taurians, because she was able to speak to them in their own language. See Diodorus Siculus, *Works*, trans. C. H. Oldfather, 10 vols, Loeb Classical Library (London: Heinemann, 1933–67), vol. 2, 4.47.2–4 and 4.48.1–3.

16. Sarah Iles Johnston, 'Introduction', in James J. Clauss and Sarah Iles Johnston (eds), *Medea: Essays on Medea in Myth, Literature, Philosophy and Art* (Princeton: Princeton University Press, 1997), pp. 3–17 (4).

17. For cinematic versions of Medea, see Ian Christie, 'Between Magic and Realism: Medea on Film', in Edith Hall, Fiona Macintosh and Oliver Taplin (eds), *Medea in Performance 1500–2000* (Oxford: Legenda, 2000), pp. 144–65.

18. Marianne McDonald, 'Medea as Politician and Diva: Riding the Dragon into the Future', in Clauss and Johnston (eds), *Medea*: 297–323, 301, 311. Kennelly's play receives an extended discussion by McDonald at pp. 305–12.

19. McDonald, 'Medea', p. 302.

20. McDonald, 'Medea', p. 301. Theodorakis's opera is discussed by McDonald at pp. 314–22.

21. John Kerrigan, *Revenge Tragedy: Aeschylus to Armageddon* (Oxford: Clarendon Press, 1996), p. 98.
22. Iles Johnston, 'Introduction', p. 4.
23. Kerrigan, *Revenge Tragedy*, pp. 321–4, 329.
24. Kerrigan, *Revenge Tragedy*, p. 329.
25. Nicola McDonald, '"Diverse Folk Diversely They Seyde": A Study of the Figure of Medea in Medieval Literature' (D.Phil. Thesis: Oxford University, 1994). My thanks to Dr McDonald for permission to quote from this work. Ruth Morse, *The Medieval Medea* (Cambridge: D. S. Brewer, 1996); Diane Purkiss, 'Medea in the English Renaissance', in Hall, Macintosh and Taplin (eds), *Medea in Performance*, pp. 32–48.
26. Examples include Clauss and Johnston (eds), *Medea*; Heike Bartel and Anne Simon (eds), *Unbinding Medea: Interdisciplinary Approaches to a Classical Myth from Antiquity to the 21st Century* (Oxford: Legenda, 2010); Domnica Radulescu, *Sisters of Medea: The Tragic Heroine across Cultures* (New Orleans: University Press of the South, 2002); and Lillian Corti, *The Myth of Medea and the Murder of Children* (Westport: Greenwood Press, 1998). Corti discusses Pierre Corneille's seventeenth-century French tragedy *Médée* in Chapter 4, while early modern French renderings are also covered by Amy Wygant, *Medea, Magic, and Modernity in France* (Aldershot: Ashgate, 2007).
27. Purkiss, 'Medea in the English Renaissance', pp. 32–3.
28. Sarah Iles Johnston, 'Corinthian Medea and the Cult of Hera Akraia', in Clauss and Johnston (eds), *Medea*, pp. 44–70.
29. Hall, *Inventing the Barbarian*, p. 200.
30. Seneca, *Tragedies I: 'Hercules', 'Trojan Women', 'Phoenician Women', Medea', Phaedra'*, ed. and trans. John G. Fitch, 8 vols (Cambridge, Mass.: Harvard University Press, 2002). Unless otherwise stated, all Latin quotations from Seneca's *Medea*, and all modern translations, are from this edition.
31. Stephen Orgel, 'Nobody's Perfect: Or Why Did the English Stage Take Boys for Women?', *South Atlantic Quarterly* 88.1 (1989), pp. 7–29 (13).
32. Dolores O'Higgins, 'Medea as Muse: Pindar's *Pythian 4*', in Clauss and Johnston (eds), *Medea*, pp. 103–26 (103).
33. For Effrosini Spentzou, the constantly fleeing Medea is 'a paradigm of displacement' (*Readers and Writers in Ovid's 'Heroides': Transgressions of Genre and Gender* (Oxford: Oxford University Press, 2003), p. 41).
34. Linda Hutcheon, *A Theory of Adaptation* (New York: Routledge, 2006), p. 116; for the 'knowing' versus 'unknowing' auditor, see p. 120. On the 'sense of play' in adaptation, see Julie Sanders, *Adaptation and Appropriation* (New York: Routledge, 2006), pp. 7, 14 and 25.
35. Seneca, *Medea*, trans. Edward Sherburne (London: 1648), Wing S2513. Unless otherwise stated, all quotations are from the 1648 edition.
36. William Webbe, *A Discourse of English Poetrie* (London: 1586), STC (2nd edn) 25172.
37. Natale Conti, *Mythologiae*, trans. and ed. John Mulryan and Steven Brown, 2 vols (Tempe, Ariz.: Arizona Center for Medieval and Renaissance Studies, 2006), p. 488.
38. The tragedy is discussed at greater length in Chapter 3. For the text, see William Alabaster, *Roxana*, ed. Dana F. Sutton, hypertext edition (Irvine, Calif.: University of California, 1998; copyright University of Birmingham).

39. Lisa Jardine, *Still Harping on Daughters: Women and Drama in the Age of Shakespeare* (Hemel Hempstead: Harvester Wheatsheaf, 1983), p. 97.
40. Jardine, *Still Harping on Daughters*, p. 97.
41. Mark Breitenberg, *Anxious Masculinity in Early Modern England* (Cambridge: Cambridge University Press, 1996), p. 23.
42. Stephen Greenblatt, *Renaissance Self-Fashioning: From More to Shakespeare* (Chicago: University of Chicago Press, 1980), p. 9.
43. Richard Robinson, *The Rewarde of Wickednesse* (London: 1574), STC (2nd edn) 21121.7.
44. Kerrigan, *Revenge Tragedy*, p. 89.
45. Hutcheon, *Theory of Adaptation*, p. 18; Sanders, *Adaptation and Appropriation*, p. 20.
46. Thomas M. Greene, *The Light in Troy: Imitation and Discovery in Renaissance Poetry* (New Haven and London: Yale University Press, 1982), p. 50.
47. Gérard Genette, *Palimpsests: Literature in the Second Degree*, trans. Channa Newman and Claude Doubinsky (Lincoln, Nebr.: University of Nebraska Press, 1997), p. 5.
48. Ruth Morse, *Truth and Convention in the Middle Ages: Rhetoric, Representation, and Reality* (Cambridge: Cambridge University Press, 1991), p. 108.
49. Morse, *Truth and Convention*, p. 5.
50. Stephen Hinds, *Allusion and Intertext: Dynamics of Appropriation in Roman Poetry*, Roman Literature and Its Contexts (Cambridge: Cambridge University Press, 1998), p. 46.
51. Hutcheon, *Theory of Adaptation*, p. 139.
52. On Jessica as a more knowing reader, one who appreciates, on some level, the darker implications of her comparison, see Purkiss, 'Medea in the English Renaissance', p. 41.
53. Breitenberg, *Anxious Masculinity*, p. 33.
54. Purkiss notes that the rejuvenation of Aeson could be invoked in Jacobean comedy, to poke fun at men (usually elderly, lecherous men) who hope to regain their own youth and potency: however, she points out that knowledge of Medea's full story will almost inevitably make such references disturbing as well as comical ('Medea in the English Renaissance', pp. 39–40).
55. Colin Burrow, *Shakespeare and Classical Antiquity* (Oxford: Oxford University Press, 2013) p. 130.
56. See Sanders, *Adaptation and Appropriation*, p. 9; and Hardwick, *Reception Studies*, ch. 3. On the politicisation of Lucrece's story, see Ian Donaldson, *The Rapes of Lucretia: A Myth and Its Transformations* (Oxford: Clarendon Press, 1982).
57. Susan Wiseman, 'Exemplarity, Women and Political Rhetoric', in Jennifer Richards and Alison Thorne (eds), *Rhetoric, Women and Politics in Early Modern England* (London: Routledge, 2007), pp. 129–48 (146).
58. Thomas Heywood, *The Brazen Age*, *Works*, vol. 3, ed. J. H. Pearson (New York: Russell and Russell, 1964, reprinted from the edition of 1874). Compare Ovid, *Ovid's 'Metamorphoses' translated by Arthur Golding*, ed. Madeleine Forey (Baltimore: Johns Hopkins University Press, 2001) 7.277 and 7.265-6; and Shakespeare, *The Tempest*, 5.1.34.
59. Horace, 'On the Art of Poetry', in Dorsch, *Classical Literary Criticism*, pp. 79–95 (83).
60. Ibid., p. 83.

1 Medieval Medea

1. John Gower, *The English Works, The Complete Works*, ed. G. C. Macaulay, 4 vols (Oxford: Clarendon Press, 1899–1902).
2. Kathryn L. McKinley notes that manuscripts of the *Metamorphoses* enjoyed much wider circulation in fifteenth-century England than did Ovid's other works: see *Reading the Ovidian Heroine: 'Metamorphoses' Commentaries 1100–1618* (Leiden: Brill, 2001), pp. 108–9. On use of the *Heroides* (and commentaries on the poems) in medieval education, see Ralph J. Hexter, *Ovid and Medieval Schooling: Studies in Medieval School Commentaries on Ovid's Ars Amatoria, Epistulae ex Ponto, and Epistulae Heroidum* (Munich: Arbeo-Gesellschaft, 1986), pp. 1–13 and Part 3.
3. While Benoît refers to Dares in his recounting of Jason and Medea's story, the sixth-century work does not actually mention her. For the medieval enthusiasm for citing Dares (whether or not he had actually been consulted), and another work that claimed to be an eyewitness account of the war, by Dictys of Crete, see A. J. Minnis, *Chaucer and Pagan Antiquity* (Cambridge: D. S. Brewer, 1982), pp. 23–4. For Dares' text, see Dictys of Crete and Dares the Phrygian, *The Trojan War*, trans. and ed. R. M. Frazer (Bloomington: Indiana University Press, 1966).
4. Benoît de Sainte-Maure, *Le Roman de Troie*, vol. 1, ed. L. Constans, 6 vols (Paris: Firmin-Didot, 1904–12). Translations my own.
5. Barbara Nolan, *Chaucer and the Tradition of the 'Roman Antique'* (Cambridge: Cambridge University Press, 1992), pp. 33–5.
6. However, see Nicola McDonald, who points out that Medea is made less alarming than her classical predecessor, since '[her] powers are seen to derive from diligent study', rather than from an inherent affinity with the supernatural ('"Diverse Folk Diversely They Seyde": A Study of the Figure of Medea in Medieval Literature' (D.Phil. Thesis: Oxford University, 1994), p. 112).
7. Ruth Morse, *The Medieval Medea* (Cambridge: D. S. Brewer, 1996), p. 88.
8. Nolan, *Chaucer and the Tradition of the 'Roman Antique'*, p. 102. On Benoît's interest in this theme, as demonstrated by Medea's story, see further pp. 99–102.
9. For the popularity of later versions of the *Roman*, see *Le Roman de Troie en Prose*, ed. Françoise Vielliard (Cologny-Genève: Martin Bodmer, 1979), p. 8.
10. Kathleen Chesney has shown that Guido's source was probably a particular prose redaction of Benoît's poem, written in southern Europe. See Morse, *Medieval Medea*, p. 92, and Kathleen Chesney, 'A Neglected Prose Version of the *Roman de Troie*', *Medium Aevum* 11 (1942), pp. 46–67.
11. Guido de Columnis (Guido delle Colonne), *Historia Destructionis Troiae*, ed. Nathaniel Edward Griffin (Cambridge, Mass.: Mediaeval Academy of America, 1936). Translations are from Guido delle Colonne, *Historia Destructionis Troiae*, trans. and ed. Mary Elizabeth Meek (Bloomington: Indiana University Press, 1974).
12. Ovid, *Metamorphoses*, trans. Frank Justus Miller, rev. G. P. Goold, 2 vols (Cambridge, Mass.: Harvard University Press, 1916, rev. 1977). All quotations from Ovid's *Metamorphoses*, and all modern translations, are from this edition.
13. Quotations from the Vatican Mythographers are from *Scriptores Rerum Mythicarum Latini Tres Romae Nuper Reperti*, ed. G. H. Bode (Hildesheim: Georg Olms, 1968; repr. 1996). Translations are my own.

14. See *The Myths of Hyginus*, trans. and ed. Mary Grant, University of Kansas Publications, Humanistic Studies 34 (Lawrence: University of Kansas Press, 1960), p. 43.
15. Giovanni di Garlandia (John of Garland), *Integumenta Ovidii: Poemetto Inedito del Secolo XIII*, ed. Fausto Ghisalberti (Messina: Giuseppe Principato, 1933). Translations of John of Garland are my own.
16. McKinley, *Reading the Ovidian Heroine*, p. 70.
17. Ibid., p. 70.
18. See ibid., pp. 67, 98, 110.
19. McDonald, '"Diverse Folk"', p. 80.
20. Ibid., p. 94.
21. *Ovide moralisé, poème du commencement du quatorzième siècle*, vol. 3, ed. C. de Boer, 5 vols (Amsterdam : Noord-Hollandsche Uitgevers-Maatschapperij, 1915–38). Translations my own.
22. See Morse, *Medieval Medea*, pp. 135–40, and also Joel N. Feimer, 'Medea in Ovid's *Metamorphoses* and the *Ovide moralisé*: Translation as Transmission', *Florilegium* 8 (1986), pp. 40–55, for further discussion of the poem's treatment of Medea.
23. *Ovide moralisé en prose, texte du quinzième siècle*, ed. C de Boer (Amsterdam: North-Holland Pub. Co., 1954). Translations my own. For further summaries of medieval commentaries on and interpretations of Ovid, see Don Cameron Allen, *Mysteriously Meant: The Rediscovery of Pagan Symbolism and Allegorical Interpretation in the Renaissance* (Baltimore: Johns Hopkins University Press, 1970), ch. 7, and Robert Earl Kaske, Arthur Groos and Michael W. Twomey (eds), *Medieval Christian Literary Imagery: A Guide to Interpretation* (Toronto: University of Toronto Press, 1988), pp. 122–6.
24. Pierre Bersuire, *Metamorphosis Ovidiana moraliter … explanata: Paris, 1509*, ed. Stephen Orgel (New York: Garland, 1979). Translation my own.
25. McDonald, '"Diverse Folk"', pp. 87–8, 90.
26. Thomas Elyot, *Bibliotheca Eliotae, Eliotis Librarie* (London: 1542; STC (2nd edn) 76595), Eiii^v. The definition remains unchanged in subsequent versions, revised by Thomas Cooper. E.g., see *Bibliotheca Eliotae: Eliotes dictionarie by Thomas Cooper the third tyme corrected* (London: 1559), STC (2nd edn) 7663. The influence of continental 'manuals' of mythology in the English Renaissance is discussed briefly by Jean Seznec, *The Survival of the Pagan Gods: The Mythological Tradition and Its Place in Renaissance Humanism and Art*, trans. Barbara F. Sessions (Princeton: Princeton University Press, 1953, repr. 1972), pp. 312–15, and more extensively in DeWitt T. Starnes and Ernest William Talbert, *Classical Myth and Legend in Renaissance Dictionaries: A Study of Renaissance Dictionaries in Relation to the Classical Learning of Contemporary English Writers* (Chapel Hill: University of North Carolina Press, 1955).
27. See Thomas Blount, *Glossographia* (London: 1656; Wing (2nd edn) B3334), B2 3^r, who quotes Thomas Browne's hugely popular reference work that aimed to debunk a wide range of myths and superstitions, *Pseudodoxia epidemica* (London: 1646; Wing B5159), pp. 22–3. See also Palaephatus, *On Unbelievable Tales*, trans. and ed. Jacob Stern, with notes and Greek text from the 1902 B. G. Teubner edition (Wauconda, Ill.: Bolchazy-Carducci, 1996), pp. 75–6.
28. On this literary tradition, see Glenda McLeod, *Virtue and Venom: Catalogs of Women from Antiquity to the Renaissance* (Ann Arbor: University of

Michigan Press, 1991). She briefly discusses Medea as an *exemplum* in works by Boccaccio, Christine de Pizan, Chaucer and the twelfth-century author Walter Map, whose 'Dissuasion to Rufinus, that he should not take a Wife', part of *De Nugis Curialium*, playfully suggests that a man should seek out Ovid's lost tragedy *Medea*, if he wants to understand more about women's malign capabilities.

29. Giovanni Boccaccio, *Famous Women*, trans. Virginia Brown (Cambridge, Mass.: Harvard University Press, 2001), pp. 75–9. Medea's reunion with Jason, also recounted by Boccaccio in *De Genealogia Deorum Gentilium Libri*, is described by the second-century mythographer Apollodorus, in *The Library of Greek Mythology*, and by the Roman historian Justin, in *The Philippic History of Pompeius Trogus*.
30. Janet Cowen, 'Women as Exempla in Fifteenth-Century Verse of the Chaucerian Tradition', in Julia Boffey and Janet Cowen (eds), *Chaucer and Fifteenth-Century Poetry* (London: Centre for Late Antique and Medieval Studies, King's College London: 1991), pp. 51–65 (56).
31. Christine de Pizan, *The Book of the City of Ladies*, trans. Earl Jeffrey Richards (New York: Persea, 1998).
32. Cowen, 'Women as Exempla', pp. 58, 57.
33. *The Seege or Batayle of Troye*, ed. Mary Elizabeth Barnicle (Oxford: Oxford University Press, 1927).
34. Joseph of Exeter, *The Trojan War I–III*, ed. and trans. A. K. Bate (Warminster: Aris & Phillips, 1986).
35. *The 'Gest Hystoriale' of the Destruction of Troy*, ed. George A. Panton and David Donaldson, Early English Text Society OS 39, 56 (London: Trübner and Co., 1869–74). The poem is usually dated to the late fourteenth century. See McKay Sundwall, '*The Destruction of Troy*, Chaucer's *Troilus and Criseyde*, and Lydgate's *Troy Book*', *RES*, New Series 26.103 (1975), pp. 313–17; and James Simpson, 'The Other Book of Troy: Guido delle Colonne's *Historia Destructionis Troiae* in Fourteenth- and Fifteenth-Century England', *Speculum* 73.2 (1998), pp. 397–423; on its author see Thorlac Turville-Petre, 'The Author of the *Destruction of Troy*', *Medium Aevum* 57 (1988), pp. 264–8; and Edward Wilson, 'John Clerk, Author of *The Destruction of Troy*', *Notes and Queries* 37.4 (1990), pp. 391–6. Panton and Donaldson identify 'Eydos' as *Heroides* 12 (p. 467n.), but in fact neither Hypsipyle nor Medea, in their letters, make mention of the rejuvenation, and if the poet did go directly to Ovid for this detail it must have been to the *Metamorphoses*.
36. Nicky Hallett, 'Women', in Peter Brown (ed.), *A Companion to Chaucer* (Oxford: Blackwell, 2000), pp. 480–94 (482–3).
37. Geoffrey Chaucer, *The Riverside Chaucer*, ed. Larry D. Benson (Oxford: Oxford University Press, 1988), p. 1069. All quotations from Chaucer's work are from this edition.
38. However, see McDonald, '"Diverse Folk"', who argues that the Flavian *Argonautica* 'suffered a prolonged oblivion until 1417, when the first three-and-a-half books were rediscovered by the Italian humanist Poggio' (p. 43 n.18). She asserts that the epic does not influence any medieval renderings of the story.
39. See 'The Man of Law's Prologue', lines 72–4, and *The Book of the Duchess*, lines 726–7, *The Riverside Chaucer*, ed. Benson.

40. As Priscilla Martin puts it, 'Virtue is equated with victimization. No wonder the heroines of the Legend look rather stupid' (*Chaucer's Women: Nuns, Wives and Amazons* (London: Macmillan, 1990), p. 203).
41. Carolyn Dinshaw, *Chaucer's Sexual Poetics* (Madison: University of Wisconsin Press, 1989), p. 77.
42. Cowen, 'Women as Exempla', p. 53.
43. Suzanne C. Hagedorn, *Abandoned Women: Rewriting the Classics in Dante, Boccaccio and Chaucer* (Ann Arbor: University of Michigan Press, 2004), p. 165. For this kind of catalogue tradition, see McLeod, *Virtue and Venom*; and Cowen, 'Women as Exempla', pp. 52–3.
44. Lisa J. Kiser, *Telling Classical Tales: Chaucer and the 'Legend of Good Women'* (Ithaca: Cornell University Press, 1983), p. 97. See also John M. Fyler, *Chaucer and Ovid* (New Haven and London: Yale University Press, 1979), p. 104.
45. Morse, *Medieval Medea*, p. 223. Conversely, Derek Pearsall sees in Gower's work the desire to limit these stereotypical romance images ('Gower's Narrative Art', *PMLA* 87.1 (1966), pp. 475–84 (482)).
46. It also appears in the *Historia*, but Guido gives it a typically unsympathetic emphasis, suggesting that Medea was only making pretence of modesty.
47. Morse, *Medieval Medea*, p. 223.
48. John Kerrigan (ed.), *Motives of Woe: Shakespeare and 'Female Complaint', a Critical Anthology* (Oxford: Clarendon Press, 1991), p. 28.
49. The date is uncertain, but the poem seems to have been composed in the late fourteenth or early fifteenth century. See Simpson, 'Other Book of Troy', pp. 404–5.
50. *The Laud Troy Book*, ed. J. Ernst Wülfing, Early English Text Society OS 121–2 (London: Kegan Paul, Trench, Trübner & Co., 1902).
51. Dorothy Kempe, 'A Middle English Tale of Troy', *Englische Studien* 29 (1901), pp. 1–26 (8).
52. McDonald, '"Diverse Folk"', pp. 270–1.
53. Ibid., p. 266.
54. John Lydgate, *Troy Book*, ed. Henry Bergen, 4 vols, Early English Text Society XS 97, 126 (London: Kegan Paul, Trench, Trübner & Co., 1906–35).
55. For Laurent's expansion of Medea's story as he found it in Boccaccio, see Patricia M. Gathercole, 'Laurent de Premierfait: The Translator of Boccaccio's *De Casibus Virorum Illustrium*', *French Review* 27.4 (1954), pp. 245–52 (248–9). Gathercole points to what she calls Laurent's 'passion to instruct' (p. 249) though his additions tend to be factual, whereas Lydgate's are very often more judgemental. For Lydgate's expansion of Laurent, see also Morse, *Medieval Medea*, pp. 209–13.
56. Laurent de Premierfait, *'Des Cas des Nobles Hommes et Femmes', Book 1: Translated from Boccaccio. A Critical Edition Based on Six MSS*, ed. Patricia M. Gathercole (Chapel Hill: University of North Carolina Press, 1968). Translations from Laurent de Premierfait are my own.
57. John Lydgate, *The Fall of Princes*, ed. Henry Bergen, 4 vols, Early English Text Society XS 121–4 (London: Oxford University Press, 1924–7).
58. He credits 'Ovidius' and 'Senec' (1.2383–4) for the story that they were reconciled: of course, neither Ovid nor Seneca give any such account.
59. Raoul Lefèvre, *The Recuyell of the Historyes of Troye*, trans. William Caxton, 2nd edn (Bruges: William Caxton and [?] Colard Mansion, 1473–4), STC (2nd edn) 15375. No signatures or pagination.

60. Raoul Lefèvre, *L'Histoire de Jason*, trans. William Caxton, ed. John Munro, Early English Text Society XS 111 (Kegan Paul, Trench, Trübner & Co. and Oxford University Press, 1913). For the French text, see Raoul Lefèvre, *L'Histoire de Jason*, ed. Gert Pinkernell (Frankfurt: Athenäum Verlag, 1971). While authors like Lydgate could alter their sources drastically, while claiming simply to render them English, McDonald notes that Caxton's translation is 'remarkably close, virtually word-for-word', and that 'For the most part Caxton's additions have no bearing on the portrayal of Medea' ('"Diverse Folk"', pp. 266–7).
61. See Ruth Morse, 'Problems of Early Fiction: Raoul Lefèvre's *Histoire de Jason*', *MLR* 78.1 (1980), pp. 34–45 (35). She notes that Philippe's choice of Jason as a kind of figurehead for the Order could well have invited ridicule, and that this informs Lefèvre's determined rewriting of his hero (and heroine).
62. For 'inverse coverture', see Frances E. Dolan, *Whores of Babylon: Catholicism, Gender, and Seventeenth Century Print Culture* (Ithaca and London: Cornell University Press, 1999), p. 61.
63. Timothy Hampton, *Writing from History: The Rhetoric of Exemplarity in Renaissance Literature* (Ithaca and London: Cornell University Press, 1990), p. 26.
64. McDonald, '"Diverse Folk"', p. 267, notes this as one of the only changes Caxton makes to Lefèvre in his representation of Medea. Lefèvre's version reads, 'Elle lui promist et jura que jamais mal ne feroit' (she promised and vowed to him that she would never more commit evil deeds) (21.5.28; translation my own). Caxton's minor alteration more vigorously underscores Medea's ceding of control to Jason, as well as containing the intriguing suggestion that she might still use her powers in the future, but only with Jason's 'knowlech'.
65. Morse notes that Caxton adds to his source, here and in the prologue, with references to Boccaccio and Statius, to give a fuller account (*Medieval Medea*, pp. 182–3).
66. McDonald, '"Diverse Folk"', p. 267.
67. I quote from the facsimile edition of the manuscript, which is now held at Magdalene College Cambridge: Ovid, *Metamorphoses of Ovid*, trans. William Caxton, 2 vols (New York: George Braziller in association with Magdalene College Cambridge, 1968). For a discussion of the text, including examples of Caxton's anxious approach to other female figures in the *Metamorphoses*, see Liz Oakley-Brown, *Ovid and the Cultural Politics of Translation in Early Modern England* (Aldershot: Ashgate, 2006), ch. 6.
68. See Ovid, 'Echo and Narcissus', trans. William Caxton, in Sarah Annes Brown and Andrew Taylor (eds), *Ovid in English, 1480–1625, Part 1: 'Metamorphoses'* (London: Modern Humanities Research Association, 2013), p. 19.

2   Translating Medea

1. Tanya Pollard, 'What's Hecuba to Shakespeare?', *Shakespeare Quarterly* 65.4 (2012), pp. 1060–93 (1064 n.15).
2. H. B. Charlton, 'The Growth of the Senecan Tradition in Renaissance Tragedy', in William Alexander, *The Poetical Works of Sir William Alexander*, ed. L. E. Kastner and H. B. Charlton, 2 vols (Manchester: Manchester University Press, 1921), vol. 1, pp. xvii–cc (xlix). Alfred Harbage notes an English prose summary of Euripides' tragedy, in manuscript, by Cornelius Schonaeus (1540–1611) ('Elizabethan and Seventeenth Century Play Manuscripts', *PMLA* 50.3 (1935), pp. 687–99 (694)).

3. E. M. Spearing notes that unlike some other Elizabethan translations of Seneca, the 1566 and 1581 versions of the *Medea* are virtually identical (*The Elizabethan Translations of Seneca's Tragedies* (Cambridge: W. Heffer and Sons, 1912), p. 35). Two anonymous early modern manuscript translations of Seneca's *Medea* into English are also extant: these are in the British Library (MS Sloane 911) and in the Bodleian (MS eng. poet. e.34). My thanks to Dr Martin Wiggins for bringing the first of these to my attention. See Alfred Harbage, *Annals of English Drama 975–1700*, rev. S. Schoenbaum, 3rd edn rev. Sylvia Stoler Wagonheim (London: Routledge, 1989), p. 372.

4. Linda Hutcheon, *A Theory of Adaptation* (New York: Routledge, 2006), p. 149.

5. Charlton, 'Growth of the Senecan Tradition', pp. xxxi–xxxii. See also Gordon Braden, who notes that Seneca's plays enjoyed 'a fair circulation by the mid-thirteenth century' (*Renaissance Tragedy and the Senecan Tradition: Anger's Privilege* (New Haven: Yale University Press, 1985), p. 101). E. M. Spearing suggests that Studley used the 1541 Lyon edition of *Medea* for his translation, rather than the Aldine or Venetian editions of 1517. John Studley, *Translations of Seneca's 'Agamemnon' and 'Medea'*, ed. E. M. Spearing (Louvain: A. Uystpruyst, 1913), p. xii. Continental knowledge of Seneca's tragedy before 1500 is also reflected by its quotation in the *Malleus Maleficarum* of 1486, where it is used to demonstrate the dangerously unbridled nature of women: Keith Thomas has shown, however, that the *Malleus* was not widely known in medieval or early modern England (*Religion and the Decline of Magic: Studies in Popular Beliefs in Sixteenth and Seventeenth Century England* (London: Weidenfeld and Nicolson, 1971, repr. 1997), p. 440). For references to Seneca's *Medea*, see Heinrich Kramer and James (or sometimes Jacob) Sprenger, *Malleus Maleficarum*, ed. and trans. Montague Summers (London: Hogarth, 1928, repr. 1969), pp. 45–6.

6. See J. W. Binns, 'Seneca and Neo-Latin Tragedy in England', in C. D. N. Costa (ed.), *Seneca* (London: Routledge and Kegan Paul, 1974), pp. 205–34 (205–6); and George Charles Moore Smith, *College Plays: Performed at the University of Cambridge* (Cambridge: Cambridge University Press, 1923), pp. 57 and 106. Both Studley's and Sherburne's translations are categorised as closet dramas in Harbage, *Annals of English Drama*, pp. 40–1, 148–9. David Gowen suggests tentatively, however, that Sherburne's *Medea* may have been performed in 1648 ('*Medeas* on the Archive Database', in Edith Hall, Fiona Macintosh and Oliver Taplin (eds), *Medea in Performance 1500–2000* (Oxford: Legenda, 2000), pp. 232–74 (234)).

7. G. K. Hunter, 'Seneca and English Tragedy', in Costa (ed.), *Seneca*, pp. 166–204 (187).

8. Studley, *Translations of Seneca's 'Agamemnon' and 'Medea'*. The text is that of the 1566 octavo edition, and references are to line numbers in Spearing's edition.

9. On domesticating translation, see Lawrence Venuti, *The Translator's Invisibility: A History of Translation*, 2nd edn (Abingdon: Routledge, 2008), pp. 26, 57–8 and *passim*. The type of the 1566 edition is difficult to decipher, and Thomas L. Berger and Sonia Massai suggest 'prophane Fooles'. Berger and Massai, *Paratexts in English Printed Drama to 1642*, 2 vols (Cambridge: Cambridge University Press, 2014), vol. 1, p. 61. The preface to the reader is omitted from the 1581 edition.

10. Frederick Kiefer, *Fortune and Elizabethan Tragedy* (San Marino, Calif.: Huntington Library Press, 1983), p. 60.
11. On Studley's Medea as pitiable, see also Allyna E. Ward, *Women and Tudor Tragedy: Feminizing Counsel and Representing Gender* (Madison: Fairleigh Dickinson University Press, 2013), pp. 99–102.
12. Seneca, *Seneca His Tenne Tragedies*, comp. Thomas Newton (London: 1581), STC (2nd edn) 22221.
13. Fiona Macintosh, 'Introduction: The Performer in Performance', in Hall, Macintosh and Taplin (eds), *Medea in Performance*, pp. 1–31 (10).
14. Braden, *Renaissance Tragedy*, p. 110.
15. Ibid., p. 110.
16. Quoted in Kiefer, *Fortune and Elizabethan Tragedy*, p. 69.
17. Robert S. Miola, *Shakespeare and Classical Tragedy: The Influence of Seneca* (Oxford: Clarendon Press, 1992), p. 105.
18. Braden, *Renaissance Tragedy*, p. 172.
19. Studley, *Translations of Seneca's 'Agamemnon' and 'Medea'*, p. xiii.
20. Evelyn M. Spearing, 'The Elizabethan *Tenne Tragedies* of Seneca', *MLR* 4.4 (1909), pp. 437–61 (460).
21. Braden, *Renaissance Tragedy*, p. 172.
22. Thomas Adams, *The Devills Banket Described in Foure Sermons* (London: 1614), STC (2nd edn) 110.5.
23. J. W. Cunliffe, *The Influence of Seneca on Elizabethan Tragedy* (London: Macmillan, 1893); Miola, *Shakespeare and Classical Tragedy*; M. L. Stapleton, *Fated Sky: The 'Femina Furens' in Shakespeare* (Newark: University of Delaware Press, 2000).
24. Peter Ure, 'On Some Differences between Senecan and Elizabethan Tragedy', *Elizabethan and Jacobean Drama: Critical Essays*, ed. J. C. Maxwell (Liverpool: Liverpool University Press, 1974), p. 74; Howard Baker, *Induction to Tragedy: A Study in a Development of Form in 'Gorboduc', 'The Spanish Tragedy' and 'Titus Andronicus'* (Louisiana: Louisiana State University Press, 1939), pp. 5 and 140–53; and G. K. Hunter, 'Seneca and the Elizabethans: A Case-Study in Influence', *Dramatic Identities and Cultural Tradition: Studies in Shakespeare and His Contemporaries* (Liverpool: University of Liverpool Press, 1978).
25. Miola, *Shakespeare and Classical Tragedy*, p. 10.
26. Noted in Cunliffe, *Influence of Seneca*, p. 101. Quotations from the play are from John Marston, *Antonio and Mellida*, ed. W. Reavley Gair (Manchester: Manchester University Press, 1991, repr. 2004). Reavley Gair also notes this parallel: see p. 141.
27. Noted in Cunliffe, *Influence of Seneca*, p. 101, and also in Marston, *Antonio and Mellida*, p. 106.
28. The comparisons between early modern drama and Seneca's *Medea* are noted in Cunliffe, *Influence of Seneca*. The comparisons with Studley's translation are my own.
29. Noted in Cunliffe, *Influence of Seneca*, p. 147. Quotations from the play are from Thomas Hughes and others, *The Misfortunes of Arthur*, ed. John S. Farmer (London: Tudor Facsimile Texts, 1911), p. 59.
30. J. L. Simmons, 'Shakespeare and the Antique Romans', in P. A. Ramsey (ed.), *Rome in the Renaissance: The City and the Myth* (Binghamton, NY: Center for Medieval and Early Renaissance Studies, 1982), pp. 77–92 (84). Quotations from the play are from John Marston, *Antonio's Revenge*, ed. W. Reavley Gair (Manchester: Manchester University Press, 1978, repr. 1999).

31. Reuben A. Brower, *Hero and Saint: Shakespeare and the Graeco-Roman Heroic Tradition* (Oxford: Clarendon Press, 1971), p. 148. He accepts that Shakespeare had probably encountered Newton's collection, despite arguing that he makes little use of it. Miola, *Shakespeare and Classical Tragedy*, p. 105; Inga-Stina Ewbank, 'The Fiend-Like Queen: A Note on *Macbeth* and Seneca's *Medea*', in Kenneth Muir (ed.), *Shakespeare Survey 19* (Cambridge: Cambridge University Press, repr. 2002), pp. 82–94.

32. Seneca, *Medea*, trans. E. S. (Edward Sherburne) (London: 1648), Wing S2513. Unless otherwise stated, all quotations are from the 1648 edition.

33. On Sherburne as a translator, see T. R. Steiner, *English Translation Theory 1650–1800* (Amsterdam: Van Gorcum, 1975), pp. 19–20 and 28.

34. Seneca, *The Tragedies of Lucius Annaeus Seneca, the Philosopher; viz. 'Medea', 'Phaedra and Hippolytus', 'Troades, or The Royal Captives', and 'The Rape of Helen', out of the Greek of Coluthus*, trans. Edward Sherburne (London: S. Smith and B. Walford, 1701).

35. The list of addenda to the 1701 edition terms this new final address to Medea 'ungrateful and scelestous' (Bb4ᵛ).

36. Hunter, 'Seneca and English Tragedy', p. 194; and on Sherburne, Gordon Braden, 'Tragedy', in Gordon Braden, Robert Cummings and Stuart Gillespie (eds), *The Oxford History of Literary Translation in English: vol. 2, 1550–1660*, 5 vols (Oxford: Oxford University Press, 2010), pp. 262–79 (270–2).

37. Robert Cummings, 'Dictionaries and Commentaries', in Braden, Cummings and Gillespie (eds), *Oxford History of Literary Translation in English: vol. 2, 1550–1660*, pp. 101–8 (105).

38. See Susan Wiseman, 'Perfectly Ovidian? Dryden's *Epistles*, Behn's "Oenone", Yarico's Island', *Renaissance Studies* 22.3 (2008), pp. 417–32 (423), who notes the criticism of paraphrase in the wake of the Dryden-Tonson Ovid, which had recommended the method.

39. Lorna Hardwick, *Reception Studies* (Oxford: Oxford University Press, 2003), p. 5.

40. Jonathan Bate, *Shakespeare and Ovid* (Oxford: Clarendon Press, 1993), p. 29.

41. Ovid, *Ovid's 'Metamorphoses' translated by Arthur Golding*, ed. Madeleine Forey (Baltimore: Johns Hopkins University Press, 2001). All quotations are taken from this translation.

42. Lee T. Pearcy, *The Mediated Muse: English Translations of Ovid 1560–1700* (Hamden, Conn.: Archon Books, 1984), p. 7.

43. Justin (Marcus Junianus Justinus), *Thabridgment of the histories of Trogus Pompeius, collected and wrytten in the Laten tonge, by the famous historiographer Iustine, and translated into English by Arthur Goldyng* (London: 1564), STC (2nd edn) 24290.

44. Gordon Braden, *The Classics and English Renaissance Poetry: Three Case Studies* (New Haven: Yale University Press, 1978), p. 12. On Golding's moralizing, see Louis Golding, *An Elizabethan Puritan: Arthur Golding the Translator of Ovid's Metamorphoses and also of John Calvin's Sermons* (New York: Richard R. Smith, 1937), p. 55. He suggests that Golding was disheartened by 'his failure to impress Elizabethans with the fundamental ethical purpose that he saw in the *Metamorphoses*'.

45. Ovid, *Metamorphoses*, trans. Frank Justus Miller, rev. G. P. Goold, 2 vols (Cambridge, Mass.: Harvard University Press, 1916, rev. 1977).

46. For an account of Ovid's use of the figure of the *strix*, see P. G. Maxwell-Stuart, *Witchcraft: A History* (Stroud: Tempus, 2004), pp. 35–6. In the notes to his *Masque of Queens*, Ben Jonson cites *Fasti* VI.135–8 as an Ovidian example of the *strix* attacking infants and drinking their blood (*Selected Masques*, ed. Stephen Orgel (New Haven and London: Yale University Press, 1970), p. 357).

47. Ovid, *P. Ovidii Nasonis Metamorphoseos libri quindecim, cum commentariis Raphaelis Regii. Adiectis etiam annotationibus J. Micylli* (Basle, 1543). For a brief survey of Golding's use of this edition and its notes, see Grundy Steiner, 'Golding's Use of the Regius-Micyllus Commentary upon Ovid', *JEGP* 49.3 (1950), pp. 317–23.

48. Translation given by Forey, p. 484.

49. Venuti, *Translator's Invisibility*, p. 26.

50. On the early modern association between the crimes of witchcraft and child murder, see Peter C. Hoffer and N. E. H. Hull, *Murdering Mothers: Infanticide in England and New England, 1558–1803* (New York: New York University Press, 1981), pp. 28–31.

51. Raphael Lyne, *Ovid's Changing Worlds: English 'Metamorphoses', 1567–1632* (Oxford: Oxford University Press, 2001), p. 73.

52. Ovid, *Ovid's 'Metamorphoses'*, ed. Forey, p. xv.

53. Stuart Gillespie, *English Translation and Classical Reception: Towards a New Literary History* (Oxford: Wiley-Blackwell, 2011), p. 39.

54. Louis Kelly, 'Pedagogical Uses of Translation', in Braden, Cummings and Gillespie (eds), *Oxford History of Literary Translation, vol. 2: 1550–1660*, pp. 12–16 (14).

55. Liz Oakley-Brown, *Ovid and the Cultural Politics of Translation in Early Modern England* (Aldershot: Ashgate, 2006), pp. 73–4. For an account of how Sandys's translation was geared towards careful instruction of the King, see Heather James, 'Ovid and the Question of Politics in Early Modern England', *ELH* 70.2 (2003), pp. 343–73.

56. Ovid, *Ovids Metamorphosis Englished, mythologiz'd, and represented in figures by George Sandys* (London: 1632), STC (2nd edn) 18966.

57. Sandys cites the Regius-Micyllus edition of the *Metamorphoses* that had been used by Golding, but Cummings argues that in fact, 'it is Sabinus who is the controlling influence on Sandys's commentary', while Deborah Rubin points to his use of Conti's *Mythologiae*. Cummings, 'Dictionaries and Commentaries', p. 106; Deborah Rubin, *Ovid's Metamorphoses Englished: George Sandys as Translator and Mythographer* (New York: Garland, 1985), p. 127. Elsewhere, Rubin lists Giraldus, Comes, Sabinus, Pontanus, Ficino, Vives, Scaliger, Bacon and Valeriano Bolzari as Sandys's principal early modern sources (Deborah Rubin, 'Sandys, Ovid, and Female Chastity: The Encyclopedic Mythographer as Moralist', in Jane Chance (ed.), *The Mythographic Art: Classical Fable and the Rise of the Vernacular in Early France and England* (Gainesville: University of Florida Press, 1990), pp. 257–77 (272 n.4)).

58. Lyne, *Ovid's Changing Worlds*, p. 72.

59. Rubin, *Ovid's Metamorphoses*, p. 159.

60. On the belief that witches made pacts with the Devil, see Thomas, *Religion and the Decline of Magic*, pp. 438–9.

61. For a range of other seventeenth-century writers who saw witches as more deluded than genuinely powerful (but still deserving of punishment) see Thomas, *Religion and the Decline of Magic*, pp. 523–4.

62. For Diodorus' explanation of the bulls in the *Bibliotheca Historica*, see Diodorus Siculus, *Works*, trans. C. H. Oldfather, 10 vols, Loeb Classical Library (London: Heinemann, 1933–67), vol. 2, 4.47.2–4 and 4.48.1–3.

63. Quotations are from a facsimile of the 1589 Frankfurt edition: Georgius Sabinus, *Metamorphosis seu fabulae* (1589), ed. Stephen Orgel (New York and London: Garland, 1976). Diodorus' explanation of the guardian of the Fleece as a man named Dracon is at 4.47.3 of the *Bibliotheca Historica*.

64. Translations my own.

65. Thomas Heywood, *Londini Status Pacatus, or Londons Peaceable Estate, Thomas Heywood's Pageants: A Critical Edition*, ed. David M. Bergeron (New York and London: Garland Publishing, 1985), lines 347–8.

66. Richard F. Hardin, 'Ovid in Seventeenth-Century England', *Comparative Literature* 24.1 (1972), pp. 44–62 (48–9).

67. Pearcy, *Mediated Muse*, p. 63.

68. Oakley-Brown notes Sandys's interest in emphasising the strangeness of foreign lands, and the turmoil of England's medieval past (*Ovid and the Cultural Politics of Translation*, p. 85).

69. Ovid, *Ovid's Metamorphosis Englished by G[eorge] S[andys]* (London: 1626), STC (2nd edn) 18964.

70. Lyne, *Ovid's Changing Worlds*, p. 252.

71. Oakley-Brown, *Ovid and the Cultural Politics of Translation*, pp. 78–81. She uses Philomela, Marsyas and Pentheus as examples of this tendency.

72. Oakley-Brown notes that in 1626 Sandys was given 'the sole right to produce the English translation' for twenty-one years, and that his 1632 version went through seven editions between 1638 and 1690 (*Ovid and the Cultural Politics of Translation*, pp. 81–2 and 105).

73. For a discussion of this translation, of the first three books of the *Tristia*, as reflecting Churchyard's sense of isolation, especially from court life, see Liz Oakley-Brown, 'Elizabethan Exile after Ovid: Thomas Churchyard's *Tristia*', in Jennifer Ingleheart (ed.), *Two Thousand Years of Solitude: Exile after Ovid* (Oxford: Oxford University Press, 2011), pp. 103–17.

74. Ovid, *Tristia*, trans. A. L. Wheeler, rev. G. P. Goold, Loeb Classical Library (Cambridge, Mass.: Harvard University Press, 1924, rev. 1988).

75. Ovid, *The three first bookes of Ovid de Tristibus translated into English*, trans. Thomas Churchyard (London: 1580), STC (2nd edn) 18978. I quote from the 1580 edition, since the 1572 description of this episode (at Fol. 24ʳ) is often illegible.

76. Ovid, *Ovids Tristia containinge five bookes of mournfull elegies*, trans. W. S. (Wye Saltonstall) (London: 1633), STC (2nd edn) 18979.

77. Ovid, *De tristibus* ... , trans. Zachary Catlin (London: 1639), STC (2nd edn) 18981. On the sense of anxiety and inadequacy that often pervades the prefaces to Renaissance translations into English, see Neil Rhodes, 'Status Anxiety and English Renaissance Translation', in Helen Smith and Louise Wilson (eds), *Renaissance Paratexts* (Cambridge: Cambridge University Press, 2011), pp. 107–20.

78. Laurel Fulkerson, *The Ovidian Heroine as Author: Reading, Writing, and Community in the 'Heroides'* (Cambridge: Cambridge University Press, 2005), pp. 43–8, and see also Effrosini Spentzou, *Readers and Writers in Ovid's 'Heroides': Transgressions of Genre and Gender* (Oxford: Oxford University Press, 2003). At the same time, Elizabeth Harvey is more circumspect: Ovid

'insinuates ... that he has liberated the heroines from the tyrannical bonds of the narratives that had confined and defined them ... *ostensibly* allowing them to assume control over their own representations through their manipulation of language' (*Ventriloquized Voices: Feminist Theory and English Renaissance Texts* (London: Routledge, 1992), p. 119, emphasis added).

79. On 'transvestite ventriloquism', see Harvey, *Ventriloquized Voices*, pp. 1–9, ch. 4, and *passim*.

80. The original epistles do not survive: for a discussion of Turberville's translations, see Raphael Lyne, 'Writing Back to Ovid in the 1560s and 1570s', *Translation and Literature* 13.2: *Versions of Ovid* (2004), pp. 143–64. M. L. Stapleton notes the Aldus Manutius/Andreas Navigerius edition of Ovid, incorporating the *Heroides* (1502), as 'the standard for English readers such as Spenser' ('Edmund Spenser, George Turberville, and Isabella Whitney Read Ovid's *Heroides*', *Studies in Philology* 105.4 (2008), pp. 487–519 (494).

81. Ovid, *The heroycall epistles of the learned poet Publius Ouidius Naso ...* , trans. George Turberville (London: 1567), STC (2nd edn) 18940.

82. Ovid, *'Heroides' and 'Amores'*, trans. Grant Showerman, rev. G. P. Goold, Loeb Classical Library (Cambridge, Mass.: Harvard University Press, 1914, rev. 1977). Unless otherwise stated, all Latin quotations from the *Heroides*, and all modern translations, are from this edition.

83. Patricia B. Phillippy, '"Loytering in Love": Ovid's *Heroides*, Hospitality, and Humanist Education in *The Taming of the Shrew*', *Criticism* 40.1 (1998), pp. 27–53 (33–4). For Deborah S. Greenhut, in contrast, this translation 'affirms a long-standing, misogynist tradition', and she argues 'Tudor feminine literary speech does not resemble a truly independent voice, for feminine rhetorical culture remains bound by a duty to moral consequences' (*Feminine Rhetorical Culture: Tudor Adaptations of Ovid's 'Heroides'* (New York: Peter Lang, 1988), pp. 190 and 139).

84. Hypsipyle and Medea never meet, but Hypsipyle's wish to see Medea begging for food is particularly intriguing in the light of Phillippy's argument, that Turberville's *Heroides* approach Ovid 'through a filter comprised of early modern ideas of hospitality and its violation' ('"Loytering in Love"', p. 34).

85. For example, see *Publii Ovidii Nasonis Heroides. Cum interpretibus Crescentio et Iano Parrhasio* (Venice, 1543), col. 156, lines 42–3; *P. Ovidii Nasonis Poetae Sulmonensis Opera* (Basle, 1549), p. 74; *P. Ovidii Nasonis Poetae Sulmonensis, Heroides Epistolae, cum interpretibus Hubertino Crescent. Et Iano Parrhasio* (Venice, 1558), p. 41ʳ; *Publii Ovidii Nasonis Poeta Sulmonensis, Heroides Epistolae: cum interpretibus Hubertino Crescentinatis, & Iano Parrhasio* (Venice, 1574), p. 41ʳ. However, 'caede ... sua', glossed by Antonio Volsce as 'suorum morte' (their deaths) is also frequently provided alongside Crescentino's note, an annotation which suggests that Medea is stained by the blood of her loved ones, rather than her own blood. Thanks to Stephen Jenkin for discussion of these passages, and for assistance with translation.

86. On suicide as the last resort of an abandoned woman, see John Kerrigan (ed.), *Motives of Woe: Shakespeare and 'Female Complaint', a Critical Anthology* (Oxford: Clarendon Press, 1991), p. 48. More than one modern re-envisioning of the Medea story has ended in her suicide: see Isabelle Torrance, 'Retrospectively Medea: The Infanticidal Mother in Alejandro Amenábar's Film *The Others'*, in Heike Bartel and Anne Simon (eds), *Unbinding Medea: Interdisciplinary*

Approaches to a Classical Myth from Antiquity to the 21st Century (Oxford: Legenda, 2010), pp. 124–34 (127–8).

87. Diane Purkiss, 'Women's Stories of Witchcraft in Early Modern England: The House, the Body, the Child', in Brian P. Levack (ed.), *New Perspectives on Witchcraft, Magic, and Demonology*, 6 vols (New York: Routledge, 2001), vol. 4, pp. 278–302 (281), reprinted from *Gender and History* 7.3 (1995), pp. 408–32.

88. Of course, in their furious reactions to Jason's betrayal, Hypsipyle and Medea are perhaps not so very different: see Fulkerson, *Ovidian Heroine*, pp. 43–8.

89. See Ovid, *P. Ovidii Nasonis Opera omnia in tres tomos divisa, cum ... Nicolai Heinsii ... notis: quibus non pauca ... accesserunt, studio Borchardi Cnippingii* (Lugduni-Batavorum, 1670).

90. Michael Drayton, *Works*, ed. J. William Hebel, Kathleen Tillotson and Bernard H. Newdigate, 5 vols (Oxford: Shakespeare Head Press, 1931–41), vol. 5, p. 98.

91. Of course, for the reader who knows that this is a hopeless wish on Hypsipyle's part, Hypsipyle becomes a more pitiful figure, one who wishes in vain that Medea will exact vengeance on herself.

92. See Stuart Gillespie and Robert Cummings, 'A Bibliography of Ovidian Translations and Imitations in English', *Translation and Literature* 13.2 (2004), pp. 207–18 (208).

93. Ovid, *Ovids heroical epistles*, trans. John Sherburne (London: 1639), STC (2nd edn) 18947.

94. Timothy Raylor, *Cavaliers, Clubs, and Literary Culture: Sir John Mennes, James Smith and the Order of the Fancy* (Cranbury, NJ: Associated University Presses, 1994), p. 149.

95. Ovid, *Ovids heroicall epistles*, trans. W. S. (Wye Saltonstall) (London: 1636), STC (2nd edn) 18945.5. On early modern anxiety about women reading Ovid, or Ovidian works such as *Venus and Adonis*, see Sasha Roberts, *Reading Shakespeare's Poems in Early Modern England* (Basingstoke: Palgrave Macmillan, 2003), pp. 20–1 and 36–7; and Phillippy, '"Loytering in Love"', pp. 32–3. Simultaneously, however, Phillippy shows that annotated vernacular translations of Ovid might be used to educate young women about moral virtue ('"Loytering in Love"', pp. 31–2).

96. Wiseman, 'Perfectly Ovidian', p. 426.

97. Harold Love, 'Some Restoration Treatments of Ovid', in Antony Coleman and Antony Hammond (eds), *Poetry and Drama 1570–1700: Essays in Honour of Harold F. Brooks* (London: Methuen, 1981), pp. 136–55 (138). See also Raylor, *Cavaliers, Clubs, and Literary Culture*, p. 151, for the suggestion that it was the particular interests of an 'emergent, middle-class market' which accounted for the success of Saltonstall's translation over that of Sherburne.

98. Harriette Andreadis, 'The Early Modern Afterlife of Ovidian Erotics: Dryden's *Heroides*', *Renaissance Studies* 22.3 (2008), pp. 401–16 (405). Raylor, *Cavaliers, Clubs, and Literary Culture*, p. 150.

99. On the rather haphazard production of the collection, see Stuart Gillespie, 'The Early Years of the Dryden-Tonson Partnership: The Background to Their Composite Translations and Miscellanies of the 1680s', *Restoration: Studies in English Literary Culture, 1660–1700* 12.1 (1988), pp. 10–19 (11–12). On the popularity of the translation, and its frequent reprinting through the eighteenth century, see Andreadis, 'Early Modern Afterlife of Ovidian Erotics', pp. 404–5. The article includes an appendix detailing printed editions of the translation to 1720.

100. Gillespie, 'Early Years', p. 11.
101. Garth Tissol, 'Ovid', in Stuart Gillespie and David Hopkins (eds), *The Oxford History of Literary Translation in English, vol. 3: 1660–1790* (Oxford: Oxford University Press, 2005), pp. 204–17 (205).
102. Ovid, *Ovid's Epistles Translated by Several Hands*, Preface by John Dryden (London: 1680), Wing 0659.
103. Tissol, 'Ovid', p. 205.
104. In her discussion of the translation of Sappho's epistle, Andreadis suggests that vernacular translations of the *Heroides* in the late seventeenth and early eighteenth centuries, which were often, like Saltonstall's, aimed at women, contributed to a process whereby female readers are 'screened from at least textual sexual knowledge', and Ovid's text is 'cleansed of … erotic vitality' ('Early Modern Afterlife of Ovidian Erotics', p. 406).
105. Dryden's and Davenant's Sycorax is the daughter of the island's original Sycorax, the Medea-figure who haunts the periphery of Shakespeare's play, but never appears. *The Enchanted Island* is discussed more fully in Chapter 4.
106. For a discussion of the controversial Ovidian line, see Florence Verducci, *Ovid's Toyshop of the Heart: Epistulae Heroidum* (Princeton: Princeton University Press, 1985), pp. 69–71. She notes that 'The textually unassailable word *credulitatis* proved so objectionable that the unmetrical but morally preferable *crudelitatis* entered the manuscript tradition' and that 'The objectionable noun [credulitatis] is wholly deleted from Tate's translation' (p. 69). Cnipping's 1670 Ovid, which may have been used by Tate and other translators who contributed to the collection,   reads 'credulitatis' (vol. 1, p. 160), and passes over the line without comment.
107. Howard D. Weinbrot, 'Translation and Parody: Towards the Genealogy of the Augustan Imitation', *ELH* 33.4 (1966): 434–47 (440).
108. Gillespie, *English Translation and Classical Reception*, p. 12.

3   Tragic Medea

1. Phaeton, son of Helios, was allowed to drive his father's sun chariot, but lost control of it and was killed by Zeus to prevent the destruction of earth. Althea (or Althaea) was the mother of Meleager: having heard a prophecy that he would die when a brand was consumed by fire, she initially sought to protect him by concealing this. After Meleager brought about the deaths of her two brothers during a boar hunt, however, Althea retrieved and burned the brand, causing her son's death.
2. Charles Gildon, *Phaeton, or, The Fatal Divorce a tragedy as it is acted at the Theatre Royal in imitation of the antients* (London: 1698), Wing G735. Gildon refers to Dryden's complaint in the *Essay of Dramatick Poesie* (1668), about Medea's implausible escape.
3. Julie Sanders, *Adaptation and Appropriation* (New York: Routledge, 2006), p. 28.
4. Fiona Macintosh, 'Introduction: The Performer in Performance', in Edith Hall, Fiona Macintosh and Oliver Taplin (eds), *Medea in Performance 1500–2000* (Oxford: Legenda, 2000), pp. 1–31 (10). On the fall in convictions for infanticide after 1700, see Peter C. Hoffer and N. E. H. Hull, *Murdering Mothers: Infanticide in England and New England, 1558–1803* (New York: New York University

Press, 1981), pp. ix–xi; and J. R. Dickinson and J. A. Sharpe, 'Infanticide in Early Modern England: The Court of Great Sessions at Chester, 1650–1800', in Mark Jackson (ed.), *Infanticide: Historical Perspectives on Child Murder and Concealment, 1550–2000* (Aldershot: Ashgate, 2002), pp. 35–51. On the contrastive Elizabethan enthusiasm for detecting and prosecuting the crime, see Hoffer and Hull, *Murdering Mothers*, ch. 1.

5. On insanity as a successful defence in the eighteenth century, see Hoffer and Hull, *Murdering Mothers*, p. 70; and Dana Rabin, 'Bodies of Evidence, States of Mind: Infanticide, Emotion and Sensibility in Eighteenth-Century England', in Jackson (ed.), *Infanticide*, pp. 73–92.

6. Compare Medea's first words in Euripides' tragedy: 'Ah, wretch! Ah, lost in my sufferings, / I wish, I wish I might die' (Euripides, *Medea*, trans. Rex Warner, *The Complete Greek Tragedies*, ed. David Grene and Richmond Lattimore, 3 vols (Chicago: University of Chicago Press, 1955), vol. 1, lines 96–7).

7. See Pausanias, *Description of Greece*, vol. 1, trans. W. H. S. Jones and H. A. Omerod, 6 vols, Loeb Classical Library (London: Heinemann, 1918–35), 2.3.6–8, and Aelian, *Historical Miscellany*, ed. and trans. N. G. Wilson, Loeb Classical Library (Cambridge, Mass.: Harvard University Press, 1997), 5.21.

8. Euripides' description of Glauce's grisly death is given at 1168–96. Gildon's account of Lybia's death, at sig. E3ᵛ, is quoted in my conclusion.

9. John Kerrigan, *Revenge Tragedy: Aeschylus to Armageddon* (Oxford: Clarendon Press, 1996), p. 98.

10. Horace, in T. S. Dorsch (trans.), *Classical Literary Criticism* (Harmondsworth: Penguin, 1965), p. 85.

11. Matteo Bandello, *Certaine Tragicall Discourses*, trans. Geoffrey Fenton (London: 1567), STC (2nd edn) 1356.1; and Bandello, *Opere*, ed. Francesco Flora, 2 vols (Milan: Arnoldo Mondadori, 1935), vol. 2, p. 515. On the ways in which Bandello's individual tales were mediated through French translations, by François de Belleforest or Pierre Boiastuau, before being translated into English by authors such as Painter and Fenton, see the very useful table in René Pruvost, *Matteo Bandello and Elizabethan Fiction* (Paris: Librairie ancienne Honoré Champion, 1937), pp. 1–2. The tale of Pandora, originally the fifty-second tale in Bandello's third volume, became the ninth tale of de Belleforest's *Histoires Tragiques*. For the French, see *Xviii histoires tragiques, extraictes des œuvres Italiennes de Bandel, & mises en langue Françoise. Tome Premier* (Lyon: 1596), pp. 207ᵛ–226ᵛ.

12. See Ovid, *Heroides* 6.123–4.

13. Helen Hackett, *Women and Romance Fiction in the English Renaissance* (Cambridge: Cambridge University Press, 2000), p. 41. Peter Lake sees a similar balance between edification and titillation at work in some of the goriest seventeenth-century murder pamphlets, although he argues that 'The very extremity of the events retold in the pamphlets militated against … an internalisation or personal application of the pamphlet's message' ('Deeds against Nature: Cheap Print, Protestantism and Murder in Early Seventeenth-Century England', in Kevin Sharpe and Peter Lake (eds), *Culture and Politics in Early Stuart England* (Basingstoke: Macmillan, 1994), pp. 257–83 (283)).

14. On Fenton's interest in the transgressive woman, see R. W. Maslen, *Elizabethan Fictions: Espionage, Counter-Espionage, and the Duplicity of Fiction in Early Elizabethan Prose Narratives* (Oxford: Clarendon Press, 1997), p. 86. On Pandora, see Maslen, *Elizabethan Fictions*, pp. 108–111.

15. See Jonathan Gibson, 'Tragical Histories, Tragical Tales', in Mike Pincombe and Cathy Shrank (eds), *The Oxford Handbook of Tudor Literature 1485–1603* (Oxford: Oxford University Press, 2009), pp. 521–36 (527); and Maslen, *Elizabethan Fictions*, pp. 97–9.
16. Edith Hall notes that Euripides seems to have been the first to make Medea a barbarian (that is, non-Greek), and her barbarism is stressed by Ovid, in *Heroides* 6 and 12 (*Inventing the Barbarian: Greek Self-Definition through Tragedy* (Oxford: Clarendon Press, 1989, repr. 2004), p. 35).
17. On Hind's (or Hynd's) use of Greene's works in *Eliosto Libidinoso*, see Helen Moore, 'Hynd, John (*fl. c.*1592–1606)', *Oxford Dictionary of National Biography* (Oxford University Press, 2004) <http://www.oxforddnb.com/view/article/14341>, accessed 31 May 2013.
18. John Hind, *Eliosto Libidinoso* (London: 1606), STC (2nd edn) 13509.
19. On early modern anxiety about maternity, see Joanna Levin, 'Lady Macbeth and the Daemonologie of Hysteria', *ELH* 69.1 (2002), pp. 21–55; Janet Adelman, 'Born of Woman: Fantasies of Maternal Power in *Macbeth*', in Marjorie Garber (ed.), *Cannibals, Witches, and Divorce: Estranging the Renaissance* (Baltimore: Johns Hopkins University Press, 1987), pp. 90–121; Karen L. Raber, 'Murderous Mothers and the Family/State Analogy in Classical and Renaissance Drama', *Comparative Literature Studies* 37.3 (2000), pp. 298–320; Dympna Callaghan, 'Wicked Women in *Macbeth*: A Study of Power, Ideology, and the Production of Motherhood', in Mario A. Di Cesare (ed.), *Reconsidering the Renaissance* (Binghamton, NY: Center for Medieval and Early Renaissance Studies, 1992), pp. 355–69; Susan C. Staub, *Nature's Cruel Stepdames: Murderous Women in the Street Literature of Seventeenth-Century England* (Pittsburgh, Pa.: Duquesne University Press, 2005), ch. 3; and Staub, 'Early Modern Medea: Representations of Child Murder in the Street Literature of Seventeenth-Century England', in Naomi J. Miller and Naomi Yavneh (eds), *Maternal Measures: Figuring Caregiving in the Early Modern Period* (Aldershot: Ashgate, 2000), pp. 333–47. For the precarious balance between woman's reproductive capabilities as at once comforting and threatening, see Hélène Cixous and Catherine Clément, *The Newly-Born Woman*, trans. Betsy Wing (Manchester: Manchester University Press, 1986), pp. 7–8.
20. On the growing interest of male authors in addressing the female reader of Elizabethan prose fiction, see Hackett, *Women and Romance Fiction*, ch. 3.
21. Katharine Wilson, 'Revenge and Romance: George Pettie's *Palace of Pleasure* and Robert Greene's *Pandosto*', in Pincombe and Shrank (eds), *Oxford Handbook of Tudor Literature*, pp. 687–703 (690).
22. Gibson, 'Tragical Histories, Tragical Tales', p. 526. On Pandora as a woman who 'evade[s] moral containment', see Maslen, *Elizabethan Fictions*, p. 111.
23. Staub, *Nature's Cruel Stepdames*, p. 77.
24. See also Maslen, *Elizabethan Fictions*, p. 110.
25. Drawing on the work of Catherine Belsey, she notes that, while such women might seem empowered by their final speeches, they are crucially unable to control how their final words are transmitted and presented to eager readers. Frances E. Dolan, '"Gentlemen, I Have One Thing More to Say": Women on Scaffolds in England, 1563–1680', *Modern Philology* 92.2 (1994), pp. 157–78 (160–1). Belsey argues that the scaffold gave women convicted of witchcraft 'a place from which to speak in public with a hitherto unimagined

authority which was not diminished by the fact that it was demonic', but acknowledges that 'the social body required that they paid a high price for the privilege of being heard' (Catherine Belsey, *The Subject of Tragedy: Identity and Difference in Renaissance Drama* (London: Methuen, 1985), pp. 190–1).

26. Although Garthine Walker argues that the primary focus of early modern murder pamphlets is not necessarily the female criminal's gender: 'Rather, murderous women and their deeds symbolize the inevitable consequences of the subversion of patriarchal and familial authority' ('"Demons in Female Form": Representations of Women and Gender in Murder Pamphlets of the Late Sixteenth and Early Seventeenth Centuries', in William Zunder and Suzanne Trill (eds), *Writing and the English Renaissance* (London: Longman, 1996), pp. 123–39 (125).

27. *A pittilesse mother That most unnaturally at one time, murthered two of her owne children at Acton within sixe miles from London uppon holy thursday last 1616* (London: 1616), STC (2nd edn) 24757. Euripides' Medea kills her children in part out of concern that they will suffer if she is exiled. Edith Hall has shown how Victorian dramatisations of Medea's story also sought to explain her infanticide as misguided concern for her children, while Dolan has demonstrated that maternal love, rather than anger, often motivated real-life infanticides in the early modern period. See Edith Hall, 'Medea and British Legislation before the First World War', *Greece and Rome* 46.1 (1999), pp. 42–77 (67); and Frances E. Dolan, *Dangerous Familiars: Representations of Domestic Crime in England, 1550–1700* (Ithaca and London: Cornell University Press, 1994), pp. 141–2. On early modern alarm at the figure of the overly loving (as opposed to cruel) mother, see Mary Beth Rose, 'Where Are the Mothers in Shakespeare? Options for Gender Representation in the English Renaissance', *Shakespeare Quarterly* 42.3 (1991), pp. 291–314 (301).

28. Dolan sees the pamphlet as essentially sympathetic towards Margaret: Dolan, *Dangerous Familiars*, pp. 145–50. See also Staub, *Nature's Cruel Stepdames*, pp. 47–9. In contrast, Keith M. Botelho sees her as a mother who forgets her children, and he and Randall Martin argue that she is condemned more harshly by the pamphlet's author (Keith M. Botelho, 'Maternal Memory and Murder in Early-Seventeenth-Century England', *Studies in English Literature* 48.1 (2008), pp. 111–30 (116–18); and Randall Martin, *Women, Murder, and Equity in Early Modern England* (New York: Routledge, 2008), p. 168).

29. Although Staub has argued that married women were more likely to be the subject of popular accounts of infanticides, despite apparently committing the crime less frequently (*Nature's Cruel Stepdames*, p. 15). On the typical profile of infanticides in early modern England, see Dolan, *Dangerous Familiars*, p. 132; Keith Wrightson, 'Infanticide in Earlier Seventeenth-Century England', *Local Population Studies* 15 (1975), pp. 10–22; and on the history of infanticide, see Mark Jackson, 'The Trial of Harriet Vooght: Continuity and Change in the History of Infanticide', in Jackson (ed.), *Infanticide: Historical Perspectives on Child Murder and Concealment, 1550–2000* (Aldershot: Ashgate, 2002), pp. 1–17. On the tendency of early modern England to suspect poor, elderly or vulnerable woman of witchcraft, see Dolan, *Dangerous Familiars*, pp. 171, 197; Alan MacFarlane, *Witchcraft in Tudor and Stuart England: A Regional and Comparative Study*, 2nd edn (London: Routledge, 1970, repr. 1999), pp. 150–1 and 161–4; and Keith Thomas, *Religion and the Decline of*

Magic: Studies in Popular Beliefs in Sixteenth and Seventeenth Century England (London: Weidenfeld and Nicolson, 1971, repr. 1997), pp. 520 and 562–3. On the perceived connection between the crimes of witchcraft and infanticide, see Hoffer and Hull, *Murdering Mothers*, pp. 28–31.

30. See Martin, *Women, Murder, and Equity*, ch. 2 and p. 112.

31. Sasha Roberts has shown how the seventeenth-century headings and contents pages added to Shakespeare's *Rape of Lucrece* direct the reader's understanding in very similar ways, although their intention was to stress Lucrece's virtue, rather than her wickedness (*Reading Shakespeare's Poems in Early Modern England* (Basingstoke: Palgrave Macmillan, 2003), ch. 3).

32. On Robinson's Protestantism, see Götz Schmitz, *The Fall of Women in Early English Narrative Verse* (Cambridge: Cambridge University Press, 1990), p. 61. For a discussion of the poem as a whole, see the introduction to Richard Robinson, *The Rewarde of Wickednesse*, ed. Allyna E. Ward (London: Modern Humanities Research Association, 2009).

33. The letting of a witch's blood was supposed to break her enchantments, a belief which may contribute to the bloodthirsty description of Medea's punishment here. See Dolan, *Dangerous Familiars*, p. 188; Anthony Harris, *Night's Black Agents: Witchcraft and Magic in Seventeenth-Century English Drama* (Manchester: Manchester University Press, 1980), p. 104; and Thomas, *Religion and the Decline of Magic*, p. 544. Dolan notes that real women were never punished by disembowelling – however, using Medea allows Robinson free reign to indulge in such gruesome fantasies ('"Gentlemen, I Have One Thing More to Say"', p. 166).

34. See Gail Kern Paster's very useful discussion of the murder of Julius Caesar, in Shakespeare's play: she notes that when they stab Caesar and provoke bleeding, 'To the conspirators go all the phlebotomist's skill, self-mastery, and therapeutic praxis; to Caesar a passivity, uncontrol, and bodily wastefulness gendered female' (*The Body Embarrassed: Drama and the Disciplines of Shame in Early Modern England* (Ithaca, NY: Cornell University Press, 1993), p. 104).

35. Dolan, *Dangerous Familiars*, p. 50.

36. Dolan, *Dangerous Familiars*, p. 50.

37. J. A. Sharpe, '"Last Dying Speeches": Religion, Ideology and Public Execution in Seventeenth-Century England', *Past and Present* 107 (1985), pp. 144–67 (156). See also Stuart A. Kane, 'Wives with Knives: Early Modern Murder Ballads and the Transgressive Commodity', *Criticism* 38.2 (1996), pp. 219–37 (227).

38. Sharpe, 'Last Dying Speeches', p. 156.

39. See Pruvost, *Matteo Bandello*, p. 2. For Bandello's version, see Matteo Bandello, *Opere*, ed. Francesco Flora, 2 vols (Milan: Arnoldo Mondadori, 1935), vol. 1, pp. 496–508. For Boiastuau's version, see Pierre Boiastuau, *Histoires Tragiques*, ed. Richard A. Carr (Paris: Librairie Honoré Champion, 1977), pp. 139–67.

40. Painter calls her 'an other Medea' at this point in the tale (Mmi^r). William Painter, *The palace of pleasure beautified, adorned and well furnished, with pleasaunt histories and excellent nouelles, selected out of diuers good and commendable authors* (London: 1566), STC (2nd edn) 19121. Painter is repeating the single reference in Boiastuau, which describes her as 'comme une Medée' (*Histoires Tragiques*, p. 162); Bandello's tale has no reference to Medea.

41. The poem is discussed by Schmitz, *The Fall of Women in Early English Narrative Verse*, pp. 205–7, who sees the Medea of the *Metamorphoses* as one of Achelley's inspirations.

42. George Whetstone, *The Rocke of Regard* (London: 1576), STC (2nd edn) 25348.

43. John Kerrigan (ed.), *Motives of Woe: Shakespeare and 'Female Complaint', a Critical Anthology* (Oxford: Clarendon Press, 1991), p 8.

44. Kerrigan (ed.), *Motives of Woe*, p. 27.

45. See introduction to William Alabaster, *Roxana*, ed. Dana F. Sutton, hypertext edition (Irvine, Calif.: University of California, 1998), sections 4, 8–9, 19, 25–6, 34–7, based on William Alabaster, *Roxana* (London: 1632) and a contemporary English translation. Copyright University of Birmingham.

46. Translations of *Roxana* are from the *c.* seventeenth-century English version, edited by Sutton. For discussion of the Latin text, see the introduction, pp. 38–40.

47. J. W. Binns, 'Seneca and Neo-Latin Tragedy in England', in C. D. N. Costa (ed.), *Seneca* (London: Routledge and Kegan Paul, 1974), pp. 205–34 (213).

48. Sutton notes that this speech was greatly altered in the English translation (Alabaster, *Roxana*, ed. Sutton, n. to lines 1737–56 of the translation).

49. Hall argues that Medea 'only exerted a subterranean influence on Renaissance, Jacobean, and Restoration tragedy' ('Medea and British Legislation', p. 47).

50. Thomas Norton [and Thomas Sackville], *The tragedie of Gorboduc* (London: 1565), STC (2nd edn) 18684.

51. Betty S. Travitsky notes how the play builds on its chronicle sources to emphasise the role of Videna, who is 'responsible for additional dimensions of disorder, unnaturalness and retribution' ('Child Murder in English Renaissance Life and Drama', in Leeds Barroll (ed.), *Medieval and Renaissance Drama in England* 6 (New York: AMS, 1993), pp. 63–84 (71 and 83).

52. On the spectre of disorder in the play, and how this is turned to instructive ends, see also Michael Ullyot, 'Seneca and the Early Elizabethan History Play', in Teresa Grant and Barbara Ravelhofer (eds), *English Historical Drama, 1500–1660: Forms outside the Canon* (Basingstoke: Palgrave Macmillan, 2008), pp. 98–124 (108–11).

53. John Higgins, *The first parte of the Mirour for magistrates* (London: 1574), STC (2nd edn) 13443.

54. Dermot Cavanagh suggests that while *Gorboduc* does encourage its Elizabethan audience to appreciate the ruler they have in the queen by presenting the contrastive woe of Gorboduc's reign, it simultaneously complicates matters by probing the question of how and why monarchs choose their successors: a question that would, of course, become ever more pressing as Elizabeth aged ('Political Tragedy in the 1560s: *Cambises* and *Gorboduc*', in Pincombe and Shrank (eds), *Oxford Handbook of Tudor Literature*, pp. 488–503.

55. Like Lady Macbeth, Videna meets her end offstage: Dolan argues that tragedy was more concerned with 'eliminating rather than displaying' such sinful women, but the crucial point is that the Medea-like woman is (almost) always punished ('"Gentlemen, I Have One Thing More to Say"', p. 163).

56. For Raber, what is particularly troubling and destabilising is Videna's 'irrational and inexplicable attachment to Ferrex' over his brother: this choice of one son over another, without good reason and with such bloody results, 'emphasizes the resistance of women's "nature" to the rational dictates of disciplined government'. At the same time, as Raber notes, the motive Videna is given distances her in some ways from Medea, who does not differentiate between her sons (Raber, 'Murderous Mothers', pp. 312–13 and 299).

57. W. S., *The Lamentable Tragedie of Locrine* (London: 1595), STC (2nd edn) 21528. George Peele or Robert Greene have been named as possible authors.

See Thomas L. Berger, William C. Bradford and Sidney L. Sondergard, *An Index of Characters in Early Modern English Drama: Printed Plays, 1500–1660* (Cambridge: Cambridge University Press, 1998), p. 111.

58. Kerrigan (ed.), *Motives of Woe*, p. 27–8.

59. Other examples of women who are compared to Medea, but allowed to survive their play's conclusions because they do not actually carry out or commission acts of violence, include Charlotte in George Chapman's *The Revenge of Bussy d'Ambois* (printed 1613) and Lepida in Nathanael Richards's *Messalina* (printed 1640).

60. Cavanagh, 'Political Tragedy', p. 490.

61. Adelman ends her essay on *Macbeth* by comparing the vanquishing of troubling female power, and the establishment of a 'purely male realm', to the similar movement achieved in *The Tempest*: as I shall show, in both the tragedy and the tragicomedy, Medea haunts the plays' conception of female and/or magical power (Adelman, 'Born of Woman', p. 111).

62. Cathy Shrank, '"This fatall Medea", "this Clytemnestra": Reading and the Detection of Mary Queen of Scots', *Huntington Library Quarterly* 73.3 (2010), pp. 523–41 (537).

63. William Shakespeare, *The Norton Shakespeare*, ed. Stephen Greenblatt et al. (New York: Norton, 1997), p. 376. See also Marion Wynne-Davies, '"The Swallowing Womb": Consumed and Consuming Women in *Titus Andronicus*', in Valerie Wayne (ed.), *The Matter of Difference: Materialist Feminist Criticism of Shakespeare* (Hemel Hempstead: Harvester Wheatsheaf, 1991), pp. 129–51 (146).

64. On Shakespeare's use of the *Metamorphoses* in *Titus Andronicus*, see R. W. Maslen, 'Myths Exploited: The Metamorphoses of Ovid in Early Elizabethan England', in A. B. Taylor (ed.), *Shakespeare's Ovid: The 'Metamorphoses' in the Plays and Poems* (Cambridge: Cambridge University Press, 2000), pp. 15–30.

65. Robert S. Miola, *Shakespeare and Classical Tragedy: The Influence of Seneca* (Oxford: Clarendon Press, 1992), p. 24.

66. Edward Ravenscroft, *Titus Andronicus, or, The Rape of Lavinia acted at the Theatre Royall* (London: 1687), Wing S2949. Ravenscroft's preface makes clear that the work was first performed at the time of the Popish Plot. For a discussion of Ravenscroft's attitude to Shakespeare's play, see John W. Velz, 'Topoi in Edward Ravenscroft's Indictment of Shakespeare's *Titus Andronicus*', *Modern Philology* 83.1 (1985), pp. 45–50.

67. On Shakespeare's Tamora as threatening mother, see Dorothea Kehler, 'That Ravenous Tiger Tamora': *Titus Andronicus'* Lusty Widow, Wife, and M/Other', in Philip C. Kolin (ed.), *Titus Andronicus: Critical Essays* (New York: Garland, 1995), pp. 317–32, and, in the same volume, David Willbern, 'Rape and Revenge in *Titus Andronicus*', pp. 171–94.

68. For a discussion of how Shakespeare's play introduces and then quietly sidelines the equally alarming female classical revenger that is Procne, see Mariangela Tempera, '"Worse than Procne": The Sister as Avenger in the English Renaissance', in Michele Marrapodi and A. J. Hoenselaars (eds), *The Italian World of English Renaissance Drama: Cultural Exchange and Intertextuality* (Cranbury, NJ, and London: Associated University Presses, 1998), pp. 71–88.

69. Willbern, 'Rape and Revenge', pp. 187–8.

70. Liz Oakley-Brown, '"My lord, be ruled by me": Shakespeare's Tamora and the Failure of Queenship', in Liz Oakley-Brown and Louise J. Wilkinson (eds),

The Rituals and Rhetoric of Queenship: Medieval to Early Modern (Dublin: Four Courts Press, 2009), pp. 222–37 (227–8).

71. Inga-Stina Ewbank, 'The Fiend-Like Queen: A Note on *Macbeth* and Seneca's *Medea*', in Kenneth Muir (ed.), *Shakespeare Survey 19* (Cambridge: Cambridge University Press, repr. 2002), pp. 82–94 (84–5).

72. Colin Burrow, *Shakespeare and Classical Antiquity* (Oxford: Oxford University Press, 2013), p. 193. For a brief but fascinating analysis of how Lady Macbeth's lexical and grammatical choices differentiate her from Studley's more proactive Medea, see pp. 193–4.

73. Miola, *Shakespeare and Classical Tragedy*, p. 107.

74. Shakespeare, *Norton Shakespeare*, ed. Greenblatt, p. 2557.

75. Burrow, *Shakespeare and Classical Antiquity*, p. 194.

76. Miola, *Shakespeare and Classical Tragedy*, p. 106.

77. Ewbank notes that the Weird Sisters' description of their concocting potions may be indebted to Medea's magical power as it is outlined in either Seneca's *Medea* or Ovid's *Metamorphoses 7*. Ewbank, 'Fiend-Like Queen', n.93. Wills argues that Shakespeare uses the Latin of both Ovid and Seneca in Macbeth's appeal to the witches in 4.1 (Gary Wills, *Witches and Jesuits: Shakespeare's 'Macbeth'* (New York: Oxford University Press, 1995), p. 184 n.26).

78. For a defence of the importance of the Hecate scenes (which may be taken from Middleton's *The Witch*) see Wills, *Witches and Jesuits*, pp. 43–9. A. C. Bradley identifies these lines, with their '[i]dea of sexual relation' between Macbeth and the witches, as more in keeping with Middleton's play than with Shakespeare's: either way, the scene recalls the anger of the Senecan Medea, or the Medea of Ovid's *Heroides*, both of whom furiously detail all they have done for the faithless and ungrateful Jason (A. C. Bradley, *Shakespearean Tragedy: Lectures on 'Hamlet', 'Othello', 'King Lear', 'Macbeth'*, 2nd edn (London: Macmillan, 1905, repr. 1978), p. 466).

79. Janet Adelman, *Suffocating Mothers: Fantasies of Maternal Origin in Shakespeare's Plays, 'Hamlet' to 'The Tempest'* (London: Routledge, 1992), p. 134.

80. For a comparison of the 1563 and 1604 statutes, see Macfarlane, *Witchcraft in Tudor and Stuart England*, pp. 14–15; and Thomas, *Religion and the Decline of Magic*, pp. 442–3.

81. Harry Berger Jr, 'Text against Performance in Shakespeare: The Example of *Macbeth*', in Stephen Greenblatt (ed.), *The Power of Forms in the English Renaissance* (Norman, Okla.: Pilgrim Books, 1982), pp. 49–79 (67). Dolan, *Dangerous Familiars*, p. 211. See also Adelman, 'Born of Woman', p. 99. For a survey of critics who see the witches as somehow comical or trivialised, see Adelman, 'Escaping the Matrix: The Construction of Masculinity in *Macbeth*', *Suffocating Mothers*, and reprinted in William Shakespeare, *Macbeth*, ed. Robert S. Miola (New York: Norton, 2004), pp. 293–315 (302).

82. Karin S. Coddon '"Unreal Mockery": Unreason and the Problem of Spectacle in *Macbeth*', *ELH* 56.3 (1989), pp. 485–501 (489). See also Levin, 'Lady Macbeth', p. 45.

83. Taylor argues that 'scarcely a trace' of the influence of Turberville's *Heroides* has been found in Shakespeare's work, but Lady Macbeth's suicide, in particular, is a realisation of the punishment which Turberville's Hypsipyle wishes on her rival (A. B. Taylor, 'Introduction', in Taylor (ed.), *Shakespeare's Ovid*, pp. 1–12 (3)). For a discussion of Elizabethan use of the *Heroides*, see Helen Moore, 'Elizabethan Fiction and Ovid's *Heroides*', *Translation and*

Literature 9.1 (2000), pp. 40–64. Moore's survey of Shakespearean borrowings from the *Heroides*, identified by critics including Baldwin, Bate and Zielinski, can be found on p. 43. On Shakespeare's use of Turberville's *Heroides* in *The Taming of the Shrew*, see Patricia B. Phillippy, '"Loytering in Love": Ovid's *Heroides*, Hospitality, and Humanist Education in *The Taming of the Shrew*', *Criticism* 40.1 (1998), pp. 27–53.

84. Stephen Orgel, '*Macbeth* and the Antic Round', *Shakespeare Survey* 52 (1999), pp. 143–53, reprinted in Shakespeare, *Macbeth*, ed. Miola, pp. 342–56 (353).
85. Adelman, 'Escaping the Matrix', pp. 295, 313.
86. While the robe is the more famous of Medea's weapons, Euripides specifically refers to a poisoned crown (1160, 1186–7), and Seneca's Medea mentions 'gemmarum nitor / distinguit aurum, quo solent cingi comae' (the golden thing set off with bright gems that usually encircles my hair) (573–4). Studley's Medea names a 'precyous fulgent gorget ... that brauelye glytters bryght' (1724–5) as one of the gifts that she intends to poison, while Sherburne specifically mentions a crown in the argument to his later translation.
87. Henry Chettle, *The Tragedy of Hoffman*, ed. J. D. Jowett (Nottingham: Nottingham Drama Texts, 1983). The quarto sometimes names Charles as Otho: see Jowett's textual appendix, p. 75.
88. On such eighteenth-century treatments of Medea, see Hall, 'Medea and British Legislation', esp. pp. 47–50.
89. The play is traditionally dated to 1647: but see Matthew Birchwood, *Staging Islam in England: Drama and Culture 1640–1685* (Cambridge: D. S. Brewer, 2007), pp. 77–8. He argues that, though preparation on the work could have begun long before, the printed version of *Mirza* should be dated to 1655.
90. Robert Baron, *Mirza a Tragedie* (London: 1655), STC (2nd edn) Wing B892.
91. See Hall, 'Medea and British Legislation', pp. 67, 70; and 'Divine and Human in Euripides' *Medea*', in David Stuttard (ed.), *Looking at Medea: Essays and a Translation of Euripides' Tragedy* (London: Bloomsbury, 2014), pp. 139–55 (148).
92. Henry Neville Payne, *The Siege of Constantinople* (London: 1675), Wing P893.
93. Jean I. Marsden, 'Tragedy and Varieties of Serious Drama', in Susan J. Owen (ed.), *A Companion to Restoration Drama* (Oxford: Blackwell, 2001, repr. 2008), pp. 228–42 (236).
94. Hall, 'Medea and British Legislation', p. 70.
95. Nathaniel Lee, *The Rival Queens* (London: 1677), Wing L865.
96. Edith Hall, '*Medea* on the Eighteenth-Century London Stage', in Hall, Macintosh and Taplin (eds), *Medea in Performance*, pp. 49–74 (65).
97. On *The Rival Queens* as registering doubts about Charles II's rule, through the inadequate kingship of Alexander, see Jessica Munns, 'Images of Monarchy on the Restoration Stage', in Owen (ed.), *Companion to Restoration Drama*, pp. 109–25 (118), and, in the same volume, Paulina Kewes, 'Otway, Lee and the Restoration History Play', pp. 355–77 (365).
98. See Elizabeth Howe, *The First English Actresses: Women and Drama 1660–1700* (Cambridge: Cambridge University Press, 1992), pp. 109–13.
99. Jean I. Marsden, *Fatal Desire: Women, Sexuality, and the English Stage, 1660–1720* (Ithaca and London: Cornell University Press, 2006), pp. 84–5. Marsden does not see Statira and Roxana as pathetic figures before Bracegirdle and Barry take over, but if Roxana's treatment is compared with that of earlier Medea-figures she is certainly treated more sympathetically.

4   Comic Medea

1. Sir Philip Sidney, *The Defence of Poesie*, in Allan H. Gilbert (ed.), *Literary Criticism: Plato to Dryden* (Detroit: Wayne State University Press, 1962), pp. 406–58.
2. Sir Thomas Elyot, *The Governor*, in Gilbert, ed. *Literary Criticism*, pp. 233–41.
3. See Thomas Heywood, *An Apology for Actors* (1612), in Gilbert (ed.), *Literary Criticism*, pp. 552–64; Sidney, *Defence of Poesie*, pp. 451–2.
4. Heywood, *Apology for Actors*.
5. Giambattista Guarini, *The Compendium of Tragicomic Poetry*, trans. Gilbert, in Gilbert (ed.), *Literary Criticism*, pp. 504–33.
6. See T. S. Dorsch (trans.), *Classical Literary Criticism* (Harmondsworth: Penguin, 1965), p. 37.
7. Susan Snyder, 'The Genres of Shakespeare's Plays', in Margreta De Grazia and Stanley William Wells (eds), *The Cambridge Companion to Shakespeare* (Cambridge and New York: Cambridge University Press, 2001), pp. 83–97 (94).
8. Ben Jonson, *The Alchemist*, *The Complete Works*, ed. David Bevington, Martin Butler and Ian Donaldson, 7 vols (Cambridge and New York: Cambridge University Press, 2012), vol. 3.
9. Ben Jonson, *'The Alchemist' and Other Plays*, ed. Gordon Campbell (Oxford: Oxford University Press, 1995), p. 489. For Jonson's use of 'Chrysognus Polydorus', a sixteenth-century alchemist who repeats and extends Suidas' classical explanation of the Fleece as an alchemical treatise, see Supriya Chaudhuri, 'Jason's Fleece: The Source of Sir Epicure Mammon's Allegory', *RES* New Series, 35.137 (1984), pp. 71–3.
10. Margaret Healy, 'Alchemy, Magic and the Sciences', in Julie Sanders (ed.), *Ben Jonson in Context* (Cambridge: Cambridge University Press, 2010), pp. 322–9 (322).
11. George Pettie, *A Petite Pallace of Pettie his Pleasure* (London: 1576), STC (2nd edn) 19819.
12. Paul Salzman, 'Placing Tudor Fiction', *Yearbook of English Studies* 38 1/2, *Tudor Literature* (2008), pp. 136–49 (146).
13. Robert Greene, *Arbasto, The Anatomie of Fortune* (London: 1584), STC (2nd edn) 12217.
14. John Kerrigan (ed.), *Motives of Woe: Shakespeare and 'Female Complaint', a Critical Anthology* (Oxford: Clarendon Press, 1991), p. 65.
15. Robert Greene, *Mamillia* (London: 1583), STC (2nd edn) 12269.
16. Katharine Wilson, *Fictions of Authorship in Late Elizabethan Narratives: Euphues in Arcadia* (Oxford: Clarendon Press, 2006), p. 16; on Greene's use of the *Heroides* in this romance, see pp. 78–9. See also Helen Moore, 'Elizabethan Fiction and Ovid's *Heroides*', *Translation and Literature* 9.1 (2000), pp. 40–64.
17. Caroline Lucas, *Writing for Women: The Example of Woman as Reader in Elizabethan Romance* (Milton Keynes: Open University Press, 1989), p. 26.
18. Timothy Hampton, *Writing From History: The Rhetoric of Exemplarity in Renaissance Literature* (Ithaca and London: Cornell University Press, 1990), p. 25.
19. Linda Hutcheon, *A Theory of Adaptation* (New York: Routledge, 2006), p. 116.
20. Wilson, *Fictions of Authorship*, p. 79.
21. Wilson, *Fictions of Authorship*, p. 83.
22. Lucas, *Writing for Women*, p. 81. See also Helen Hackett, *Women and Romance Fiction in the English Renaissance* (Cambridge: Cambridge University Press,

2000), p. 97, who notes Greene's 'supposed championing of women's cause' in his early works.
23. Robert Greene, *The defence of conny-catching* (London: 1592), STC (2nd edn) 5656.
24. On the mutilation of a man's nose and ears as symbolic of castration, see Garthine Walker, *Crime, Gender and Social Order in Early Modern England* (Cambridge: Cambridge University Press, 2003), pp. 91–3.
25. Constance C. Relihan, *Fashioning Authority: The Development of Elizabethan Novelistic Discourse* (Kent, OH: Kent State University Press, 1994), p. 80.
26. *The Academy of Pleasure* (London: 1656), Wing A159.
27. Adam Smyth, *'Profit and Delight': Printed Miscellanies in England, 1640–1682* (Detroit: Wayne State University Press, 2004), p. 69.
28. Ibid., p. 70.
29. Frances E. Dolan, *Dangerous Familiars: Representations of Domestic Crime in England, 1550–1700* (Ithaca and London: Cornell University Press, 1994), p. 217.
30. H. W. Herrington, 'Witchcraft and Magic in the Elizabethan Drama', *Journal of American Folklore* 32.126 (1919), pp. 447–85 (477); Dolan, *Dangerous Familiars*, p. 204. See also Diane Purkiss, 'Witchcraft in Early Modern Literature', in Brian P. Levack (ed.), *The Oxford Handbook of Witchcraft in Early Modern Europe and Colonial America* (Oxford: Oxford University Press, 2013), pp. 122–40 (135–8).
31. Robert Greene, *The Comicall Historie of Alphonsus, King of Aragon* (London: 1599), STC (2nd edn) 12233.
32. Heather Dubrow, *Genre* (London: Methuen, 1982), p. 31.
33. On the problem of maternal involvement in courtship and love plots in Shakespearean drama, see Mary Beth Rose, 'Where Are the Mothers in Shakespeare? Options for Gender Representation in the English Renaissance', *Shakespeare Quarterly* 42.3 (1991), pp. 291–314 (308–9).
34. Dubrow, *Genre*, p. 108.
35. Jonathan Bate, *Shakespeare and Ovid* (Oxford: Clarendon Press, 1993), pp. 155–6.
36. Ibid., p. 153.
37. As in Chapter 2, I quote from Madeleine Forey's edition of Golding's translation.
38. Bate, *Shakespeare and Ovid*, p. 9.
39. Leonard Barkan, *The Gods Made Flesh: Metamorphosis and the Pursuit of Paganism* (New Haven and London: Yale University Press, 1986), pp. 287–8.
40. William Shakespeare, *The Tempest*, ed. Frank Kermode (London: Methuen, 1954), p. 150.
41. Colin Burrow, *Shakespeare and Classical Antiquity* (Oxford: Oxford University Press, 2013), pp. 131 and 130.
42. Charles Martindale and Michelle Martindale, *Shakespeare and the Uses of Antiquity: An Introductory Essay* (London: Routledge, 1990), p. 23.
43. As Burrow points out, in this famous passage 'magical mastery is renounced even at the level of syntax, but ... the threatening potential of Medea remains just a distant possibility' (*Shakespeare and Classical Antiquity*, p. 132).
44. Kermode argues that the magic of Sycorax and Prospero is fundamentally different: see *The Tempest*, ed. Kermode, pp. xli, 145, 149. Others see their magic as harder to separate: see Shakespeare, *The Tempest*, ed. Stephen Orgel (Oxford: Clarendon Press, 1987), pp. 19–23; and Paul Brown, '"This Thing of Darkness I Acknowledge Mine": *The Tempest* and the Discourse

of Colonialism', in Jonathan Dollimore and Alan Sinfield (eds), *Political Shakespeare: Essays in Cultural Materialism*, 2nd edn (Manchester: Manchester University Press, 1994), pp. 48–71 (61).

45. Although Anthony Harris suggests that this choice of trees indicates an 'essential difference' between the magic of Prospero and Sycorax, because of the oak's historical association with 'priest-like figures', while pine forests supposedly attracted 'trolls and other demonic figures' (*Night's Black Agents: Witchcraft and Magic in Seventeenth-Century English Drama* (Manchester: Manchester University Press, 1980), p. 145). By and large, though, he sees Prospero's magic as dark. Jonathan Bate notes that Prospero's later mention of 'Jove's stout oak', in his renunciation speech, indicates a use of Ovid rather than Golding, as the former specifically refers to *robora* (oak) while the latter does not (*Shakespeare and Ovid*, p. 8).

46. Diane Purkiss, *The Witch in History: Early Modern and Twentieth-Century Representations* (London: Routledge, 1996), p. 269.

47. See Shakespeare, *The Tempest*, ed. Orgel, pp. 19–20; Bate, *Shakespeare and Ovid*, p. 9.

48. Daniel Vitkus, '"Meaner Ministers": Mastery, Bondage, and Theatrical Labor in *The Tempest*', in Richard Dutton and Jean E. Howard (eds), *A Companion to Shakespeare's Works Volume IV: The Poems, Problem Comedies, Late Plays* (Oxford: Blackwell, 2003), pp. 408–26 (422).

49. Lawrence Danson, *Shakespeare's Dramatic Genres* (Oxford: Oxford University Press, 2000), p. 63.

50. Parallels between Medea and Miranda, who turns 'very slightly' against her father in her desire for Ferdinand, are noted by Raphael Lyne, 'Ovid, Golding, and the "Rough Magic" of *The Tempest*', in Taylor (ed.), *Shakespeare's Ovid*, pp. 150–64 (159). See also Kirilka Stavreva, '"There's Magic in Thy Majesty", Queenship and Witch-Speak in Jacobean Shakespeare', in Carole Levin, Jo Eldridge Carney and Debra Barrett-Graves (eds), *High and Mighty Queens of Early Modern England: Realities and Representations* (New York: Palgrave, 2003), pp. 151–68 (164).

51. Christine M. Neufeld suggests that John Lyly seeks to create a comparable sense of discomfort, of disorder apparently banished but never entirely forgotten, in his *Endymion*, an 'ostensibly panegyric' Elizabethan drama of the mid-1580s, which draws disturbing parallels between the Ovidian Medea and the play's female characters (including its queen-figure, Cynthia) ('Lyly's Chimerical Vision: Witchcraft in *Endymion*', *Forum for Modern Language Studies* 43.4 (2007), pp. 351–69 (352, 357, 365).

52. James Shirley, *The Schoole of Complement* (London: 1631), Wing (2nd edn) 22456.

53. Verna A. Foster, *The Name and Nature of Tragicomedy* (Aldershot: Ashgate, 2004), p. 61.

54. Thomas Meriton, *The Wandring Lover* (London: 1658), Wing M1824. The main plot sees Euphrates rescue his kidnapped beloved, Graecana, and, in the process, apparently kill one of her kidnappers, Perco. Medea is not involved in this climactic moment, and its tragic power is deliberately undercut by the fact that it is not shown or properly described, and because Euphrates is disguised in women's clothes when he ambushes his rival.

55. Laurie Maguire, *Shakespeare's Names* (Oxford: Oxford University Press, 2007), p. 119.

56. Harris, *Night's Black Agents*, p. 176.

57. James Shirley, *The Triumph of Beautie* (London: 1646), Wing (2nd edn) S3488.
58. Often, authors telling the story of the Fleece try their hardest to ignore Medea's crucial role, and shape it into a myth of masculine triumph and fortitude: Shirley, by contrast, deliberately stresses Medea's part here.
59. Similarly, Nicholas Brooke argues that much of the comedy at the end of Thomas Middleton's *Women Beware Women* springs from the 'sheer incompetence' of unsuitable characters trying to put on a classicised story for their superiors (*Horrid Laughter in Jacobean Tragedy* (London: Open Books, 1979), pp. 97 and 106).
60. Julie Sanders, *Adaptation and Appropriation* (New York: Routledge, 2006), p. 29.
61. Charles Cotton, *Erotopolis, The Present State of Betty-Land* (London: 1684), Wing E3242.
62. See Palaephatus, *On Unbelievable Tales*, trans. and ed. Jacob Stern, with notes and Greek text from the 1902 B. G. Teubner edition (Wauconda, Ill.: Bolchazy-Carducci, 1996), pp. 75–6. Seventeenth-century rationalisations of this aspect of the myth are mentioned briefly in Chapter 1 of the current work.
63. See Keith Thomas, *Religion and the Decline of Magic: Studies in Popular Beliefs in Sixteenth and Seventeenth Century England* (London: Weidenfeld and Nicolson, 1971, repr. 1997), p. 452. He notes that the last hanging of a witch in England took place in 1685.
64. John Dryden and William Davenant, *The Tempest, or The Enchanted Island*, in Dryden, *Works*, vol. 10, ed. Maximillian E. Novak and George Robert Guffey.
65. Shakespeare, *The Tempest*, ed. Kermode, p. 130. See also Dryden, *Works*, vol. 10, pp. 376–7.
66. On the potential political applications of the Restoration *Tempest*, see Matthew H. Wikander, '"The Duke My Father's Wrack": The Innocence of the Restoration *Tempest*', *Shakespeare Survey* 43, ed. Stanley Wells (Cambridge: Cambridge University Press, 1990), pp. 91–8.
67. Douglas Bush, *Mythology and the Renaissance Tradition in English Poetry* (New York: Pageant, 1932, repr. 1957), pp. 293 and 287.
68. See Susan Wiseman, 'Perfectly Ovidian? Dryden's *Epistles*, Behn's 'Oenone', Yarico's Island', *Renaissance Studies* 22.3 (2008), pp. 417–32 (423–6). For an earlier general discussion of Stevenson's and Radcliffe's collections, see Richard F. Hardin, 'Ovid in Seventeenth Century England', *Comparative Literature* 24.1 (1972), pp. 44–62 (52–3).
69. Susan Wiseman, 'Rome's Wanton Ovid: Reading and Writing Ovid's *Heroides* 1590–1712', *Renaissance Studies* 22.3 (2008), pp. 295–306 (301).
70. Matthew Stevenson, *The Wits paraphras'd or, Paraphrase upon paraphrase in a burlesque on the several late translations of Ovids Epistles* (London: 1680), Wing (2nd edn) S5513.
71. Wiseman, 'Perfectly Ovidian', p. 424. On the experimental nature of Tonson's multi-authored approach, see Stuart Gillespie, 'The Early Years of the Dryden-Tonson Partnership: The Background to Their Composite Translations and Miscellanies of the 1680s', *Restoration: Studies in English Literary Culture, 1660–1700* 12.1 (1988), pp. 10–19 (11–12).
72. Alexander Radcliffe, *Ovid travestie, a burlesque upon Ovid's Epistles* (London: 1680), Wing R125. This burlesque was also printed by Jacob Tonson, who had produced the 1680 *Ovid's Epistles*.
73. Radcliffe is usually accounted the victor: see Hardin, 'Ovid in Seventeenth-Century England', p. 53; Wiseman, 'Perfectly Ovidian', p. 424.
74. Kerrigan, *Motives of Woe*, pp. 72–3.

75. Kerrigan, *Motives of Woe*, p. 65; Harvey, *Ventriloquized Voices*, p. 1.
76. The choice of 'Bunting' as an apparent term of endearment for Jason is curious: a nautical term, referring to the filling of a ship's sails with wind, there may also be a suggestion of obscenity associated with the idea of swelling. (In the eighteenth-century nursery rhyme, 'Bye Baby Bunting', the term refers affectionately to the plumpness of the child.) 'bunting, adj.', OED Online. December 2013 (Oxford: Oxford University Press, 17 January 2014 <http://www.oed.com/view/Entry/24841?rskey=l7Kp42&result=5&isAdvan ced=false>, accessed 22 July 2014. Settle has Hypsipyle complain, 'a Witch destroys / My fancied pleasures, and my promis'd Joys' (M5ʳ).
77. Kerrigan, *Motives of Woe*, p. 73.
78. 'Maunder' means to beg or grumble. 'Glaunders' was an equine disease, characterised by discharge of mucous from the nostrils: 'maunder, v. 1', OED Online. December 2013 (Oxford: Oxford University Press, 17 January 2014) <http://www.oed.com/view/Entry/115177?rskey=UeNvyk&result= 3&isAdvanced=false>, accessed 22 July 2014. 'glander, n.', OED Online. December 2013 (Oxford: Oxford University Press, 17 January 2014) <http:// www.oed.com/view/Entry/78711?redirectedFrom=glaunders>, accessed 22 July 2014.
79. 'placket, n. 1', OED Online. December 2013 (Oxford: Oxford University Press, 17 January 2014) <http://www.oed.com/view/Entry/144921?rskey= NDHdXR&result=1&isAdvanced=false>, accessed 22 July 2014.
80. See Herrington, 'Witchcraft and Magic', p. 469. Thomas argues that the belief that witches had sexual relations with the Devil, or with incubi and succubi, declined in the eighteenth century, which preferred to see women as passive rather than demonise them as sexually insatiable (*Religion and the Decline of Magic*, p. 569).
81. Here 'pintle' means penis. 'pintle, n.', OED Online. December 2013 (Oxford: Oxford University Press, 17 January 2014) <http://www.oed.com/view/ Entry/144335?rskey=t3DX08&result=5&isAdvanced=false>, accessed 22 July 2014.
82. On the split or mutilated nose as a 'whore's mark', see Walker, *Crime, Gender and Social Order*, p. 92.
83. This couplet is omitted from the 1681 edition.
84. On the use of contemporary references in translation, see Harold Love, 'Some Restoration Treatments of Ovid', in Antony Coleman and Antony Hammond (eds), *Poetry and Drama 1570–1700: Essays in Honour of Harold F. Brooks* (London: Methuen, 1981), pp. 136–55 (139); and Harold F. Brooks, 'The "Imitation" in English Poetry, Especially in Formal Satire, before the Age of Pope', RES 25.98 (1949), pp. 124–40. On parody's use of contemporary additions, see Howard D. Weinbrot, 'Translation and Parody: Towards the Genealogy of the Augustan Imitation', ELH 33.4 (1966), pp. 434–47; and Julie Candler Hayes, *Translation, Subjectivity, and Culture in France and England, 1600–1800* (Stanford: Stanford University Press, 2009), p. 80.
85. C. S. Lewis, *An Experiment in Criticism* (Cambridge: Cambridge University Press, 1961), p. 43.
86. Dubrow, *Genre*, p. 25.
87. Edith Hall, 'Medea and British Legislation before the First World War', *Greece and Rome* 46.1 (1999), pp. 42–77 (53). On the latter's attribution see n. 74.

5 Political Medea

1. Anthony Munday, *The Triumphs of the Golden Fleece, Pageants and Entertainments of Anthony Munday: A Critical Edition*, ed. David M. Bergeron (New York and London: Garland Publishing, 1985), pp. 137–43.
2. Anthony Munday, *Metropolis Coronata, The Triumphs of Ancient Drapery, Pageants and Entertainments of Anthony Munday*, ed. Bergeron, pp. 85–99.
3. Tracey Hill, *Anthony Munday and Civic Culture: Theatre, History and Power in Early Modern London, 1580–1633* (Manchester: Manchester University Press, 2004), p. 157.
4. Thomas Heywood, *Londini Status Pacatus, or Londons Peaceable Estate, Thomas Heywood's Pageants: A Critical Edition*, ed. David M. Bergeron (New York and London: Garland Publishing, 1985), pp. 123–41.
5. Peter Elmer, '"Saints or Sorcerers": Quakerism, Demonology and the Decline of Witchcraft in Seventeenth-Century England', in Jonathan Barry, Marianne Hester and Gareth Roberts (eds), *Witchcraft in Early Modern Europe: Studies in Culture and Belief* (Cambridge: Cambridge University Press, 1996), pp. 145–79 (160). See also Peter Lake, 'Anti-popery: The Structure of a Prejudice', in Richard Cust and Ann Hughes (eds), *Conflict in Early Stuart England: Studies in Religion and Politics, 1603–1642* (London: Longman, 1989), pp. 72–106 (75, 93).
6. On the Protestant perception that Catholicism 'inappropriately empower[ed] women, spiritually, symbolically, and socially', see Frances E. Dolan, *Whores of Babylon: Catholicism, Gender, and Seventeenth-Century Print Culture* (Ithaca and London: Cornell University Press, 1999), p. 8.
7. Ruth Morse, *The Medieval Medea* (Cambridge: D. S. Brewer, 1996), p. 15.
8. Excerpts from Elizabeth's speech are from Janet M. Green, '"I My Self": Elizabeth I's Oration at Tilbury Camp', *Sixteenth Century Journal* 28.2 (Summer 1997), pp. 421–45 (426). In her consideration of the ways in which tyranny might be aligned with the feminine, Rebecca Bushnell notes that Elizabeth privileges her masculine aspects here: 'while she admits that her body is that of a woman, she stresses that her "affections" or emotions are masculine, thus implicitly at once both strong and under control' ('Tyranny and Effeminacy in Early Modern England', in Mario A. Di Cesare (ed.), *Reconsidering the Renaissance* (Binghamton, NY: Center for Medieval and Early Renaissance Studies, 1992), pp. 339–54 (341).
9. On Elizabeth's presentation as both masculine and feminine, and unlike other women, see Louis A. Montrose, '"Shaping Fantasies": Figurations of Gender and Power in Elizabethan Culture', *Representations* 2 (1983), pp. 61–94 (78–80).
10. For an alternative view of Studley's *Medea*, which argues that the play does speak to Elizabeth's rule, by presenting 'the pitfalls of an uncounseled woman in power' and 'a warning about the risks of a female monarch manipulated in matters of marriage and divorce', see Allyna E. Ward, *Women and Tudor Tragedy: Feminizing Counsel and Representing Gender* (Madison: Fairleigh Dickinson University Press, 2013), pp. 100 and 102. For me, this reading is problematic because it is Creon, not Medea, who enjoys monarchical power in Corinth.
11. M. L. Stapleton, *Fated Sky: The 'Femina Furens' in Shakespeare* (Newark: University of Delaware Press, 2000), p. 41.
12. See Christine M. Neufeld, 'Lyly's Chimerical Vision: Witchcraft in *Endymion*', *Forum for Modern Language Studies* 43.4 (2007), pp. 351–69 (352), for the

suggestion that *Endymion*, a play that makes repeated reference to Medea, 'communicates a profound anxiety about the monstrous shadow cast by the Virgin Queen', notwithstanding the play's ostensible interest in quashing or containing Medea's power.

13. Mihoko Suzuki, *Metamorphoses of Helen: Authority, Difference, and the Epic* (Ithaca: Cornell University Press, 1989), p. 178; Bart van Es, *Spenser's Forms of History* (Oxford: Oxford University Press, 2002), pp. 150–1.

14. Heather Dubrow notes that at points, Paridell and Britomart begin to seem uncomfortably similar to one another in the selective way that they recount history, but insists that finally 'Britomart's versions of history and of love are indisputably different from and superior to those of Paridell' ('The Arraignment of Paridell: Tudor Historiography in *The Faerie Queene*, III.IX', *Studies in Philology* 87.3 (1990), pp. 312–27 (325). On Paridell and Britomart as very different narrators of their common Trojan history, see Dubrow, 'Arraignment of Paridell', pp. 320–1.

15. Edmund Spenser, *The Faerie Queene*, ed. A. C. Hamilton, 2nd edn, text ed. Hiroshi Yamashita and Toshiyuki Suzuki (Harlow: Pearson Longman, 2007).

16. On the gate of ivory as a purveyor of false dreams, see *Odyssey* 19.560–9 and *Aeneid* 6.893–8. Spenser had also used the idea in Book 1 of his epic.

17. Diane Purkiss sees the blood-stained gold and ivory as bearing a warning about imperial ambition, suggesting that 'empire is only manageable for men who can obliterate every trace of its seductive otherness and bring it fully under control' ('Medea in the English Renaissance', in Edith Hall, Fiona Macintosh and Oliver Taplin (eds), *Medea in Performance 1500–2000* (Oxford: Legenda, 2000), pp. 32–48 (38)).

18. Syrithe Pugh, *Spenser and Ovid* (Aldershot: Ashgate, 2005), p. 84. She notes that Acrasia is also an echo of the Virgilian Dido, herself an adaptation of Apollonius Rhodius' Medea (*Spenser and Ovid*, p. 83).

19. Pugh compares the trembling, blushing Britomart and Malecasta, described in 3.2 and 3.1, to the Medea of the *Metamorphoses* (*Spenser and Ovid*, pp. 126–7). Britomart's lovesickness is described by Spenser at 3.2.22–39; Radigund's at 5.5.26–34.

20. Suzuki, *Metamorphoses of Helen*, p. 180.

21. For Radigund as representative of Mary, see Michael O'Connell, *Mirror and Veil: The Historical Dimension of Spenser's 'Faerie Queene'* (Chapel Hill: University of North Carolina Press, 1977), p. 140. For Radigund as representative of Elizabeth's 'strict control' over her male courtiers, see Suzuki, *Metamorphoses of Helen*, p. 190. On the blurring of distinctions between Radigund and Britomart, see Elizabeth D. Harvey, *Ventriloquized Voices: Feminist Theory and English Renaissance Texts* (London: Routledge, 1992), pp. 41–2; and Mary Villeponteaux, '"Not as Women Wonted Be": Spenser's Amazon Queen', in Julia M. Walker (ed.), *Dissing Elizabeth: Negative Representations of Gloriana* (Durham, NC: Duke University Press, 1998), pp. 209–25.

22. For the comparison with Penelope, see 5.7.39. On Britomart's re-establishment of order by 'putting other women in their places', see Montrose, '"Shaping Fantasies"', p. 76; and see also Harvey, *Ventriloquized Voices*, p. 42.

23. Justin Kolb, '"In th'armor of a Pagan knight": Romance and Anachronism East of England in Book V of *The Faerie Queene* and *Tamburlaine*', *Early Theatre* 12.2 (2009), pp. 194–207 (196); Judith H. Anderson, 'Spenser's *Faerie Queene*,

Book V: Poetry, Politics and Justice', in Michael Hattaway (ed.), *A Companion to English Renaissance Literature and Culture* (Oxford: Blackwell, 2003), pp. 195–205 (203). See also Richard F. Hardin, 'Adicia, Souldan', in A. C. Hamilton (ed.), *The Spenser Encyclopedia* (London: Routledge, 1990), pp. 7–8.

24. For works published in Edinburgh and Oxford that use Medea to criticise Mary, see James Emerson Phillips, *Images of a Queen: Mary Stuart in Sixteenth-Century Literature* (Berkeley: University of California Press, 1964), pp. 44, 261.

25. On the debate over the letters' veracity, see Hans Villius, 'The Casket Letters: A Famous Case Reopened', *Historical Journal* 28.3 (1985), pp. 517–34, esp. 523 and 534.

26. Mary's letter is reproduced by Wilson in George Buchanan, *Ane Detectioun of the Duinges of Marie Quene of Scottes* (London: 1571), STC (2nd edn) 3981.

27. See Morse, *Medieval Medea*, n.164, for the intriguing suggestion that Mary owned an early printed copy of Lefèvre's *Histoire de Jason*, which features a Medea who is similarly possessive (and yet wholly unsympathetic).

28. Cathy Shrank, '"This fatall Medea", "this Clytemnestra": Reading and the Detection of Mary Queen of Scots', *Huntington Library Quarterly* 73.3 (2010), pp. 523–41 (527).

29. Shrank, '"This fatall Medea"', pp. 527–8. On the widespread equation of Mary and Medea in ballads and pamphlets printed in Scotland and on the Continent during the 1560s and 70s, see this article and also John D. Staines, *The Tragic Histories of Mary Queen of Scots, 1560–1690: Rhetoric, Passions, and Political Literature* (Farnham: Ashgate, 2009), pp. 58, 69, 79.

30. Staines, *Tragic Histories of Mary Queen of Scots*, p. 46.

31. Marianne McDonald, 'Medea as Politician and Diva: Riding the Dragon into the Future', in James J. Clauss and Sarah Iles Johnston (eds), *Medea: Essays on Medea in Myth, Literature, Philosophy and Art* (Princeton: Princeton University Press, 1997), pp. 297–323 (301–2).

32. See, e.g., the Calvinist Richard Crakanthorpe, *The Defence of Constantine with a Treatise of the Popes Temporall Monarchie* (London: 1621; STC (2nd edn) 5974), Ss3^{r-v}. Crakanthorpe quotes the Senecan line to argue that even 'Heathenish poets' can be used to demonstrate that 'pietie, and prosperitie in Princes ... doe stand and fall, flourish and fade together'. Of course, Creon's piety is not what concerns Medea at this point.

33. Van Es, *Spenser's Forms of History*, p. 143.

34. Michael Drayton, *Works*, ed. J. William Hebel, Kathleen Tillotson and Bernard H. Newdigate, 5 vols (Oxford: Basil Blackwell, for the Shakespeare Head Press, 1931–41), vol. 2. All quotations from Drayton's poems are from this edition.

35. Danielle Clarke, 'Ovid's *Heroides*, Drayton and the Articulation of the Feminine in the English Renaissance', *Renaissance Studies* 22.3 (2008), pp. 385–400 (400). See also Alison Thorne, 'Large Complaints in Little Papers: Negotiating Ovidian Genealogies of Complaint in Drayton's *Englands Heroicall Epistles*', *Renaissance Studies* 22.3 (2008), pp. 368–84 (381–2). She suggests that, for Elinor, Medea's story is a 'beguiling fantasy' of 'a woman triumphing over personal and political humiliation by dint of her indomitable capacity to wreak destruction on her enemies'. The word 'fantasy' is crucial here: as Drayton's readers would be aware, things were not so easy for Elinor, and thus the threatening spectre of Medea's power is implicitly neutralised even as it

is represented. On the Elizabethan male-authored complaint which makes use of the female voice, see John Kerrigan (ed.), *Motives of Woe: Shakespeare and 'Female Complaint', a Critical Anthology* (Oxford: Clarendon Press, 1991); and Wendy Wall, *The Imprint of Gender: Authorship and Publication in the English Renaissance* (Ithaca and London: Cornell University Press, 1993), ch. 4. She argues that in complaints which make use of the *Heroides*, the Elizabethan female speaker 'acts as a more complex literary figure' than her classical forebear, moving ' in a complicated fashion between justification and penitence'. This is a fitting description of Drayton's Elinor, although the Heroidean Medea is not simply the 'lamenting and powerless paramour' who, Wall argues, is typical of Ovid's collection (*Imprint of Gender*, p. 252).

36. Drayton, *Works*, vol. 1.
37. Drayton, *Works*, vol. 2.
38. Medieval accounts which describe the origins of Jason's and Medea's relationship often dwelt at length on her youth and beauty. On the supposed erotic powers of witches, documented in the Middle Ages and Renaissance, see Gareth Roberts, 'The Descendants of Circe: Witches and Renaissance Fictions', in Barry, Hester and Roberts (eds), *Witchcraft in Early Modern Europe*, pp. 183–206 (200–1).
39. Medea's method of murdering Pelias, by encouraging his daughters to stab him and then slitting his throat, would have been particularly troubling for an early modern male readership: see Mark Breitenberg, *Anxious Masculinity in Early Modern England* (Cambridge: Cambridge University Press, 1996), p. 52, for the supposedly feminising nature of bleeding and blood-letting in the early modern imagination. See also Gail Kern Paster, *The Body Embarrassed: Drama and the Disciplines of Shame in Early Modern England* (Ithaca and London: Cornell University Press, 1993), p. 92.
40. Jonathan Bate, *Shakespeare and Ovid* (Oxford: Clarendon Press, 1993), pp. 155–6.
41. Drayton, *Works*, vol. 1.
42. Louis A. Montrose, 'Gifts and Reasons: The Contexts of Peele's *Araygnement of Paris*', *ELH* 47.3 (1980), pp. 433–61 (441). Through an account of George Peele's use of the mythical Judgement of Paris, Montrose shows how entertainments presented to the queen gradually moved from promoting marriage to singing the praises of virginity and chastity, as it became increasingly clear that Elizabeth would not marry. Richard F. Hardin notes that the 'self-centred Plantagenet monarchs' such as Henry II are presented 'groaning in a most unkingly fashion': their susceptibility to desire means that they are not examples to be followed ('Convention and Design in Drayton's *Heroicall Epistles*', *PMLA* 83.1 (1968), pp. 35–41 (39)).
43. Clarke, 'Ovid's *Heroides*', p. 391.
44. Philip Edwards, *Threshold of a Nation: A Study in English and Irish Drama* (Cambridge: Cambridge University Press, 1979), p. 110.
45. William Shakespeare, *The Second Part of King Henry VI*, ed. Michael Hattaway (Cambridge: Cambridge University Press, 1991), p. 5.
46. T. W. Baldwin, *William Shakspere's Small Latine and Less Greeke*, 2 vols (Urbana, Ill.: University of Illinois Press, 1944), vol. 2, p. 420. DeWitt T. Starnes and Ernest William Talbert, *Classical Myth and Legend in Renaissance Dictionaries: A Study of Renaissance Dictionaries in Relation to the Classical*

Learning of Contemporary English Writers (Chapel Hill: University of North Carolina Press, 1955), p. 112. Inga-Stina Ewbank argues that Studley's *Medea* is the likely source of Shakespeare's knowledge of the fratricide. Inga-Stina Ewbank, 'The Fiend-Like Queen: A Note on *Macbeth* and Seneca's *Medea*', in Kenneth Muir (ed.), *Shakespeare Survey 19* (Cambridge: Cambridge University Press, repr. 2002), pp. 82–94 (88). Studley's play mentions the crime several times, for example at 978–9 and 1374–5; and Yves Peyré notes that he adds an extra gruesome detail, having Medea claim to have cut off her brother's genitals ('Absyrtus', 2014, in Yves Peyré (ed.), *A Dictionary of Shakespeare's Classical Mythology* (2009–), <http://www.shakmyth.org/myth/1/absyrtus/analysis>, accessed 12 August 2014).

47. Edward Hall, *The union of the two noble and illustre famelies of Lancastre & Yorke* (London: 1548), STC (2nd edn) 12722.

48. On Margaret herself as a Medea-figure, on account of her cruelty to Rutland's father, see Janet Adelman, *Suffocating Mothers: Fantasies of Maternal Origin in Shakespeare's Plays, 'Hamlet' to 'The Tempest'* (London: Routledge, 1992), p. 3.

49. Ronald S. Berman, 'Fathers and Sons in the *Henry VI* Plays', *Shakespeare Quarterly* 13 (1962), pp. 487–97 (491). He suggests, 'The juxtaposition of the myths of Aeneas and Medea by Clifford condenses the intermingling of piety and barbarity' (p. 494).

50. Shakespeare, *Second Part of King Henry VI*, ed. Hattaway, p. 1.

51. For a classic discussion of how, in Shakespeare's history plays, 'actions that should have the effect of radically undermining authority turn out to be the props of that authority', and how in the two parts of *Henry IV*, 'moral values – justice, order, civility – are secured paradoxically through the apparent generation of their subversive contraries', see Stephen Greenblatt, 'Invisible Bullets: Renaissance Authority and Its Subversion, *Henry IV* and *Henry V*', in Jonathan Dollimore and Alan Sinfield (eds), *Political Shakespeare: Essays in Cultural Materialism*, 2nd edn (Manchester: Manchester University Press, 1994), pp. 18–47 (39–40). For an argument that sees the history plays as more genuinely subversive, see David Scott Kastan, 'Proud Majesty Made a Subject: Shakespeare and the Spectacle of Rule', *Shakespeare Quarterly* 37.4 (1986), pp. 459–75.

52. John Crown (John Crowne), *The misery of civil-war a tragedy, as it is acted at the Duke's theatre, by His Royal Highnesses servants* (London: 1680), Wing C7395.

53. Page duBois, *Trojan Horses: Saving the Classics from Conservatives* (New York and London: New York University Press, 2001), pp. 16–17. There is, perhaps, a comparison to be made here between modern, conservative rewriting of myth and the medieval catalogue tradition (lampooned by Chaucer in the *Legend of Good Women*) that sought to present such a contentious figure as Medea simply as an example of women's suffering for love, and made no mention of her crimes.

54. Matthew H. Wikander, 'The Spitted Infant: Scenic Emblem and Exclusionist Politics in Restoration Adaptations of Shakespeare', *Shakespeare Quarterly* 37.3 (1986), pp. 340–58 (346). Compare the avowal of Aaron, in Ravenscroft's adaptation of *Titus Andronicus*, that he will eat the body of the infant that Tamora has killed. At other points, too, Crowne enthusiastically embellishes the witchcraft scene in *2 Henry VI*, and adds extra scenes describing and depicting robbery, rape and violence. See Stuart Hampton-Reeves and

Carol Chillington Rutter, *The Henry VI Plays* (Manchester: Manchester University Press, 2006), pp. 27–9.

55. Julie Sanders, *Adaptation and Appropriation* (New York: Routledge, 2006), p. 107.

56. Susan J. Owen, *Restoration Theatre and Crisis* (Oxford: Clarendon Press, 1996), p. 76. The conflicted political attitudes of Crowne's plays are discussed by Owen in Chapter 3, and by Nancy Klein Maguire, 'Factionary Politics: John Crowne's *Henry VI*', in Gerald MacLean (ed.), *Culture and Society in the Stuart Restoration: Literature, Drama, History* (Cambridge: Cambridge University Press, 1995), pp. 70–92.

57. For a very useful account of how Restoration adaptations of Shakespeare were tailored to reflect the conflicts of the Civil Wars and more contemporary instability, see Wikander, 'Spitted Infant'.

58. Sanders, *Adaptation and Appropriation*, p. 97. For her discussion of *Wide Sargasso Sea* (just one of many fascinating examples), see pp. 100–6.

59. Wikander, 'Spitted Infant', p. 357.

60. Thomas Gainsford, *The True and Wonderfull History of Perkin Warbeck, Proclaiming himselfe Richard the fourth* (London: 1618), STC (2nd edn) 11525. George Buchanan had translated Euripides' *Medea* into Latin during the reign of Henry VIII, but his is not the version Gainsford uses here.

61. See Euripides, *Medea*, trans. Rex Warner, *The Complete Greek Tragedies*, ed. David Grene and Richmond Lattimore, 3 vols (Chicago: University of Chicago Press, 1955), vol. 1, lines 408–9. All translations from this edition.

62. 'On the one hand was love, on the other, fear; and fear increased my very love' (*Heroides* 12.61). Here, Medea describes wrestling with her fears for Jason, and her growing feelings towards him, as she decides whether to offer him her assistance.

63. Thomas May, *The Reign of King Henry II Written in Seaven Bookes* (London: 1633), STC (2nd edn) 17715.

64. In the 1640s May allied himself with the Parliamentarians, and his works begin to reflect anxiety about the extent of monarchical power: however, up to 1640 he published several works either commissioned by the King, or dedicated to him. Speaking of his *Henry II* and *Edward III* (1635), David Norbrook notes, 'These poems, while they do not follow an obvious Caroline propaganda purpose, are sympathetic to the dilemmas of royal power'. See David Norbrook, 'May, Thomas (*b.* in or after 1596, *d.* 1650)', *Oxford Dictionary of National Biography*, Oxford University Press, 2004; online edn, Jan 2008 <http://www.oxforddnb.com/view/article/18423>, accessed 1 May 2014.

65. Reginald Scot, *The Discoverie of Witchcraft* (London: 1584), STC (2nd edn) 21864.

66. Luc Racaut, 'Accusations of Infanticide on the Eve of the French Wars of Religion', in Mark Jackson (ed.), *Infanticide: Historical Perspectives on Child Murder and Concealment, 1550–2000* (Aldershot: Ashgate, 2002), pp. 18–34.

67. As well as noting the association of witchcraft with Catholicism, Peter Lake sees its foreignness as a 'central characteristic of popery in the eyes of English Protestants' ('Anti-popery', p. 79). See also William S. Maltby, *The Black Legend in England: The Development of Anti-Spanish Sentiment, 1558–1660* (Durham, NC: Duke University Press, 1968).

68. Edith Hall, *Inventing the Barbarian: Greek Self-Definition through Tragedy* (Oxford: Clarendon Press, 1989, repr. 2004), p. 35.

69. On the perceived foreignness of even English Catholics, see Frances E. Dolan, *Whores of Babylon: Catholicism, Gender, and Seventeenth Century Print Culture* (Ithaca and London: Cornell University Press, 1999), pp. 34 and 37. On Catholicism and racial difference, see pp. 39–41. For the Puritan association between the Catholic and the barbaric, see Mary Nyquist, '"Profuse, proud Cleopatra": "Barbarism" and Female Rule in Early Modern English Republicanism', *Women's Studies* 24 (1994), pp. 85–130 (92).

70. Francis Herring, *Mischeefes Mysterie: or, Treasons Master-peece*, trans. John Vicars (London: 1617), STC (2nd edn) 13247.

71. Martin Butler, *Theatre and Crisis, 1632–1642* (Cambridge: Cambridge University Press, 1984), p. 87.

72. Francis Herring, *Pietas pontificia* (London: 1606), STC (2nd edn) 13244. For a useful account of Herring's original, see the introduction by Estelle Haan to another treatise on the Gunpowder Plot, Phineas Fletcher's *Locustae* (1627). Phineas Fletcher, *Locustae, vel, pietas Jesuitica*, ed. and trans. Estelle Haan (Louvain: Leuven University Press, 1996), pp. xxxiv–xxxix.

73. A. P., *Popish pietie, or The first part of the historie of that horrible and barbarous conspiracie, commonly called the powder-treason* (London: 1610), STC (2nd edn) 13246.

74. Medea is one of many classical figures likened to Fawkes and his fellow conspirators by Vicars: to underscore his treacherous nature Fawkes is elsewhere described as 'Dissembling Sinon' and 'Neptunes Proteus' (F3ʳ), while Catesby is 'Medusa's son' (C3ᵛ). On the tendency to insert stories of female conspirators into accounts of the Plot, see Dolan, *Whores of Babylon*, p. 12.

75. Dolan notes that the lack of remorse expressed by the conspirators was frequently stressed in official accounts of the Plot: the refusal of the Senecan Medea to repent her crimes against Jason and Creon may thus have prompted Vicars to add her to his narrative (*Whores of Babylon*, p. 77).

76. Henry Burton, *The baiting of the Popes bull* (London: 1627), STC (2nd edn) 4137.3.

77. Thomas Ady, *A candle in the dark shewing the divine cause of the distractions of the whole nation of England and of the Christian world* (London: 1655), Wing A673.

78. Dagmar Freist, 'The King's Crown Is the Whore of Babylon: Politics, Gender and Communication in Mid-Seventeenth-Century England', *Gender and History* 7.3 (1995), pp. 457–81 (465); and Dolan, *Whores of Babylon*, pp. 94 and 124–5. See also Susan Wiseman, '"Adam, the Father of all Flesh": Porno-Political Rhetoric and Political Theory in and after the English Civil War', in James Holstun (ed.), *Pamphlet Wars: Prose in the English Revolution* (London: Frank Cass, 1992), pp. 134–57. On suspicion of Charles's Catholic queen Henrietta Maria in particular, see Dolan, *Whores of Babylon*, pp. 97–101.

79. Anthony Milton points to the 'hysterical fears' about Catholicism that are evident in the 1640s, though he cautions that such hysteria was not necessarily universal: 'English people did not suffer from a simple allergic reaction to all things popish' ('A Qualified Intolerance: The Limits and Ambiguities of Early Stuart Anti-Catholicism', in Arthur F. Marotti (ed.), *Catholicism and Anti-Catholicism in Early Modern English Texts* (Basingstoke: Palgrave Macmillan, 1999), pp. 85–115 (85–6).

80. A. B. C. D. E., *Novembris monstrum, or, Rome brought to bed in England* (London: 1641), Wing E3.

81. Fabian Philipps, *King Charles the First, no man of blood: but a martyr for his people* (London: s.n., 1649), Wing (2nd edn) P2008.

82. Elmer, '"Saints or Sorcerers"', pp. 163–6 and 174; and Diane Purkiss, 'Desire and Its Deformities: Fantasies of Witchcraft in the English Civil War', in Brian P. Levack (ed.), *New Perspectives on Witchcraft, Magic, and Demonology*, 6 vols (New York: Routledge, 2001), vol. 3, pp. 271–300 (274–7); reprinted from the *Journal of Medieval and Early Modern Studies* 27.1 (1997), pp. 103–32. See also Purkiss, 'Women's Stories of Witchcraft', in Levack (ed.), *New Perspectives on Witchcraft*, vol. 4, pp. 278–302 (280); reprinted from *Gender and History* 7.3 (1995), pp. 408–32.

83. For example, see John Thornborough (and/or John Bristol), *A Discourse Shewing the Great Happiness that Hath and May Still Accrue to His Majesties Kingdomes of England and Scotland by Re-uniting them into one Great Britain* (London: 1641), Wing (2nd edn) T1042A, H7^v; and Edmund Calamy, *An Indictment Against England because of her Selfe-murdering Divisions* (London: 1645; STC (2nd edn) C256), C4^r.

84. *The Turne of time, or, The period of rebellion dedicated, to the infamous members late sitting at Westminster* (London: 1648?), Wing (2nd edn) T3266.

85. A rare example of a Parliamentarian use of Medea can be found appended to a 1650 account of a Parliamentarian victory in Scotland: the author assures his readers that the majority of people in Yorkshire, Cumberland, Sunderland and Durham support their cause, but that there are those who, like Medea, 'endeavour to alienate and withdraw the hearts of the people, from their due obedience to the *present Authority*' (p. 5). Once again, it is Medea's deception of the daughters of Pelias that is employed as a specific example, and here it is made into a warning about the naive masses being seduced into believing treacherous lies. Peter Michel, *A victory obtained by Lieut: Gen: David Lesley, in the north of Scotland, against Colonell Hurrey and his forces* (London: 1650), Wing (2nd edn) M1963, A4^r. Thomas Hobbes also uses the same part of the myth, in *Leviathan* (1651), to warn against the power of rhetoric, which might lead to overzealous attempts to reform governments, just as Pelias' daughters were deliberately misled by Medea. See Thomas Hobbes, *Leviathan*, ed. Richard Tuck (Cambridge: Cambridge University Press, 1991), p. 234.

86. Stuart Clark, 'Inversion, Misrule and the Meaning of Witchcraft', *Past & Present* 87 (1980), pp. 98–127 (119); and see Elmer, '"Saints or Sorcerers"', pp. 165 and 178, for sermons that associated witchcraft with rebellion.

87. Nancy Klein Maguire notes that 'The Restoration propaganda machine relentlessly exploited the guilt association with the act of regicide' (*Regicide and Restoration: English Tragicomedy, 1660–1671* (Cambridge: Cambridge University Press, 1992), p. 6).

88. Henry Glover, *CAIN and ABEL PARALLEL'D With King CHARLES and his Murderers. IN A SERMON Preached in S. Thomas Church in Salisbury, Jan. 30. 1663* (London: 1664), Wing G889.

89. Cimelgus Bonde, *Salmasius his buckler, or, A royal apology for King Charles the martyr dedicated to Charles the Second, King of Great Brittain* (London: 1662), Wing S411.

90. John Allington, *The regal proto-martyr, or, The memorial of the martyrdom of Charles the First in a sermon preached upon the first fast of publick appointment for it* (London: 1672), Wing A1214.

91. Linda Hutcheon, *A Theory of Adaptation* (New York: Routledge, 2006), p. 145.

92. On preoccupation with the memory of the English Civil Wars in the last years of Charles's reign, see for example Elizabeth Clarke, 'Re-reading the

Exclusion Crisis', *Seventeenth Century* 21.1 (2006), pp. 141–59 (146); Peter Hinds, '"A Vast Ill-Nature": Roger L'Estrange, Reputation, and the Credibility of Political Discourse in the Late Seventeenth Century', *Seventeenth Century* 21.2 (2006), pp. 335–63 (354); Hinds, '*The Horrid Popish Plot': Roger L'Estrange and the Circulation of Political Discourse in Late Seventeenth-Century London* (Oxford: Oxford University Press for the British Academy, 2010), p. 292; Jonathan Scott, 'England's Troubles: Exhuming the Popish Plot', in Tim Harris, Paul Seaward and Mark Goldie (eds), *The Politics of Religion in Restoration England* (Oxford: Basil Blackwell, 1990), pp. 107–31 (123–4).

93. Elmer, '"Saints or Sorcerers"', p. 178.
94. Robert Dixon, *Canidia, or, the Witches a Rhapsody, in Five Parts* (London: 1683), Wing D1745. On the poem's attribution to Dixon, see Jason McElligott, 'Dixon, Robert (1614/15–1688)', *Oxford Dictionary of National Biography*, Oxford University Press, 2004; online edn, January 2008 <http://www.oxforddnb.com/view/article/7705>, accessed 6 August 2014.
95. Here Jason is an error for Aeson. Nathaniel Johnston, *The excellency of monarchical government, especially of the English monarchy wherein is largely treated of the several benefits of kingly government, and the inconvenience of commonwealths* (London: 1686), Wing J877.

Conclusion

1. Joshua Poole (comp.), *The English Parnassus, or, A helpe to English poesie* (London: 1657), Wing P2814.
2. On various kinds of women's translations in the early modern period, see Luise von Flotow, *Translation and Gender: Translating in the 'Era of Feminism'* (Manchester: St Jerome Publishing, 1997), pp. 66–70; Suzanne Trill, 'Sixteenth-century Women's Writing: Mary Sidney's *Psalmes* and the '"Femininity" of Translation', in William Zunder and Suzanne Trill (eds), *Writing and the English Renaissance* (London: Longman, 1996), pp. 140–58; Christa Knellwolf, 'Women Translators, Gender and the Cultural Context of the Scientific Revolution', in Roger Ellis and Liz Oakley-Brown (eds), *Translation and Nation: Towards a Cultural Politics of Englishness*, Topics in Translation 18 (Clevedon: Multilingual Matters, 2001), pp. 85–119; and Sarah Annes Brown, 'Women Translators', in Stuart Gillespie and David Hopkins (eds), *The Oxford History of Literary Translation in English, vol. 3: 1660–1790* (Oxford: Oxford University Press, 2005), pp. 111–20. On women's translations of Ovid, see Liz Oakley-Brown, *Ovid and the Cultural Politics of Translation in Early Modern England* (Aldershot: Ashgate, 2006), ch. 5.
3. Christine de Pizan, *The Book of the City of Ladies*, trans. Earl Jeffrey Richards (New York: Persea, 1998).
4. The text here is the Middle English rendering of Stephen Scrope. Christine de Pisan, *The Epistle of Othea*, trans. Stephen Scrope, ed. Curt F. Bühler, Early English Text Society OS 264 (London: Oxford University Press, 1970).
5. For a more positive assessment of Christine's treatments of classical women, including Medea, see Rosalind Brown-Grant, *Christine de Pizan and the Moral Defence of Women: Reading beyond Gender* (Cambridge: Cambridge University Press, 1999), pp. 55, 79 and 85–6.

6. Isabella Whitney, *The copy of a letter, lately written in meeter, by a yonge gentilwoman: to her unconstant lover* (London: 1567), STC (2nd edn) 25439.

7. Elizabeth Cary, *The Tragedy of Mariam, The Fair Queen of Jewry*, ed. Stephanie Hodgson-Wright (Letchworth: Broadview Publishing, 2000).

8. For example, the Chorus's statement at the close of Act 3: 'And every mind, though free from thought of ill, / That out of glory seeks a worth to show, / When any's ears but one therewith they fill, / Doth in a sort her pureness overthrow' (31–4).

9. Mary Pix, *The False Friend* (London: 1699), Wing P2328.

10. On correspondences between family and state in the early modern imagination, see Jonathan Goldberg, 'Fatherly Authority: The Politics of Stuart Family Images', in Margaret W. Ferguson, Maureen Quilligan and Nancy J. Vickers (eds), *Rewriting the Renaissance: The Discourses of Sexual Difference in Early Modern Europe* (Chicago: University of Chicago Press, 1986), pp. 3–32 (5); and Natalie Zemon Davis, 'Women on Top', *Society and Culture in Early Modern France: Eight Essays* (Cambridge: Polity Press, 1987), pp. 124–51.

11. On the alarm felt by early modern commentators, such as Stephen Gosson, at the idea of the theatre-going woman, see Jean E. Howard, 'Women as Spectators, Spectacles, and Paying Customers', in David Scott Kastan and Peter Stallybrass (eds), *Staging the Renaissance: Reinterpretations of Elizabethan and Jacobean Drama* (New York: Routledge, 1991), pp. 68–74, and her 'Scripts and/versus Playhouses: Ideological Production and the Renaissance Public Stage', *Renaissance Drama* New Series 20 (1989), pp. 31–49.

12. See Diane Purkiss, 'Women's Stories of Witchcraft', in Brian P. Levack (ed.), *New Perspectives on Witchcraft, Magic, and Demonology*, 6 vols (New York: Routledge, 2001), vol. 4, pp. 278–302 (284); reprinted from *Gender and History* 7.3 (1995), pp. 408–32.

13. Derek Hughes, *English Drama 1660–1700* (Oxford: Clarendon Press, 1996), quoted in Jean I. Marsden, *Fatal Desire: Women, Sexuality, and the English Stage, 1660–1720* (Ithaca and London: Cornell University Press, 2006), p. 106.

14. Marsden, *Fatal Desire*, p. 112.

15. On Garth's translation see David Hopkins, 'Dryden and the Garth-Tonson *Metamorphoses*', *RES* New Series 39.153 (1988), pp. 64–74; and Oakley-Brown, *Ovid and the Cultural Politics of Translation*, ch. 4.

16. Ovid, *Ovid's Metamorphoses in fifteen books. Translated by the most eminent hands*, comp. Samuel Garth (London: Jacob Tonson, 1717).

17. Hopkins notes that Jacob Tonson had already published Tate's translation of this part of Book 7, in 1704's *Poetical Miscellanies: The Fifth Part* ('Garth-Tonson *Metamorphoses*', p. 65).

18. Richard Glover, *Medea: A Tragedy* (London: 1761).

19. Marion Wynne-Davies, '"The Swallowing Womb": Consumed and Consuming Women in *Titus Andronicus*', in Valerie Wayne (ed.), *The Matter of Difference: Materialist Feminist Criticism of Shakespeare* (Hemel Hempstead: Harvester Wheatsheaf, 1991), pp. 129–51 (146).

Select Bibliography

Note

For the sake of saving space, early modern titles have generally been abbreviated. Names beginning with 'Mac' and 'Mc' have been interfiled.

A. B. C. D. E., *Novembris monstrum, or, Rome brought to bed in England* (London: 1641), Wing E3.

The Academy of Pleasure (London: 1656), Wing A159.

Achelley, Thomas, *The Most Lamentable and Tragicall Historie of Didaco and Violenta* (London: 1576), STC (2nd edn) 1356.4.

Adams, Thomas, *The Devills Banket Described in Foure Sermons* (London: 1614), STC (2nd edn) 110.5.

Adelman, Janet, 'Born of Woman: Fantasies of Maternal Power in *Macbeth*', in Garber (ed.), *Cannibals, Witches, and Divorce*, pp. 90–121.

———, 'Escaping the Matrix: The Construction of Masculinity in *Macbeth*', *Suffocating Mothers*, and reprinted in William Shakespeare, *Macbeth*, ed. Robert S. Miola (New York: Norton, 2004), pp. 293–315.

———, *Suffocating Mothers: Fantasies of Maternal Origin in Shakespeare's Plays, 'Hamlet' to 'The Tempest'* (London: Routledge, 1992).

Ady, Thomas, *A candle in the dark shewing the divine cause of the distractions of the whole nation of England and of the Christian world* (London: 1655), Wing A673.

Aelian, *Historical Miscellany*, ed. and trans. N. G. Wilson, Loeb Classical Library (Cambridge, Mass.: Harvard University Press, 1997).

Alabaster, William, *Roxana*, ed. Dana F. Sutton, hypertext edition (Irvine, Calif.: University of California, 1998); copyright University of Birmingham.

Alexander, William, *The Poetical Works of Sir William Alexander*, ed. L. E. Kastner and H. B. Charlton, 2 vols (Manchester: Manchester University Press, 1921).

Allen, Don Cameron, *Mysteriously Meant: The Rediscovery of Pagan Symbolism and Allegorical Interpretation in the Renaissance* (Baltimore: Johns Hopkins University Press, 1970).

Allington, John, *The regal proto-martyr, or, The memorial of the martyrdom of Charles the First in a sermon preached upon the first fast of publick appointment for it* (London: 1672), Wing A1214.

Anderson, Judith H., 'Spenser's *Faerie Queene*, Book V: Poetry, Politics and Justice', in Hattaway (ed.), *Companion to English Renaissance Literature and Culture*, pp. 195–205.

Andreadis, Harriette, 'The Early Modern Afterlife of Ovidian Erotics: Dryden's *Heroides*', *Renaissance Studies* 22.3 (2008), pp. 401–16.

Annes Brown, Sarah, 'Women Translators', in Gillespie and Hopkins (eds), *Oxford History of Literary Translation in English, Vol. 3: 1660–1790*, pp. 111–20.

———, and Taylor, Andrew (eds), *Ovid in English, 1480–1625, Part 1: 'Metamorphoses'* (London: Modern Humanities Research Association, 2013).

A. P., *Popish pietie, or The first part of the historie of that horrible and barbarous conspiracie, commonly called the powder-treason* (London: 1610), STC (2nd edn) 13246.

Apollodorus, *The Library*, trans. J. G. Frazer, 2 vols, Loeb Classical Library (Cambridge, Mass.: Harvard University Press, 1921).

——, *The Library of Greek Mythology*, trans. Robin Hard (Oxford: Oxford University Press, 1997).

Apollonius Rhodius, *The Argonautica*, trans. and ed. Richard Hunter (Oxford: Clarendon Press, 1993).

Aristotle, 'On the Art of Poetry', in Dorsch (trans.), *Classical Literary Criticism*, pp. 31–75.

Baker, Howard, *Induction to Tragedy: A Study in a Development of Form in 'Gorboduc', 'The Spanish Tragedy' and 'Titus Andronicus'* (Louisiana: Louisiana State University Press, 1939).

Baldwin, T. W., *William Shakspere's Small Latine and Less Greeke*, 2 vols (Urbana, Ill.: University of Illinois Press, 1944).

Bandello, Matteo, *Certaine Tragicall Discourses*, trans. Geoffrey Fenton (London: 1567), STC (2nd edn) 1356.1.

——, *Opere*, ed. Francesco Flora, 2 vols (Milan: Arnoldo Mondadori, 1935).

Barkan, Leonard, *The Gods Made Flesh: Metamorphosis and the Pursuit of Paganism* (New Haven and London: Yale University Press, 1986).

Baron, Robert, *Mirza a Tragedie* (London: 1655), Wing (2nd edn) B892.

Barry, Jonathan, Hester, Marianne, and Roberts, Gareth (eds), *Witchcraft in Early Modern Europe: Studies in Culture and Belief* (Cambridge: Cambridge University Press, 1996).

Bartel, Heike, and Simon, Anne (eds), *Unbinding Medea: Interdisciplinary Approaches to a Classical Myth from Antiquity to the 21st Century* (Oxford: Legenda, 2010).

Bate, Jonathan, *Shakespeare and Ovid* (Oxford: Clarendon Press, 1993).

Belsey, Catherine, *The Subject of Tragedy: Identity and Difference in Renaissance Drama* (London: Methuen, 1985).

Benoît de Sainte-Maure, *Le Roman de Troie*, ed. L. Constans, 6 vols (Paris: Firmin-Didot, 1904–12).

Berger, Harry, Jr, 'Text against Performance in Shakespeare: The Example of *Macbeth*', in Greenblatt (ed.), *The Power of Forms in the English Renaissance* (Norman, Okla.: Pilgrim Books, 1982), pp. 49–79.

Berger, Thomas L., and Massai, Sonia (eds), *Paratexts in English Printed Drama to 1642*, 2 vols (Cambridge: Cambridge University Press, 2014).

——, Bradford, William, and Sondergard, Sidney L., *An Index of Characters in Early Modern English Drama: Printed Plays, 1500–1660* (Cambridge: Cambridge University Press, 1998).

Berman, Ronald S., 'Fathers and Sons in the *Henry VI* Plays', *Shakespeare Quarterly* 13.4 (1962), pp. 487–97.

Bersuire, Pierre, *Metamorphosis Ovidiana moraliter ... explanata: Paris, 1509*, ed. Stephen Orgel (New York: Garland, 1979).

Binns, J. W., 'Seneca and Neo-Latin Tragedy in England', in Costa (ed.), *Seneca*, pp. 205–34.

Birchwood, Matthew, *Staging Islam in England: Drama and Culture 1640–1685* (Cambridge: D. S. Brewer, 2007).

Blount, Thomas, *Glossographia* (London: 1656), Wing (2nd edn) B3334.

Boccaccio, Giovanni, *Famous Women*, trans. Virginia Brown (Cambridge, Mass.: Harvard University Press, 2001).

Boffey, Julia, and Cowen, Janet (eds), *Chaucer and Fifteenth-Century Poetry* (London: Centre for Late Antique and Medieval Studies, King's College London, 1991).
Boiastuau (or Boaistuau), Pierre, *Histoires Tragiques*, ed. Richard A. Carr (Paris: Librairie Honoré Champion, 1977).
Bonde, Cimelgus, *Salmasius his buckler, or, A royal apology for King Charles the martyr dedicated to Charles the Second, King of Great Brittain* (London: 1662), Wing S411.
Botelho, Keith M., 'Maternal Memory and Murder in Early-Seventeenth-Century England', *Studies in English Literature* 48.1 (2008), pp. 111–30.
Braden, Gordon, *The Classics and English Renaissance Poetry: Three Case Studies* (New Haven: Yale University Press, 1978).
——, *Renaissance Tragedy and the Senecan Tradition: Anger's Privilege* (New Haven and London: Yale University Press, 1985).
——, 'Tragedy', in Braden, Cummings and Gillespie (eds), *Oxford History of Literary Translation in English, Vol. 2: 1550–1660*, pp. 262–79.
——, Cummings, Robert, and Gillespie, Stuart (eds), *The Oxford History of Literary Translation in English: Vol. 2, 1550–1660*, 5 vols (Oxford: Oxford University Press, 2010).
Bradley, A. C., *Shakespearean Tragedy: Lectures on 'Hamlet', 'Othello', 'King Lear', 'Macbeth'*, 2nd edn (London: Macmillan, 1905, repr. 1978).
Breitenberg, Mark, *Anxious Masculinity in Early Modern England* (Cambridge: Cambridge University Press, 1996).
Brooke, Nicholas, *Horrid Laughter in Jacobean Tragedy* (London: Open Books, 1979).
Brooks, Harold F., 'The "Imitation" in English Poetry, Especially in Formal Satire, before the Age of Pope', *RES* 25.98 (1949), pp. 124–40.
Brower, Reuben A., *Hero and Saint: Shakespeare and the Graeco-Roman Heroic Tradition* (Oxford: Clarendon Press, 1971).
Brown, Paul, '"This Thing of Darkness I Acknowledge Mine": The Tempest and the Discourse of Colonialism', in Dollimore and Sinfield (eds), *Political Shakespeare*, pp. 48–71.
Brown, Peter (ed.), *A Companion to Chaucer* (Oxford: Blackwell, 2000).
Browne, Thomas, *Pseudodoxia epidemica* (London: 1646), Wing B5159.
Brown-Grant, Rosalind, *Christine de Pizan and the Moral Defence of Women: Reading beyond Gender* (Cambridge: Cambridge University Press, 1999).
Buchanan, George, *Ane Detectioun of the Duinges of Marie Quene of Scottes* (London: 1571), STC (2nd edn) 3981.
——, *Tragedies*, ed. P. Sharratt and P. G. Walsh (Edinburgh: Scottish Academic Press, 1983).
Burrow, Colin, *Shakespeare and Classical Antiquity* (Oxford: Oxford University Press, 2013).
Burton, Henry, *The baiting of the Popes bull* (London: 1627), STC (2nd edn) 4137.3.
Bush, Douglas, *Mythology and the Renaissance Tradition in English Poetry* (New York: Pageant, 1932, repr. 1957).
Bushnell, Rebecca, 'Tyranny and Effeminacy in Early Modern England', in Di Cesare (ed.), *Reconsidering the Renaissance*, pp. 339–54.
Butler, Martin, *Theatre and Crisis, 1632–1642* (Cambridge: Cambridge University Press, 1984).
Calamy, Edmund, *An Indictment Against England because of her Selfe-murdering Divisions* (London: 1645), STC (2nd edn) C256.

Callaghan, Dympna, 'Wicked Women in *Macbeth*: A Study of Power, Ideology, and the Production of Motherhood', in Di Cesare (ed.), *Reconsidering the Renaissance*, pp. 355–69.

Cary, Elizabeth, *The Tragedy of Mariam, The Fair Queen of Jewry*, ed. Stephanie Hodgson-Wright (Letchworth: Broadview Publishing, 2000).

Cavanagh, Dermot, 'Political Tragedy in the 1560s: *Cambises* and *Gorboduc*', in Pincombe and Shrank (eds), *Oxford Handbook of Tudor Literature*, pp. 488–503.

Chance, Jane (ed.), *The Mythographic Art: Classical Fable and the Rise of the Vernacular in Early France and England* (Gainesville: University of Florida Press, 1990).

Charlton, H. B., 'The Growth of the Senecan Tradition in Renaissance Tragedy', in Alexander, *Poetical Works of Sir William Alexander*, ed. Kastner and Charlton, pp. xvii–cc.

Chaucer, Geoffrey, *The Riverside Chaucer*, ed. Larry D. Benson (Oxford: Oxford University Press, 1988).

Chaudhuri, Supriya, 'Jason's Fleece: The Source of Sir Epicure Mammon's Allegory', *RES* New Series, 35.137 (1984), pp. 71–3.

Chesney, Kathleen, 'A Neglected Prose Version of the *Roman de Troie*', *Medium Aevum* 11 (1942), pp. 46–67.

Chettle, Henry, *The Tragedy of Hoffman*, ed. J. D. Jowett (Nottingham: Nottingham Drama Texts, 1983).

Christie, Ian, 'Between Magic and Realism: Medea on Film', in Hall, Macintosh and Taplin (eds), *Medea in Performance*, pp. 144–65.

Christine de Pizan, *The Book of the City of Ladies*, trans. Earl Jeffrey Richards (New York: Persea, 1998).

———, *The Epistle of Othea*, trans. Stephen Scrope, ed. Curt F. Bühler, Early English Text Society OS 264 (London: Oxford University Press, 1970).

Cixous, Hélène, and Clément, Catherine, *The Newly-Born Woman*, trans. Betsy Wing (Manchester: Manchester University Press, 1986).

Clark, Stuart, 'Inversion, Misrule and the Meaning of Witchcraft', *Past & Present* 87 (1980), pp. 98–127.

Clarke, Danielle, 'Ovid's *Heroides*, Drayton and the Articulation of the Feminine in the English Renaissance', *Renaissance Studies* 22.3 (2008), pp. 385–400.

Clarke, Elizabeth, 'Re-reading the Exclusion Crisis', *Seventeenth Century* 21.1 (2006), pp. 141–59.

Clauss, James J., and Johnston, Sarah Iles (eds), *Medea: Essays on Medea in Myth, Literature, Philosophy and Art* (Princeton: Princeton University Press, 1997).

Coddon, Karin S., '"Unreal Mockery": Unreason and the Problem of Spectacle in *Macbeth*', *ELH* 56.3 (1989), pp. 485–501.

Coleman, Antony, and Hammond, Antony (eds), *Poetry and Drama 1570–1700: Essays in Honour of Harold F. Brooks* (London: Methuen, 1981).

Conti, Natale, *Mythologiae*, trans. and ed. John Mulryan and Steven Brown, 2 vols (Tempe, Ariz.: Arizona Center for Medieval and Renaissance Studies, 2006).

Corti, Lillian, *The Myth of Medea and the Murder of Children* (Westport: Greenwood Press, 1998).

Costa, C. D. N. (ed.), *Seneca* (London: Routledge and Kegan Paul, 1974).

Cotton, Charles, *Erotopolis, The Present State of Betty-Land* (London: 1684), Wing E3242.

Cowen, Janet, 'Women as Exempla in Fifteenth Century Verse of the Chaucerian Tradition', in Boffey and Cowen (eds), *Chaucer and Fifteenth-Century Poetry*, pp. 51–65.

Crakanthorpe, Richard, *The Defence of Constantine with a Treatise of the Popes Temporall Monarchie* (London: 1621), STC (2nd edn) 5974.

Crown [Crowne], John, *The misery of civil-war a tragedy, as it is acted at the Duke's theatre, by His Royal Highnesses servants* (London: 1680), Wing C7395.

Cummings, Robert, 'Dictionaries and Commentaries', in Braden, Cummings and Gillespie (eds), *Oxford History of Literary Translation in English: Vol. 2, 1550–1660*, pp. 101–8.

Cunliffe, J. W., *The Influence of Seneca on Elizabethan Tragedy* (London: Macmillan, 1893).

Cust, Richard, and Hughes, Ann (eds), *Conflict in Early Stuart England: Studies in Religion and Politics, 1603–1642* (London: Longman, 1989).

Danson, Lawrence, *Shakespeare's Dramatic Genres* (Oxford: Oxford University Press, 2000).

De Belleforest, François, *XVIII histoires tragiques, extraictes des œuvres Italiennes de Bandel, & mises en langue Françoise. Tome premier* (Lyon: 1596).

De Grazia, Margreta, and Wells, Stanley William (eds), *The Cambridge Companion to Shakespeare* (Cambridge: Cambridge University Press, 2001).

Di Cesare, Mario A. (ed.), *Reconsidering the Renaissance* (Binghamton, NY: Center for Medieval and Early Renaissance Studies, 1992).

Dickinson, J. R., and Sharpe, J. A., 'Infanticide in Early Modern England: The Court of Great Sessions at Chester, 1650–1800', in Jackson (ed.), *Infanticide*, pp. 35–51.

Dictys of Crete and Dares the Phrygian, *The Trojan War*, trans. and ed. R. M. Frazer (Bloomington: Indiana University Press, 1966).

Dinshaw, Carolyn, *Chaucer's Sexual Poetics* (Madison: University of Wisconsin Press, 1989).

Diodorus Siculus, *Works*, trans. C. H. Oldfather, 10 vols, Loeb Classical Library (London: Heinemann, 1933–67).

Dixon, Robert, *Canidia, or, the Witches a Rhapsody, in Five Parts* (London: 1683), Wing D1745.

Dolan, Frances E., *Dangerous Familiars: Representations of Domestic Crime in England, 1550–1700* (Ithaca and London: Cornell University Press, 1994).

———, '"Gentlemen, I Have One Thing More to Say": Women on Scaffolds in England, 1563–1680', *Modern Philology* 92.2 (1994), pp. 157–78.

———, *Whores of Babylon: Catholicism, Gender, and Seventeenth Century Print Culture* (Ithaca and London: Cornell University Press, 1999).

Dollimore, Jonathan, and Sinfield, Alan (eds), *Political Shakespeare: Essays in Cultural Materialism*, 2nd edn (Manchester: Manchester University Press, 1994).

Donaldson, Ian, *The Rapes of Lucretia: A Myth and Its Transformations* (Oxford: Clarendon Press, 1982).

Dorsch, T. S. (trans.), *Classical Literary Criticism* (Harmondsworth: Penguin, 1965).

Drayton, Michael, *Works*, ed. J. William Hebel, Kathleen Tillotson and Bernard H. Newdigate, 5 vols (Oxford: Basil Blackwell, for the Shakespeare Head Press, 1931–41).

Dryden, John, *Works*, ed. E. N. Hooker and H. T Swedenberg, 20 vols (Berkeley: University of California Press, 1956–2002).

———, and Davenant, William, *The Tempest, or The Enchanted Island*, in Dryden, *Works*, vol. 10, ed. Maximillian E. Novak and George Robert Guffey.

DuBois, Page, *Trojan Horses: Saving the Classics from Conservatives* (New York and London: New York University Press, 2001).

Dubrow, Heather, 'The Arraignment of Paridell: Tudor Historiography in *The Faerie Queene*, III.IX', *Studies in Philology* 87. 3 (1990), pp. 312–27.

———, *Genre* (London: Methuen, 1982).

Durham, Carolyn A., 'Medea: Hero or Heroine?', *Frontiers: A Journal of Women's Studies* 8.1 (1984), pp. 54-9.

Dutton, Richard, and Howard, Jean E. (eds), *A Companion to Shakespeare's Works*, 4 vols (Oxford: Blackwell, 2003).

Edwards, Philip, *Threshold of a Nation: A Study in English and Irish Drama* (Cambridge: Cambridge University Press, 1979).

Ellis, Roger, and Oakley-Brown, Liz (eds), *Translation and Nation: Towards a Cultural Politics of Englishness*, Topics in Translation 18 (Clevedon: Multilingual Matters, 2001).

Elmer, Peter, '"Saints or Sorcerers": Quakerism, Demonology and the Decline of Witchcraft in Seventeenth-Century England', in Barry, Hester and Roberts (eds), *Witchcraft in Early Modern Europe*, pp. 145–79.

Elyot, Sir Thomas, *Bibliotheca Eliotae, Eliotis Librarie* (London: 1542), STC (2nd edn) 76595.

———, *Bibliotheca Eliotae: Eliotes dictionarie by Thomas Cooper the third tyme corrected* (London: 1559), STC (2nd edn) 7663.

———, *The Governor*, in Gilbert (ed.), *Literary Criticism*, pp. 233–41.

Euripides, *Medea*, trans. Rex Warner, *The Complete Greek Tragedies*, ed. David Grene and Richmond Lattimore, 3 vols (Chicago: University of Chicago Press, 1955), vol. 1.

Ewbank, Inga-Stina, 'The Fiend-Like Queen: A Note on *Macbeth* and Seneca's *Medea*', in Kenneth Muir (ed.), *Shakespeare Survey 19* (Cambridge: Cambridge University Press, repr. 2002), pp. 82–94.

Feimer, Joel A., 'Medea in Ovid's *Metamorphoses* and the *Ovide moralisé*: Translation as Transmission', *Florilegium* 8 (1986), pp. 40–55.

Ferguson, Margaret W., Quilligan, Maureen, and Vickers, Nancy J. (eds), *Rewriting the Renaissance: The Discourses of Sexual Difference in Early Modern Europe* (Chicago: University of Chicago Press, 1986).

Fletcher, Phineas, *Locustae, vel, pietas Jesuitica*, ed. and trans. Estelle Haan (Louvain: Leuven University Press, 1996).

Foster, Verna A., *The Name and Nature of Tragicomedy* (Aldershot: Ashgate, 2004).

France, Peter, and Gillespie, Stuart (general eds), *The Oxford History of Literary Translation in English*, 5 vols (Oxford: Oxford University Press, 2005–).

Freist, Dagmar, 'The King's Crown Is the Whore of Babylon: Politics, Gender and Communication in Mid-Seventeenth-Century England', *Gender and History* 7.3 (1995), pp. 457–81.

Fulkerson, Laurel, *The Ovidian Heroine as Author: Reading, Writing, and Community in the 'Heroides'* (Cambridge: Cambridge University Press, 2005).

Fyler, John M., *Chaucer and Ovid* (New Haven and London: Yale University Press, 1979).

Gainsford, Thomas, *The True and Wonderfull History of Perkin Warbeck, Proclaiming himselfe Richard the fourth* (London: 1618), STC (2nd edn) 11525.

Garber, Marjorie (ed.), *Cannibals, Witches, and Divorce: Estranging the Renaissance* (Baltimore: Johns Hopkins University Press, 1987).

Gathercole, Patricia M., 'Laurent de Premierfait: The Translator of Boccaccio's *De Casibus Virorum Illustrium*', *French Review* 27.4 (1954), pp. 245–52.

Genette, Gérard, *Palimpsests: Literature in the Second Degree*, trans. Channa Newman and Claude Doubinsky (Lincoln, Nebr.: University of Nebraska Press, 1997).

The 'Gest Hystoriale' of the Destruction of Troy ... ed. George A. Panton and David Donaldson, Early English Text Society OS 39, 56 (London: Trübner and Co., 1869–74).

Gibson, Jonathan, 'Tragical Histories, Tragical Tales', in Pincombe and Shrank (eds), *Oxford Handbook of Tudor Literature*, pp. 521–36.

Gilbert, Allan H. (ed.), *Literary Criticism: Plato to Dryden* (Detroit: Wayne State University Press, 1962).

Gildon, Charles, *Phaeton, or, The Fatal Divorce a tragedy as it is acted at the Theatre Royal in imitation of the antients* (London: 1698), Wing G735.

Gillespie, Stuart, 'The Early Years of the Dryden-Tonson Partnership: The Background to Their Composite Translations and Miscellanies of the 1680s', *Restoration: Studies in English Literary Culture, 1660–1700* 12.1 (1988), pp. 10–19.

———, *English Translation and Classical Reception: Towards a New Literary History* (Oxford: Wiley-Blackwell, 2011).

———, and Cummings, Robert, 'A Bibliography of Ovidian Translations and Imitations in English', *Translation and Literature* 13.2 (2004), pp. 207–18.

———, and Hopkins, David (eds), *The Oxford History of Literary Translation in English: Vol. 3: 1660–1790* (Oxford: Oxford University Press, 2005).

Giovanni di Garlandia (John of Garland), *Integumenta Ovidii: Poemetto Inedito del Secolo XIII*, ed. Fausto Ghisalberti (Messina: Giuseppe Principato, 1933).

Glover, Henry, *CAIN and ABEL PARALLEL'D With King CHARLES and his Murderers. IN A SERMON Preached in S. Thomas Church in Salisbury, Jan. 30. 1663* (London: 1664), Wing G889.

Glover, Richard, *Medea: A Tragedy* (London: 1761).

Goldberg, Jonathan, 'Fatherly Authority: The Politics of Stuart Family Images', in Ferguson, Quilligan and Vickers (eds), *Rewriting the Renaissance*, pp. 3–32.

Golding, Louis, *An Elizabethan Puritan: Arthur Golding the Translator of Ovid's Metamorphoses and also of John Calvin's Sermons* (New York: Richard R. Smith, 1937).

Gowen, David, '*Medeas* on the Archive Database', in Hall, Macintosh and Taplin (eds), *Medea in Performance*, pp. 232–74.

Gower, John, *The Complete Works*, ed. G. C. Macaulay, 4 vols (Oxford: Clarendon Press, 1899–1902).

Grant, Teresa, and Ravelhofer, Barbara (eds), *English Historical Drama, 1500–1660: Forms outside the Canon* (Basingstoke: Palgrave Macmillan, 2008).

Green, Janet M., '"I My Self": Elizabeth I's Oration at Tilbury Camp', *Sixteenth Century Journal* 28.2 (Summer 1997), pp. 421–45.

Greenblatt, Stephen, 'Invisible Bullets: Renaissance Authority and Its Subversion, *Henry IV* and *Henry V*', in Dollimore and Sinfield (eds), *Political Shakespeare*, pp. 18–47.

——— (ed.), *The Power of Forms in the English Renaissance* (Norman, Okla.: Pilgrim Books, 1982).

———, *Renaissance Self-Fashioning: From More to Shakespeare* (Chicago: University of Chicago Press, 1980).

Greene, Robert, *Arbasto, The Anatomie of Fortune* (London: 1584), STC (2nd edn) 12217.

——, *The Comicall Historie of Alphonsus, King of Aragon* (London: 1599), STC (2nd edn) 12233.

——, *The Defence of conny-catching* (London: 1592), STC (2nd edn) 5656.

——, *Mamillia* (London: 1583), STC (2nd edn) 12269.

Greene, Thomas M., *The Light in Troy: Imitation and Discovery in Renaissance Poetry* (New Haven and London: Yale University Press, 1982).

Greenhut, Deborah S., *Feminine Rhetorical Culture: Tudor Adaptations of Ovid's 'Heroides'* (New York: Peter Lang, 1988).

Guarini, Giambattista, *The Compendium of Tragicomic Poetry*, trans. Gilbert, in Gilbert (ed.), *Literary Criticism*, pp. 504–33.

Guido delle Colonne, *Historia Destructionis Troiae*, ed. Nathaniel Edward Griffin (Cambridge, Mass.: Mediaeval Academy of America, 1936).

——, *Historia Destructionis Troiae*, trans. and ed. Mary Elizabeth Meek (Bloomington: Indiana University Press, 1974).

Hackett, Helen, *Women and Romance Fiction in the English Renaissance* (Cambridge: Cambridge University Press, 2000).

Hagedorn, Suzanne C., *Abandoned Women: Rewriting the Classics in Dante, Boccaccio and Chaucer* (Ann Arbor: University of Michigan Press, 2004).

Hall, Edith, 'Divine and Human in Euripides' *Medea*', in Stuttard (ed.), *Looking at Medea*, pp. 139–55.

——, *Inventing the Barbarian: Greek Self-Definition through Tragedy* (Oxford: Clarendon Press, 1989, repr. 2004).

——, '*Medea* and British Legislation before the First World War', *Greece and Rome* 46.1 (1999), pp. 42–77.

——, '*Medea* on the Eighteenth-Century London Stage', in Hall, Macintosh and Taplin (eds), *Medea in Performance*, pp. 49–74.

——, Macintosh, Fiona, and Taplin, Oliver (eds), *Medea in Performance 1500–2000* (Oxford: Legenda, 2000).

Hall, Edward, *The union of the two noble and illustre famelies of Lancastre & Yorke* (London: 1548), STC (2nd edn) 12722.

Hallett, Nicky, 'Women', in Brown (ed.), *Companion to Chaucer*, pp. 480–94.

Hamilton, A. C. (ed.), *The Spenser Encyclopedia* (London: Routledge, 1990).

Hampton, Timothy, *Writing from History: The Rhetoric of Exemplarity in Renaissance Literature* (Ithaca and London: Cornell University Press, 1990).

Hampton-Reeves, Stuart, and Rutter, Carol Chillington, *The Henry VI Plays* (Manchester: Manchester University Press, 2006).

Harbage, Alfred, *Annals of English Drama 975–1700*, rev. S. Schoenbaum, 3rd edn rev. Sylvia Stoler Wagonheim (London: Routledge, 1989).

——, 'Elizabethan and Seventeenth-Century Play Manuscripts', *PMLA* 50.3 (1935), pp. 687–99.

Hardin, Richard F., 'Adicia, Souldan', in Hamilton (ed.), *Spenser Encyclopedia*, pp. 7–8.

——, 'Convention and Design in Drayton's *Heroicall Epistles*', *PMLA* 83.1 (1968), pp. 35–41.

——, 'Ovid in Seventeenth-Century England', *Comparative Literature* 24.1 (1972), pp. 44–62.

Hardwick, Lorna, *Reception Studies* (Oxford: Oxford University Press, 2003).

Harris, Anthony, *Night's Black Agents: Witchcraft and Magic in Seventeenth-Century English Drama* (Manchester: Manchester University Press, 1980).

Harris, Tim, Seaward, Paul, and Goldie, Mark (eds), *The Politics of Religion in Restoration England* (Oxford: Basil Blackwell, 1990).

Harvey, Elizabeth D., *Ventriloquized Voices: Feminist Theory and English Renaissance Texts* (London: Routledge, 1992).

Hattaway, Michael (ed.), *A Companion to English Renaissance Literature and Culture* (Oxford: Blackwell, 2003).

Hayes, Julie Candler, *Translation, Subjectivity, and Culture in France and England, 1600–1800* (Stanford: Stanford University Press, 2009).

Healy, Margaret, 'Alchemy, Magic and the Sciences', in Sanders (ed.), *Ben Jonson in Context*, pp. 322–9.

Herring, Francis, *Mischeefes Mysterie: or, Treasons Master-peece*, trans. John Vicars (London: 1617), STC (2nd edn) 13247.

———, *Pietas pontificia* (London: 1606), STC (2nd edn) 13244.

Herrington, H. W., 'Witchcraft and Magic in the Elizabethan Drama', *Journal of American Folklore* 32.126 (1919), pp. 447–85.

Hexter, Ralph J., *Ovid and Medieval Schooling: Studies in Medieval School Commentaries on Ovid's Ars Amatoria, Epistulae ex Ponto, and Epistulae Heroidum* (Munich: Arbeo-Gesellschaft, 1986).

Heywood, Thomas, *The Brazen Age, Works*, vol. 3, ed. J. H. Pearson (New York: Russell and Russell, 1964, reprinted from the edition of 1874).

———, *An Apology for Actors*, in Gilbert (ed.), *Literary Criticism*, pp. 552–64.

———, *Londini Status Pacatus* (London: 1639), STC (2nd edn) 13350.

———, *Londini Status Pacatus, or Londons Peaceable Estate, Thomas Heywood's Pageants: A Critical Edition*, ed. David M. Bergeron (New York and London: Garland Publishing, 1985).

Higgins, John, *The first parte of the Mirour for magistrates* (London: 1574), STC (2nd edn) 13443.

Hill, Tracey, *Anthony Munday and Civic Culture: Theatre, History and Power in Early Modern London, 1580–1633* (Manchester: Manchester University Press, 2004).

Hind, John, *Eliosto Libidinoso* (London: 1606), STC (2nd edn) 13509.

Hinds, Peter, *'The Horrid Popish Plot': Roger L'Estrange and the Circulation of Political Discourse in Late Seventeenth-Century London* (Oxford: Oxford University Press for the British Academy, 2010).

———, '"A Vast Ill-Nature": Roger L'Estrange, Reputation, and the Credibility of Political Discourse in the Late Seventeenth Century', *Seventeenth Century* 21.2 (2006), pp. 335–63.

Hinds, Stephen, *Allusion and Intertext: Dynamics of Appropriation in Roman Poetry*, Roman Literature and Its Contexts (Cambridge: Cambridge University Press, 1998).

Hobbes, Thomas, *Leviathan*, ed. Richard Tuck (Cambridge: Cambridge University Press, 1991).

Hoffer, Peter C., and Hull, N. E. H., *Murdering Mothers: Infanticide in England and New England, 1558–1803* (New York: New York University Press, 1981).

Holstun, James (ed.), *Pamphlet Wars: Prose in the English Revolution* (London: Frank Cass, 1992).

Hopkins, David, 'Dryden and the Garth-Tonson *Metamorphoses*', *RES* New Series 39.153 (1988), pp. 64–74.

Horace, 'On the Art of Poetry', in Dorsch, *Classical Literary Criticism*, pp. 79–95.

Howard, Jean E., 'Scripts and/versus Playhouses: Ideological Production and the Renaissance Public Stage', *Renaissance Drama* New Series 20 (1989), pp. 31–49.

———, 'Women as Spectators, Spectacles, and Paying Customers', in Kastan and Stallybrass (eds), *Staging the Renaissance: Reinterpretations of Elizabethan and Jacobean Drama*, pp. 68–74.

Howe, Elizabeth, *The First English Actresses: Women and Drama 1660–1700* (Cambridge: Cambridge University Press, 1992).

Hughes, Derek, *English Drama 1660–1700* (Oxford: Clarendon Press, 1996).

Hughes, Thomas, and others, *The Misfortunes of Arthur*, ed. John S. Farmer (London: Tudor Facsimile Texts, 1911).

Hunter, G. K., *Dramatic Identities and Cultural Tradition: Studies in Shakespeare and His Contemporaries* (Liverpool: Liverpool University Press, 1978).

———, 'Seneca and English Tragedy', in Costa (ed.), *Seneca*, pp. 166–204.

Hutcheon, Linda, *A Theory of Adaptation* (New York: Routledge, 2006).

Hyginus, *Myths*, trans. and ed. Mary Grant, University of Kansas Publications, Humanistic Studies 34 (Lawrence: University of Kansas Press, 1960).

Ingleheart, Jennifer (ed.), *Two Thousand Years of Solitude: Exile after Ovid* (Oxford: Oxford University Press, 2011).

Jackson, Mark (ed.), *Infanticide: Historical Perspectives on Child Murder and Concealment, 1550–2000* (Aldershot: Ashgate, 2002).

———, 'The Trial of Harriet Vooght: Continuity and Change in the History of Infanticide', in Jackson (ed.), *Infanticide*, pp. 1–17.

Jacobson, Howard, *Ovid's 'Heroides'* (Princeton: Princeton University Press, 1974).

James, Heather, 'Ovid and the Question of Politics in Early Modern England', *ELH* 70.2 (2003), pp. 343–73.

Jardine, Lisa, *Still Harping on Daughters: Women and Drama in the Age of Shakespeare* (Hemel Hempstead: Harvester Wheatsheaf, 1983).

Johnston, Nathaniel, *The excellency of monarchical government, especially of the English monarchy wherein is largely treated of the several benefits of kingly government, and the inconvenience of commonwealths* (London: 1686), Wing J877.

Johnston, Sarah Iles, 'Corinthian Medea and the Cult of Hera Akraia', in Clauss and Johnston (eds), *Medea*, pp. 44–70.

———, 'Introduction', in Clauss and Johnston (eds), *Medea*, pp. 3–17.

Jonson, Ben, *'The Alchemist' and Other Plays*, ed. Gordon Campbell (Oxford: Oxford University Press, 1995).

———, *The Complete Works*, ed. David Bevington, Martin Butler and Ian Donaldson, 7 vols (Cambridge and New York: Cambridge University Press, 2012).

———, *Selected Masques*, ed. Stephen Orgel (New Haven and London: Yale University Press, 1970).

Joseph of Exeter, *The Trojan War I–III*, ed. and trans. A. K. Bate (Warminster: Aris & Phillips, 1986).

Justin (Marcus Junianus Justinus), *Thabridgment of the histories of Trogus Pompeius, collected and wrytten in the Laten tonge, by the famous historiographer Iustine, and translated into English by Arthur Goldyng* (London: 1564), STC (2nd edn) 24290.

Kane, Stuart A., 'Wives with Knives: Early Modern Murder Ballads and the Transgressive Commodity', *Criticism* 38.2 (1996), pp. 219–37.

Kaske, Robert Earl, Groos, Arthur, and Twomey, Michael W. (eds), *Medieval Christian Literary Imagery: A Guide to Interpretation* (Toronto: University of Toronto Press, 1988).

Kastan, David Scott, 'Proud Majesty Made a Subject: Shakespeare and the Spectacle of Rule', *Shakespeare Quarterly* 37.4 (1986), pp. 459–75.

——, and Stallybrass, Peter (eds), *Staging the Renaissance: Reinterpretations of Elizabethan and Jacobean Drama* (New York: Routledge, 1991).

Kehler, Dorothea, 'That Ravenous Tiger Tamora': *Titus Andronicus'* Lusty Widow, Wife, and M/Other', in Kolin (ed.), *Titus Andronicus*, pp. 317–32.

Kelly, Louis, 'Pedagogical Uses of Translation', in Braden, Cummings and Gillespie (eds), *Oxford History of Literary Translation, Vol. 2: 1550–1660*, pp. 12–16.

Kempe, Dorothy, 'A Middle English Tale of Troy', *Englische Studien* 29 (1901), pp. 1–26.

Kerrigan, John (ed.), *Motives of Woe: Shakespeare and 'Female Complaint', a Critical Anthology* (Oxford: Clarendon Press, 1991).

——, *Revenge Tragedy: Aeschylus to Armageddon* (Oxford: Clarendon Press, 1996).

Kewes, Paulina, 'Otway, Lee and the Restoration History Play', in Owen (ed.), *Companion to Restoration Drama*, pp. 355–77.

Kiefer, Frederick, *Fortune and Elizabethan Tragedy* (San Marino, Calif.: Huntington Library Press, 1983).

Kiser, Lisa J., *Telling Classical Tales: Chaucer and the 'Legend of Good Women'* (Ithaca: Cornell University Press, 1983).

Knellwolf, Christa, 'Women Translators, Gender and the Cultural Context of the Scientific Revolution', in Ellis and Oakley-Brown (eds), *Translation and Nation*, pp. 85–119.

Kolb, Justin, '"In th'armor of a Pagan knight": Romance and Anachronism East of England in Book V of *The Faerie Queene* and *Tamburlaine'*, *Early Theatre* 12.2 (2009), pp. 194–207.

Kolin, Philip C. (ed.), *Titus Andronicus: Critical Essays* (New York: Garland, 1995).

Kramer, Heinrich, and Sprenger, Jacob, *Malleus Maleficarum*, ed. and trans. Montague Summers (London: Hogarth, 1928, repr. 1969).

Lake, Peter, 'Anti-popery: The Structure of a Prejudice', in Cust and Hughes (eds), *Conflict in Early Stuart England*, pp. 72–106.

——, 'Deeds against Nature: Cheap Print, Protestantism and Murder in Early Seventeenth-Century England', in Sharpe and Lake (eds), *Culture and Politics in Early Stuart England*, pp. 257–83.

The Laud Troy Book, ed. J. Ernst Wülfing, Early English Text Society OS 121–122 (London: Kegan Paul, Trench, Trübner & Co., 1902).

Laurent de Premierfait, *'Des Cas des Nobles Hommes et Femmes', Book 1: Translated from Boccaccio. A Critical Edition Based on Six MSS*, ed. Patricia M. Gathercole (Chapel Hill: University of North Carolina Press, 1968).

Lee, Nathaniel, *The Rival Queens* (London: 1677), Wing L865.

Lefèvre, Raoul, *L'Histoire de Jason*, ed. Gert Pinkernell (Frankfurt: Athenäum Verlag, 1971).

——, *L'Histoire de Jason*, trans. William Caxton, ed. John Munro, Early English Text Society XS 111 (London: Kegan Paul, Trench, Trübner & Co. and Oxford University Press, 1913).

——, *The Recuyell of the Historyes of Troye*, trans. William Caxton, 2nd edn (Bruges: William Caxton and [?] Colard Mansion, 1473–4), STC (2nd edn) 15375.

Levack, Brian P. (ed.), *New Perspectives on Witchcraft, Magic, and Demonology*, 6 vols (New York: Routledge, 2001).

—— (ed.), *The Oxford Handbook of Witchcraft in Early Modern Europe and Colonial America* (Oxford: Oxford University Press, 2013).

Levin, Carole, Carney, Jo Eldridge, and Barrett-Graves, Debra (eds), *High and Mighty Queens of Early Modern England: Realities and Representations* (New York: Palgrave, 2003).

Levin, Joanna, 'Lady Macbeth and the Daemonologie of Hysteria', *ELH* 69.1 (2002), pp. 21–55.

Lewis, C. S., *An Experiment in Criticism* (Cambridge: Cambridge University Press, 1961).

Love, Harold, 'Some Restoration Treatments of Ovid', in Coleman and Hammond (eds), *Poetry and Drama 1570–1700*, pp. 136–55.

Lucas, Caroline, *Writing for Women: The Example of Woman as Reader in Elizabethan Romance* (Milton Keynes: Open University Press, 1989).

Lydgate, John, *The Fall of Princes*, ed. Henry Bergen, 4 vols, Early English Text Society XS 121–4 (London: Oxford University Press, 1924–7).

———, *Troy Book*, ed. Henry Bergen, 4 vols, Early English Text Society XS 97, 126 (London: Kegan Paul, Trench, Trübner & Co., 1906–35).

Lyne, Raphael, 'Ovid, Golding, and the "Rough Magic" of *The Tempest*', in Taylor (ed.), *Shakespeare's Ovid*, pp. 150–64.

———, *Ovid's Changing Worlds: English 'Metamorphoses', 1567–1632* (Oxford: Oxford University Press, 2001).

———, 'Writing Back to Ovid in the 1560s and 1570s', *Translation and Literature* 13.2: *Versions of Ovid* (2004), pp. 143–64.

McDonald, Marianne, 'Medea as Politician and Diva: Riding the Dragon into the Future', in Clauss and Johnston (eds), *Medea*, pp. 297–323.

McDonald, Nicola. '"Diverse Folk Diversely They Seyde": A Study of the Figure of Medea in Medieval Literature' (D.Phil. Thesis: Oxford University, 1994).

McElligott, Jason, 'Dixon, Robert (1614/15–1688)', *Oxford Dictionary of National Biography*, Oxford University Press, 2004; online edn, January 2008 <http://www.oxforddnb.com/view/article/7705>, accessed 6 August 2014.

MacFarlane, Alan, *Witchcraft in Tudor and Stuart England: A Regional and Comparative Study*, 2nd edn (London: Routledge, 1970, repr. 1999).

Macintosh, Fiona, 'Introduction: The Performer in Performance', in Hall, Macintosh and Taplin (eds), *Medea in Performance*, pp. 1–31.

McKinley, Kathryn L., *Reading the Ovidian Heroine: 'Metamorphoses' Commentaries 1100–1618* (Leiden: Brill, 2001).

MacLean, Gerald (ed.), *Culture and Society in the Stuart Restoration: Literature, Drama, History* (Cambridge: Cambridge University Press, 1995).

McLeod, Glenda, *Virtue and Venom: Catalogs of Women from Antiquity to the Renaissance* (Ann Arbor: University of Michigan Press, 1991).

Maguire, Laurie, *Shakespeare's Names* (Oxford: Oxford University Press, 2007).

Maguire, Nancy Klein, 'Factionary Politics: John Crowne's *Henry VI*', in MacLean (ed.), *Culture and Society in the Stuart Restoration*, pp. 70–92.

———, *Regicide and Restoration: English Tragicomedy, 1660–1671* (Cambridge: Cambridge University Press, 1992).

Maltby, William S., *The Black Legend in England: The Development of Anti-Spanish Sentiment, 1558–1660* (Durham, NC: Duke University Press, 1968).

Marotti, Arthur F. (ed.), *Catholicism and Anti-Catholicism in Early Modern English Texts* (Basingstoke: Palgrave, now Palgrave Macmillan, 1999).

Marrapodi, Michele, and Hoenselaars, A. J. (eds), *The Italian World of English Renaissance Drama: Cultural Exchange and Intertextuality* (Cranbury, NJ, and London: Associated University Presses, 1998).

Marsden, Jean I., *Fatal Desire: Women, Sexuality, and the English Stage, 1660–1720* (Ithaca and London: Cornell University Press, 2006).

——, 'Tragedy and Varieties of Serious Drama', in Owen (ed.), *Companion to Restoration Drama*, pp. 228–42.

Marston, John, *Antonio and Mellida*, ed. W. Reavley Gair (Manchester: Manchester University Press, 1991, repr. 2004).

——, *Antonio's Revenge*, ed. W. Reavley Gair (Manchester: Manchester University Press, 1978, repr. 1999).

Martin, Priscilla, *Chaucer's Women: Nuns, Wives and Amazons* (London: Macmillan, 1990).

Martin, Randall, *Women, Murder, and Equity in Early Modern England* (New York: Routledge, 2008).

Martindale, Charles, and Martindale, Michelle, *Shakespeare and the Uses of Antiquity: An Introductory Essay* (London: Routledge, 1990).

Maslen, R. W., *Elizabethan Fictions: Espionage, Counter-Espionage, and the Duplicity of Fiction in Early Elizabethan Prose Narratives* (Oxford: Clarendon Press, 1997).

——, 'Myths Exploited: The Metamorphoses of Ovid in Early Elizabethan England', in Taylor (ed.), *Shakespeare's Ovid*, pp. 15–30.

Maxwell-Stuart, P. G., *Witchcraft: A History* (Stroud: Tempus, 2004).

May, Thomas, *The Reign of King Henry II Written in Seaven Bookes* (London: 1633), STC (2nd edn) 17715.

Meriton, Thomas, *The Wandring Lover* (London: 1658), Wing M1824.

Michel, Peter, *A victory obtained by Lieut: Gen: David Lesley, in the north of Scotland, against Colonell Hurrey and his forces* (London: 1650), Wing (2nd edn) M1963.

Miller, Naomi J., and Yavneh, Naomi (eds), *Maternal Measures: Figuring Caregiving in the Early Modern Period* (Aldershot: Ashgate, 2000).

Milton, Anthony, 'A Qualified Intolerance: The Limits and Ambiguities of Early Stuart Anti-Catholicism', in Marotti (ed.), *Catholicism and Anti-Catholicism in Early Modern English Texts*, pp. 85–115.

Minnis, A. J., *Chaucer and Pagan Antiquity* (Cambridge: D. S. Brewer, 1982).

Miola, Robert S., *Shakespeare and Classical Tragedy: The Influence of Seneca* (Oxford: Clarendon Press, 1992).

Montrose, Louis A., 'Gifts and Reasons: The Contexts of Peele's *Araygnement of Paris*', *ELH* 47.3 (1980), pp. 433–61.

——, '"Shaping Fantasies": Figurations of Gender and Power in Elizabethan Culture', *Representations* 2 (1983), pp. 61–94.

Moore, Helen, 'Elizabethan Fiction and Ovid's *Heroides*', *Translation and Literature* 9.1 (2000), pp. 40–64.

——, 'Hynd, John (*fl. c.*1592–1606)', *Oxford Dictionary of National Biography* (Oxford: Oxford University Press, 2004) <http://www.oxforddnb.com/view/article/14341>, accessed 31 May 2013.

Moore Smith, George Charles, *College Plays: Performed at the University of Cambridge* (Cambridge: Cambridge University Press, 1923).

Morse, Ruth, *The Medieval Medea* (Cambridge: D. S. Brewer, 1996).

——, 'Problems of Early Fiction: Raoul Lefèvre's *Histoire de Jason*', *MLR* 78.1 (1980), pp. 34–45.

——, *Truth and Convention in the Middle Ages: Rhetoric, Representation, and Reality* (Cambridge: Cambridge University Press, 1991).

Munday, Anthony, *Metropolis Coronata, Pageants and Entertainments of Anthony Munday.*
———, *Pageants and Entertainments of Anthony Munday: A Critical Edition,* ed. David M. Bergeron (New York and London: Garland Publishing, 1985).
———, *The Triumphs of the Golden Fleece, Pageants and Entertainments of Anthony Munday.*
Munns, Jessica, 'Images of Monarchy on the Restoration Stage', in Owen (ed.), *Companion to Restoration Drama,* pp. 109–25.
Neufeld, Christine M., 'Lyly's Chimerical Vision: Witchcraft in *Endymion*', *Forum for Modern Language Studies* 43.4 (2007), pp. 351–69.
Nikolaidis, A. G. 'Some Observations on Ovid's Lost *Medea*', *Latomus* 44.2 (1985), pp. 383–7.
Nolan, Barbara, *Chaucer and the Tradition of the 'Roman Antique'* (Cambridge: Cambridge University Press, 1992).
Norbrook, David, 'May, Thomas (*b.* in or after 1596, *d.* 1650)', *Oxford Dictionary of National Biography,* Oxford University Press, 2004; online edn, January 2008 <http://www.oxforddnb.com/view/article/18423>, accessed 1 May 2014.
Norton, Thomas, [and Sackville, Thomas], *The tragedie of Gorboduc* (London: 1565), STC (2nd edn) 18684.
Nyquist, Mary, '"Profuse, proud Cleopatra": "Barbarism" and Female Rule in Early Modern English Republicanism', *Women's Studies* 24 (1994), pp. 85–130.
Oakley-Brown, Liz, 'Elizabethan Exile after Ovid: Thomas Churchyard's *Tristia*', in Ingleheart (ed.), *Two Thousand Years of Solitude,* pp. 103–17.
———, '"My lord, be ruled by me": Shakespeare's Tamora and the Failure of Queenship', in Oakley-Brown and Wilkinson (eds), *Rituals and Rhetoric of Queenship,* pp. 222–37.
———, *Ovid and the Cultural Politics of Translation in Early Modern England* (Aldershot: Ashgate, 2006).
———, and Wilkinson, Louise J. (eds) *The Rituals and Rhetoric of Queenship: Medieval to Early Modern* (Dublin: Four Courts Press, 2009).
O'Connell, Michael, *Mirror and Veil: The Historical Dimension of Spenser's 'Faerie Queene'* (Chapel Hill: University of North Carolina Press, 1977).
O'Higgins, Dolores, 'Medea as Muse: Pindar's *Pythian 4*', in Clauss and Johnston (eds), *Medea,* pp. 103–26.
Orgel, Stephen, '*Macbeth* and the Antic Round', *Shakespeare Survey* 52 (1999), pp. 143–53, reprinted in Shakespeare, *Macbeth,* ed. Miola, pp. 342–56.
———, 'Nobody's Perfect: Or Why Did the English Stage Take Boys for Women?', *South Atlantic Quarterly* 88.1 (1989), pp. 7–29.
Ovid, *De tristibus ...,* trans. Zachary Catlin (London: 1639), STC (2nd edn) 18981.
———, '*Heroides*' *and* '*Amores*', trans. Grant Showerman, rev. G. P. Goold, Loeb Classical Library (Cambridge, Mass.: Harvard University Press, 1914, rev. 1977).
———, *The heroycall epistles of the learned poet Publius Ouidius Naso ... ,* trans. George Turberville (London: 1567), STC (2nd edn) 18940.
———, *Metamorphoses,* trans. Frank Justus Miller, rev. G. P. Goold, 2 vols, Loeb Classical Library (Cambridge, Mass.: Harvard University Press, 1916, rev. 1977).
———, *Metamorphoses of Ovid,* trans. William Caxton, 2 vols (New York: George Braziller in association with Magdalene College Cambridge, 1968).
———, *Opere,* 3 vols (Venice: 1502–3).
———, *Ovid's Epistles Translated by Several Hands,* Preface by John Dryden (London: 1680), Wing 0659.

————, *Ovids heroical epistles*, trans. John Sherburne (London: 1639), STC (2nd edn) 18947.

————, *Ovids heroicall epistles* , trans. W. S. (Wye Saltonstall) (London: 1636), STC (2nd edn) 18945.5.

————, *Ovids Metamorphosis Englished, mythologiz'd, and represented in figures by George Sandys* (London: 1632), STC (2nd edn) 18966.

————, *Ovid's Metamorphosis Englished by G[eorge] S[andys]* (London: 1626), STC (2nd edn) 18964.

————, *Ovid's Metamorphoses in fifteen books. Translated by the most eminent hands,* comp. Samuel Garth (London: Jacob Tonson, 1717).

————, *Ovid's 'Metamorphoses' translated by Arthur Golding*, ed. Madeleine Forey (Baltimore: Johns Hopkins University Press, 2001).

————, *Ovids Tristia containinge five bookes of mournfull elegies*, trans. W. S. (Wye Saltonstall) (London: 1633), STC (2nd edn) 18979.

————, *P. Ovidii Nasonis Metamorphoseωs libri quindecim, cum commentariis Raphaelis Regii. Adiectis etiam annotationibus J. Micylli* (Basle: 1543).

————, *P. Ovidii Nasonis Opera omnia in tres tomos divisa, cum ... Nicolai Heinsii ... notis: quibus non pauca ... accesserunt, studio Borchardi Cnippingii* (Lugduni-Batavorum: 1670).

————, *P. Ovidii Nasonis Poetae Sulmonensis, Heroides Epistolae, cum interpretibus Hubertino Crescent. Et Iano Parrhasio* (Venice: 1558).

————, *P. Ovidii Nasonis Poetae Sulmonensis Opera* (Basle: 1549).

————, *Publii Ovidii Nasonis Heroides. Cum interpretibus Hubertino Crescentio et Iano Parrhasio* (Venice: 1543).

————, *Publii Ovidii Nasonis Poeta Sulmonensis, Heroides Epistolae: cum interpretibus Hubertino Crescentinatis, & Iano Parrhasio* (Venice: 1574).

————, *The three first bookes of Ovid de Tristibus translated into English*, trans. Thomas Churchyard (London: 1580), STC (2nd edn) 18978.

————, *Tristia*, trans. A. L. Wheeler, rev. G. P. Goold, Loeb Classical Library (Cambridge, Mass.: Harvard University Press, 1924, rev. 1988).

Ovide moralisé en prose, texte du quinzième siècle, ed. C. de Boer (Amsterdam: North-Holland Pub. Co., 1954).

Ovide moralisé, poème du commencement du quatorzième siècle, ed. C. de Boer, 5 vols (Amsterdam: Noord-Hollandsche Uitgevers-Maatschapperij, 1915–38).

Owen, Susan J. (ed.), *A Companion to Restoration Drama* (Oxford: Blackwell, 2001, repr. 2008).

————, *Restoration Theatre and Crisis* (Oxford: Clarendon Press, 1996).

Painter, William, *The palace of pleasure beautified, adorned and well furnished, with pleasaunt histories and excellent nouelles, selected out of diuers good and commendable authors* (London: 1566), STC (2nd edn) 19121.

Palaephatus, *On Unbelievable Tales*, trans. and ed. Jacob Stern, with notes and Greek text from the 1902 B. G. Teubner edition (Wauconda, Ill.: Bolchazy-Carducci, 1996).

Paster, Gail Kern, *The Body Embarrassed: Drama and the Disciplines of Shame in Early Modern England* (Ithaca, New York: Cornell University Press, 1993).

Pausanias, *Description of Greece*, trans. W. H. S. Jones and H. A. Omerod, 6 vols, Loeb Classical Library (London: Heinemann, 1918–35).

Payne, Henry Neville, *The Siege of Constantinople* (London: 1675), Wing P893.

Pearcy, Lee T., *The Mediated Muse: English Translations of Ovid 1560–1700* (Hamden, Conn.: Archon Books, 1984).

Pearsall, Derek, 'Gower's Narrative Art', *PMLA* 87.1 (1966), pp. 475–84.

Pettie, George, *A Petite Pallace of Pettie his Pleasure* (London: 1576), STC (2nd edn) 19819.

Peyré, Yves (ed.), *A Dictionary of Shakespeare's Classical Mythology* (2009–), <http://www.shakmyth.org/myth/1/absyrtus/analysis>, accessed 12 August 2014.

Philipps, Fabian, *King Charles the First, no man of blood: but a martyr for his people* (London: 1649), Wing (2nd edn) P2008.

Phillippy, Patricia B., '"Loytering in Love": Ovid's *Heroides*, Hospitality, and Humanist Education in *The Taming of the Shrew*', *Criticism* 40.1 (1998), pp. 27–53.

Phillips, James Emerson, *Images of a Queen: Mary Stuart in Sixteenth-Century Literature* (Berkeley: University of California Press, 1964).

Pincombe, Mike, and Shrank, Cathy (eds), *The Oxford Handbook of Tudor Literature 1485–1603* (Oxford: Oxford University Press, 2009).

A pittilesse mother That most unnaturally at one time, murthered two of her owne children at Acton within six miles from London uppon holy thursday last 1616 (London: 1616), STC (2nd edn) 24757.

Pix, Mary, *The False Friend* (London: 1699), Wing P2328.

Pollard, Tanya, 'What's Hecuba to Shakespeare?', *Shakespeare Quarterly* 65.4 (2012), pp. 1060–93.

Poole, Joshua (comp.), *The English Parnassus, or, A helpe to English poesie* (London: 1657), Wing P2814.

Pruvost, René, *Matteo Bandello and Elizabethan Fiction* (Paris: Librairie ancienne Honoré Champion, 1937).

Pugh, Syrithe, *Spenser and Ovid* (Aldershot: Ashgate, 2005).

Purkiss, Diane, 'Desire and Its Deformities: Fantasies of Witchcraft in the English Civil War', in Levack (ed.), *New Perspectives on Witchcraft, Magic, and Demonology*, vol. 3, pp. 271–300; reprinted from the *Journal of Medieval and Early Modern Studies* 27.1 (1997), pp. 103–32.

——, 'Medea in the English Renaissance', in Hall, Macintosh and Taplin (eds), *Medea in Performance*, pp. 32–48.

——, *The Witch in History: Early Modern and Twentieth-Century Representations* (London: Routledge, 1996).

——, 'Witchcraft in Early Modern Literature', in Levack (ed.), *Oxford Handbook of Witchcraft in Early Modern Europe and Colonial America*, pp. 122–40.

——, 'Women's Stories of Witchcraft in Early Modern England: The House, the Body, the Child', in Levack (ed.), *New Perspectives on Witchcraft*, vol. 4, pp. 278–302; reprinted from *Gender and History* 7.3 (1995), pp. 408–32.

Quintilian, *The Orator's Education*, ed. and trans. Donald A. Russell, 5 vols, Loeb Classical Library (Cambridge, Mass.: Harvard University Press, 2001).

Raber, Karen L., 'Murderous Mothers and the Family/State Analogy in Classical and Renaissance Drama', *Comparative Literature Studies* 37.3 (2000), pp. 298–320.

Rabin, Dana, 'Bodies of Evidence, States of Mind: Infanticide, Emotion and Sensibility in Eighteenth-Century England', in Jackson (ed.), *Infanticide*, pp. 73–92.

Racaut, Luc, 'Accusations of Infanticide on the Eve of the French Wars of Religion', in Jackson (ed.), *Infanticide*, pp. 18–34.

Radcliffe, Alexander, *Ovid travestie, a burlesque upon Ovid's Epistles* (London: 1680), Wing R125.

Radulescu, Domnica, *Sisters of Medea: The Tragic Heroine across Cultures* (New Orleans: University Press of the South, 2002).

Ramsey, P. A. (ed.), *Rome in the Renaissance, the City and the Myth* (Binghamton, NY: Center for Medieval and Early Renaissance Studies, 1982).

Ravenscroft, Edward, *Titus Andronicus, or, The Rape of Lavinia acted at the Theatre Royall* (London: 1687), Wing S2949.

Raylor, Timothy, *Cavaliers, Clubs, and Literary Culture: Sir John Mennes, James Smith and the Order of the Fancy* (Cranbury, NJ: Associated University Presses, 1994).

Relihan, Constance C., *Fashioning Authority: The Development of Elizabethan Novelistic Discourse* (Kent, OH: Kent State University Press, 1994).

Rhodes, Neil, 'Status Anxiety and English Renaissance Translation', in Smith and Wilson (eds), *Renaissance Paratexts*, pp. 107–20.

Roberts, Gareth, 'The Descendants of Circe: Witches and Renaissance Fictions', in Barry, Hester and Roberts (eds), *Witchcraft in Early Modern Europe*, pp. 183–206.

Roberts, Sasha, *Reading Shakespeare's Poems in Early Modern England* (Basingstoke: Palgrave Macmillan, 2003).

Robinson, Richard, *The Rewarde of Wickednesse*, ed. Allyna E. Ward (London: Modern Humanities Research Association, 2009).

———, *The Rewarde of Wickednesse* (London: 1574), STC (2nd edn) 21121.7.

Roisman, Hanna M., 'Medea's Vengeance', in Stuttard (ed.), *Looking at Medea*, pp. 111–22.

Le Roman de Troie en Prose, ed. Françoise Vielliard (Cologny-Genève: Martin Bodmer, 1979).

Rose, Mary Beth, 'Where Are the Mothers in Shakespeare? Options for Gender Representation in the English Renaissance', *Shakespeare Quarterly* 42.3 (1991), pp. 291–314.

Rubin, Deborah, *Ovid's Metamorphoses Englished: George Sandys as Translator and Mythographer* (New York: Garland, 1985).

———, 'Sandys, Ovid, and Female Chastity: The Encyclopedic Mythographer as Moralist', in Chance (ed.), *Mythographic Art*, pp. 257–77.

Sabinus, Georgius, *Metamorphosis seu fabulae* (1589), ed. Stephen Orgel (New York and London: Garland, 1976).

Salzman, Paul, 'Placing Tudor Fiction', *Yearbook of English Studies* 38 1/2, *Tudor Literature* (2008), pp. 136–49.

Sanders, Julie, *Adaptation and Appropriation* (New York: Routledge, 2006).

——— (ed.), *Ben Jonson in Context* (Cambridge: Cambridge University Press, 2010).

Schmitz, Götz, *The Fall of Women in Early English Narrative Verse* (Cambridge: Cambridge University Press, 1990).

Scot, Reginald, *The Discoverie of Witchcraft* (London: 1584), STC (2nd edn) 21864.

Scott, Jonathan, 'England's Troubles: Exhuming the Popish Plot', in Harris, Seaward and Goldie (eds), *Politics of Religion in Restoration England*, pp. 107–31.

Scriptores Rerum Mythicarum Latini Tres Romae Nuper Reperti, ed. G. H. Bode (Hildesheim: Georg Olms, 1968, repr. 1996).

The Seege or Batayle of Troye, ed. Mary Elizabeth Barnicle (Oxford: Oxford University Press, 1927).

Seneca, *L. Annei Senecae Cordubensis Tragoediae Septem* (Lyon: 1541).

———, *Medea*, trans. E. S. (Edward Sherburne) (London: 1648), Wing S2513.

———, *Medea*, trans. H. M. Hine (Warminster: Aris and Phillips, 2000).

———, *Seneca His Tenne Tragedies*, comp. Thomas Newton (London: 1581), STC (2nd edn) 22221.

———, *Tragedies I: 'Hercules', 'Trojan Women', 'Phoenician Women', Medea', Phaedra'*, ed. and trans. John G. Fitch, 8 vols, Loeb Classical Library (Cambridge, Mass.: Harvard University Press, 2002).

———, *The Tragedies of Lucius Annaeus Seneca, the Philosopher, viz. 'Medea', 'Phaedra and Hippolytus', 'Troades, or The Royal Captives', and 'The Rape of Helen', out of the Greek of Coluthus*, trans. Edward Sherburne (London: S. Smith and B. Walford, 1701).

———, *Translations of Seneca's 'Agamemnon' and 'Medea'*, trans. John Studley, ed. E. M. Spearing (Louvain: A. Uystpruyst, 1913).

Seznec, Jean, *The Survival of the Pagan Gods: The Mythological Tradition and Its Place in Renaissance Humanism and Art*, trans. Barbara F. Sessions (Princeton: Princeton University Press, 1953, repr. 1972).

Shakespeare, William, *Macbeth*, ed. Robert S. Miola (New York: Norton, 2004).

———, *The Norton Shakespeare*, ed. Stephen Greenblatt et al. (New York: Norton, 1997).

———, *The Second Part of King Henry VI*, ed. Michael Hattaway (Cambridge: Cambridge University Press, 1991).

———, *The Tempest*, ed. Frank Kermode (London: Methuen, 1954).

———, *The Tempest*, ed. Stephen Orgel (Oxford: Clarendon Press, 1987).

Sharpe, J. A., '"Last Dying Speeches": Religion, Ideology and Public Execution in Seventeenth-Century England', *Past and Present* 107 (1985), pp. 144–67.

Sharpe, Kevin, and Lake, Peter (eds) *Culture and Politics in Early Stuart England* (Basingstoke: Macmillan, 1994).

Shirley, James, *The Schoole of Complement* (London: 1631), Wing (2nd edn) 22456.

———, *The Triumph of Beautie* (London: 1646), Wing (2nd edn) S3488.

Shrank, Cathy, '"This fatall Medea", "this Clytemnestra": Reading and the Detection of Mary Queen of Scots', *Huntington Library Quarterly* 73.3 (2010), pp. 523–41.

Sidney, Sir Philip, *The Defence of Poesie*, in Gilbert (ed.), *Literary Criticism*, pp. 406–58.

Simmons, J. L., 'Shakespeare and the Antique Romans', in Ramsey (ed.), *Rome in the Renaissance: The City and the Myth*, pp. 77–92.

Simpson, James, 'The Other Book of Troy: Guido delle Colonne's *Historia Destructionis Troiae* in Fourteenth- and Fifteenth-Century England', *Speculum* 73.2 (1998), pp. 397–423.

Smith, Helen, and Wilson, Louise (eds), *Renaissance Paratexts* (Cambridge: Cambridge University Press, 2011).

Smyth, Adam, *'Profit and Delight': Printed Miscellanies in England, 1640–1682* (Detroit: Wayne State University Press, 2004).

Snyder, Susan, 'The Genres of Shakespeare's Plays', in De Grazia and Wells (eds), *Cambridge Companion to Shakespeare*, pp. 83–97.

Sowerby, Robin, *The Classical Legacy in Renaissance Poetry* (London: Longman, 1994).

Spearing, Evelyn M., 'The Elizabethan "Tenne Tragedies" of Seneca', *MLR* 4.4 (1909), pp. 437–61.

———, *The Elizabethan Translations of Seneca's Tragedies* (Cambridge: W. Heffer and Sons, 1912).

Spenser, Edmund, *The Faerie Queene*, ed. A. C. Hamilton, 2nd edn, text ed. Hiroshi Yamashita and Toshiyuki Suzuki (Harlow: Pearson Longman, 2007).

Select Bibliography 261

Spentzou, Effrosini, *Readers and Writers in Ovid's 'Heroides': Transgressions of Genre and Gender* (Oxford: Oxford University Press, 2003).

Staines, John D., *The Tragic Histories of Mary Queen of Scots, 1560–1690: Rhetoric, Passions, and Political Literature* (Farnham: Ashgate, 2009).

Stapleton, M. L., 'Edmund Spenser, George Turberville, and Isabella Whitney Read Ovid's *Heroides*', *Studies in Philology* 105.4 (2008), pp. 487–519.

———, *Fated Sky: The 'Femina Furens' in Shakespeare* (Newark: University of Delaware Press, 2000).

Starnes, DeWitt T., and Talbert, Ernest William, *Classical Myth and Legend in Renaissance Dictionaries: A Study of Renaissance Dictionaries in Relation to the Classical Learning of Contemporary English Writers* (Chapel Hill: University of North Carolina Press, 1955).

Staub, Susan C., 'Early Modern Medea: Representations of Child Murder in the Street Literature of Seventeenth-Century England', in Miller and Yavneh (eds), *Maternal Measures*, pp. 333–47.

———, *Nature's Cruel Stepdames: Murderous Women in the Street Literature of Seventeenth-Century England* (Pittsburgh, Pa.: Duquesne University Press, 2005).

Stavreva, Kirilka, '"There's Magic in Thy Majesty", Queenship and Witch-Speak in Jacobean Shakespeare', in Levin, Carney and Barrett-Graves (eds), *High and Mighty Queens of Early Modern England*, pp. 151–68.

Steiner, Grundy, 'Golding's Use of the Regius-Micyllus Commentary upon Ovid', *JEGP* 49.3 (1950), pp. 317–23.

Steiner, T. R., *English Translation Theory 1650–1800* (Amsterdam: Van Gorcum, 1975).

Stevenson, Matthew, *The Wits paraphras'd or, Paraphrase upon paraphrase in a burlesque on the several late translations of Ovids Epistles* (London: 1680), Wing (2nd edn) S5513.

Stuttard, David (ed.), *Looking at Medea: Essays and a Translation of Euripides' Tragedy* (London: Bloomsbury, 2014).

Sundwall, McKay, 'The Destruction of Troy, Chaucer's *Troilus and Criseyde*, and Lydgate's *Troy Book*', *RES*, New Series 26.103 (1975), pp. 313–17.

Suzuki, Mihoko, *Metamorphoses of Helen: Authority, Difference, and the Epic* (Ithaca: Cornell University Press, 1989).

Taylor, A. B., 'Introduction', in Taylor (ed.), *Shakespeare's Ovid*, pp. 1–12.

——— (ed.), *Shakespeare's Ovid: The 'Metamorphoses' in the Plays and Poems* (Cambridge: Cambridge University Press, 2000).

Tempera, Mariangela, '"Worse than Procne": The Sister as Avenger in the English Renaissance', in Marrapodi and Hoenselaars (eds), *Italian World of English Renaissance Drama*, pp. 71–88.

Thomas, Keith, *Religion and the Decline of Magic: Studies in Popular Beliefs in Sixteenth and Seventeenth Century England* (London: Weidenfeld and Nicolson, 1971, repr. 1997).

Thornborough, John (or John Bristol), *A Discourse Shewing the Great Happiness that Hath and May Still Accrue to His Majesties Kingdomes of England and Scotland by Re-uniting them into one Great Britain* (London: 1641), Wing (2nd edn) T1042A.

Thorne, Alison, 'Large Complaints in Little Papers: Negotiating Ovidian Genealogies of Complaint in Drayton's *Englands Heroicall Epistles*', *Renaissance Studies* 22.3 (2008), pp. 368–84.

Tissol, Garth, 'Ovid', in Gillespie and Hopkins (eds), *Oxford History of Literary Translation in English, Vol. 3: 1660–1790*, pp. 204–17.

Torrance, Isabelle, 'Retrospectively Medea: The Infanticidal Mother in Alejandro Amenábar's Film *The Others*', in Bartel and Simon (eds), *Unbinding Medea*, pp. 124–34.

Travitsky, Betty S., 'Child Murder in English Renaissance Life and Drama', in Leeds Barroll (ed.), *Medieval and Renaissance Drama in England* 6 (New York: AMS, 1993), pp. 63–84.

Trill, Suzanne, 'Sixteenth-century Women's Writing: Mary Sidney's *Psalmes* and the "Femininity" of Translation', in Zunder and Trill (eds), *Writing and the English Renaissance*, pp. 140–58.

Trinacty, Christopher, 'Seneca's Heroides: Elegy in Seneca's *Medea*', *Classical Journal* 103.1 (2007), pp. 63–78.

The Turne of time, or, The period of rebellion dedicated, to the infamous members late sitting at Westminster (London: 1648?), Wing (2nd edn) T3266.

Turville-Petre, Thorlac, 'The Author of the *Destruction of Troy*', *Medium Aevum* 57 (1988), pp. 264–8.

Ullyot, Michael, 'Seneca and the Early Elizabethan History Play', in Grant and Ravelhofer (eds), *English Historical Drama, 1500–1660*, pp. 98–124.

Ure, Peter, *Elizabethan and Jacobean Drama: Critical Essays* (Liverpool: University of Liverpool Press, 1974).

Valerius Flaccus, *Argonautica*, trans. and ed. J. H. Mozley, Loeb Classical Library (Cambridge, Mass.: Harvard University Press, 1934).

Van Es, Bart, *Spenser's Forms of History* (Oxford: Oxford University Press, 2002).

Velz, John W., 'Topoi in Edward Ravenscroft's Indictment of Shakespeare's *Titus Andronicus*', *Modern Philology* 83.1 (1985), pp. 45–50.

Venuti, Lawrence, *The Translator's Invisibility: A History of Translation*, 2nd edn (Abingdon: Routledge, 2008).

Verducci, Florence, *Ovid's Toyshop of the Heart: Epistulae Heroidum* (Princeton: Princeton University Press, 1985).

Villeponteaux, Mary, '"Not as Women Wonted Be": Spenser's Amazon Queen', in Julia M. Walker (ed.), *Dissing Elizabeth: Negative Representations of Gloriana* (Durham, NC: Duke University Press, 1998), pp. 209–25.

Villius, Hans, 'The Casket Letters: A Famous Case Reopened', *Historical Journal* 28.3 (1985), pp. 517–34.

Vitkus, Daniel, '"Meaner Ministers": Mastery, Bondage, and Theatrical Labor in *The Tempest*', in Dutton and Howard (eds), *Companion to Shakespeare's Works Volume IV: The Poems, Problem Comedies, Late Plays* (Oxford: Blackwell, 2003), pp. 408–26.

Von Flotow, Luise, *Translation and Gender: Translating in the 'Era of Feminism'* (Manchester: St Jerome Publishing, 1997).

Walker, Garthine, *Crime, Gender and Social Order in Early Modern England* (Cambridge: Cambridge University Press, 2003).

———, '"Demons in Female Form": Representations of Women and Gender in Murder Pamphlets of the Late Sixteenth and Early Seventeenth Centuries', in Zunder and Trill (eds), *Writing and the English Renaissance*, pp. 123–39.

Walker, Julia M. (ed.), *Dissing Elizabeth: Negative Representations of Gloriana* (Durham, NC: Duke University Press, 1998).

Wall, Wendy, *The Imprint of Gender: Authorship and Publication in the English Renaissance* (Ithaca: Cornell University Press, 1993).

Ward, Allyna E., *Women and Tudor Tragedy: Feminizing Counsel and Representing Gender* (Madison: Fairleigh Dickinson University Press, 2013).

Wayne, Valerie (ed.), *The Matter of Difference: Materialist Feminist Criticism of Shakespeare* (Hemel Hempstead: Harvester Wheatsheaf, 1991).

Webbe, William, *A Discourse of English Poetrie* (London: 1586), STC (2nd edn) 25172.

Weinbrot, Howard D., 'Translation and Parody: Towards the Genealogy of the Augustan Imitation', *ELH* 33.4 (1966), pp. 434–47.

Whetstone, George, *The Rocke of Regard* (London: 1576), STC (2nd edn) 25348.

Whitney, Isabella, *The copy of a letter, lately written in meeter, by a yonge gentil-woman: to her unconstant lover* (London: 1567), STC (2nd edn) 25439.

Wikander, Matthew H., '"The Duke My Father's Wrack": The Innocence of the Restoration *Tempest*', *Shakespeare Survey* 43, ed. Stanley Wells (Cambridge: Cambridge University Press, 1990), pp. 91–8.

———, 'The Spitted Infant: Scenic Emblem and Exclusionist Politics in Restoration Adaptations of Shakespeare', *Shakespeare Quarterly* 37.3 (1986), pp. 340–58.

Willbern, David, 'Rape and Revenge in *Titus Andronicus*', in Kolin (ed.), *Titus Andronicus*, pp. 171–94.

Wills, Gary, *Witches and Jesuits: Shakespeare's 'Macbeth'* (New York: Oxford University Press, 1995).

Wilson, Edward, 'John Clerk, Author of *The Destruction of Troy*', *Notes and Queries* 37.4 (1990), pp. 391–6.

Wilson, Katharine, *Fictions of Authorship in Late Elizabethan Narratives: Euphues in Arcadia* (Oxford: Clarendon Press, 2006).

———, 'Revenge and Romance: George Pettie's *Palace of Pleasure* and Robert Greene's *Pandosto*', in Pincombe and Shrank (eds), *Oxford Handbook of Tudor Literature 1485–1603*, pp. 687–703.

Wiseman, Susan, '"Adam, the Father of all Flesh": Porno-Political Rhetoric and Political Theory in and after the English Civil War', in Holstun (ed.), *Pamphlet Wars*, pp. 134–57.

———, 'Exemplarity, Women and Political Rhetoric', in Jennifer Richards and Alison Thorne (eds), *Rhetoric, Women and Politics in Early Modern England* (London: Routledge, 2007), pp. 129–48.

———, 'Perfectly Ovidian? Dryden's *Epistles*, Behn's "Oenone", Yarico's Island', *Renaissance Studies* 22.3 (2008), pp. 417–32.

———, 'Rome's Wanton Ovid: Reading and Writing Ovid's *Heroides* 1590–1712', *Renaissance Studies* 22.3 (2008), pp. 295–306.

Wrightson, Keith, 'Infanticide in Earlier Seventeenth-Century England', *Local Population Studies* 15 (1975), pp. 10–22.

W. S.[?], *The Lamentable Tragedie of Locrine* (London: 1595), STC (2nd edn) 21528.

Wygant, Amy, *Medea, Magic, and Modernity in France: Stages and Histories, 1553–1797* (Aldershot: Ashgate, 2007).

Wynne-Davies, Marion, '"The Swallowing Womb": Consumed and Consuming Women in *Titus Andronicus*', in Wayne (ed.), *Matter of Difference*, pp. 129–51.

Zemon Davis, Natalie, *Society and Culture in Early Modern France: Eight Essays* (Cambridge: Polity Press, 1987).

Zunder, William, and Trill, Suzanne (eds), *Writing and the English Renaissance* (London: Longman, 1996).

Index

Note: passing or very minor references, particularly to authors (e.g. Ovid) and characters (e.g. Aeson) are not included.

CPSIA information can be obtained at www.ICGtesting.com
Printed in the USA
LVOW04*2000310315

432761LV00009B/204/P